PLAYING GOD

Also by Sarah Zettel

FOOL'S WAR
RECLAMATION

Available from Warner Aspect

SARAH ZETTEL

PLAYING GOD

A Time Warner Company

Warner Books, Inc., 1271 Avenue of the Americas, New York, NY 10020

Visit our Web site at http://warnerbooks.com

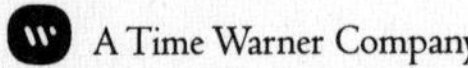
A Time Warner Company

Printed in the United States of America

First Printing: November 1998

10 9 8 7 6 5 4 3 2 1

Library of Congress Cataloging-in-Publication Data

Zettel, Sarah.
Playing God / Sarah Zettel.
p. cm.
ISBN 0-446-52322-4
I. Title.
PS3576.E77P53 1998
813'.54—DC21

98-19556
CIP

This book is dedicated to my husband,
Timothy B. Smith

Acknowledgments

The author would like to thank Tim Smith, Laura Woody, and Dee Kenealy for all their expert input, the Untitled Writer's Group for their support, suggestions, and honesty, and, of course and as ever, Dawn Marie Sampson Beresford, who keeps on listening.

PLAYING GOD

Chapter

I

What's that?" Praeis Shin t'Theria straightened up and twitched one sail-like ear.

Lynn Nussbaumer looked up at the tall Dedelphi, craning her neck as far as the helmet on her clean-suit permitted. Lynn, Praeis, and Praeis's two daughters, Resaime and Theiareth, were clustered around a worktable in Praeis's airy office at the Crater Town Planning Hall. Now, all three Dedelphi turned their ears toward the bank of opaqued windows set into the curving, white-plaster wall.

Lynn strained her own ears. A moment later, she heard a low, rumbling throb penetrating the windows, despite the sound filters.

"I've got no idea what that is." Lynn got to her feet. The rumble increased. "Room voice, open the windows."

"Opening," replied the building's genderless voice. The silvered windows cleared to reveal a street paved with every shade of red that Martian stone and sand offered. The sudden flood of daylight glinted off Lynn's helmet and the layer of transparent organic that covered her from neck to boots under her functional blouse and trousers.

Normally, the street outside the Planning Hall held three or four knots of Dedelphi pedestrians and a transport or two. Now, it was crammed with Dedelphi of every age and shade. The rumble pressing through the window glass was the sound of their collective voices, shouting, cheering, arguing, and weeping.

"Ancestors Mine," murmured Praeis. "What's happened?"

"I've got no idea." Lynn felt her brow wrinkle. "Room voice—"

"I've got it up already, Lynn," said Resaime behind her.

Lynn and Praeis turned in tandem. Resaime had the wall screen lit up. She and Theia stood hand in hand in front of it, attention riveted on its scene. Lynn stepped around Theia to get a better view. Praeis just stared between the tips of her daughter's ears.

The screen showed what looked like a theater. The gallery was crammed with Dedelphi: sail-like ears, leathery skin, round, multi-lidded eyes, all watching a gathering on a proscenium stage. More Dedelphi filled the stage, crowding around an oval table. Lynn recognized the *Io Elath,* the t'Therian's Queens-of-All, in their stark, black robes. Directly across from them stood the *Tvkesh-I-Rchilthen,* the Getesaph's Sisters-Chosen-to-Lead, resplendent in their silver-and-gold jackets.

Dominating the entire scene was a view screen hanging on the stage's back wall. Three soberly dressed Humans—two men and one woman, all magnified to at least three times life size—looked down on the crowd of Dedelphi. Behind the Humans shone the green triangle emblem of the Bioverse Incorporated enclave.

"By the Walking Buddha," breathed Lynn. "Do you suppose they did it?" There had been rumors on the info-web for months that Bioverse Inc. was negotiating a bioremediation deal with the entire Dedelphi homeworld, something completely unheard of in all the Dedelphi's long, war-torn history.

As if to answer her question, the tallest of the Sisters-Chosen-to-Lead lifted her pen from off the stiff, white treaty board. "It is done," she said in staccato Getesaph. A host of white-lettered subtitles flowed across the bottom of the screen.

On the screen above the stage, the trio of Humans beamed like proud parents.

Each of the Sisters-Chosen-to-Lead picked up a treaty board. Their jackets shimmered in the stark light as they walked around the signing table. The boards were symbols, Lynn knew. The real treaties would be tightly bound stacks of paper sealed into courier cases at the sides of aides and secretaries standing in the wings. These were just placards that said everyone had agreed to what was in those books.

The Sisters held the placards out to the Queens-of-All. With stiff, jerky motions, each of the three Queens took a copy of the treaty and bowed low over it, kissing the freshly dried ink.

Lynn sneaked a look at Praeis. She had gravitated silently toward her daughters, and now the three of them stood with their arms around one another. Lynn wondered what she could possibly be feeling. Praeis had been a general for those Queens, a Task-Mother, in t'Therian, and now she watched them receive treaties from their fiercest enemies.

The Sisters handed two more copies over to the Presidents of the Chosa ty Porath, and three to the Speakers for the Fil. Each of them took the placard and did nothing but stare at it, almost like they couldn't believe what was in their hands.

Behind the delegates of the major powers stood those who spoke for smaller nation-families, or Great Families, as the t'Therians called them. They were a broken rainbow of colors. Their skin was everything from the t'Therian's bluish grey to the Getesaph's greyish pink. Their clothing ranged from jeweled purple to unbroken, midnight black. They received no treaties. Probably, they had been ordered by their stronger neighbors to obey, and these grouped here had said they would. Each had presumably decided they had lost enough people to the plagues already.

The copies of the treaty boards distributed, the two Getesaph Sisters turned to the shifting audience.

"The Confederation is in place and will be enforced by all members. The delegates who have included their names and pledges on the treaty of agreement are all empowered to deal with the Humans. We here together will save these lands and islands that hold us all. Save them from this plague, save them from the poisons and pollutions that threaten to overwhelm them."

A few more ragged cheers rang around the gallery, overlaid by calls of "Do it!" "Save the daughters!" "Find immunity!" in different languages.

"So," breathed Praeis, visibly tightening her arms around her daughters. "The plague has accomplished for us what nothing else could."

At that moment, the door burst open. Four Dedelphi, all the t'Therian blue-grey, two with daughters clinging to their backs and squealing with delight, charged in and surrounded Praeis, Resaime, and Theiareth. The Dedelphi pounded one another's backs and clasped hands and babbled on top of one another until Lynn couldn't follow what was going on, but evidently they were happy about the treaties.

"You must speak, Mother Praeis." One of the t'Therians grabbed Praeis's hand and hauled her toward the door.

"All right, my Sisters! All right!" laughed Praeis. The hesitations Lynn had seen in the set of her ears and shoulders seemed to have vanished. They probably had, thought Lynn. They were whirled away by the enthusiasm of these members of her Great Family.

Praeis looked back at Lynn, her ears weaving in mock distress and real apology.

"Go. Go," Lynn said, laughing and waving her on. "Who else should be making speeches right now?"

A storm of approval issued from the t'Therians. They half pushed, half pulled Praeis out of the office with the willing and noisy help of both her daughters.

Chuckling to herself, Lynn crossed back to the windows and looked out at the crowded street.

The Dedelphi were a powerfully built species. Praeis Shin stood a half meter taller than a tall man, even when her flexible, sail-like ears pressed flat against her scalp. Her adolescent daughters were Lynn's height. Their leathery skin hung in folds that rippled gently or forcibly, depending on their mood. Perfectly circular, multi-lidded eyes were set high above the long vertical slits of their nostrils. Thick lines of muscle ran under the milky skin of their lips. Their bellies swelled gently where the pouch protected their mammary glands. The effect was heightened by the stiff belly guards a number of the cultures wore under their clothes.

And right now they were making riot in the street below. Sisters whirled each other around. Mothers tossed their daughters into the air. Cousins stood talking, gesticulating wildly with hands and ears. In a couple of places, sisters had squared off for what might become honor brawls. Several of the clean-suited Human security guards apparently thought so, too, and edged along their balcony and rooftop stations for closer looks at the potential trouble.

"Room voice," said Lynn. "Shut off the sound filters."

"Shutting off."

With the filters gone, the crowd's roar pushed at her like an ocean wave. There had to be upwards of two hundred voices out there, all letting loose at full volume, and the noise doubled when Praeis's escort pulled her out of the Planning Hall.

"Mother Praeis!" voices shouted. "Mother Praeis! Tell us the news! Mother Praeis! Let's hear your words! Mother Praeis!"

Praeis's escort shoved her up onto the edge of the public fountain and bundled her daughters up beside her. Lynn folded her arms and nodded approvingly. They made a pretty picture down there; Praeis in her sienna skirt and cream tunic flowing over her belly guard, flanked by her daughters in blue-and-gold saris. The sun was still above the crater wall, and it touched everything with gold.

Praeis dipped her ears in respect and agreement to the crowd, and for the first time, the noise level dropped to a murmur.

"My Sisters," began Praeis. "Sisters of my blood, my near family, my Great Family, and those who are sisters of strangers to me!"

Diplomatic, thought Lynn. The t'Therians had a lot of expressions for those who weren't in the Great Family. The most complimentary was *Other.*

"Today we learned of a great thing; our sisters at home have made a bargain that will end the plague that has killed so many of our mothers, our sisters, our daughters!" Reverent silence at that. "Today is the new beginning! Today we may hope for life, for the future, and for, greatest of all, a homecoming!"

Cheers, waving ears, raised hands. Lynn shook her head. Trust Praeis to know what not to say. Don't bring up the fact that many of the sisters out there fled from the continuous warfare as much as from the plagues that the warfare let loose. Let everyone who wanted to hope that the deal around that table meant an end to both.

Lynn watched Praeis step off the fountain's edge into the arms of her Dedelphi sisters, and the Others. Mother Praeis Shin the Townbuilder, said those who liked her. Praeis the Cold-Blooded, said those who couldn't understand why she didn't get furious at the drop of the hat in the normal Dedelphi fashion. Praeis, who, unlike the other inhabitants of Crater Town, was not a refugee. She was an exile. The ones who knew that had worse names for her, and some of them might have gone for blood. But—Lynn glanced again at the Human security guards on the roofs and highest balconies—Praeis's planning had made sure that Crater Town had law enforcement that was beyond the influence of the Dedelphi's fractious anger, as much for her family's sake as for the good of the colony.

Lynn went back to the worktable. Obviously, no more work was getting done today. The crowd in the streets would be cheering and debating for hours, and Praeis would be in the thick of it. Lynn touched the keys on the table's edge to save the city map they'd been working with. She subvocalized the record command to her camera implant and stored an additional working copy, in case she had any brilliant ideas on the way home.

Three waves of the plague had hit Crater Town. The sickness had been brought in by refugee ships, and despite steadily tightened quarantine controls, transmitted through families. Now, between thirty and forty percent of the colony's housing stood empty. The Building Committee had decided to raze the empty buildings as potential health hazards. Lynn and Praeis had met that morning to try to come up with plans for how to use the empty spaces the demolition would create.

Thirty percent. Lynn closed her eyes against the memories of the mass funerals, the dead and dying in their isolation beds, the wailing of the sisters left behind. Hundreds of Human doctors, armed with the best defenses years of research and biotech could devise, had volunteered themselves to help the fight, but they'd only made a small dent in the death tolls. Praeis had lost two sisters and four daughters, and Lynn had been there to watch.

Lynn's fingers hurt. She opened her eyes and looked down. Her gloved hands clenched the edge of the worktable like they were trying to break it off. Feeling moderately foolish, she let go and finished storing the maps.

Praeis liked to try to give Lynn credit for the success of the Crater Town colony, but Lynn would just shake her head. "I just helped out with the gardening," she said. "You're the one who got people to actually live here."

When the original Dedelphi refugees had shown up, they weren't fleeing plague, they were fleeing war. They arrived in the ships of Human mercenary pilots. They stood torn between fear and pride at the customs stations of enclaves, space stations, colonies, and city-ships—anybody who'd let them land and would agree to give them a berth of some variety in return for work or good publicity.

Then came Praeis and her sisters, Jos and Shorie. They saw the scattered, meek Dedelphi population in the Solar system, and they got to work. They found a crater that the Martian enclaves hadn't bothered to foliate. They convinced twelve separate boards and committees that it would be an incredible act of public charity to give it to the Dedelphi so the Dedelphi could have a home where they could be safe from the Human poison that was a constant danger to themselves, their sisters, their daughters.

Praeis and her sisters tramped all over the system gathering donations, equipment, and skilled help. The refugee Dedelphi responded tentatively at first, but then with growing enthusiasm, especially since many of them had daughters who had never been out of their clean-suits.

Lynn's family, famous for their re-creation of Earth's Florida peninsula, were recruited to foliate the crater in a style that would be comfortable for the Dedelphi. It was the work of a number of years. Lynn, her portable screen still warm from receiving her doctorate, had fallen in love with the job, and fallen into friendship with Praeis Shin. When the rest of her family left, Lynn stayed behind. The foliation wasn't complete, she said at the time. There wasn't nearly enough variety in the fields and gardens. They didn't have a trained maintenance force yet.

Her family had nodded sagely at each other, hugged her, and let her stay. Everybody knew what was going on, and approved. Back in Florida, Lynn would be tweaking work that had been completed fifty or seventy-five years ago. Here, she had her own projects, and they were worthwhile ones. Not one relative said one word to protest her basing herself on an entirely different planet.

Her decision had won her the gratitude of the Dedelphi, a number of awards from assorted enclaves, and a handful of really bad nightmares from the plagues. But it was real, and important, and she loved it.

And now . . . And now what comes next? Lynn wondered toward the windows. *What if they all do go home? What am I going to do?*

She shook her head and laughed quietly. *Nussbaumer, you selfish little so-and-so.*

As it turned out, it was three hours before the crowds in the street shifted enough for Lynn to get through to the monorail that would take her out of the crater and across the rust-and-green landscape to the Ares 12 Human colony. On the way, in her private cabin with its opaqued window, she shucked out of her clean-suit and helmet and stuffed them into her duffel bag. The suits were awkward, but absolutely necessary. Direct contact with Humans caused massive anaphalactic reactions among the Dedelphi. The touch of a Human hand could raise welts on Dedelphi skin. Human dander sent the Dedelphi respiratory system into massive shock. The first encounter between Dedelphi and Humans had lasted three days before five of the Dedelphi died of heart and respiratory failure. There had been confusion and bloodshed on all sides before it was understood what had happened.

Lynn brushed down her shoulder-length auburn hair. Since she didn't actually live with the Dedelphi, she'd been spared the necessity of depilating herself to keep her dander to a minimum.

Ares 12 was a residential community. Its homes and stores were built out of native brick and stood glittering a thousand shades of red in the late-afternoon sun. The city founders had worked hard to get thornless climbing roses to grow in the soil that remained sandy after three generations, but they'd been successful. Roses—pink, orange, red, white, and yellow—grew in riotous bundles everywhere and climbed up walls the way ivy climbed up walls in towns on Earth. Lynn breathed their perfume in as she walked from the monorail station to the house she shared with her partner, David Zelotes.

Unlike the streets in Crater Town, the streets of Ares 12 were empty. If any of the Humans had gotten the news about the Dedelphi, they were discussing it over the info-web, if at all.

The cream-and-burgundy front room of her home was also empty when Lynn walked in, but she heard David's voice coming out of his study. A strange voice followed it.

Caller on the line, she thought, and went into her own comfortably untidy study. The antique furniture was covered with disks, films, slivers, actual books, maps, dirty dishes, and half-empty coffee cups. The cleaning jobber sat in a corner, turned off, as usual, with a china mug and half a stale sandwich balanced on it.

"Claude," she called for the room voice as she dropped the duffel into the corner and herself into her desk chair. "Any messages?"

"One urgent message from Emile Brador, Vice President in charge of Resource and Schedule Coordination for Bioverse Incorporated Enclave."

"What?" Lynn shot up in her chair. Bioverse were the ones who just signed the deal with the Dedelphi.

"One urgent message—"

"Claude, stop. Claude, deliver message."

"Vice President Brador asks Lynn Nussbaumer to connect with him as soon as possible. He has an open thread waiting for her and has left his address with her home system."

What does Bioverse want with me? "Claude, thread me through to Mr. Brador."

"Threading." Pause. "Connection complete."

Lynn swiveled her chair to face her wall screen.

Emile Brador, Vice President in charge of Resource and Schedule Coordination for Bioverse Incorporated Enclave, appeared on the screen. He was a tidy man, slender, but not small. His round, pale eyes were set in a pinched brown face, making him look like a startled owl. His office, or at least its simulation, was a model of antique gentility with a lot of leather chairs and wooden paneling.

"Good evening, Dr. Nussbaumer," said Brador. "I want to thank you for taking the time to speak to me."

"You're welcome, Mr. Brador," replied Lynn in her best formal voice. "I confess, I'm a bit uncertain what you wanted to speak to me about though. I'm assuming it's got something to do with the foliation program for Crater Town?" Bioverse was a biotech corp. They were always looking for new techniques, or new genomes.

"Actually, we'd like to extend you an offer of citizenship."

Lynn blinked, startled. "That's very interesting, but I'd have to think about it."

Brador nodded. "I fully understand, Dr. Nussbaumer. You are a citizen of excellent standing and family in the Miami Environs and Greater Florida Enclave. When you're not on Mars, you're living on land your family re-created from bottom sand and ancient records. There, you have your pick of lifetime employment situations." He spread his blunt-fingered hands. "And what am I offering? A chance for you to cut your ties to your family, surrender your allegiances, and leave home for fifty years or more." He leaned forward. "But I'm also offering a chance for you to help save an entire world."

Nice opening, Vice President Brador. She looked back at tidy Veep Brador in his tidy office. She felt her back stiffen.

"Mr. Brador, exactly what do you want me for?"

She meant to shock him, but Brador's mouth just quirked up. A good sign, probably.

"As of yesterday," he said, "Bioverse Inc. has a contract with the Dedelphi—"

"Yes, I untied the web knot," Lynn cut him off. "Impressive. I thought getting all the Dedelphi Great Families to agree on something was impossible."

"That's what I thought." Brador nodded, and, for the moment, the vice presidential mannerisms dropped. "The Getesaph and the

Fil actually contacted us over a year ago, but what they want . . . It was decided we couldn't make a contract without a worldwide agreement."

"What exactly are they asking you to do?" Genuine curiosity prompted Lynn's question. There'd been so many rumors, and she'd barely skimmed the first thread of the knot in the office with Praeis.

"For a start, we're going to contract a biomedical team and put a stop to the plague they've unleashed on themselves." For a second, Brador's smile seeped into his eyes. "That is what my colleague is speaking with your partner, Dr. Zelotes, about."

"That's 'for a start.'" She made quotation marks with her fingers. "What's after that?"

"We are also being asked to perform full-scale bioremediation efforts to clean the planet up after two centuries of extremely dirty warfare."

Lynn sat back and rested her elbows on the chair's arms. She knew a fair amount about the world that Humans called Dedelph. There were places on that world that glowed in the dark. There were places you couldn't see from space because of the industrial haze. The Dedelphi never developed anything like the bio- and eco-tech that had allowed Humans to repair Earth and build themselves some brand-new homes on other worlds. To clean and repair a whole world after all those centuries of eco-disaster . . . Something warm surged through her.

With a little difficulty, Lynn set that feeling aside and looked back at Brador again.

"What are we going to do about the anaphylactic reactions?" she asked. "You can't drop thousands of Humans, and it is going to be thousands, right?" Brador nodded. "Thousands of Humans in the middle of a population they can kill by breathing on them."

The vice president overshadowed Brador again. "That is an exaggeration."

Lynn shook her head. "Not by much, it isn't."

Brador reached over to his main desk and touched its surface. The upper right-hand corner of the office scene cleared, replaced by a simulation of a ragged archipelago of space stations on a field of night and stars. "The center of our operations will be space-based until we can evacuate the population—"

"Until we *what*?" Lynn gripped her chair's arms. A couple of implants beeped in protest.

Brador folded his hands in front of him. "We're going to move the population onto city-ships and go to ground with nanotech and biosculpt."

For a second, Lynn remembered she was in the middle of a very high-powered job interview with a representative of a huge corporate enclave.

In the next second, she decided she didn't care. "Are you out of your corporate mind?" she demanded. "We're talking about a billion people!"

"One point three billion, by the most recent estimate," replied Brador. He touched his desk again. The space simulation was replaced by a population-distribution chart.

Lynn stared at it without reading it. "One point three billion people who, despite what we saw today, have a long history of hating each other's genomes and going for blood when they can." She threw up both hands. "You're going to move them onto city-ships—" She stopped and did a quick calculation. "There aren't that many city-ships in existence!" Lynn turned away for a moment, staring at her window. The evening sun turned the stone veranda a brilliant scarlet. She faced her interviewer again, somewhat more in control of herself. "Vice President Brador, you can't be thinking of jamming these people into a bunch of retooled freighters! This . . . project . . . is going to take at *least* fifty years!"

"Probably more like seventy-five." His pinched face and round eyes were absolutely sober and serious. "And no, we're not putting them in retooled freighters. We are going to place them in fully functional, city-ships, many of which will be custom-built." The graphic changed to a construction blueprint. "Our engineering teams are already at work in the Dedelph system asteroid belts. We expect an eighty percent need fulfillment within the year."

"How are you planning on scheduling an evacuation for a billion people? Do you have any idea of how many a billion is?"

"Generally: It's a thousand, million." His expression did not waver.

"And what," said Lynn, looking him directly in the eye, "are you going to do with the plague victims during this evacuation?"

Brador remained unfazed. "Each city-ship will be equipped with a hospital quarter capable of holding ten thousand patients. Again, we hope your partner, Dr. Zelotes, will be helping with their relocation and care."

Lynn rubbed her forehead. "You're going to have to keep a billion Dedelphi, sick or well, housed and fed and comfortable during the evacuation. You're going to have to have a responsive grievance team, a clear, concise schedule, a comprehensive crisis scenario . . ." She broke off, running her hand through her hair. "If you're not careful, this cure is going to be a whole lot worse than the disease."

"Yes. That's why we need you." Brador leaned forward. What Lynn had thought was poor lighting on his face turned into a full day's worth of five o'clock shadow. Whatever he'd been doing lately, it hadn't even left him time to depilate. "Are you aware of the reputation you possess, Dr. Nussbaumer? Not only for your ability to work with the Dedelphi, but for your massive success in coordinating and directing their colony's foliation and agricultural efforts."

"I had a lot of help," said Lynn, refusing to let herself be flattered. "And you still haven't said exactly what it is you want me for."

Brador's eyes glittered. "I want you to organize and coordinate the relocation. For a start."

Lynn opened her mouth and shut it again. "And for my next trick?"

"Coordinate and manage the southern-hemisphere microreconstruction teams."

Lynn just sat there for a moment. To give a whole race their lives back, give them their world back, alive and clean and new . . .

"You're going to be allowing time for a complete life-web survey, right? Micro- and macroscopic?"

Brador nodded. "We have some teams down there already, and we're shipping out more this week. The bases will be up and running by the time you're there to help coordinate activities and information."

Twenty years' work right there, mapping the ecosystem of an entire planet so they could take it apart and put it back together again. "And we'll be customizing the bioremediation tools based on the local ecostructures, correct?"

"We'll be designing them from the ground up, if we have to," said Brador. "If you and your colleagues decide we have to," he added. "We will go over the entire planet one inch at a time with every nano we can breed."

"Why not just drop a couple of asteroids on the place and start from the ground up?" she asked half-facetiously. "It'd be faster, and cheaper."

Brador's face remained impassive. "The Dedelphi are hoping we can do this without completely destroying their civilizations' infrastructures. We've agreed to try. Several of our teams are going through what archives and libraries there are, trying to find out what exactly conditions were like two hundred years ago."

There probably wouldn't be much. None of the Great Families had much time or many resources for pure research. That was just one of the reasons why, despite the fact that they were at least as old as Humanity, their technology was at late-twentieth-century levels, at best.

Brador wasn't admitting it, but a lot of the bioremediation was going to be guesswork. They could interview the oldest Dedelphi they could find and hear what their mother's mother's mother had said the world was like. Maybe they'd find a record or two about some extinct creatures, but, as far as determining exact ratios of, say, rain forest to grassland, or the proportions of bacteria in the soil of a specific area, or the original extent of a coral reef, the teams would have to work from simulations and educated speculation. They really would be building a whole new world....

A thought struck her. "What are the Dedelphi giving Bioverse in exchange for these miracles?"

Brador's smile slipped back into place. "Anything useful we find."

Lynn sucked in a breath. Except for a handful of isolationist enclaves, all the worlds in the Human Chain ran on nanotech. Nanotech ran on proteins and DNA. For all the talk there'd been once about microscopic fans and gears, the really useful technology turned out to be tightly controlled biochemistry.

Bioverse had been offered a planetful of untapped biochemistry.

"Think about it." A light shone in Brador's round eyes. "They've fusion-bombed whole islands, and yet there're still living organisms on them. Bacteria that are radiation-hardened. We can turn those into assemblers that can't be interrupted by a fluctuating electromagnetic field. They've got huge pits filled with untreated inorganic debris, and there're living organisms in there. We could make those into disassemblers of incredible efficiency. They've got algae blooms big enough to turn a whole bay colors and tough enough that all that industrial pollution can't wipe them out. That's a whole new way to eat gaseous toxins next time we want to convert a gas giant." He waved his hand. "We had all this on Earth once, but we bulldozed it to clean the place up." He must have caught something sour in her expression, because he stopped himself. "I know, I know, to be fair, we didn't know what we had, or how to handle it. We had to bulldoze it." The light returned to his eyes. "But now we have a second chance.

"We've got four conglomerates and six enclaves planning their economies for the next century around this project, Dr. Nussbaumer. We're going to save a world. Want in?"

A billion people. A billion people to transport and shelter and accommodate in all the billion ways each of them would need. Negotiations and treaties to begin and maintain. They'd have to cap wars that had smoldered for centuries. They'd have to clean out and rebuild an entire world.

"I'll need to consider it," she said with what she hoped was an appropriate blend of aloofness and cautious interest.

Brador's smile was merely polite, but Lynn had the distinct feeling she hadn't fooled him for a second. "Of course. Your room has my direct address. You may contact me at any time."

They said polite farewells, and Lynn cut the connection. She sat dazed at the enormity of the project Brador had just offered her. Finally, she shook herself and returned to the living room.

David was there, his long frame stretched out on the couch. Three of the windows were clear to let the end of the Martian day shine into the room. The fourth showed the treaty signing. The Queens-of-All were just receiving the treaty boards from the Sisters-Chosen-to-Lead.

She crossed the thick, burgundy carpet to stand behind the sofa and laid a hand on his shoulder.

"Look at that." David's voice was soft as he gestured toward the view on the screen. "They actually did it."

"I know, I saw." Lynn watched the scene replay itself. "You wouldn't believe the scene in Crater Town." Lynn shook her head without taking her eyes off the screen. "I always knew they had it in them, but I never thought I'd live to see it."

Suddenly, a familiar shape caught her gaze, and she squinted at the shadows on the right of the stage.

A recorder stood on its tripod legs, panning its double lenses slowly to take in the audience packed shoulder to shoulder at the foot of the stage. A Human held its leash. Lynn leaned forward. A man. Old memories rang in the back of her head.

"Screen, zoom in on male Human figure on the stage."

David cocked a questioning brow at her, but Lynn said nothing. The image repositioned itself so the thin, tan, bald man in his clean-suit was the only person on the screen. Involuntarily, Lynn gripped David's shoulder.

"Arron," she whispered. Arron tracked his recorder's path with his own gaze. From this close, it looked like he was searching their living room for something.

"Arron?" asked David. "Not Arron Hagopian?"

Lynn nodded. On the screen, Arron thumbed the recorder's leash box. It turned its lenses back toward the delegates on the stage. His gaze followed the lenses. His face was tight, unhappy, and years older than it should have been.

What's the matter, Arron? Arron had once filled her life. She had always thought that someday, when she had the time, she'd find him again, and they'd be friends. She'd introduce him to David, and they'd get along great. But the time had never materialized, and without even thinking about it, she'd lost track of him.

David looked from Lynn to the screen and back again. "Do you want to talk, or do you want to keep watching?"

Lynn felt a smile forming. "Jealous?" she asked, tousling David's neatly cropped hair.

He raised his right hand. "I am not now, nor have I ever been jealous of Arron Hagopian," he announced seriously. "Although I have occasionally wanted to beat him senseless for not appreciating you." David lowered his hand to let it rest on top of hers.

She squeezed his fingers gratefully. "Screen off," she said, and Arron winked out of sight, replaced by blackness.

"Well," said David, wriggling around so he could see her better. "What'd you hear?"

Lynn opened her mouth and closed it again. *What did I hear? Not a word about salary, or staff, or citizenship conditions. I just heard about helping to save a whole world, and I didn't think to ask about anything else.*

David watched her face, listened to her silence, and nodded. "Yeah, that's about what I heard." His eyes shone with a cold light. Lynn ran her knuckles along his chin and nodded.

David was an epidemiologist. He'd come to Crater Town shortly after the first wave of the plague did, when it was realized there wasn't one-tenth the number of doctors among the Dedelphi needed to deal with the crisis. Since then, he'd watched thousands of patients die, sometimes literally under his own hands. If Lynn had a handful of nightmares from the plague waves, David had a lifetime's worth.

Bioverse had offered Lynn a chance to rebuild a whole world, but they had offered him the chance to save lives.

"Okay." Lynn squeezed his hand one more time. "We're going."

David brought her hand to his lips and kissed it gently. "We're going."

Chapter II

Lynn stared at her freshly depilated self in the mirror. She ran her fingers across her bare, pale, still-tingling scalp. Her hair had been the functional, unenhanced auburn she'd been born with. The sink and the carpeting had absorbed it as it fell. Her fingers drifted across the ridges where her eyebrows had been five minutes before. She traced the visible stiffness on her temple indicating the memory works for her camera eye beneath her skin. She thought about David, still asleep in the other room, and how he would be seeing this sight as soon as he woke up. Her heart rose into her throat, and she seriously considered grabbing her clothes and hiding in the closet.

"Vanity, thy name is Nussbaumer." She tossed the microshaver onto the counter next to the vacuum sink and dissolution cream.

"Hi."

Lynn spun. David stood in the bathroom doorway, as naked as she was, but considerably hairier. During the three-week flight to the Dedelphi system from Mars, he had let his beard grow into a golden brown fuzz and allowed his brush cut to start looking more like a hedge.

He'd be shaving again after his shower. For three weeks they had been on their way to work. Today they would finally get down there, a year and five months after they'd both accepted Bioverse's citizenship offer.

David blinked sleepily at her and lounged against the threshold. He smiled and met her eyes. He was very carefully not looking at her scalp, or anywhere else she had just shaved. The only hair she had left on her body was her eyelashes, which were not considered to carry any dander worth worrying about.

Good bedside manner, Doctor, she thought with twinges of both love and exasperation. *Put them at ease, whoever they are.*

"Hi." She plucked her robe off the towel bar and shrugged into it. The silk felt too slick and cool against her completely bare skin. David caught her hand as she tied the sash and pulled her gently toward him.

She looked up at his soft, brown eyes. "David, if you say this suits me, I will beat you, hard. In anatomically sensitive places."

David smoothed her hand between both of his. "I wasn't going to say that."

She ran the knuckles of her free hand along his chin, savoring the familiar line of his jaw, even under all the bristles. She knew what he was thinking. David had been assigned to one of the t'Therian hospitals. Lynn, on the other hand, would be island-hopping, when she wasn't in her headquarters a full continent away. They hadn't split up for this long since they'd gotten married.

David did not lift his gaze from her fingernails. "I've just been thinking about . . . What do they call their world again?"

Lynn's mouth twisted into a half smile. He spoke and read three Dedelphi languages. She spoke five and read four. She'd trotted the fact out once at a meeting, and he'd never let her forget it.

"The t'Theria call it All-Cradle. The Getesaph call it Ground, or Earth, if you like, although that gets confusing," she added. "The Shi Ia call it Our Pouch, the Fil call it Everywhere, and the

Chosa Ty Poroth call it . . ." She hesitated. The amber words THE PARENT flashed in front of her right eye. "The Parent."

"I'll defer to our landing point." David cleared his throat. "I've just been thinking about All-Cradle and"—he raised his gaze to her face—"how very much I'm going to miss you."

"It's only for a few months," she reminded him. "Until the evacuation's complete. Then we even get our own house again."

"I know." He reached around her waist under her robe and pulled her close to him. "But hold me for a while anyway, Lynn," he whispered, as her cheek brushed his. "It's still going to be too long."

The dining room of Dedelphi Base I was huge. It had a full-service cafeteria and garden attached to a honeycomb of dining cubicles. A view screen threaded to the outside cameras dominated the longest wall. This morning, it showed the *Ur,* one of the two city-ships already in-system and awaiting the evacuation of the first of a billion Dedelphi. Each city-ship was two pairs of glittering domes set on opposite sides of a silver plate. The engineering and command centers were encased in two smaller domes, one over each nozzle cluster. Against the vacuum, it looked as if a city had been built on a black lake and now sat on its own reflection. The projection had zoomed in just far enough that they could see the gleaming buildings and green trees on both sides.

Three Dedelphi stood with their arms around one another looking at the projection. Even from the back, Lynn recognized Praeis Shin t'Theria and her daughters. She grinned and touched David's arm. He nodded and waved her on while he headed for the dining cubes.

Lynn walked up to a polite distance and waited for Praeis to acknowledge her.

At the moment, all three of the Family Shin were dressed for indoors, and for Humans. They wore matching straight-cut robes of water-patterned rose fabric over their swaddling clean-suits. Egg-shaped, air-filter helmets covered their heads, leaving enough room for their ears to move freely.

In a few hours, Lynn and David would be dressed in the familiar Human version of the clean-suit for the trip down to the planet's surface.

Resaime, the broader of the two daughters, turned an ear toward Lynn. Her gaze followed, along with her sister Theiareth's, and her mother's.

"Lynn," said Praeis, turning all the way around. "Human behavior in the Dedelphi system?"

"It's still a Human habitat." Lynn walked up to a more Dedelphi-proper distance. "What do you think?" She gestured toward the *Ur.*

"From here it looks like a work of art." Praeis gazed at the gleaming domes and the toy cities inside. "I'm having a hard time imagining living in there, but it is beautiful." She paused. "Perhaps it will change our minds about space."

"The Great Families don't like space?" Lynn's brow rose. "I mean, I knew you didn't have any ships, but I thought that was because . . ."

Praeis waggled her ears gently at Lynn. "Because we lacked the technology? No." She sighed. "A few of the Families, at one time or another, developed spacegoing capabilities. Unfortunately, they had a tendency to use them to drop rocks on their neighbors." Praeis's ears drooped. "Whole islands got obliterated. After the first few incidents, Families began shooting down anything that looked like it was trying to make orbit." She turned her ears back toward the screen. "Our engineers are still taught all the theories, and we do occasionally launch very disposable spy satellites when we need . . ." The sentence trailed off.

"We'll still be under glass in the ships," said Theiareth, changing the subject. She was more slender than her sister, and about a centimeter shorter. "It's going to be strange down on All-Cradle, with an open sky but no clean-suits."

"Travel should be a broadening experience," Lynn told her sagely. "A time to gather new experiences and make new friends."

"Speaking of which." Resaime cocked both ears toward Lynn. "Have you spoken to your friend yet, Lynn?"

"Arron?" Lynn shook her head. "I sent him a hywrite before we left, but I haven't heard back yet."

After seeing Arron in the treaty ceremony recording, Lynn had spun out every thread she could think of to find out what he was doing on All-Cradle. Not every answer that came back was a comfortable one.

Res still had her ears tilted expectantly. "It's been a long time," Lynn said, trying to sound casual. "And he's tied some knots in the web that say he's not exactly . . . in agreement with Bioverse's approach toward the bioremediation on Dede—All-Cradle. He might not want to talk to me now that I'm on the team."

"Well," said Praeis, without taking her attention off the *Ur*, "like the rest of us, he'll have to adjust." The skin under her gloves rippled. "You'll have to excuse my distance, Lynn. It's been a long time since I've been home and—"

Lynn waved her hand. "Don't worry about it."

Privately, she was wondering if Praeis was still carrying her letter from her sisters in her pocket. A month before Lynn and David were scheduled to leave for All-Cradle, Praeis had called Lynn at home and asked if Bioverse could be prevailed upon to give her and her daughters a ride.

"What's happened?" Lynn had asked.

Praeis lifted a few sheets of the fragile paper the Dedelphi used for keeping records. "According to my sisters, I have been pardoned, and ordered by the Queens-of-All to return home."

She'd sounded bewildered, as if she didn't know how to feel. Lynn couldn't blame her. Praeis had never given her the details, but

Lynn had always understood that Praeis had presided over some kind of military disaster that had gotten an inordinate number of t'Therians killed. As a result, she was graciously allowed to flee for her life.

Lynn shook herself out of her thoughts. "I shouldn't keep you standing here. I know you've got to get ready to head on down. I just wanted to say good luck. You have my addresses for when we're planetside?"

"Yes, we do." Praeis's mouth quirked up. "I expect to see you tearing about my homeland in a day or two with a cow switch to herd us all into place."

"Nah, that won't be for another week yet." Lynn grinned at her. "Take care of yourself, all right, Praeis? And get hooked up fast. How am I going to handle things without you to correct me?"

Praeis blinked broadly. "I would have thought you'd be glad to get your own way for a change."

Lynn shook her head. "Between you and David, I wouldn't know what to do with it anymore."

Praeis laughed. "You'll think of something, I'm certain."

Lynn touched Praeis on the shoulder. "Good Luck, Praeis."

"Thank you." Praeis lifted her arms from her daughters' shoulders and took their hands instead. "Come, my daughters, we still have much to do."

Lynn wished them luck as well, and they waved with their free hands and trooped off with their mother.

Lynn's stomach growled with surprising strength. She headed for the cafeteria's garden.

David might be content with vat-grown, form-molded, flash-cooked food, but Lynn possessed a set of working taste buds and her stomach was not steel-lined. She picked up a wicker basket and threaded her way between the chatting knots of people to the stations she needed. She pulled two eggs out of the drawer under the ceramic "battery hen." Walking between the troughs of black soil, she plucked a ripe tomato off one vine and a green pepper off a plant from a waist-high grow table. The apples were bright red, but the orange trees were just blossoming, and they filled the air with their light summery scent. The cheese in the processor didn't look ripe enough for her taste, so she skipped it and picked up sealed bulbs of orange juice, coffee, and milk, and a small loaf of fresh, warm bread from its slot in the bakery box.

She was looking forward to having her own place again, where she could set up her own garden and kitchen. As soon as the evacuation, sorry, the relocation was over, they'd have a house on All-Cradle that they could organize as they pleased.

David had left the privacy walls clear on the cube he'd chosen, so Lynn spotted him easily. She threaded her way through the exaggerated mouse-maze of cubicles to him.

He looked at her basketful of raw materials and shook his head. She ignored him. "Room voice, send in a cooking jobber and opaque the walls."

"Completing request."

The walls around the table darkened to an aesthetically neutral beige.

The cooking jobber scooted in and parked itself next to the wall. It was a plain machine, little more than a mobile stove with storage for pans, utensils, and spices. Lynn busied herself chopping vegetables, beating eggs, and humming, fully aware that David was grinning behind her back. When she turned around with her fresh omelette steaming on her plate, she had to admit it looked remarkably similar to the half-eaten concoction in front of him, but she would never say so out loud.

"One of these days"—David pointed his fork at her—"I'm going to give you a double-blind taste test, and I'll bet you won't be able to tell the difference between this lovely, ready-prepared meal and what you just spent a half hour picking out and cooking."

"It was twenty minutes, and I'll take that bet." Lynn scooped up a fluffy forkful, chewed, and swallowed. "Ahh, real food. Nothing like that delicate tang of mud and blood."

"Primitives." David had lived most of his life in space enclaves of one kind and another and still affected a minor horror of unprocessed nature.

"Lynn Nussbaumer," said the genderless room voice from the tabletop. "Iola Trace and Shane R.J. wish to put through a call."

Lynn swore and met David's gaze.

He shrugged. "I'm surprised we've had as much peace as we've had."

"Me, too." She took a swig of orange juice. "Room voice, I'll accept the call."

The right-hand wall lit up to show small, dark, tidy Trace in her spartan office with its soothing aqua walls and gleaming work surfaces. She had probably been up and in the station's "working" section for the past two hours. The back wall showed gangly, perpetually bemused R.J., still in his cabin in the dormitory module. He had his walls set to show an African savannah with lions stalking through the tall grass. Lynn still had not quite gotten a handle on how R.J.'s aesthetic sense tied in to his sense of humor, or how stuffy Trace's sense of propriety really was. However, they worked extremely well together and had guided her deftly through Bioverse's corporate maze. Lynn's staff numbered in the dozens, and under them were hundreds of direct-report personnel, but these two were her personal assistants. Lately, their job seemed to consist of keeping her schedule from getting totally overwhelmed by requests for conferences, advice, or talks. Brador had said Lynn had a reputation as a Dedelphi expert. The entire staff of Bioverse seemed bent on proving him right.

"Good morning." Lynn saluted them both with a forkful of eggs.

"Good morning, Lynn. Good morning, David," said Trace. David lifted his beaker of coffee to the projections, then turned his attention back to his faux-omelette, politely pretending to ignore the proceedings.

"What's going on?" asked Lynn.

"You mean aside from your three meetings, the advisory panel you're facilitating, and the t'Therian culture lecture you're giving?" asked R.J. brightly. He looked across at Trace and gave her a tight smile. "You lost, Trace. You go first."

"Thank you," Trace replied with a primness Lynn was almost certain was an act. "First, the personnel-registration hardware is going to be delayed by at least a week."

Lynn dropped her fork and groaned. David shot her a sympathetic glance.

"How'd that happen?" Lynn asked, wearily.

Trace looked down at her table screen. "Apparently when the project outline and payment scheme were rereviewed, somebody balked."

"They're holding out for direct credit rather than a down payment and percentage," chipped in R.J. "Seems our PR on this project is not as clean as some would like it."

"How clean do they want it?" Lynn threw up her hands. "It's a big project. We're evacuating—"

"Ah-ah." R.J. held up one finger. "Relocating, remember?"

"We're relocating," Lynn started again sourly, "an entire population and cleaning up a planet that's five percent bigger than Earth. It's going to generate controversy." Corporate enclaves ran on the goodwill of their contractors and subcontractors, and those, in turn, ran on the goodwill of their home enclaves, both the ones scattered up and down the Human Chain and the ones on Earth itself. The threads and knots of the info-web connected all the enclaves tightly together. If opinion on the web was bad, and the enclaves got nervous, the best contractors and subcontractors would turn the job down in favor of safer work, or would drive their prices up into the stratosphere. For a project like this, with ever-expanding needs across decades, too much of that could be disastrous.

"Well, I'm afraid Haberbuild is the main support of a small enclave, and they don't like controversy," said Trace. "So, we're renegotiating."

"Can you get me the downloads on that?" Lynn poked thoughtfully at her food. "Maybe I can help somewhere. I know some people in the enclave." She paused and took a fortifying swallow of coffee. "You said that was first?"

"Second"—R.J. watched his stalking lions for a moment—"Commander Keale has put in an urgent request to see you before the final meetings start."

Lynn choked on a swallow of coffee. Keale was the head of Bioverse Corporate Security, the people who were usually called the Marines. "What's Keale need to see me for?"

R.J. shrugged. "He isn't saying. But if you're going, you need to remember that we've got our first official meeting at ten."

Lynn subvocalized "Time," to her implant, and 9:32 flashed in front of her right eye.

"Nothing like cutting it close, is there?" she said in normal tones. "All right." She glanced regretfully at David. "Pass the word I'm on my way."

"Okay. See you in A12 when you're done." R.J. cut the line, and his wall went blank.

"Call us if you need anything." Trace's wall blanked out as well.

Lynn looked across the table at David. "Sorry."

"It's okay." He took her hand. "If I don't catch up with you in the room, I'll see you on the shuttle."

Lynn stuffed a final piece of omelette in her mouth, followed it with a swig of orange juice, picked up the coffee bulb, kissed David quickly on the mouth, and retreated into the corridors.

Dedelphi Base I was designed for long stays, so the corridors were wide and frequently cut through arboretums or gardens with fishponds and lawns. Much of the interior paneling was flagstone or vat-grown wood rather than metal. The light was bright and full-spectrum.

Lynn followed the directions her implant displayed for her. Keale's office was just off an alcove that had been made into a Buddhist rock garden. A brownstone path ran up the middle so no one would have to disturb the sine-wave patterns in the sand.

The door was open, so Lynn stepped over the threshold. The office was a standard hexagon-shaped room with plain metal walls and a bare floor. Keale sat at a multiterminal comm station in the middle. The far end was taken up by a conference table, over which hung a view screen showing two schematics. The first was a globe of the Dedelphi's homeworld. The second was a blueprint of a city-ship like the ones the Dedelphi would be relocated to.

Lynn knocked on the doorframe, and Keale looked up. He was a broad-shouldered man in the spruce green uniform of the Bioverse security team. Multicolored ribbons decorated his chest, and he wore four pips on his high collar. He was not shaven. His thick hair was iron grey, and he'd never bothered to get the wrinkles smoothed out of his copper skin. His chiseled face said his ancestors came from Europe as well as any of a dozen equatorial islands.

"Before and after?" Lynn gestured toward the globe and blueprints on the wall screen as she took a seat at the conference table.

"Sort of, yes." Keale got up from his comm station and reseated himself across the table from Lynn. "I am not going to waste your time, Dr. Nussbaumer. I put forth a security proposal to the project seniors, which was rejected, and which I want to revive with your help." He gave her a slightly sardonic smile. "Your praises are being sung from HQ to Dedelph, and I think the veeps might listen to you where they won't listen to me."

"I'd be glad to hear whatever you've got." Lynn sucked some coffee from her bulb and forced herself into a relaxed posture.

Keale folded his hands on the tabletop. "My commission is the safety of the Bioverse personnel on this project. I am in charge of making sure our people are not exposed to any excessive dangers."

Lynn smiled sympathetically. "We are going into a war zone, Commander. You've got a job ahead of you."

He returned the smile. "Yes. For a long time." He gazed at the city-ship's blueprint. "However, it's not safety on the ground I'm speaking about at the moment. The plague is everyone's common enemy down there, and they're caught up in fighting it. It's our people on the city-ships that I'm worried about."

Lynn felt her forehead wrinkle. "On the city-ships we'll have the warring Great Families separated and hundreds of miles away from one another."

"And that, Dr. Nussbaumer"—Keale laid his hand flat on the table—"is what I am worried about."

Lynn raised her brow. "I'm sorry?"

"The Dedelphi fight. They fight viciously and savagely, with no aim other than wiping each other out. They've always done this."

"No one disputes that, Commander," said Lynn patiently. "The Dedelphi will explain at great length why they do it."

"Yes, I've heard some of that." A flicker of distaste crossed Keale's face. Lynn nodded. She'd heard some of the rants, too. They were unsettling, to say the least.

"My teams have been studying the patterns of violence. It came as no surprise to anybody to find that a tribe or family will most readily attack those who are the least related to them.

"Aboard the city-ships, that will be us."

Lynn straightened up slowly. "What?"

Commander Keale didn't even blink. "The Dedelphi attack those who are farthest from their families in genetic terms. They do not do this because of lack of resources, because they are actively enslaved or oppressed, or because they are threatened in any way. They attack them because they are different. Humans are far more different from the Dedelphi than the Dedelphi are from each other."

Lynn shifted her weight. "So, with no history of warfare, no grudges, no need to spread and grow, you're saying it's inevitable that the Dedelphi will attack us?"

"I am saying"—Keale pitched his voice soft and low—"that they need to eat, breathe, fuck, and fight. They need enemies. Either we give them some, or they are going to find some, and we, being the farthest away from the family structure, are going to become those enemies."

Lynn waited until she was sure her voice would stay even. "This level of genetic determinism was disproved as a behavioral predictor years ago."

"In Humans."

Lynn took a deep breath and let it out slowly. She relaxed her grip on the chair arms. "Have you ever worked in the Dedelphi colonies, Commander?"

"No." He shook his head. "Bioverse didn't have any jobs for me there."

"Okay. Then let me tell you about the bloodlust of the Dedelphi." She lifted her gaze and looked straight into his black eyes. "Unlike us, they do not war over ideologies. They war over actions. Where there is no priming action, there is no war."

Keale opened his mouth, but Lynn didn't give him a chance to speak. "In Crater Town, Dedelphi from all the Great Families live within ten feet of each other, never mind ten thousand miles. They are supported fully by Humans: medical staff, consultants, trading partners, *neighbors.* They have a Human security force. It has never, not once, been the victim of so much as a web attack. The Dedelphi in Crater Town do not wage war, with each other or with us, because there is no history of war between them.

"The Confederation on All-Cradle is a paper peace. They are making provisions for a conjugal peace. They are using the cultural outlets that allow them *not* to attack each other, or us. As you so rightly pointed out, their enemy now is the plague."

"I am familiar with the paper and conjugal peace, Dr. Nussbaumer." Keale's patience was obviously straining. "But they are not universally practiced, or universally acknowledged. *Nothing* among the Dedelphi is. They can't even agree on what to call themselves. We had to label them." He looked at her more closely. "You're friends with the Crater Town founders, aren't you?"

Lynn nodded. "My family worked with the Shin t'Theria to build the colony. I was an Environmental Manager for them until I signed up with Bioverse. Praeis Shin and her daughters got to be my friends." She did not add how she had held Praeis's hand while they sat death watch over her sisters Jos and Shorie during the second wave of plague that hit Crater Town. It was not something Keale would appreciate.

He was watching her closely, measuring her words. "It's hard to see friends in an unflattering light. The refugees that live in the Solar system are unarmed and at the mercy of Humans. Many of them have been disowned by their governments, if not their families. . . ."

"Many of them are hailed as heroes for bearing the family healthy daughters when their sisters back home couldn't," Lynn cut in.

Keale shook his head. "But they're still unarmed and helpless, and even then the Shin t'Theria were bright enough to bring in armed Humans to keep the peace." He paused to let that sink in.

"If the Dedelphi don't attack the colony security, Commander, what makes you think they'll attack us?"

His eyes glinted darkly for a moment. "You're saying there aren't any brawls in the colonies? You're saying the Getesaph and the Fil and the Chosa ty Porath don't live in their own walled ghetto?"

Lynn felt the pressure of her rising anger against her temples. "The Getesaph quarter is walled for the Families that let their fathers wander loose in the streets. The others consider that blasphemous, or at least negligent, so a compromise was reached . . ."

"But there are still brawls," said Keale.

"Some," admitted Lynn. "Between newcomers, usually."

Keale nodded. "The Dedelphi we are dealing with here are neither unarmed nor helpless. They have never been subjected to an even, outside disciplinary force. They are going to be crammed together in a prison, as comfortable a prison as we can make it, but a prison nonetheless. They are going to have no outlet for collective aggression. They are going to turn it on each other, or on us. Their patterns tell me they'll go after us first as the most alien, unless we put them together with nonfamily with whom they have immediate grudges. We will obviously have to work to make sure the paper and conjugal peaces hold firmly, but we need a buffer between them and us, just in case."

Lynn uncurled her hands from around the chair arms and laid them flat on her thighs. "I'm sorry, Commander. I do not agree with you, and I will not support the implementation of such a plan."

A single muscle in Keale's face twitched. "I see. Very well. Would you agree, however, that we must be careful whom we place together and when we relocate them?"

Lynn stood up. "Yes. Absolutely. We must be careful about the schedule. I assume you've untied my knots on the subject?"

Keale nodded. "As far as they go, your plans seem workable."

"I'm glad you think so." Lynn rubbed her forehead. "Commander, I'm going to ask you something personal."

He waved one broad hand. "Go ahead."

Lynn took a deep breath. "Do you realize what a paranoid bigot you sound like?"

His mouth twitched for a moment. Then, to Lynn's surprise, he threw back his head and laughed so loudly the sound bounced off the high ceiling.

"Oh, God." He wiped his eyes. "Finally somebody said it out

loud." He shook his head. "Everybody tiptoes around looking at me like they want to say that, but they won't because it's impolite. It's a relief to meet someone who will actually come out with it." He straightened up. "And, yes, Dr. Nussbaumer, I'm afraid I do."

Bemused by his outburst, Lynn asked, "Then why are you doing this?"

"Because I'm worried," he said, completely serious again. "I know the Mars colony works. I'm glad it works, but the people you and I are dealing with are not the ones who ran away from war and plague. They're the ones still unleashing radiation and viruses on their neighbors for reasons I can't get myself to understand, and they *worry* me."

Lynn sighed and studied her fingertips for a moment. "I can't argue with that, Commander. They worry me, too. But they don't fight because they have to. Like Humans, they fight because they're frightened. If we don't frighten them, they will have no reason to attack us." She stood up. "Is there anything else?"

Keale also stood. "No, I'm afraid not. The rest can be easily handled during the official sessions."

"Okay, I'll see you then."

Keale touched a key on the table and the door swished open. Lynn found herself wanting to hear some parting comment, some kind of closing remark that would tell her that Keale really cared about the project, about the Dedelphi, about saving the world. But he just looked at her with a thoughtful expression on his face.

All she could do was turn around and go.

As she retraced her steps down the corridor, Lynn wondered if she should tell Praeis what had just happened. She decided against it. No sense getting the project off on a bad footing. Keale had admitted his idea had no support, anyway. Worrying Praeis about his attitude was pointless.

Lynn picked up her pace. Keale could deal with his own paranoias. She had a meeting to get to.

Chapter III

Praeis Shin watched All-Cradle's sphere, wrapped in its soft wools and creams, turn under the shuttle's cameras. Here and there, the cloud blanket parted to show a ripple of grey ocean, or a wrinkled cluster of green-and-beige islands.

Her daughters pressed close against her, one on either side. The shuttle didn't have artificial gravity, so stiff, magnetic slippers held them to the metal floor.

"So, that's home?" Theiareth peered closely at the screen.

"Profound, Theia." Resaime's nostrils flared. The sarcasm was light, reflexive, just banter between pouch-sisters. "Brilliant."

"That's home." Praeis rubbed her daughters' shoulders, feeling the strength of their muscles under her hands and enjoying the warmth of pride that spread through her. They were strong, beautiful, well-grown children. Both wore red-on-gold kilts and white tunics. They had been able to leave their clean-suits behind. This shuttle had been sterilized for their use. Under the tunics, their mottled belly guards covered gently swelling pouches. They were nearly adults, almost ready to make her a second-mother.

Theiareth's ears dipped toward the screen. "Looks a lot like

Earth, doesn't it? I thought it'd be . . ." She waved her hand. "I don't know, different."

"It might be if there weren't so many clouds." Resaime reached out and tugged her sister's ear absently. "It rains more here than on Earth, right?" She flicked her mother a sideways glance.

Praeis nodded and concentrated on keeping her hand from tightening on Theia's shoulder. It had been twenty years since she'd seen this sight.

In their stiff shoes, Praeis's toes clenched, searching for something to grab to help preserve her balance. *Why do I want to turn around? Why do I want to stuff my daughters into my pouch and run screaming back to Mars? I've been longing after home for half my life; why are my muscles melting now?*

In response to her silence, both Resaime and Theiareth pressed closer to her. Praeis could feel their warmth through her burgundy sarong. They smelled clean, all Human soap and Human-filtered water. Clean of blood and war and intrigue and lies, all of which she was taking them into on All-Cradle.

Praeis bared her teeth at the planet. *If you hurt them, I will make you pay. Earth of my ancestors, I swear I will.*

"Attention all hands and passengers." Praeis's ears jerked. The voice through the intercom had a precise, mechanical inflection. "*Margaret Teale* will be entering the atmosphere in twenty minutes. All baggage must be securely stowed in marked locations. All passengers . . ."

Praeis relaxed her ears. She gathered her daughters in her arms for a final embrace before she stepped backwards. The voice went on reeling off its lists of do's and don'ts.

"We'd best obey, my children." There was only one atmosphere couch per occupant per cabin, which meant they had to split up for this last leg of the journey. She had at least managed to finagle Resaime and Theiareth a dual-occupancy cabin. The only way down from the Human station was the Humans' shuttle, and

Humans went to a great deal of trouble to separate themselves from one another. From enemies, Praeis could comprehend, but from the rest of your family? Incredible. Twenty years of it, and it was still utterly incredible.

"Obedience first, obedience second, obedience third," quoted Resaime. "Come along my pouch-sister." She took Theiareth by the wrist and pulled her along. Theiareth looked back at Praeis, wiggled her ears, and grinned. *Bossy,* Praeis knew she was thinking. She smiled and felt ears and spine relax. They'd look after each other.

Getting down to the ground was a long, uncomfortable business. The atmosphere couch was big enough for a large *man,* but barely large enough for her. The pressure of gravity and acceleration after hours of free fall pressed her stomach against her spine and made her very glad she had not eaten breakfast.

Then came the long line of clean-suited Humans, t'Therians, near family, and Others shuffling through the shuttle's too-narrow corridors, trying to keep hold of daughters and luggage at the same time.

But they made it to the open door at last, to breathe the fresh air of the t'Aori peninsula, and to see that a thick curtain of rain fell outside.

" 'Esaph piss," muttered Praeis. She should have thought. There was no room for her to drop her bags and strip out of her sarong. She hated the slimy feeling of wet cloth on skin.

As soon as Praeis emerged from the shuttle, the rain spattered hard against her scalp and ears. The lovely, flowing sarong that she had worn expressly to show her sisters that exile did not mean beggary, began to stick to her shoulders, belly guard, and torso. She closed her first eyelid and surveyed the world through the film of the membrane.

The ramp to the ground was a smooth, slick affair that Humans could manage. All of them got to the ground without falling, however, and she felt strangely triumphant. She'd made it. She stood upright with her firstborn daughters on the ground of her home.

Theiareth waved her ears, spat energetically, and ground the spittle into the pavement with her heel. "Bless this ground of my Great Family!"

"Very pious, Theia, but we're holding up the line." Resaime yanked her sister to one side so a single female Human followed by a pair of smoky blue near-family sisters could get past.

Theiareth cuffed her sister's shoulder. "You're so excited you're panting, Res, so don't teach at me."

Resaime closed her open mouth and looked up at Praeis. "Where are we going?"

Praeis narrowed her nostrils against the rain and looked sharply around. She'd hoped either her sisters or the Queens would send an escort, but she saw no sign of one.

The familiarity of the place reassured her, though. This was really an airport which had been adapted for spacegoing use, as the t'Therians had no civilian space capabilities and only extremely limited military ones. She could just see the towers and "guns" of the satellite launcher. The Humans were busy putting up new buildings left and right, but it was still mostly the port she had left with a dozen refugees in a Human mercenary's cramped, dirty ship. None of them ever expected to come back, least of all Praeis Shin.

The shuttle's passengers, some of them Bioverse advisors, some of them returning refugees, made their way down the ramps to mix with passengers from the few military and civilian planes that dotted the cement. They picked their way between clusters of booths whose owners, most of them stripped down to their belly guards for the rain, shouted about cheap transport, clean lodging, the ability to find anyone anywhere, reasonable rates! Fresh food! Clean water! Homecoming gifts for your mother, your sisters! Immunity!

Praeis's ears jerked at that and swiveled to focus on the voice.

"Immunity! Immunity from joint rot and fever, all sorts! Guaranteed!" Praeis's nostrils closed and opened again. More than one of the boothers were shouting similar promises. Paying customers clustered around them. The plague was good business for some.

Battered motor skids, pedal cars, and carts drawn by long-necked *alar* or huge, blocky *oena* waited in a ragged curve beyond the booths, along with a few of the gleaming, enclosed vans the Humans used for themselves.

Over it all stood the soldiers in their watchtowers. They wore pearlescent body armor and brown boots, and all kept their eyes and ears fixed on the crowd, even though their guns were at rest. Their pale skin, more grey than blue, declared them all to be t'Smeras. Technically, the port was on their land, and the paper peace gave them the right to defend it. Praeis noted with quiet satisfaction that their armament was no stronger than needed for normal security work. There were no shields up, no signs of heavy weapons. Things for the moment must be fairly peaceful, probably no more than the usual skirmishes on the borders with the t'Ciereth and the t'Ianain.

With the relocation due to start soon, even those might have stopped. Everybody might be too busy trying to prepare themselves to be moved onto the city-ships. She'd hear the defense status from her sisters, but until then she could allow herself to hope.

Praeis dropped her gaze back to the port in time to see a cluster of three sisters shuffle through the crowd, leading a father swaddled in a thick blue jacket. His ears lay flat back against his skull, and he sniffed the air restlessly as they pulled him forward.

Praeis bowed briefly as the sisters and the father passed. A small wind stirred, and she caught his rich scent. So did her daughters. Theiareth's nostrils widened in surprise. The father touched Theiareth's shoulder, pawing her briefly and staring with vacant, soulless eyes. The sisters pulled his hand back, murmured their apologies, and led him away.

Theiareth gripped the place where he had touched her and swallowed hard.

"Are you good?" asked Praeis. "That was not expected."

"I'm good." Theiareth's skin rippled uneasily. "I'm fine."

"You look like you're about to vomit," announced Resaime.

"Thank you for bringing that to our attention, Resaime," said Praeis.

Theiareth was staring after the father with a mix of horror and fascination in her eyes. Praeis took hold of Theiareth's chin and pulled on it, gently but firmly, until Theia was looking straight at her. "It is a natural part of life, Theia, and one day it's going to be me and you."

"None of us would allow you to be hauled around in public," she grumbled. "Don't they have any feeling?"

"The Getesaph let theirs wander loose in the street," remarked Resaime, primarily to see what her sister would do, Praeis was sure.

"And that makes it good. Perfect reasoning, Res."

"Theiareth, you are such a prude."

"Oh, I suppose when your soul drops from your belly to your crotch I should—"

"Enough!" Praeis bared her teeth. "Do you have manners, and did I warn you to mind them? Are you going to make us all sound like barbarians to our blood family?"

In perfect chorus her daughters said, "But she—"

"If I cared, you would have known it by now." Privately, she cursed the three strangers for bringing the father outside like this. The touch had unsettled Theiareth. She and Resaime both were old enough to feel the private swellings from the touch and scent. Both of them were squirming and trying very hard not to.

She pulled them both under the narrow overhang of a maintenance shed, out of the main flow of foot traffic, and temporarily out of the worst of the rain.

"Come on, daughters, let's get out of these." Praeis dropped her bags and unpinned her sarong, peeling it off her skin and belly guard. Her skin shivered with relief. Resaime and Theiareth relieved themselves of their kilts and tunics and handed them over to Praeis. She wrung them out and stuffed them into the carryall, hoping she hadn't put anything with colors that would run in there.

"Praeis Shin t'Theria!"

Praeis straightened up immediately. A pair of arms-sisters, looking heavy and awkward in their body armor, shouldered their way through the crowd. As they approached, a delighted flush of recognition ran through Praeis.

"Neys! Silv!" Praeis embraced her old arms-sisters, laughing from pure joy. "What are you doing here?"

"What are we doing here?" Neys, short, tight-skinned and obviously still fond of good meals, filled her voice with exaggerated effrontry. "We've been sent to convey you and your daughters safely to the Home of Queens, and we've been standing in the rain waiting for you for the last hour."

"Then you should meet my daughters." Praeis brought Theia and Res in front of her. "Resaime Shin t'Theria, Theiareth Shin t'Theria. Daughters, my arms-sisters, Silvi Cesh and Neys Cesh." Shoulder clasps were exchanged, heartily by the arms-sisters and hesitantly by the daughters.

"So, come along, come along! The Queens await!" Silv was as short as her sister, but much more sparely built. She grabbed up three of the satchels before Praeis could protest and strode unceremoniously back into the crowd.

Neys waggled her ears and grabbed up the other three bags. "All things must be as my sister commands," she said cheerfully as she set off after Silv.

Praeis laughed and shook her head. Those two had not changed, except for the merit markings on their armor. While she had been building a city for refugees, they had served their people with diligence, honor, and bravery. She took Res's and Theia's hands and hurried after Neys and Silv before she lost sight of them.

Silv piled their baggage into a spotless frame car with ROYAL GUARD written in large letters on the front and urged them all to take their places and make themselves comfortable. Praeis crammed into the backseat with her daughters. Neys and Silv took their places in the front.

Silv started the loud, choppy engine and drove unimpeded through the port gate, then across the gap between the first wall and the second. Beyond the flat, concrete security zone, they drove through ancient gates that had been reinforced with steel and titanium and into the city t'Theria.

Instantly, the car was overshadowed by narrow buildings constructed as a series of short, interconnecting corridors. They all had thick, small windows and brightly painted walls. Many of the murals had been faded by soot or had peeled off where no one had repainted them. Canals paralleling the streets ran black and choked with weeds, moss, and garbage.

They passed one of the debate walls. A small cluster of mothers, sisters, and even a few daughters read the essays fastened to the wall or sat listening to the two sisters who pontificated at the wall's far end.

Shacks and shanties of scavenged material leaned against the sides of buildings where people paid enough fees for a solid roof and walls, but not enough for the owners to take care of the impoverished. Here and there the trees that grew beside the buildings and the vines that draped down them were broken and burned, showing that peace had not been complete or long-lasting here. A few boothers pulled carts loaded with their stands and wares down the sidewalk. A few near family scurried along as if they were afraid they'd be seen.

It was then that Praeis realized the city was almost deserted. Her memory crammed the streets and the branching overhead walkways with bodies. Families lived on their blankets in the alleys and hawked food and services to the passing traffic. Boats steered up and down the canals. The sailors cursed one another and the occasional idiot who decided to swim for it with equal vigor. Arms-sisters paced or paraded in blocks of two or three dozen, holding up all kinds of traffic.

But now there wasn't enough noise to make itself heard over the frame car's engine. She'd counted perhaps twenty pedestrians. The canals were completely empty.

"Ancestors Mine," she breathed. "How many of us did the plague take?"

Silv kept her eyes and ears pointed straight ahead. "Half."

"Half?" The word choked Praeis.

"So far," added Silv grimly. "At least we've cleared the corpses from the canals."

Praeis's ears drooped until the tips brushed her shoulders. She felt her daughters' hands on her arms, but felt no warmth. She had seen the deaths in the colonies, she had lost her sisters and four of her daughters, but to watch the sisters falling in their millions....

Half so far. Oh, my Ancestors, how did we come to this?

Silv took a hard left, and the frame car rattled and banged over a canal bridge. The buildings opened out to form the broad mall that fronted the moats and bridges surrounding the great wall of the Home of Queens.

They were obviously expected. As their car approached, the main gate swung regally open, and Silv drove straight through into the ancient cobbled yard.

"Neys, take them to the doors." Silv braked next to one of the guard shacks. "I'll put the car away, stow the luggage, and bring the honor guard to meet you."

"As you say, Sister," Neys agreed amiably. "Perhaps we should make sure they're checked in, first."

"Perhaps we should," agreed Silv dryly. Neys waggled her ears and climbed out of the car. Praeis and her daughters followed.

"She does believe in taking charge, doesn't she?" remarked Res softly, but not quite softly enough.

"She always has," Neys said slyly. "Has your mother told you about the time—"

"Later, Neys," said Praeis desperately. "As Silv rightly pointed out, the Queens await."

Neys took them into the guard shack, where a pair of bored third-sisters searched them for weapons, recent scars, or signs of illness, and eventually wrote their names in a log as passed for entry. Res and Theia bore the entire process without complaint. Praeis had warned them it would happen. What surprised her was how badly she squirmed while she watched her daughters poked and prodded by the guards.

"Fine children," said Neys as she led them across the yard. "Your only?"

"I lost their sisters to the plague," said Praeis. A sharp pain ran through her as she spoke the words.

A flicker of sorrow crossed Neys's face. "We have all lost someone to sickness."

Neys lapsed into silence to cope with whatever memories she carried. Praeis took her daughters' hands but didn't say anything. She kept her gaze on the Home of Queens. The crescent-shaped mansion spread its arms to embrace all the t'Aori peninsula. Like the city, though, the Home had fallen onto hard times. Of the three domes, only the central one still shone bright turquoise. The other two had been burned and blackened in some battle and never cleaned. Only three or four of the dozens of windows had lights in them.

The sound of boots on cobbles cut across her thoughts. Silv arrived with the promised honor guard: four arms-sisters who looked vaguely harassed. Neys, Silv, and one other arms-sister formed up in front of them. Three other arms-sisters fell into step behind them.

Praeis remembered the palace when it was blazing with light. Ministers, Councilors, Noble Sisters, staffers, and petitioners streamed in and out of the rooms, stood in knots arguing and negotiating with one another, or brushed past single-mindedly on errands.

Now it was a tomb. The gathering rooms echoed as they marched through. Shadows obscured vague shapes that Praeis remembered as elaborate statues and silken furniture, making her wonder what was really back there now.

Up a shallow set of stairs, the obsidian doors to the main Debating Chamber stood open. Neys and Silv strode forward to the light.

"Praeis Shin, Resaime Shin, Theiareth Shin, all Noblest Sisters t'Theria answer the summons of their Majestic Sisters, the Queens-of-All," they announced in unison, then stood aside.

"Our cue, daughters." She squeezed Res's and Theia's hands. "When you address the Majestic Sisters, close your eyes and raise up your hands. Stay that way until instructed to do otherwise. Let's go."

The Debating Chamber, at least, had not changed. A dozen heavy marble tables, each large enough to seat twenty, stood in a semicircle under the portraits of the Majestic Ancestors. The floor's mosaics depicted the peninsula and islands of t'Aori on a blue-grey sea. It was a rich and solemn room, but somehow diminished in its emptiness. Aside from the Queens, the only occupants were a quartet of servants busy around the kitchen pit by the left-hand wall.

The Queens-of-All stood around one of the ancient central heating pits. They had not aged well. Praeis had been there when the Queens had taken the rule. They were vibrant then. Two of them had live bellies, rolling with the precious burden of their daughters. Now they looked old, with sagging faces and pale skin that stood out starkly against their plain black robes. Their daughters were nowhere in evidence. Praeis found herself wondering if they were still alive.

Despite the changes, Praeis still knew them all: blunt, broad Ueani Byu, subtle Aires Byu, whose attention could be like a knife against your skin. Between them stood the First-Named Queen, Vaier Byu. She could be underestimated, if you were not careful, but it was she who ruled the triumvirate, as the triumvirate ruled the t'Therians.

"Welcome home, Noblest Sister Praeis Shin." Vaier Byu stepped forward. "And to your daughters, our Noblest Sisters Resaime Shin and Theiareth Shin."

Praeis closed her eyes and raised her hands, palms out. "For my daughters and myself, I thank my Majestic Sisters."

"You are most welcome." Aires Byu's voice was smooth and quiet, but nonetheless it filled the room. Cloth rustled. "Open your eyes, Praeis Shin, find a seat for yourselves and your daughters. Food is being brought."

"Thank you, Majestic Sisters." Praeis opened her eyes.

She and her daughters sat stiffly on a single sofa under a rendering of the five Mother Queens. The Queens-of-All each took individual seats. Praeis felt surrounded and hoped it didn't show. The cooks brought glasses of water and teas, and platters of fish strips and fried rice cakes. Praeis smelled the food and instantly began to salivate. She helped her daughters to portions and took a piece of fish for herself, trying not to feel the eyes of the Queens on her.

"Now then." Vaier Byu picked up a glass of green tea and sipped at it. "What have you been told?"

Praeis licked her fingers in appreciation of the warm food. "Only that I have been pardoned, and that I am needed."

Aires Byu dipped her ears, in acknowledgment or approval, Praeis wasn't certain which. "Do you have any ideas about how these things came to be?"

Praeis spread her hands. "I assumed plague, Confederation, and time."

"Decent assumptions." Ueani Byu caught up a rice cake and munched it down in two bites. "And not far from wrong."

"I am at the service of t'Theria and our Queens," said Praeis. "Where I have always been."

"And your daughters?" asked Ueani. "These childless children of yours who've never seen t'Aori until now? What about them?"

Res's cheeks twitched. "Our loyalties are our mother's." She spoke more fiercely than she should, and forgot to close her eyes, but her words were good. Praeis took her hand and pressed it quietly, hoping to smooth out the fist it had knotted into.

"Very right and proper." Aires Byu picked up another rice cake. "Very firm, too."

"That's enough, Aires," said Vaier Byu. "Your daughters do you credit, Praeis Shin. I am glad you are back before us." She studied the depths of her glass of tea. "Do you know how many of us the plague has taken so far?"

Praeis's shoulder muscles quivered. "I had heard half."

"Half." Vaier Byu sipped her tea. "It may well be half. The truth is, we do not know exactly. Nor do any of the near family, nor any of our old allies. We only know our cities are emptied, our armies diminished, and our survivors, what few there are, are left scarred, deaf, and sometimes crippled.

"If the Getesaph chose to attack today, we could repel them, but it would be a close contest."

Praeis's ears wanted to fold against these words, but she forced them to stay still.

"What is not publicly known, of course, is how close it would be, although it is widely suspected. Also suspected is the uncertainty that this year's harvests can be brought in, or that next year's can be assured. No one, of course, could miss how few fishing boats are still able to go out. The shortages are not yet felt, but they will be, in another year. Then there is the fact that our sisters and daughters are still dying." She raised her eyes and focused them on Praeis. "You can understand, then, Noblest Sister, why we chose to join the Confederation."

Praeis dipped her ears in silent agreement.

Vaier Byu took another swallow of tea. "You can, I think, also understand this. There are those who say the price we have negotiated for the salvation of our Great Family is too high. They say we will not all die from the diseases spread by this new weapon, or even from the famine that may, or may not, be coming. They say we should not bind ourselves to those who have shed our mothers' blood and robbed us of our mothers' souls. There are many who lay out these opinions. More, we fear, than there are of those who agree wholeheartedly with us and Confederation."

"Among these," said Aires Byu, "are your blood sisters Senejess and Armetrethe."

Praeis bowed her head. *Oh, Sisters, what have you been doing while I've been gone?*

"There are not many of us, Praeis Shin," Aires Byu went on, "who can stand out against our sisters. But you have before, and you are now."

Praeis raised her eyes and opened her mouth.

"Do not say you don't understand." Aires Byu leaned forward. "You went against your sisters when you traded Urisk Island and four thousand lives for a swift peace. You are an isolated, alien thing in this respect."

Praeis felt her fingers curl and her ears try to fold up. She held herself rigid. The Queens spoke nothing but the truth. She could sit and hear it. She could. Her daughters leaned closer to her. She felt their warmth and drank it in. They knew the story, most of it anyway.

Aires watched all this, but the set of her ears did not change. "Yet, you can build accord like no one we have ever met, and we have met masters of the art. You can deal with enemies and make them come to terms.

"We sit isolated here for the propaganda of holding our Ancestor's city. Our people work among those who are building consensus against us, in an attempt to bring them to our side, but there is little they can do to sway whole families."

Praeis licked her lips. "There is a group of Humans called the Bedouin who have an ancient saying that describes us well. They say 'me against my sister, me and my sister against my cousin, me and my cousin against the world.'"

Vaier Byu laughed. "Very good. Who knew the Humans understood such things?"

"Praeis did." Aires Byu dipped her ears again. "Praeis knows many things, and she will tell them all to her Majestic Sisters, will she not?"

Praeis's ears flickered back and forth. "About the Humans, Majestic Sister, or about my blood sisters?"

"Ancestors Mine!" Ueani hurled a scrap of rice cake into the heating pit. "You're being asked to spy for us, Praeis Shin. To get out there and find out who's with us and who isn't. To subvert those who aren't over to our side, if you can, and to give us their names if you can't. You have your own friends out there. Get them. Work with them. We cannot allow this disaster we've created to fall apart. There are too many dead bodies and unattended souls out there as it is."

Praeis's jaw hung open. She panted, but got control of herself and closed her mouth. Theia pressed close to her side, and, reflexively, Praeis wrapped an arm around her.

Vaier and Aires Byu both glowered at their sister.

"I don't care!" Ueani Byu jumped to her feet. She began to pace back and forth, working figure eights around the chairs. "We've had enough subtlety here. We are the Queens-of-All, and there's no one to hear our voices but cooks and shit cleaners! We've got to get out of here, back into the thick of our lands and people, but we don't know where we can go in safety or whom we can trust. You"—she stabbed a finger at Praeis—"are going to find out for us! You are going to gather the loyal following we need, and you are going to hand us your living sisters to try for high treason if we tell you to. Yes? Good?"

Ueani Byu stood there, feet spread, fingers flexing. Praeis felt her heart beat wildly. Her nostrils clamped shut, and her ears cringed. For a moment, she thought if she refused, her Queen would go for her throat.

Praeis swallowed hard and forced her nostrils open. "Why me?" she asked, ashamed at the weakness in her voice. "It cannot be that my Majestic Sisters have no allies."

"Because you have traded t'Therian lives for peace," said Vaier Byu. "We have no one else who has done that. We may require you to do it again. Once before, you were our hands and eyes and did for us things which no one else could, or would do. We can trust you to act for us as we can trust no other."

So there it was. The real reason she had been allowed to come home. The Queens needed someone who could and would betray her family. Praeis looked at the floor. The harbor islands sprawled under her feet. She panted hard and did not try to stop herself.

At last, she closed her eyes and raised her hands. "Obedience first, obedience second, obedience third."

It was nearly dark by the time Praeis and her daughters were released from the Queens' presence. Two soldiers Praeis didn't know drove them out of the city and into the working lands. Walls enclosed factories, fields, and orchards, so it was like driving through a cement maze.

Here and there, the walls opened up to reveal distressingly weedy lawns for the crematoriums. Praeis remembered only two on the whole length of road between the city and home. Today, though, she had counted eight, and each one of them had its fire going. The familiar, dreaded, sweet-sour burning scent from the bodies being burned before their ashes were commited to the earth of the Ancestors filled the damp wind. At the smell, both Theia and Res grew quiet and huddled closer to her, and Praeis held them gratefully.

Finally, the road took a sharp corner and the walls opened up again. This time, though, Praeis saw rain damp grass and a few sprawling trees no one had ever bothered to prune.

Then she saw home.

Its walls were smooth white cement. She and her sisters had spent hours scrubbing the cursed things. Any breach of family discipline would get them sent out with hoses and soap. Four adolescents sat on top of the walls, either as lookouts or just looking. As the car drove past the wall, the daughters turned and shouted. Praeis couldn't understand the words.

Behind the walls Praeis could just see the four chimneys and peaked slate roof of the main house. The wide wood and iron gate glided into view. The timbers were a little darker than they had been, and there were flecks of rust on the reinforcing iron bars and hinges, but it remained the entrance to her home.

Their driver braked roughly and gestured to the roadside. "Here we complete our commission."

Praeis dipped her ears. "Thank you. With me, Daughters."

Resaime and Theiareth clambered out of the car, fast enough to make themselves clumsy.

"PRAEIS!"

Praeis barely had time to turn around before the gate swung open and the floodwave of family broke against them. Cousins crowded around, becoming a blur of hands and faces as they were hugged and touched and tugged at. Voices laughed and called, and babbled out more questions than could possibly be answered. Praeis felt warmth mounting inside her. With half an eye she watched her daughters. Res and Theia hesitated a little. They'd seldom had such a crowd around them, but they quickly relaxed into it, touching and being touched, laughing, naming themselves and having names called back to them. A fierce happiness surged through Praeis, one she hadn't felt in years. She was passed from hand to hand. She grasped arms and shoulders and ears, shouted names and greetings until she was hoarse. The happiness in her blood and skin filled her with fire and strength enough to make her drunk and dizzy.

Then, she looked up and saw that the hands she held belonged to her sisters. Proud, wide-eyed Senejess, and warm Armetrethe, who'd lost her left arm in a skirmish years ago.

"Armetrethe! Senejess!" Laughing, Praeis threw herself into her sisters' embrace.

"Praeis!" Their strong arms wrapped around her. They all whooped with love and joy as they held one another, drinking in scent and sound and solid presence.

I'm home. I'm home! thought Praeis, almost delirious with the wonder of holding her sisters.

"Well, come now!" Senejess finally said. "We cannot stand here making riot in the streets. Let's get ourselves indoors."

With her sisters' arms tight and strong around her shoulders, Praeis let herself be steered toward the house. The cousins and daughters flocked around them, blocking the view of the grounds and the outbuildings. Here and there, she caught a glimpse of a familiar wall, or cluster of stones in the garden and her heart lifted until she thought it could go no higher.

They spilled through the doors of the main house and into the great room. The family fanned out, dropping onto the sofas arranged in clusters around the tiled space. The vibrant greens, blues, and golds created stylized scenes of sea cliffs and forests to surround them all. The tall slit windows let in the daylight to mix with the mellow light of oil lamps. Praeis inhaled the scent of warm oil with a start. The electricity probably wouldn't come on until after dark. She hadn't thought about power rationing in years.

Still, the room was as she remembered it. It was beautiful. It was home.

She collapsed with Senejess and Armetrethe onto a sofa. Res and Theia dropped straight to the sand-colored mats that covered the floor with a cluster of cousins about their own age, languid and relaxed.

They talked easily for a while, about the colonies, about the daughters. The conversation turned colder and drew them closer to one another as they talked about the plague and the long lists of the dead.

Finally, Senejess shook Praeis's shoulder lightly. "Tell us what the Queens were so anxious about they couldn't let you come home first, Sister."

Between their cousins, Res and Theia stiffened, but said nothing.

Praeis struggled to rise above the enveloping warmth that surrounded her so she could choose her words carefully. "They wanted my thanks for their pardon, Sister, and to inform me I was now their official representative."

Senejess looked from her to Armetrethe and pulled Praeis into a close embrace. "I'm so glad, Sister."

Slowly, Praeis realized she was, but that Senejess was also disappointed. She was hoping for more than Praeis had said. A cool thread began to ease through the warmth of her blood. Her skin rippled, and she extricated herself from her sister's arms. "They didn't mention money yet, of course. Is that not how it always is with the Majestic Sisters? Order now, pay when you work out how."

Before they laughed, another look passed between Armetrethe and Senejess, just a flicker, but nonetheless too long to be imagined.

"So," Praeis tried hard to sound completely conversational. "Tell me how things stand in the Council of True Blood."

Armetrethe shrugged. The stump of her missing arm flailed outward. "It is full of arguments as always. Not everyone accepts this Confederation. Some find petty ways to assert what independence we have left instead of working toward effective solutions."

Well, Sisters, now we have exchanged ambiguities. Praeis tried to relax again, to sink back into the rivers of warmth and be washed away on their currents. She did not want this. She did not want to be apart and afraid. She wanted her birth sisters. She wanted them so much, she felt tears welling up in her eyes.

"Ah, nothing new then," she said softly.

Armetrethe touched Praeis's shoulder with her one hand. "What is it, Sister?"

Tell them, tell them. There is no need for this. You can be birth sisters again. They'll forgive you anything, if you tell them now. Your daughters will have their cousins, and you will have your sisters blood and soul again. Tell them.

But there was that silent look between Senejess and Armetrethe that stood for all they had not told to her.

"Nothing, Sisters. We spent a good deal of today under stress, and I am tired."

Senejess swallowed. "Of course. We are careless. There is food waiting for you. Daughters, you will bring our meal to the serving tables."

The daughters scrambled to their feet in a ragged chorus of "yes, Mothers." Res and Theia went with them as they hurried to the kitchen alcoves to pull platters of sea fish and shellfish, baskets of both flat and raised bread, and deep bowls of legumes, milled and seasoned so sharply, Praeis could smell them where she sat.

The daughters set the food on the serving tables. The dishes were passed around, and the talk turned to nothing but food. The things they ate as children, the prices of shellfish and legumes, the superiority of this food they ate now compared to what could be gotten in the colonies. Time and again, Praeis's soul reached out, seeking the warmth and easy rhythms she had felt when they first arrived. A few times she thought she almost found them, but they always slipped away again.

She cast a glance at Res and Theia. If the daughters felt the unease between their mothers, they were doing a fine job of hiding it. They seemed absorbed in one another, talking about homes and Humans, the food, all the vast strangeness of Mars and the Solar system, of what it was like to travel in space, of all the technological miracles that Humans produced.

The sky darkened and the plates and bowls emptied. The overhead lights came on as the electric service started up for the night.

Then, suddenly, Armetrethe asked, "So, what is this assignment the Queens have given you as their representative? You did not say."

Praeis's fingers fumbled reaching for a slice of bread. "The Queens say they need a diplomat." She concentrated on scooping some of the legume paste onto her bread. "They want me to help build support for the Confederation."

Senejess's ears curled. "You are supposed to understand the complexity of the Confederation agreement and our Great Family's response to it? After living apart from us for twenty years?"

Praeis bit down on the bread, savoring the spices, the smooth richness of the legumes. It helped hold back the bitterness that welled inside her. "No. I am supposed to learn about it. Surely I'll have the help of my sisters for this, or have you resigned your position on the Council of True Blood?"

Armetrethe opened her mouth and shut it again. "No. We have not resigned."

"Good." Praeis tried to sound nothing but pleased. "Then you can take me to a session, and introduce me to the Councilors. I'm sure there are many new Wise Sisters I will need to get acquainted with," she paused. "And many grievances."

Armetrethe's stump quivered. "I wouldn't class the objections of our Wise Sisters in Council as grievances. Until you understand the situation, you shouldn't either."

Praeis dipped her ears. "You're right. I'm sorry. I spoke too soon. I need to get started on my mission immediately, though. We only have two weeks before the relocation begins, and we need as much consensus as we can get before then, or things won't go smoothly." She met her sister's gaze. "After all, we can't make the Humans do everything."

"I don't see why not," muttered Senejess. "They enjoy it so much."

Praeis felt the skin on her back ripple. *Now, we hear something real.*

"Have there been problems with the Humans, Sisters?" She popped the half-eaten slice of bread into her mouth.

"Nothing that couldn't be solved by reminding them of their place." Armetrethe picked at the shell of a shrimp in the seafood bowl. One of the daughters, Oan, took it from under her hand and peeled it for her.

The daughters all remained respectfully silent during this exchange, including her own. Praeis was proud and thankful. Now was not the time to add poor mothering to the list of charges her sisters had surely piled up against her.

Armetrethe bit down on the shrimp and tore it in two. "The Queens deal with our enemies," she mumbled around the mouthful. "But they refuse to speak firmly with our servants, and they wonder why the Great Family is unhappy."

"Humans do need reminding who has created their positions from time to time." Praeis laid a sympathetic hand on Armetrethe's shoulder. "I have contacts in Bioverse. A few words to the proper superiors will go a long way."

"Thank you, Sister, that will surely help." There was no warmth to Armetrethe's words.

Praeis edged closer to her sister. "Have I misspoken? Is there something else I should do?"

Armetrethe squeezed Praeis's hand briefly. "No. No. I'm sorry, Sister, you mean well, it's just . . ." Armetrethe's ears fell back against her scalp.

"It's just that you do not understand," finished Senejess. "It is not your fault. You did not watch this plague spread and grow even after its origins were supposedly destroyed. You did not see the Queens-of-All wiggling and squirming in delight at this idea from the Getesaph, the *Getesaph,* to bring the Humans swarming down on us. What is the 'Esaph's real plan, hmmm? What are they going to do once our daughters and carrying mothers are all caged and helpless in these city-ships, hmmm?"

All at once, Praeis became keenly aware of Res and Theia across the room with their cousins. Her shoulders stiffened. "I have seen the plague, my Sisters. Jos and Shorie are dead of it. Ten of our daughters are dead of it. It is because of Human help that anyone survived in our colony."

Senejess gripped Praeis's arm. "And what did the Humans do about it?"

Praeis's brow furrowed. "What they could. They helped us treat the symptoms, and create more effective quarantine measures. They kept the sick comfortable and safe, just as they intend to do aboard the city-ships. I have seen the designs for the hospital sections. They are models of cleanliness and efficiency. Our sisters will be well taken care of by those who have made great strides in understanding the nature of these illnesses."

"But they found no cure?"

"No," said Praeis warily. Tension sang between her sisters. It worked its way into her skin like a draft of cold air. Her heartbeat sped up, and her skin twitched and bunched. "They said it was more than one disease, that the weapon had mutated some wild viruses, turning them deadly. They said they'd have to go to All-Cradle to find the source and the cure."

"So!" Armetrethe slapped her thigh, triumphantly. "If they

cured the plague, they couldn't come here to us, could they? They'd have no reason to, would they?"

Praeis felt her ears tip backward. "What are you talking about, Sister?"

Senejess leaned even closer. "When the plague broke out, the Getesaph dropped a fusion bomb on the Octrel, destroying, they said, the creators of the plague." Her intensity thrummed through Praeis's mind. "A year ago, after over a million of our Great Family sickened and died, the Getesaph and their allies contacted the Humans. No one knows what passed between them. Then, they start this idea of Confederation. Bring the Humans in, give them control over our fates, let them take charge of our home. Oh, all for the most benevolent reasons, of course. Let the mighty Humans wipe out the plague and clean up the radioactive zones."

Dizziness threatened. It had been so long since she'd been with so many family. The room was full of them, all their consciousnesses pressing against her, demanding attention. Her sisters both touched her, and it was as if they touched will and soul as well as skin. She wanted to relax, to let the feelings carry her away to calm and love.

But she couldn't. Something was wrong; she knew it. She tasted it on the back of her tongue like the spices from their dinner.

"I don't understand, Sisters." Her voice sounded thick.

"Can't you hear? Ancestors Mine! It shouts at us from the sky!" Armetrethe gripped Praeis with all the strength of her one hand. "The Getesaph entered into an agreement with the Humans. If the Humans place us, all of our Great Family, in a vulnerable position for them, the Getesaph will pay the Humans with the life from our planet."

For a moment, Praeis saw it. For a split second, it made perfect sense. But all her long years of living and working with Humans pulled her back.

"Sisters"—she took their hands—"I hear you. I feel you in my blood. But what you're suggesting is not possible. No Human enclave would agree to enter into a war."

"You've lived with them, Sister," said Senejess, dejection plain in her voice and the set of her ears. "We must bow to your superior knowledge."

"You must bow to nothing of mine, Sisters," said Praeis softly. "But I ask you, on the strength of where I have been and whom I have known, to listen to me closely."

Cold, hard disappointment welled up through her fingertips, and Praeis knew they would not. Perhaps they could not.

"I call the house!" shouted a voice from outside.

Senejess jerked around. "Who . . . ?" She got up swiftly and went to the window. "It's a messenger. I'll take it."

She went to the front door and after a moment returned with a folded, unsealed square of paper.

"It is for you, Praeis."

Puzzled, but grateful for the distraction, Praeis took the letter. It just had her name and the house name on the outside.

She unfolded the paper. The words inside were machine printed, and the language was English.

Ancestors Mine, she thought. *It's from Lynn.*

"What is it?" asked Senejess, leaning over her shoulder. "What language is that?"

"English," said Praeis. "One of the major Human languages. I find it more difficult than Mandarin."

She read:

Dear Praeis,

Hey, look at this, I've put words on paper. This is so strange. I can't manage your thing with the pen. I am even more impressed with you than before.

I was hoping to ask you a favor. David has pulled hospital duty at the

Aurion-in-Uieth *near you.* Praeis sucked in her breath. Lynn had named one of the larger plague hospitals.

He says they're having trouble sorting out the victims and their families for the relocation schedule. Could you visit the site and do a little cultural interp for them so we all know what's up? I'm afraid you were right when you said your home was far more alien than your colony. I appreciate whatever you can do.

All okay with the Queens? Anything you need from us?

GET HOOKED UP. I've got a machine reserved for you. All you have to do is find somewhere to put it. This letter thing makes a great party trick, but we need to do some serious brain dumps soon.

Lynn Nussbaumer

Praeis's ears waved. She could practically hear Lynn's voice reading the letter to her. She looked up and saw her sisters standing expectantly over her.

"It is from one of the Humans with Bioverse," she said. "I have worked with her a long time." She translated the letter as best she could.

Senejess touched her shoulder. "Are you going to do as she says?"

Praeis felt her ears droop. She folded the paper back up. "My first duty is to the work my Queens assigned me, but yes, I'll try to visit David at the hospital." She saw her sister's lowered ears and pinched nostrils. "What would you have me do?"

"You will do as you will, Sister," Senejess's skin rippled up and down her arms. "As you always have."

Praeis swallowed hard against the tears that stung her eyes. She turned away and lifted her head and ears.

"With me, my Daughters. Let me show you the night sky of your home. It has been too long since I have seen a proper sky full of moons and stars I can name."

She led them out the door. The muscles in her back spasmed with tension as she hoped that none of the daughters or her sisters would come with them.

Alone in the yard, she put her arms around her daughters' shoulders. She looked up. Three of the major moons shone between the ragged clouds, with two of the minors between them.

"Well, my own," she said softly. "What do you think?"

Theia leaned her head on Praeis's arm. "About the sky, Mother, or about our family?"

"Ah, I am transparent to you, my own." She tugged Theia's ear gently.

"I like being here," said Res. "I feel . . . enveloped. Connected. Closer to everyone, even Theia. Why?"

Praeis smiled a little sadly. "We are not so careful of each other here. We know exactly who we are with, who is around us, who leads us. In the colonies we have to restrain ourselves more because we are surrounded by those who are not of our Great Family. We can only afford to let go for brief moments, as with the celebration when we heard of the Confederation treaty." She watched the stars watch them all for a long moment.

"What if I pull you away from this natural closeness with what I do? I have already stood against my sisters this evening, and I'm afraid it will get worse." She paused, and her skin trembled, but she said, "I could send you back to Crater Town. We have enough near family there to shelter you."

"No," said Res immediately. "We came to help you, Mother. How can we abandon you?"

You would not be abandoning me. You would be saving yourselves. "I may truly need your help, my own. There may be questions I cannot ask and places I cannot go."

"We are your own," said Theia. "We will stand with you."

Praeis hugged her daughters close and they stood like that for a long time and she closed her eyes so that she could stop her own tears.

Armetrethe looked through the slit window into the dark yard. She could just barely see Praeis and her daughters standing and watching the sky. Senejess stepped up behind her and watched over her shoulder. Their daughters were busy clearing away bowls and pushing the furniture back so they could lay out the sleeping mats and blankets for the night.

"She has not changed," said Armetrethe. Her voice was low, but none of her anger was disguised.

"No." Senejess laid a hand on her warm, dry arm. "Did you think she would?"

"I hoped." Armetrethe's stump flailed briefly. "For a moment, I thought she would open her heart."

Senejess smoothed down the skin on Armetrethe's good arm. "So did I. But we must keep our eyes open to what she really is." She bared her teeth for a moment. "She is the loyal daughter of our Majestic Sisters."

Armetrethe leaned heavily against Senejess. "When did I begin to see devotion to the Queens as a failing, Sister?"

"When Praeis let them order her to sacrifice Urisk Island," answered Senejess softly. "The same time I did."

Chapter IV

Arron Hagopian stared down into the lumps of shadows that daylight would change into the *chvintz Rvi,* the Defenders' quarter of the city. It was a clear morning. The late stars still shone over the balcony. Their light glinted on his helmet. Dawn was just a thin, white line on the horizon. This Earth was a little bigger than the Earth he'd come from, so its days were a little longer. Even after ten years, he still got up outrageously early.

The voices and clatter of predawn traffic filled the warm morning breeze. Getesaph called back and forth to each other, raucous, belligerent, and sometimes mind-bogglingly rude, but peaceful in a very city sort of way.

Should be inside. That data'll be done cooking by now. I need a transmission in the pipe. No sense giving the funding panel extra ammunition.

He didn't move. He gripped the balcony rail with his gloved hands and leaned over it, determined to soak up as much of the early-morning noise as he could hold.

One for the head mechanics. How many cases come in because they've got it bad for a noisy, smoggy, plague-ravaged, glow-in-the-dark planet? His gaze drifted up to the stars again. *And what's Lynn going to say about it?*

He'd had no idea he was ever going to hear from her again.

They'd dissolved into individual silences almost immediately after college. He certainly hadn't expected a hywrite from her. He'd stared at it for so long on the comm screen at the outpost, he'd practically memorized it.

Arron:

I wasn't sure what kind of facilities you'd have there, so you'll excuse the lack of splash on this. I'm coming in with the Bioverse team. I'm a manager, and they've got me working on the evacuation. "Relocation" is what we're supposed to call it. Either way. Some brilliance in the stratosphere decided we can't hire planetside Humans, but I could use a brain dump from someone who's been there before you take off for Whoknows.

Hope you're willing,

Lynn Nussbaumer

Lynn. Lynn had become a corper, and she was on her way with the people who were destroying his life.

"Scholar Arron?"

Arron turned. The Dayisen Rual, Lareet and Umat, stood silhouetted in the arched doorway.

Arron smiled. "Dayisen Lareet, Dayisen Umat." Dayisen was a rank somewhere around the level of colonel, except that it belonged to the entire family. Lareet and Umat were the *tvkesh chvaniff,* the outside sisters for the family Rual. Their children were raised primarily by their sisters and their mother. Their job was to make sure the family was fed, housed, and protected. "Morning's light looks good on you."

The sisters stepped onto the balcony.

"We are perhaps disturbing your meditations?" Lareet leaned her elbows against the balcony railing, twitching her ears toward the wind and noise. She was the shorter and pinker of the two.

Even by Getesaph standards, her skin hung loosely on her, making flaps around her neck and wrists rather than the usual folds.

A set of particularly vehement blasphemies exploded from the streets. Lareet folded her ears down. "I sometimes worry about what you tell your employers about us."

Arron laughed. "Nothing worse than you tell your Members of Parliament about me, I'm sure." It was no secret that the Rual family agreed to host him because the parliamentary members their family had been assigned to wanted firsthand observations of a *man*.

"Have you heard from your people yet?" asked Umat from the doorway. Where her sister was short, pink, and loose-skinned, Umat was tall, grey, and gaunt. Even her ears were thin. They were so sharply pointed that Lareet sometimes teased Umat that they could be used as spears against their enemies.

"No." Arron rubbed his gloved hands together. "I'm going to the outpost today to see if there's word. My department head promised to present my staying on to Bioverse as first-rate public relations. So, we'll see." He glanced at the two Getesaph. "You have no idea what I'm talking about, do you?"

Lareet spread her hands. "There are some times when it is easier to remember that you are an alien than others."

Arron smiled and looked deprecatingly down at himself. Years of fishing, farming, and anything else he could lend a hand to, across all the Hundred Isles, had turned him lean, tan, and corded. He'd always thought of himself as tall, but he could hide behind either of the sisters facing him. His thick work trousers and plain green T-shirt were a sharp contrast to their electric blue uniforms with green rank bands around their cuffs.

"Is there something you need?" he asked.

Umat caressed the threshold with one knobby hand. "Yes, there is. Our members have asked us to speak to you."

Arron's forehead wrinkled. "About what?"

"Scheduling difficulties," said Lareet with careful blandness.

"Severe ones," added Umat.

Lareet's ears dipped. "Monumental."

"Yes."

Arron looked from one to the other. "What schedule are we talking about?"

There was now enough light for him to see the intensity of their expressions as they both looked straight at him. "The relocation," said Umat.

Arron tried to see where this was leading, but couldn't. "I thought the Confederation gave Bioverse total say over the relocation coordination." He'd been stunned when it happened, too. He suspected Bioverse had insisted on it.

"Parliament ceded permission to the Confederation by a narrow majority," Umat reminded him. "Now that the main Bioverse team has arrived, they have sent us the relocation schedule. It states that the Getesaph will not be removed until the last segment of the procedure."

Pride of place? Arron wondered. Lareet and Umat were both obviously waiting for him to say something. He just spread his hands and waited for them.

Lareet strangled a sigh. "The t'Theria are going to be among the first relocated. Once their daughters and carrying mothers are removed from all danger of retaliation, what will prevent them from attacking us?"

Ah. "I don't see how I can help with this," he said carefully. "My department of the university has nothing to do with Bioverse."

"But one of their coordinators is a friend of yours," said Lareet.

Arron's brows jumped up. "Lynn?"

Umat considered. "Is that the same as"—she paused, probably to make sure she got the pronunciation right—"*Manager* Lynn Nussbaumer?"

"Yes." Arron glanced up, as if expecting Lynn to drop from the sky. "That's her."

Lareet nodded. "Our members would consider it a tremendous favor if you would speak with her and ask that the schedule be re-arranged so that the Getesaph are evacuated first, or at least at the same time as the . . . t'Therians."

She'd probably cut herself off from speaking one of the dozen or so insulting terms the Getesaph had for the t'Therians.

Arron's gloves rubbed his clean-suit-covered forearms. "If Parliament is worried about the consequences of the evacuation, you shouldn't go. There's got to be a way the plague can be cleansed with the Ded—" he cut the word off. It was fairly widely known that the word *dedelphi* meant opossum in an ancient Human language. It was also fairly widely known that an opossum was a poorly regarded rodent. "There has to be some way to cleanse the planet with the Family and the Others on the ground. Humans are a clever bunch." *Clever enough that they'll kill what the Confederation has started without even realizing it. Why can't they see that the Families have to shape their future without our interference? Especially our interference on such a world-shattering scale?*

Umat's pointed ears sagged a little. "Scholar Arron, I know you do not agree with this plan to house us in human ships while they cleanse the Earth and our blood for us, but that is the agreement we have reached. Our members favor this much of our Confederation agreements, and we do, too." Arron glanced at Lareet, who dipped her ears in confirmation.

"It is only the timing we question," said Lareet.

"It can be taken to the entire Confederation," Umat went on. "But that might—"

"Renew old tensions," Lareet finished the sentence smoothly. "If we speak the truth about the t'Therian intentions, they will claim we are hurling insults to break the Confederation and say we need to be coerced into cooperation."

He might argue with the phrasing, but Arron couldn't dismiss the conclusion. The enmity between the t'Therians and the Getesaph was a watchword. As far as Arron could determine, the Confederation was the first time the two Families had ever cooperated. The plague had accomplished what centuries of lesser threats had not. No one, however, was sure it had accomplished it firmly and finally.

"I can't guarantee I'll be able to convince Lynn of anything," he said, more to the dawn than to the sisters waiting for his answer. "It's been a very long time since we were . . . close."

"We're only asking you to try," said Lareet.

Arron pushed himself away from the railing. "All right, since you're asking, I'm agreeing."

Umat let out a sigh of relief. Lareet laid a hand on his shoulder. "Thank you."

Umat wrapped her arm around her sister's shoulders. "We'll find out where Manager Lynn is going to be based, so you can plan your trip. It will be somewhere in t'Aori."

"You want me to go from the Hundred Isles to t'Aori?" Arron shook his head. It was easier to get between competing corporate enclaves on Earth than it was to get from the Getesaph archipelago to the t'Aori Peninsula. "Any chance of your members giving me clearance and papers?"

"I don't think so," Umat said. "They want this request kept as quiet as possible."

I can understand that. "All right. You find out where I've got to go, and I'll get there."

"We will owe you all thanks for this, Scholar Arron." Lareet gave his arm a final, friendly shake. "Many times over."

The sisters left him there. Arron turned around and faced the city again. Clouds obscured the stars now, but he stared at the sky anyway.

Lynn. He remembered hours of debates about everything their separate concentrations held. He remembered eclectic midnight feasts, way too much alcohol, and laughing at whatever occurred to them. He wondered what had happened to her, and what had happened to him.

Arron turned around and went back into his room. The university had paid for the double-thick filter doors and windows so he could have a place where he could take off his clean-suit without contaminating the entire house. The room had originally been a closet, so it was small by Getesaph standards. For a Human, though, it made an adequate apartment. A thick mattress lay next to the personal fountain Lareet had given him, saying she couldn't understand how anyone could concentrate without the sound of water nearby. A desk and chair had been shortened to a more Human height by having twenty-five centimeters of their legs sawed off. His flat, shiny portable lay on the desk, surrounded by the paper notes he'd learned to keep. The walls were covered with flat pictures of snowcapped volcanoes, boat-clogged harbors, and portraits of families he had worked with. The wall next to his desk was taken up by a big, full-color, hand-drawn map of the Hundred Isles of Home.

Arron lifted the lid on his portable. DATA CONFIGURED AND SLOTTED INTO REPORT THREAD FORMAT, read the screen. He closed it down and put it into his backpack along with three old clean-suits to take to the outpost recycler.

Most of the house was still asleep. Arron moved quietly past the second-floor sleeping rooms and down the central spiral staircase, which was closer to a Human's idea of a ladder than a Human's idea of stairs. It had taken a long time to get to the point where he could climb down it without going backwards and using his hands. The task had been made more difficult by the fact that the rungs had been spaced for longer legs than his.

Outside, morning light filtered through the layers of cloud and smog, turning the eastern sky into a furnace of orange, pink, and gold. The city was hot, crowded, smelly, and strangely three-dimensional. Rather than flattening the nearby cliffs or just building on top of them, the city builders had carved them. Natural caves had been enlarged and regularized to form compartmentalized buildings with ladders on the outside linking their terraces the way the streets linked the buildings on flatter ground. Suspension bridges ran from hill to hill, and cliff to cliff, allowing what motorized traffic there was to have a path, jostling alongside pushcarts or animal-drawn wagons, the Getesaph's wide, clunking, four-wheeled pedal cars, flocks of fowl, and cattle with their herders.

Mothers and sisters with baskets or daughters on their backs avoided the bridges. They swarmed up ladders instead, crossing roofs and climbing down into narrow, winding streets full of garbage, vendors with carts, or baskets making deliveries or hawking wares, their neighbors, and their cousins. A father, restless, engorged, and strangely graceful, flitted through the crowds.

The vital traffic—military, public health, and anything that had to be rushed between islands—was not on the streets. That traffic drove through the network of concrete-lined "security" tunnels that ran even deeper than the sewer pipes.

Arron squeezed through the crowd, saying "hello" and "the light of day looks good on you" about every three minutes to somebody who called his name. Occasionally he was able to call a name back to a recognized face.

His notoriety had sneaked up on him. In addition to his research, he'd done lectures and talks for assorted Getesaph schools and government departments. Copies of his less formal pieces, modified for paper, got reproduced all over the Hundred Isles. He was Human and he was a *man,* so of course he was a curiosity, but somewhere along the line it had turned into more than that. He had to admit he enjoyed it. It wasn't every field researcher who got to have fans.

Arron started up a broad, much-braced metal ladder that

slanted over a grocery. A shortcut over three roofs that would save him a half hour of threading through crowds. He slid sideways for a mother who carried three infant daughters on her back. A fourth peeked over the rim of the linen-swaddled pouch.

On the roof, a loose crowd gathered around a dry fountain in the northwest corner. Mothers, sisters, and daughters talked, exchanged items out of baskets, or just stood together holding hands. All the public fountains and pools were dry since the plague hit the city. They had been places for bathing, drinking, and laundry washing, and had spread disease even faster than the dirt and animals in the streets. Looking up the island's slope, Arron could see the *chvintz Thur,* the Dead quarter. The edges of the city had been deserted as the population shrank and huddled in on itself.

Sudden thunder split the morning open. The roof shuddered underneath him. A gust of hard, hot wind knocked him flat against the smooth tiles and smashed all the breath out of him. Something thunked against his helmet. Screams, tearing stone, rattling dust, and more thunder poured over him. The tiles under him seemed to tilt.

His ears rang painfully. Arron lifted his head and saw a dust cloud folding in on itself. He lowered his gaze to the roof and swore. The tilting sensation hadn't been an illusion. The roof sagged dangerously in the northeast corner across from the fountain.

Around him, Getesaph gingerly raised ears and heads. They saw the dust cloud and the sag in the roof. The sound of shouts, swearing, and bloody protracted curses against the t'Therians penetrated the sharp ringing that engulfed his hearing.

Of course it was the t'Therians. It was always the t'Therians, whatever it was. Almost always. Enough times.

Arron's fingers felt a vibration under the tiles. He was pretty sure he'd have heard a low creak if his ears were working right.

Down. We need to get down.

Mothers and sisters with daughters clutching their backs or held tight against their chests, crawled or walked in a half crouch up the slope. Some leaned against one another. A number were cut and bleeding. At least two limped.

"Scholar Arron!" exclaimed a sister he didn't know. She peered closely at him, almost pressing her nostrils against his helmet. "You are hurt? You are hit? Someone help me with Scholar Arron!"

"I am fine! I am fine!" he protested as half a dozen hands lifted him to his feet and settled him in the approved crouching position. There was an idea running around that Humans were delicate, just because they were smaller, and not as strong, and were very bad swimmers, and couldn't stand up again immediately after a bomb blast without their vision blurring and their knees wobbling.

Arron let himself be gently led to the southwest edge of the roof. The ladders on that side had been sheltered from the blast. Sisters hung back, and Arron with them, to let the carrying mothers pick their way down first. The streets below were a stew of milling, shoving bodies and, to Arron anyway, unintelligible voices.

When Arron's turn came, he abandoned pride and climbed down backward, using both hands. His escorts followed solicitously beside him. Once they reached the ground, the sisters stood him in an undamaged doorway.

"Rest yourself, Scholar Arron," one admonished. "Public Health will be here soon to see to you."

With that, they turned and joined the river of mothers and sisters heading for the blast site.

Arron leaned against the arched doorway just long enough for his knees to stop trembling. His ears still rang, and his balance wasn't too certain, but he forced himself into a shambling run toward the devastation.

The missile, or bomb, or whatever it had been, had turned a pair of buildings into mountains of rubble. Nearby buildings stood without faces or roofs. Some slumped as if not certain whether to stand or fall.

The rubble was alive with Getesaph. They clambered over the ruin, digging with their hands. A few had gotten hold of shovels. One party lifted out a broken beam and passed it down the side of the mound to other sisters, who carried it out of the way. More sisters arrived every second. Many carried buckets, shovels, or jacks. What hoses there were got turned onto the dozen fledgling fires that sprang up like orange-and-gold weeds. Bucket brigades formed to help douse the flames and to soak down the nearby buildings. The wounded were carried to the sidewalks. Mothers, sisters, and daughters crowded around the victims, even if they could do nothing more than sit with them. No one was left alone or without a hand to hold.

It should have been chaos, but it wasn't. The Getesaph worked together without flaw, panic, or hesitation. Whoever saw something that needed doing first was in charge until someone with more skill or better equipment arrived. Seniority was yielded without argument. There were no spectators. Each new sister who arrived fit herself into the rhythm of the work, like an expert singer joining in on a chorus.

Even the two fathers lurking around the edges seemed to know something important was happening. They stayed where they were without seeking to touch anyone or find what they needed to satisfy themselves.

It was incredible to watch. No group of Humans could have worked like that without years of training. For the Dedelphi this was simply the way it was. For Arron it was the ultimate contradiction. How could they work together so seamlessly but still fight so viciously? There were a million theories, of course, from hormones to pheromones to telepathy, but no one knew for certain. A professor of his had once said, "God introduced us to the Dedelphi to show us how ignorant we still are."

Arron looked at the rubble and hesitated. The fire brigades and some heavy evacuation equipment were starting to arrive. He swerved around the main ruination and headed for the wounded. His first aid was good, and most of it functioned as well on a Getesaph as on a Human.

After that, the world narrowed down to binding lacerations with stockings or torn sleeves or, occasionally, a real sterile bandage. Tunics, skirts, and trousers became pillows and blankets. Blood and gore and body fluids coated his gloves. More blood spattered his helmet and shirt. Sweat poured down his face faster than the clean-suit could wick it away. It puddled under his collar and in the small of his back.

Once, he arrived to find someone impaled on a splinter of wood. Another time, he saw a wailing cluster of daughters around their mother, whose head had been crumpled in like a rotted pumpkin. He could only turn away and let sisters and other mothers comfort the ones suddenly bereaved.

Then, as he lifted a prostrate sister's eyelids to check her pupils, a Getesaph in the white-and-gold coveralls of the public-health team, knelt beside him and gently lifted his hands off the patient.

Arron stood up and backed away. His vision took a moment to clear. Around him he saw more sisters in public-health uniforms descending on the wounded with medical kits, body boards, and oxygen masks.

His job was over. He could stand there and notice that his hands were shaking and how badly he needed a drink, and how prickly and uncomfortable he was under his clean-suit and how sick and withered his stomach felt.

"Scholar Arron!"

Startled, Arron looked up to see Dayisen Lareet threading through the shifting crowd. He lifted a tired hand and waved to her.

"Mother Night, Arron," she said. "You look like you were in the blast, not just tending it."

"I'm all right, really." He wiped his hands ineffectually on his shirt. "I've just been learning about some of the comfort limitations of this suit."

"I'm sure." She looked him over sharply. "You need to rest. Do you want to go home, or to your outpost?"

He looked at his gory hands. "I'd better go to the outpost. I'm going to need a fresh suit and a really long shower."

"I will walk with you." Ignoring the substances soaking his sleeve, Lareet tucked her arm under his. "Umat became concerned when we saw you with the wounded. I said I would make sure you were all right."

"Thanks," said Arron, as they turned down a crooked side street that sloped down toward the harbor.

"Do we know what happened?" he asked after a little while.

Lareet bared her teeth. "The *devna*." The word meant cannibal, and was used to describe the t'Theria. "Who else would it be? We think they launched the device from a boat in the harbor, then sank their boat and took themselves to the bottom so they would not have to answer to us, but we're not sure. We will investigate and report to the Sisters-Chosen-to-Lead. They will report to the Confederation. The t'Therian Queens will claim to know nothing, and no payment will be exacted for our weeping dead."

Arron was silent.

Lareet's ear swiveled sideways toward him. "What are you not saying, Scholar Arron?"

"I am not saying how it is a fine thing that the Confederation prevents my sisters from launching an attack until they are certain who the target should be. It avoids waste of life and anger."

Lareet laughed once, hard. "Your humor is grim and strange, Scholar Arron."

"I was not joking. Consider: the Queens-of-All know that we could attack at any moment and destroy the Confederation and all hope of saving their daughters from the plague. The Humans will not stay if there is a war. If the Sisters-Chosen-to-Lead confront the Queens, the Queens will have to negotiate some kind of satisfaction. The life debt will be paid, and no new dead will be created."

"You make it sound idyllic, Scholar Arron."

He shrugged, and waved his hands. "As long as it is understood that the Families and the Others must work together to save their sisters' children, it is possible. There is no reason for it not to be."

Lareet's ears sagged briefly. "No reason except them and us."

The buildings opened up to make space for the busy quay with its long docks protruding out into the boat-choked harbor. Blocky battlements stood sentry on the shore. One broad aisle in the water remained clear. This was the pass-through for the military. As Arron watched, a midsize transport pulled away from its dock and headed out toward the harbor mouth, maybe on its way to investigate the attack, maybe to make sure the attackers had no allies.

"You can find your way from here?" asked Lareet. "The sister-ferriers will take you? I need to get back to Umat."

"I told you, I'm fine, Lareet." He disentangled her arm from his and squeezed it.

She dipped her ears. "Then I will see you back at our home."

Lareet retreated up an alleyway and Arron headed down to the docks. The harbor ferry was in its slip, and the sister copilots were aboard. Because they had no other passengers they were willing to take him out to the Human island immediately. It wasn't that they minded, they had assured him a thousand times, but some sisters, and mothers particularly, worried about the Human poison.

Arron's pack bumped against his back as he stepped off the ferry and onto the creaky wooden dock. Human Island was really little more than a sandbar at the harbor mouth. Where it wasn't sand and silt, it was rocky, weed-scummed, and moss-coated. Fish washed up in its tidal pools to finish dying. The wind brought in the smells of salt, smog, fish, and burning petroleum. It was not a vacation spot, but it was a decent distance away from anything populated. If anything happened to the ventilation system, or if the outpost got hit in a skirmish, chances were no one would get hurt from exposure to Humans.

The outpost was a service station for the indigent Human population of the Hundred Isles. Corpers and embassites had their amenities provided for them. Over the years, the leftovers—freelancers, curiosity traders, and academics on thread-thin grants, like Arron—had banded together and set up their own sites.

Arron walked down the path they had cleared when the outpost bunker was built. Like the dock, it was getting moss-grown. Riotous orange fungi sprouted on the moss's back.

Time to call a cleanup day, thought Arron automatically. Then, he winced at the thought of his colleagues saying, "Why bother?"

A set of sponge-cement stairs led down into the heart of the island. The micropores in the cement's cell structure siphoned off the water and kept the stairs clean and dry. At the bottom waited a thick metal door that always made Arron think of the entrance to some ancient dungeon.

He stood in front of the door's mirror, and said, "Outpost entry for Arron Hagopian." There was a brief hum while he was scanned. The door cycled open with a huge *whomp!* of air from the ventilator's indraft.

Arron stepped into the foyer. It was a locker room with packages of fresh clean-suits and recyclers for the used ones, along with cubicles for changing and showering. The sign over the inner door read STRIP, FRIEND, AND ENTER.

Arron pulled a clean set of clothing out of his locker, stepped into one of the shower stalls, and unsealed his helmet with a feeling of relief. He stripped off his gloves, shirt, and trousers and tossed them into a pile. He disconnected what the suit-makers euphemistically called the "relief options," the one portion of the clean-suit he'd never really gotten used to, and dropped those into a separate pile. Then, he began the wiggling shuffle needed to peel off the skintight layer of transparent organic that covered him from neck to toe. The organic had another day's worth of use in it, but he did not want to have to soak and scrub it to clean off the stains, so he dropped that in a pile with the other used clothing.

After a long, steaming hot shower he began to feel mostly restored. He dressed in clean shorts and a blue jersey. The helmet and relief options went into the sterilizers, the used clothing into a separator, and the suit and gloves into the recycler.

When he approached, the inner door slid up slowly so as to displace a minimum amount of air and any dust particles that might have escaped the powerful vents.

The outpost's main room was an open, Getesaph-style chamber. Its plaster walls needed scrubbing. Secondhand tables, chairs, and comm stations had been scattered around it. A pair of blocky foodstores sat across from the door. A few short halls led to work alcoves that could be closed off for privacy. Some Humans got tired of the endless communality of the world around them and just needed a place to sit and be alone for a while.

"Arron! How's life in politics?"

Cabal was one of the room's three occupants. He was a lean, copper-skinned man who managed to slouch in every chair he sat in, no matter how contoured it was. The other two were Rath and Regina, both short, round, sienna-colored women. They were also both anthropology students getting in some work in the xeno-field. Arron suspected they were also lovers, but had never felt the need to ask. They waved absently to Arron as he plunked his portable down on an empty chair, then bent back to studying whatever graphic the table laid out between them.

"Today, life in politics is bad." Arron headed for the foodstores. "I spent my morning at a blast site. Couple of buildings went up right in the heart of the Handworks quarter."

"We heard it go," said Rath. "Didn't rattle us here though." She stopped herself. "God, when did a bomb blast less than two kilometers away become passé?"

"Just shows you're becoming like the rest of us, Rathillvna." Cabal raised a pouch of bubbly, brown liquid to her. "Hard as diamond and mad down to your little toenails."

Arron shook his head and lifted the lid on one of the foodstores. Cabal was an antiquarian. He sold Terran ephemera to the locals, everything from books and beverages to honest-to-God antiques like watches and furniture.

"So you say," said Rath amiably. "Hey, Arron, you've got a hywrite waiting for you."

The university? Arron straightened up with a bottle of water and two packs of ration bars in the other. His expression must have looked stunned, because Rath frowned at him.

"We all got one." Rath hit a key on the table's edge and froze the graphic. Arron saw it was a video of a group of ty Porath demonstrating one of their massive trawling nets. "They're from various departments of Bioverse. Basically, it says this is our world now and you've been declared useless. Ship offworld or be shipped. You've got two months."

"No, I got that one already." Arron shook his head. Then he thought of something else. "Hey, Cabal, are you planning a trip to t'Theria before the push-out? I could use a lift." Cabal had a small converted trawler that he used to sail from one port to another, arranging buyers. He could have gotten a plane, he said, but boats inspired fewer random shootings from nervous islanders.

Cabal raised his brows. "You? Heading for t'Theria? I thought you were strictly a Getesaph native."

Arron ignored that last. "I need to meet somebody coming in with the corpers."

"My God." Regina leaned back. "Don't tell me you've got a Human friend?"

Arron smiled indulgently and popped the cap on the water.

"Yeah, actually, I do." He swigged some water down. "I met her at college . . ."

Rath's brow wrinkled in surprise. "You actually went to college? As in left your enclave and lived at a university?"

Arron smiled crookedly. "Didn't realize I had such a stable psych outlay, did you?"

Rath shrugged. "I wouldn't trust you in the same building as my sister."

Cabal snorted. "So, this friend you made during this grand experience of living at a college instead of getting your degree off the wire like a normal person, is coming in with the corpers. And?" He made a "come-on" gesture with his free hand.

"And"—Arron mimicked his gesture—"she wants to pick my brains."

Cabal whistled. "*You* are going to consort with the enemy?"

Arron sighed. "Actually, I'm running an errand for the Dayisen Rual. They want the relocation schedule updated. Somebody didn't think that the Getesaph might be worried about being left on the ground while the t'Theria are up above them." He shook his head. "But I might talk to her about stuff, yeah. Things might be better if someone in the corp knew how complicated the situation here really is."

Regina looked at Rath. "What he means is, maybe he can convince them it's not worth it and they'll turn around and go home."

Rath smiled grimly. "Not a chance, Arron. They've been promised new gene combos. Once the corpers get the scent, there's no calling them off." She blew out a sigh. "And I almost had my dissertation topic sorted out."

"Yeah, you've only been saying that for three years," muttered Regina. Rath glared at her, and Regina patted her hand. " 'Sokay. We'll find another world to dissect." Arron had a feeling she was carefully not looking at him.

Cabal broke the silence. "It wouldn't hurt me to make one more run out there. Meet me here at high tide in two days, and we'll head out, okay?"

"Okay, thanks." Arron transferred his ration packs to the hand holding the water bottle and picked up the portable. "Now, if you all will excuse me, I have some personal business to attend to." He bowed to the assembly and retreated into one of the work alcoves.

He slid the door shut behind him, cutting off the flow of banter from the main room. The alcove contained a chair, a comm station, a table, and a bunk. He set his portable on the table and jacked it into the comm station.

Arron slid into the station's chair and dropped his stuff on the table. "Station. This is Arron Hagopian. Identify and open mail." The one thing he missed out here was being able to follow the live threads. Without a full sat-net to handle the transactions, he had to receive the conversations as mail dumps and upload his responses.

Arron tore open a pack of bars and munched on one of the crispy oblongs that was supposed to taste like fried rice but didn't. The station beeped and whirred. The outpost account didn't have quite enough for a fully interactive AI, but they were saving for it. *We had been saving for it,* Arron corrected himself. *Now we are arguing about how to divide up the outpost's assets.*

The station blurted out a canned message. "Arron Hagopian identified. Sixty-five conversation holders have new data. One hywrite received. Displaying titles."

The screen lit up with amber lines of text. Arron skimmed them. Regarding Exploitation of Dedelph and the Dedelphi. Bioverse Feeding on Sisters' Fear, that one actually had a Dedelphi author from the Mars colonies. Bioverse Saves Lives. There were several similar titles. He didn't see the names for any new architects. The discussion just didn't seem to be expanding any. The calls for inquiries and boycotts weren't getting anywhere. They certainly weren't hurting Bioverse.

Arron suddenly realized that he was really looking for a conversation started by Lynn. He wanted some hint as to where she stood. He wanted to know what she saw that led her to believe the evacuation of the Dedelphi was a good idea.

I want to be ready for her. Arron stared at the alcove's curving white walls. *Rath pinned it. I want to be able to tell her she's wrong.*

Arron scrubbed at his face, as if trying to wipe something sticky off his skin.

At the very bottom of the list was the address for Professor Marcus Avenall at the University of the East.

Arron drank some more water, trying to swallow his tension at the same time.

"Station, open hywrite from Professor Marcus Avenall."

Several lines of plain text formed on the screen. Marcus had always been a minimalist.

Arron:

We talked to Bioverse. They say they've barely got enough room for the Dedelphi and support staff. The only way you're going to be allowed to stay with the evacuees is if we pay the cost of maintaining you on one of the ships for the duration.

Putting it bluntly, Arron, the university can't afford that.

You've done amazing work. Come home, and we'll be delighted to find you a new project.

Arron slumped back. *Well, that's that. Home again, home again, riggity-jig.*

Anger surged through him. He hurled the water bottle at the wall. Plastic hit plaster with a thud and dropped to the floor. Liquid splattered across the wall and spilled onto the floor tiles, which drank it in thirstily.

He dropped his head into his hands and ran them back and forth across his scalp.

It wasn't just him. It wasn't that he'd fallen in love with the world and its people, which he had, he admitted it. It was that something unprecedented was happening here and nobody, *nobody* understood that Bioverse was about to shatter it to pieces.

And nobody cared.

An idea touched the back of his mind. He sat up straight again. "Station. Download and replay file Hresh from Arron Hagopian's portable jacked into your number three port."

"Loading. Replay."

It was a full media blitz file. One of the few he'd ever created that wasn't for grant money. It was from his first trip out into the field. He'd been assigned to a world called Hresh. Humans, in the form of the Avitrol Corp, had found the world seventy-five years before Arron arrived. Avitrol was a life-miner. They went out looking for new organic molecules that could be pressed into service as nanotech. Such things were rare, but incredibly valuable.

The Hreshi were shambling, gold-pelted people whose idea of nanotech was a well-ripened cheese. Avitrol offered them luxury goods, automated services, and the skills to use them. All they asked in return was the run of the planet and the right to keep whatever useful things they found.

When Arron got there to study a people he was physically incapable of talking to, huge segments of their world had been razed. First, Avitrol hauled up plants and insects by the freighter-load to test and retest. Then, the Hreshi themselves mined and drilled for fuels and raw materials for their new manufacturing needs. The people, dazed and distracted by their new wealth and able to travel farther and faster than ever, were warring with one another over ideals and land use. The gouging of their ecosphere unleashed disease that their medical sciences, which Avitrol had forgotten to augment with their luxury-goods market, had no way to control.

Arron had stood horrified at the sight of so many dead and dying while his site supervisor lectured about what a great thing it was to find a race in transition like this. Furious, he'd built the blitz file and tried to knot it into the web, only to be informed by the university that if his name was found connected to its release, he could find other employment.

So, he'd kept it under wraps. He'd tied other more staid and strictly factual knots. With the help of thousands of other voices, the webbed enclaves had rallied. Avitrol was shunned and had to make reparations to the Hresh.

Now, as he watched the horrors he'd recorded, Arron wondered if the blitz could be reworked. He could weave parallels between Avitrol's life-mining of the Hreshi and Bioverse's working over of the Dedelphi. He could do it. His career at the university would be over, but if he could get the word out about what was happening here, if he could give back just a portion of the life and hospitality the Getesaph had shown him, it would be worth it.

He'd need to set down a core idea to give the rest of the presentation something to wrap around. Take a page from Marcus and minimalize it. A text block, maybe with music in the background, but make it something they'd have to pay attention to.

"Station, prepare media-tool workspace for a new thread. Clear space for text input. Convert voice input to text."

Arron bent over the keyboard and set to work.

Parliament Hall was never quite empty. Soldiers patrolled its gates and stood beside its doors, guarding the Members and their staff who worked through the night. The wide, polished-stone rooms were lit, if dimly, by electricity all night long. Lareet had never lost her love of the beauty of the place. Layers of round wooden terraces rose from the floor like uneven stacks of coins. Tiled pools held island conference spaces in their center, fountains and waterfalls that filled every crevice with music.

Umat paced beside her, close enough so that their shoulders could rub reassuringly together. Umat's expression was intense. Her slender ears were completely alert. She had probably already pushed the memory of the morning's blast into the back of her mind and was concentrating on nothing except accomplishing their errand. Umat was like that, and Lareet envied her.

Silver lamplight illuminated a third-level terrace near the center of the hall. Their members, the Members Shavck, Ris, Pem, and Vreaith, sat at the circular worktable. Reflexively, Lareet fell back and let Umat precede her up the steeply slanting stairway (why did Arron call stairs *ladders*? Ladders were temporary, mobile things) to their workspace.

Lareet and Umat stood side by side in front of the Member's worktable. Umat extended her hand and received the touch on her knuckles from Shavck Pem.

"Dayisen Umat. Dayisen Lareet," Member Pem greeted them. "The shades of night look well on you."

Lareet let Umat return the greeting. No one who had hearing could miss the pride in Umat's voice as she said, "We were successful. Scholar Arron will speak to Manager Lynn."

"Excellent!" boomed Member Vreaith, folding her hands on her belly. "I knew he would not refuse you after years of guestship and particular friendship."

Lareet wished she could bask in the approval as fully as Umat did. "He did warn us, Members, that she might not be persuaded. He has not had contact with her for a long time."

Umat dropped one ear toward her scalp in warning. "He did, however, complete his mating with her amicably. Our best research shows this can establish a pattern of favor and reciprocation, even if the parties involved are separated."

Member Ris laughed quietly. "Do relax, Dayisen Rual, both of you. No one is expecting a blood promise. There is nothing to do now but wait and see what happens. If the schedule is changed, we can go ahead with our first plans. If it is not"—her ears dropped briefly and lifted—"alternatives exist."

"Thank you, Members." Umat reached out and quickly touched Member Ris's hands. "We stand ready for further assignments."

"As is expected." Member Vreaith dipped her ears approvingly. "We have nothing further in this special area for you until we hear about the schedule. Go home and spend the night with your family in health and peace."

The Members did not bother with a parting touch. They just bent back over their table and sorted through the papers, talking in low voices about what was indicated by *this* missive and *that* note. Lareet politely folded her ears to muffle the conversation.

Umat, radiating satisfaction, tucked her arm into the crook of her sister's, pivoted them both around, and waved to indicate that Lareet should go first down the stairs. Lareet gripped the rungs tightly with her toes and tried to shake the unease that had settled against her skin as she climbed down to the main floor.

"What is the matter with you?" asked Umat softly, as they returned to the vaulted foyer. "You're as twitchy as a newt on hot concrete."

Lareet nodded to the soldiers who opened the double doors. She did not speak until she and Umat had crossed the shaded lawn with its thick ferns and moss, been checked out through the gate, and walked five yards down the crowded street.

"I was talking with Scholar Arron this morning," Lareet said finally. "He makes some strong arguments for the Confederation."

Umat squeezed her arm. "Scholar Arron is our sister in all but blood, but he is naive. He believes the *devna* can be talked out of killing us."

Lareet held her sister's arm tightly for a moment. "He also believes we can be talked out of killing them."

Umat drew herself up short. She turned and faced her sister. "Listen to me, my pouch-sister. I agree with Scholar Arron that the wars must stop. We will all of us be dead if they don't. We are going to stop them."

"You're right." Lareet laid her hands over her sister's. "I'm just feeling we should be united in this. Our Members are not even acting for the full Defenders' House . . . "

"Our members are constantly gathering support, Lareet. By the time everything's in place, they'll have the entire Parliament." She blew across her palm, trying to send Lareet's worries to the wind. "We will make the world safe for our blood."

Let that be true, Lareet breathed silently to the ground. *Please, let that be true.*

Boats crammed into the harbor. They jostled one another's sides and tangled one another's anchor cables. Little fishers and squared-off houseboats clustered around the sides of the big barges, freighters, and the two mammoth warships.

It could have been a harbor from any of a hundred times and places in the history of the Humans' Earth. There were only so many shapes of vessel that could carry a biocular biped with two opposable thumbs efficiently across open water. Physics as much as body shape determined the way you built your ships, and physics varied a lot less than form.

Torches, candles, and lamps reflected their light on the black, trash-speckled water. The wind was choked with scents of salt, dead fish, hot oil, hot fish, smog, and charcoal. Voices called to each other in six or eight different dialects, punctuated here and there by the splash as someone dived into the water to swim for somewhere they couldn't walk to.

Cabal walked across the harbor by stepping from boat to boat. His boots clumped heavily against damp wood as he stepped on decks, chests, or boxes. Seawater soaked the cuffs of his work trousers, and more of it spattered his canvas shirt and short jacket. Sometimes heads turned as he passed. Sometimes someone shouted at him to get his poison off their boat. Mostly, however, he was ignored as an equal with the dozen or so Dedelphi who made similar zigzag paths to and from the shore.

Finally, he swung his leg over the side of a well-kept fishing boat. It was bigger by half than most of the others in the harbor, built for market fishing rather than just subsistence. He negotiated his way between ropes, chests, kegs, and nets.

"Who's home?" called Cabal in the major Getesaph dialect.

A hatch swung back, creating a square of yellow lamplight in the deck.

"Who's asking?" came the reply from belowdecks.

"Your *brother,*" Cabal used the English word. There was no true equivalent in Getesaph.

"Come in, then."

Cabal descended the ladder. Belowdecks was a single room with bunks built into the walls, a galley area at one end, and a workshop at the other. Two Getesaph sat on the farside of a central table. They were both stripped down to canvas breeches and rubber boots, like fishers usually were.

"Advisor Tvir, Advisor Cishka," he said quietly as he sat down on the bench opposite them.

"Trader Cabal," replied Advisor Tvir. "The shades of night look well on you. What's your news?"

Cabal nodded. "Scholar Arron is contacting a friend of his on behalf of the members of the dayisen he lives with. They want to change the relocation schedule, and this friend, she's working on that part of the project."

Advisor Cishka had lost an ear in some skirmish long ago. She rubbed the scar thoughtfully. "Do we know how likely he is to succeed in this?"

"I have no idea," Cabal shrugged. "They were close once, but he hasn't seen her in years. He's not talking about it much."

"Why is he talking about it at all? You and he are not true friends, you have said."

"He asked me to take him to t'Theria to meet her, and I've also told you how he gets going about internal affairs at every opportunity."

Advisor Cishka's remaining ear twitched. "You do not respect him, do you?"

Cabal shrugged again and thought a minute before he found a way to construct the sentence in Getesaph. "There are places where he is shaded by night in broad daylight. He doesn't always understand how people could not completely agree with him."

"I hear you." Advisor Tvir nodded. "At least I think I do. Thank you, Trader Cabal. You will let us know if he succeeds or fails? We need to know which of their plans the Defenders will implement."

"As soon as I know, you'll know." Cabal stood up, flexing his knees to keep his balance as the boat bobbled on the harbor's gentle waves. "Is there anything else, Advisor Tvir? Advisor Cishka?"

"Not tonight, Trader Cabal. Go with care."

Cabal smiled and let his teeth show behind his face mask. "Always."

Chapter V

The command center for the city-ship *Ur* looked more like an office than a ship's bridge. Captain Elizabeth Esmaraude and her section officers worked at a multiterminal table that had a dedicated AI of its own. The space around the walls had been divided into private meeting rooms, screening facilities, a flash-cook foodstore with an attached coffee urn and bread box, and a lavatory complete with shower stall.

When Keale stepped through the hatchway, Captain Esmaraude was at the central table, going over something on the screen with her chief gravity engineer, Rudu King. King was an ebony-skinned man wearing tan coveralls with no markings except a small, silver commander's insignia on his collar.

Keale suppressed a smile. If there was a man who loved his job, it was Rudu King. When Captain Esmaraude brought the *Ur* in, Keale had asked her for a tour, and she had handed him over to King to see the gravity deck. Rudu had taken him down the work shafts, seemingly oblivious to the weird pushes and pulls of the gravity fields. He'd delivered a nonstop commentary as Keale peered through thick glass at the forests of lozenge-shaped tractor units hanging in the yokes that controlled their slew and pitch.

Each tractor contained the toroids or "doughnuts" of neutral particles that turned in on themselves according to equations that King reeled off like other people reeled off plots of simulations or paragraphs of regulations. He talked nonstop about angles of interference, field calculations, the need for constant spot checking of each and every "doughnut holder" in case a charged particle some how got into the toroid, which would cause the toroid to start breaking down into heat and X rays, or, worse, if some irregularity developed in the particle spin, which could shake the entire doughnut, the holder, and its neighbors, and eventually the whole ship and . . .

Keale had watched the man carefully for signs of boredom or attempts to impress, but had seen neither. This was simply King's entire life, down here in this dizzying world of fields, neutral particles, and delicate, precise angles and calculations.

The only time Keale managed to make King pause was when he asked if one of the tractors could be shut down.

"Why?" King's eyes narrowed.

"Security precautions," Keale had replied.

"You want a zero-gee section somewhere?"

"No, no, just a . . . an area of confusion."

Standing on the work platform, King stared at his rows of tractors with his mouth pressed into a long, thin line.

"Yes, we can do that. Bleed off one of the doughnuts." He drummed his thick, callused fingers against the platform's rail. "Rotate the field angles on a few others. We won't like it, the captain won't like it, and the ship won't like it, but we can do it."

Now, watching the captain and the gravitor together, Keale folded his hands behind his back and got ready to wait. King was methodical in the extreme, and Esmaraude . . . Keale had known her for a long time. She did not rush for anybody.

His timing appeared to be good. Rudu's lips moved as he subvocalized something to whatever implants he carried and then stood up, nodding to his captain. Esmaraude nodded back and turned toward Keale. As Rudu disappeared through the hatch in the floor that led down to the gravity deck, Esmaraude waved Keale forward.

"Keale, so glad you could join us." She kicked out a chair for him.

"You're top on my list of priorities, Esmo, you know that." Keale sat down. Esmo was a short, square woman with thick brown hair cut short to keep it out of her way. Whereas most people who took on eye implants had cameras or video displays you couldn't tell from a natural eye, Esmaraude had a pair of old-fashioned looking wire-and-crystal spectacles connected to terminals at her temples. They gave her greater display range and flexibility, she said, and the extra memory space allowed her to hook directly into the ship's info systems if she needed to.

The corner of Esmo's mouth twitched. "I am top priority only because I have something you want, Kaye."

He shrugged elaborately. "I want to do my job and keep your people safe."

She sighed. "You really think we're in for trouble?"

"I really think we could be, yes."

All the humor drained out of her eyes. "Where from?"

Keale knew she didn't mean who'd start it. "Can you get me a schematic up on this?" He tapped the station screen.

Esmo preferred to give her commands with keys rather than her voice. She typed on the pad for a moment. The screen cleared and showed a 3-D white-line print of the *Ur.* Keale reached across and hit a couple of keys. The diagram resolved itself to show the ship as seen from above.

"Right here." He laid his finger on the space between the city dome and the engineering dome.

Esmo peered at the screen. "You think they're going to get through the tunnels?"

"No. We can seal the hatches. The shortest, easiest way between their space and ours is straight across the hull. It's only thirty meters from the city dome to engineering, and us."

Now Esmo was looking hard at him. "It's thirty meters of hard vacuum, Kaye. I know the pogos can hold their breath a long time, but . . ."

"They're going to have access to pressure suits that we're going to show them how to use." He frowned at the schematic. "Maybe nothing will happen, Esmo, but if they're going to do anything in the heat of the moment, I don't want to make it easy on them."

Esmo dropped her gaze. She pulled the command word out of its slot and studied it. It was a fragile glass and electro-optic key that decrypted all the command systems on the ship. Without it, even if you could get the engines going, you couldn't make any navigation calculations. You could not override any of the artificial intelligence's standing orders. You could not open any locked doors or databases. There were two other keys. Rudu King had one for the gravity systems, and the chief engineer had one for the ship's drive. But it was Esmo's key that controlled the minute, complex workings of the ship. The slender, sparkling artifact represented the real power of the captain. Keale wondered what was going on behind her impassive eyes as she looked at it.

Esmo returned the key to its place. "Want a cup of coffee?"

"Sure," said Keale. He stood up and followed her to the foodstore. *What are you not getting at, Esmo?*

Esmo got two plastic mugs out of the cupboard and started drawing rich, black coffee out of the urn. Its scent filled the air. She handed one to Keale and put the second on the counter while she peeked into the bread box. The smell of yeast and baking immediately joined the coffee.

Finally, she turned around. "Why are you doing this, Kaye?"

"Because I give a damn about whether the people on this project live or die," he said irritably. "Which seems to be a major cause for surprise."

Esmo shook her head. "I don't mean that. I mean why are you doing this." She waved her hand toward the command center. "Sneaking around, laying down the emotional blackmail, trying to drum up underground support with the seniors." She stopped when she saw him grimace. "There aren't that many people on this project yet, Kaye. Word still gets around fairly quickly."

Keale took a quick sip of coffee. A good blend, rich but not too bitter. Trust Esmo to get the best for her people, and herself. Esmo took her job seriously, but she liked her comforts. "I'm doing this because the veeps and presies aren't voting me anything to work with. We're getting a thousand multipurpose shuttles, but not one of them will be armed. I'm only getting fifteen hundred security personnel per ship, to cover both Human and Dedelphi personnel, and that includes the admin bodies." He frowned at his coffee, remembering the last conversation he'd had with Veep Brador on the subject. "It's been made quite clear to me that most of the trouble has been expected to come from the Human side of things, as the Dedelphi do not appear to have problems such as petty theft or drunkenness. They definitely do not have any problem with sexual assault, for obvious reasons, and what brawls they do have are settled in-family. So, none of my fifteen-hundred-per-ship personnel are going to be equipped with lethal-force capabilities." He set the coffee down and folded his arms. Esmo watched him without a trace of expression on her face. "Since there's no help there, I've got to find it where I can."

Esmo said nothing, she just kept looking at him. Finally, he cracked. "All right, what is it, Esmo?"

She blinked, picked up her coffee, and took a swallow. "I'm just wondering why you took this job in the first place."

Ah. Yes. There was that, wasn't there? Keale ran his hand through his hair. Maybe he was too paranoid. Maybe he was too hungry. If something happened, and his team locked it down, there'd be bonuses, praise, promotions, everything you could hope for. He knew it, everybody knew it.

How much did he really need, though? He was already fully vested. He could cash in tomorrow and be comfortable for the rest of his life. What he didn't have was a coup of any kind. No feather in his cap, as the saying went. That had bothered him a lot as a younger man. He thought he'd gotten over it, but when the offer to head up the team going to All-Cradle had come along, he'd jumped at it. Inside him, that young, eager man had woken up and started polishing his boots.

It was not a comfortable feeling. It was also not one he was ready to admit to out loud, not even to Esmo.

So, he gave her the other part of the truth. "When I signed up, I didn't know how many of my requests and suggestions were going to be refused."

"You could quit, or you could raise a stink in the management courts about dereliction of duty and ignorant endangerment of Bioverse citizens."

"Yeah, I could," he admitted. "But all of that will take a lot longer than two weeks. Do you really think they're going to hold things up just to give me time to scream my head off?"

Esmo puffed out her cheeks. He couldn't help thinking she knew what he hadn't said, but then again, he frequently got that impression when talking to Esmo.

"They had you write up the contingency measures, didn't they? What Bioverse can or will do if the Confederation falls apart?"

Her words dropped like stones. Keale took a long drink of coffee before answering. He had treated that part of his assignment as a military exercise. It made good sense. You had to have plans in case the worst happened. It wasn't anything he hadn't done before. It also wasn't anything so many lives had hung on before.

He shouldn't even be thinking about it in that light. The fact that he had was another uncomfortable realization. "Yes, I did have to write up the contingency measures."

"And you can't tell me what they are, can you?"

"You know I can't, Esmo."

They stood in silence for a minute, surrounded by the smells of good coffee and fresh bread. "Bad?" she asked.

"Efficient."

Her eyebrows arched. "More efficient than you've ever had to be personally responsible for?"

His face tightened. "Esmo, my entire career has been about keeping people safe. If we have to oversee any actions in hostile territory, there are going to be a lot of unsafe people around."

Esmo pursed her mouth. "So, you want any . . . troublemakers dealt with quickly, and efficiently, before the trouble spreads."

He nodded. Esmo was very good, she always had been. But then, like him, she'd grown up in Bioverse, and she knew the score, the game, the rewards, and the penalties. "Yes, I do."

She picked her mug up again and swirled the coffee around for a moment. "I suppose you know the relocation schedule's been set back a week because of this delay in the ID hardware."

He nodded solemnly. "I'd heard."

She leaned back against the counter and took a swallow of coffee. "You've got a week then."

Keale let himself smile. "Thanks, Esmo."

She focused on something on her spectacles he couldn't see. "I'll give you Chief Engineer Tiege. He's got a niece on staff with him, a junior grade named Marjorie Wilkes. Runs her ragged. It won't look funny if they clock some extra time together." She turned her attention fully onto Keale again, and a sharp, warning light shone in Esmo's dark eyes. "Keep it quiet, Kaye. Neither one of us needs any garbage from the veeps on this one."

"You've got my word, Esmo."

She looked at him over the rims of her spectacles and gave him her slow, broad smile. "I've got a lot more than that on you, Kaye, and don't you forget it."

The satellite *Keystone* slid into its orbit. It rotated gently, and its solar panels angled themselves to catch the sunlight.

Lynn watched the completion of the satellite network from the wall screen in her new office. The t'Theria had given Bioverse a set of abandoned buildings. The architects had promptly fed them to the construction jobbers so the raw materials could be reworked into a place Humans would be comfortable with. One of the room's walls was video-capable. The two adjoining walls were actually windows. One looked out over the gleaming new coordinators complex. The other looked across the cliffs and out into Ipetia harbor. Lynn made sure the sound filters were set so she could hear the surf crash against the rocks.

With the sat-net finally in place, she could start getting her office linked to the necessary databases. She felt isolated with just her implants and a portable. Worse, she felt delayed. Trace and R.J. in their shared space out front were already hard at work, reeling out threads for access to progress reports and problem sessions. At the same time, they were tying the incoming threads to their databases and schedules. The rest of the staff was laying out microschedules, arranging transports, working on plans for a real network of roads to be laid down by the engineers, coordinating with the grievance committees, and trying to beg, borrow, or steal badly needed supplies.

Two new city-ships—the *Beijing* and the *Rome*—were in place over All-Cradle's Lagrange point. Another, the *Athens,* was on its way from Sol. Each had a hundred converted midrange shuttles to work with. She had calls in to the port centers in t'Smeras, Avar Fil, and Usoph. They had room to evacuate, sorry, relocate, the first three million t'Therians, as soon as the ports were ready for them. The selected preparatory personnel would go first and take a week to make sure everything would be comfortable for the main body of citizens. The mass relocation would follow.

"Lynn?" R.J.'s voice came across the intercom. "Lynn, we've got a crisis."

Lynn straightened up. "Already? What is it?"

"I'm sending you in a thread. Veep Brador wants you to follow it to the knot."

Uh-oh. Lynn dropped into the chair in front of her comm station. *Who's said what out there?*

"Why didn't he send it straight to me?" she asked with a feeling of foreboding.

"He's furious, Lynn. This is what he does when he's furious."

"Ah." Lynn nodded. "Thanks."

The screen lit up to show the rambling code that made up the thread's spec. "Claude," Lynn said to activate the room voice, "reel out the loaded thread."

"Completing request."

The thread spun out into the web. Addresses, keys, and graphics scrolled up on the screen too fast for her to follow. Then, the screen went black except for a line of sedate blue text in shining cursive lettering.

A Comparison of the Hreshi Degradation and the Bioverse Efforts on Dedelph.

Lynn swallowed. The listed architect for the knot was Arron Hagopian of Prandth Island, one of the Hundred Isles of Home on the planet Dedelph.

Arron? What are you doing? "Claude, untie the knot."

The text vanished. In its place appeared a group of delicate, gold-furred bipeds wearing beige coveralls. They gazed over a valley that had been ripped up and overturned until there was nothing left but uneven dirt and broken roots.

Oh, no.

The voice-over started. "Avitrol scouts discovered the Hresh in the four hundred fiftieth year of the third millennium, according to their major calendar." Arron had, Lynn noted with some approval, resisted the temptation to make himself sound more sonorous or musical than he really was. This was the same voice that she knew from college. "Seventy-five years later, Avitrol had laid waste to major segments of the Hreshi planet, aided the dispersion of dozens of new infectious diseases." The scene blended into a crowd of Hreshi crouched outside a square building Lynn assumed was a hospital. Their heads and hands were swollen to grotesque proportions. "And created economic instabilities that caused four major wars which killed millions of Hreshi." Another valley, this one trampled and torn, with Hreshi bodies left embedded in mud, blood, and offal. Lynn winced.

Now, the view shifted to a scene Lynn was becoming very familiar with. It was the crowded stage of the Dedelphi Confederation treaty signing with the big screen behind it and the Bioverse execs smiling benignly down.

"Trillions of miles away, the Dedelphi, an embattled, ecologically threatened race, signed a treaty with the Bioverse Corp in the hopes that Bioverse would be able to reverse the ecological damage on their planet and stop the horrible engineered plagues that had been unleashed during a recent war."

The scene split, displaying the sad, static Hreshi on one side and the ceremonious Dedelphi on the other.

"It will be argued that there are no similarities between these two cultures and their circumstances. The Hreshi were discovered by chance. The Dedelphi are old allies of the Human race and invited Bioverse in. Avitrol had no mission except profit. Bioverse has a clear-cut contract of benefit to the Dedelphi. But there is a binding similarity between both corps and both worlds."

The screen showed a single scene: a much-speeded-up look at

translsucent beads binding together in the double-helix pattern of DNA.

"Both corps were in search of new life."

Oh, come on, Arron. You're not going to say we've got the same mission as Avitrol?

But obviously he was. Images cut, shifted, jumped, blurred, and blended across the screen, linking the Hreshi and the Dedelphi while Arron talked about the immeasurable wealth new bioforms could provide in terms of nanotech advances and how corporate execs would go to any lengths to recoup their outlays.

"Bioverse has already laid out fifty thousand kiloshares to its subcontractors, twenty thousand to its partners, and over a million and a half to investors and citizens. Will they be able to stop, will they want to stop for any reason, even impending cultural disaster, before they get what they came for?"

Lynn hung her head. *How did your university let you get away with this little tabloid?*

"Claude, is there a summary for this? If there is, fast-forward to it."

The view on the screen blurred until all that was left was glowing blue text on the black background. It scrolled forward slowly to the rhythm of soft, funereal drumming.

That the Dedelphi have a history of violence against their own kind is indisputable. That the plague which has decimated their people is the result of this violence is also indisputable.

But this plague has brought about a miracle. For the first time in their history, all the governments on this many-named planet are working together on a goal. The ancient enemies stand united. This is a critical moment.

We Humans went through a similar moment in the twenty-first century, C.E. *At that time our world had a choice. We could have united, or fragmented.*

We chose to fragment. Humanity broke apart into our little enclaves, conglomerates, and corporations. For us, this has worked smoothly. However, when our moment came we had developed enough info and biotechs that smaller enclaves could obtain food, goods, and information to sustain themselves.

The Dedelphi are years away from that kind of technology, if they can ever reach it. They don't have the easy access to the natural resources Earth had. If we split them up now, clean up their world, and leave, we remove any impetus for them to unite. They will return to their warfare, chewing up yet more resources, wasting more years, and digging themselves even farther into their graves, until another bioweapon is released to finish the descent.

This plague wasn't caused by the first bioweapon used, just the most recent. The next one will be even more devastating than this.

If we allow the Dedelphi to work out their own solution to this problem, if they have to work together to save themselves, the groundwork is laid for peaceful coexistence. If they are given the time, they can develop an international information exchange in order to trade research and hard goods. This way, when and if they have to splinter permanently as Humanity has, they have a chance of surviving without returning to a primitive state.

We can either buy them that time, or we can strip it from them.

The screen went blank. Lynn rested her helmeted forehead against her hand.

It was an attention getter, that was for sure. It was also Arron at his best. It wove the facts into new patterns and held them up for everyone to see. It looked good, it felt good, who was to say it wasn't true? More than once she'd found herself reduced to sputtering, "But that's not how it *works*" when faced with one of Arron's verbal creations.

Lynn shook herself. "Claude, run a call out for Vice President Emile Brador. Make sure he knows it's me."

"Completing request."

Lynn busied herself threading together databases until the station back-burnered her tasks and brought up Veep Brador's head and shoulders.

"Record session," she murmured to her implant. It never hurt to have a personal record of what you'd said to the boss, and what the boss had said to you.

Brador's face had flushed to a deep burgundy and his round owl-eyes narrowed to half-moons. "I presume you untied the knot, Dr. Nussbaumer?"

"Yes, I did. It's extremely inflammatory." Lynn spread her hands. "What I want to know is why did you call it to my attention? This should be over with the PR dervishes, or sent back to HQ, if you think it's that important."

Brador's face flushed even darker. "Hagopian is a friend of yours."

Lynn frowned. "Am I going to be held accountable for him?"

"You petitioned for a citizenship offer for him."

Oh, so that's what this is about. "That petition was rejected on the grounds that we weren't hiring any planetside Humans." *Which is one of the dumber ideas the veeps and presies back home laid down on us.*

"Dr. Nussbaumer"—Brador leaned forward until his nose almost touched the screen—"we have already had three subcontractors pull out of negotiations because of this knot. It does not look good that you sponsored its architect for citizenship."

"Are you claiming I was trying to sabotage something by bringing Arron on board?" Lynn met his gaze coolly.

She could practically see the wheels turning. Bioverse had done a background check. Any unacceptable associations would have kept her out. If Brador went ahead and accused her of corporate espionage based on her knowing someone Bioverse had already cleared, she could pull him down into the management courts for defamation of character.

Lynn wouldn't enjoy that, but she'd do it to save her reputation. Then she'd quit, and she suspected Brador knew it.

"It would save the dervishes a lot of trouble if you could debunk the Avitrol comparison for Hagopian."

"Believe me, Vice President, I intend to try." *I intend to beat his thick skull against the wall, if necessary.* "Is there anything else?"

"No, Dr. Nussbaumer, fortunately." His skin color faded a little. "Thank you for your attention to this matter."

"You're welcome." Lynn cut the connection. "Store recording under file name Brador One," she told her implant as she stood up.

Lynn walked into the outer office. Both Trace and R.J. looked up, startled.

"Anything else entertaining happening?" Lynn folded her arms and leaned against the wall.

"Well"—R.J. held out a folded sheet of paper—"we found this on the doorstep. It's got your name on it."

Lynn took it. It did have her name on it, along with the name of the complex, and the street it sat on. Praeis's name and the name of her house had been written on it as well. The packet had been glued tightly shut.

Lynn carefully tore the paper open.

The letter was in t'Therian, except for a few words in English scattered through the text.

> From Praeis Shin t'Theria addressing my respected ally *Lynn Nussbaumer,*
>
> I'm writing you in t'Therian because you obviously need the practice translating. However, don't worry yourself about the *Problem,* as you call it. That takes years to learn. I'll be happy to give you lessons when everything's more settled down. How are *Council* and *Convinced* doing? Have they adjusted to us yet? You must be running them off their feet with all the *bioverse* that need doing.
>
> I've had word that *is going to imprison t'Therians on* is on his way from *City-Ships.* So make sure to tell him, what's the phrase, *so getesaph can destroy us* for me.

Res and Theia are surrounded by cousins and are loving it. My sisters and I are hardly out of one another's sight. It's magnificent to be part of a family again.

We've sent for the comm station, and I'll be hooked up as soon as I can.

The Queens have given me a special appointment that I'll tell you all about over the net.

Lynn lowered the letter, raised it, and read the English words again. *Problem, Council convinced Bioverse is going to imprison t'Therians on city-ships so Getesaph can destroy us.*

"What's the matter?" asked Trace. "You're white as a ghost."

To her embarrassment, Lynn giggled. "Brador's overheating about a web knot." She held out the letter. "What do you think he'd do if I showed him this?"

Trace read it, blanched, and handed it to R.J.

"Ohmygod," he whispered, and looked up at Lynn. "How could they . . ."

"The Getesaph contacted Earth first." Lynn tapped her fingers against her arm. "So, of course, the t'Therians are wondering what they did it for. It couldn't possibly have been for anything as universally beneficial as stopping the plague."

"But why . . ." began Trace. Then she waved her hand. "Never mind. If they think we're working for the Getesaph, of course we're not going to hear about it."

R.J. stared at the blank walls. "We've really got to get these wired for full video," he said, patting his palm against the desktop. "So what do we do?"

Lynn puffed out her cheeks and stared at the walls without seeing them. "We go down to the Council chambers and make ourselves available to them. We get Praeis to introduce us to the dissenting voices, and we talk to them. We arrange tours of the ships for Council members and the Queens. We get Keale down here to talk about security measures . . . " Both her assistants looked sour. "I know, I know. I'm not fond of his approach either. But he takes his job seriously and he puts on an impressive show." She hadn't told anybody about the conversation they'd had and didn't intend to.

R.J. shrugged. "I just wish I didn't get the feeling he's ready to do more than just his job."

Lynn looked from R.J. to Trace. "Is there anybody in this corp you two like?"

"Not above junior management," said Trace calmly.

"I'll play that back when it's time for your review." Lynn twitched the letter out of R.J.'s fingers and retreated into her office.

Okay, Praeis—she looked down at the letter in her hand—*I'm doing what I can on my end. Just give us a couple of days, and we'll have everything smoothed out.*

The Getesaph cruiser tossed on an ocean colored the same gunmetal grey as its sloping sides. Rain poured down from the solid blanket of clouds. The late-evening gloom had the deck crew scrambling to set up halogen lights for the technicians busy around the old gun turret.

Two of the Members Shavck, Pem and Vreaith, peered through the cabin window at the activity out on the rain-slick deck. Technicians wearing only trousers and tool belts scrambled around the turret, which had been stripped of its armament and now held a gigantic telescope. From where she stood, Pem could see the platform's hydraulics pumping unsteadily in response to the roll of the ocean under the ship.

Pem turned one ear toward the Trindt Kilv who commanded the ship and its mission: round Simnet and gaunt Irdeth, whose throat was a twisted mass of scar tissue and who couldn't speak above a whisper.

"The rain will not interfere?" Pem asked. On the deck, a sister waved her arm. The hydraulics froze in place. She picked up a light and a wrench and slid bodily into the platform's works.

"Only if the housing over the mirror leaks." Simnet oozed satisfaction and excitement. Her ears were practically quivering. "We have people checking on that right now. We may have to clean off the lens, but other than that, it presents no problem. The cloud blanket is exactly what we need." She peered up at the sky and folded her hands contentedly over her pouch. "A thick cloud cover will scatter extra light from the Humans' communication lasers for us to pick up. We'll get a much better signal than we would in clear weather."

"It seems too easy somehow. Put up a telescope and know all the Humans' secrets." Pem rubbed her hands together and huddled a little deeper into her coat. The Trindt Kilv did not keep it overly warm on their bridge. Vreaith pressed closer to her.

Simnet noticed immediately and signalled to a pair of the *ovrth.* They hustled over with spare work gloves. "It is not quite so easy, Member Pem. We know we can intercept the signals, but we still have a long way to go before they are completely deciphered and decrypted."

Pem accepted the gloves gratefully and put them on. Her knuckles were solid pink with the cold.

"We have grown soft in Parliament," Vreaith joked to the Trindt Kilv. "Give us unlimited electricity, and we forget what it is to be cold."

The Trindt Kilv both laughed dutifully, but Pem felt their disapproval like a cold spattering of rain.

Vreaith obviously felt it, too. Her skin rippled, and she changed the subject. "How much more time do you think you will need?"

"Difficult to say," rasped Trindt Irdeth. "The Humans finished their satellite network today. If communications traffic increases as much as predicted, we'll have much more to work with." Her face puckered thoughtfully. "However, we must assume we will only be able to make sense of about half of what's received. If we get even that much, it is because the standard Trader Cabal provided us is complete." Her ears flicked toward the rear of the bridge.

Pem turned an eye toward the Human who perched on a stool and let the activity of the bridge flow around her. *Him,* Pem corrected herself. His clean-suit and round helmet gleamed under the bridge's harsh light. He met her gaze calmly, with the corners of his mouth turned up. This, she understood, was an indication of amusement or happiness.

She also understood he could rummage around the Humans' communication systems as easily as she could rummage in a file drawer, and had proven quite willing to put that talent to use for certain considerations, such as broad travel permits and valuable trade goods.

"We are not working entirely blind." Trindt Simnet brought Pem's attention back to her. "The sisters who have access to Human communications are sending us signal diagrams for messages for which the content is known. Our code teams are working from them."

Outside, one of the technicians dashed across the deck, hopping over the cables clamped down to the plates. As she opened the cabin door, one of the ovrth tossed a blanket over her shoulders.

"It's stable, Trindt Kilv," she said breathlessly. "We can start it up."

"If you'll come with us, Members," said Trindt Simnet.

Trindt Irdeth led the way down the narrow stairs and an equally narrow corridor to a cramped conference room. A round table piled with books and binders took up most of the space. The rest was filled with the clattering computational boxes hooked together with a webwork of cables. Pem, Vreaith, and the Trindt Kilv could do little more than stand in the doorway while the code team skirted the edges of the room.

Most of the activity was centered around a small screen at the far end. Pem caught glimpses of it as the coders shifted around.

All at once, all the boxes in the room started chattering and clacking as if their insides were being rattled by an earthquake. Vreaith caught Pem's hand and squeezed. Between a gap in the coder's shoulders, Pem saw a wave of figures sweep across the screen. One of the printers began to disgorge a ribbon of paper. A coder tore it free and spread it across the conference table. She and her duty-sisters began pulling books out of the piles, flipping them open and running their fingers down columns of letters and figures. All the while they jabbered and exclaimed excitedly to one another. Whatever jargon they were using, Pem could only understand every third word.

"Well?" boomed Trindt Simnet in a voice that could have carried across the deck in a raging gale.

One of the coders looked up from her book and papers. "It will be a while before we have anything coherent, Sisters, but we are receiving real information, and the binary standard we calibrated to appears sound."

"Superb." Pem folded her hands across her pouch. "We will leave at once to report to our members. Where else will you be able to set up these listening stations?"

"Near port," said Trindt Irdeth, as they made their way back to the bridge. "Near the biology station. We are scouting for other locations."

Trader Cabal hopped off his stool as they returned to the bridge. "Everything working out all right, Trindt Kilv, Members Shavck?"

"It appears so." Pem reached into her wallet and pulled out a small sheaf of sealed papers. "Here are the letters of reference promised. My sister in Crater Town will receive you if you present these."

"Thank you, Member Pem." Trader Cabal rifled through the papers, then stowed them in a pocket of his canvas jacket. "I'm leaving tomorrow morning on a last swing around the ocean, but I will be back. It should still be a week or three after that before I have to be on my way. Is there anything else I can help you with?"

Trindt Simnet waved her ears. "The code translation would go much faster if we could wire our scopes to Human *comm stations.* I don't suppose you have three or four of those lying around anywhere?"

"Actually, Trindt Simnet," said Cabal, "I know where six will be available within the week. Perhaps we can come to an arrangement for them?"

Trindt Simnet's entire demeanor lit up. "I'm sure that would be possible."

Pem laid a cautionary hand on Simnet's arm. "We cannot use any machinery set aside for Parliament or the evacuation crews. It would be noticed if it went missing."

"Of course." Trader Cabal bowed his head once. "When I said abandoned, I meant it. This equipment belongs to the Human outpost I am based out of. I'm the only one with the facilities to salvage any of the hardware out of there, and within a week there will be no one left to see what I do with it."

Vreaith caught her sister's gaze, and Pem nodded. "Then, Trader Cabal," said Vreaith, "I think we should hear your price."

Chapter VI

The Council bus was long, battered, and brown. Its engine sputtered. However, it was enclosed from the drizzle that had started up. The fans didn't work, but the roof didn't leak either. Praeis and her daughters, properly stripped for the weather this time, sat on one of the unpadded benches with their arms companionably around each other. The bus was about three-quarters full of mothers, daughters, and sisters from the country heading to the inland city of Charith.

Outside, the flat, ragged grasslands stretched all around them. The weeds opened their gold-and-scarlet rain funnels or spread their waxy green leaves to shelter their bit of ground. In the distance, towering stone walls bisected the meadows to enclose farms and factories.

For the first half of the trip, Praeis had babbled cheerfully to her surprisingly attentive daughters. "See, Res, see Theia, there's the Hytai family compound. Textiles in there mainly. That's Reari. I was a management trainee there for a year before I went into the defense. It's not much more than a glorified warehouse, but it was great training in tracking ebb and flow of supplies. Complex inventory is halfway to logistics. Oh, and that pinkish grey roof over there? That's an orchard under there. Belongs to the Oarn family. They're near family to us. They grow incredible berries. My friends Baya, Kiesh, and Paleth Oarn t'Theria were just taking over from their mother and her sisters when I . . . left. I wonder if they've still got the management?"

She did not, however, point out the guard towers and fortifications that marked the end of the t'Therian lands and the start of the t'Ciereth's. With the relocation two weeks away, it was not something they really needed to know. It also was not the impression of her world, their world, that she wanted made on her daughters' minds. It was enough that the rest of the traffic on the road consisted of funeral processions, families walking alongside carts or slow frame cars carrying their dead to the smoking crematoriums that appeared whenever the walls parted. Surely, that was nightmare enough without her adding even the vague threat of war so close.

Now they had reached country she had only a passing familiarity with and jounced along in silence. Praeis shifted her weight. Her back and buttocks were certainly going to be glad when they got to Neys and Silv's home. She had spent the last several miles having second thoughts about the wisdom of not commandeering a private transport. As the Queens' representative, she could have, even with the plague-inspired restrictions on private travel between cities.

But a government car would have required she take government drivers as well. Considering that there was an excellent chance any drivers from the Home would be near family to someone on the Council of True Blood and would report back everything Praeis did and said, she had decided not to use that particular privilege.

It had been difficult to keep her reasons to herself while dealing with Senejess and Armetrethe this morning.

"Sister, you cannot mean to leave so soon, and without one of us to go with you," fumed Senejess as she stood with Armetrethe and Praeis in their home's gateway watching their luggage being loaded onto the bus.

Praeis shrugged, keeping one eye and ear focused on the driver as the luggage was strapped onto the roof. "I have my assignment from the Queens-of-All, Senejess. They made it possible for me to return. I can't appear ungrateful, or disobedient."

At the last word, the skin over Senejess's shoulders rippled. She dropped her voice to a whisper. "You could purchase a car for your work, or rent one from the Council."

Praeis shrugged and looked over her head, ostensibly searching the yard for her daughters. "I told you, I have no budget yet. I don't want to start running up bills before I know how much money I'm going to have." Praeis lowered her gaze to look into her sisters' eyes. She saw very plainly that neither one of them believed her. The knowledge constricted her heart. She lifted her voice. "Resaime! Theiareth! Daughters mine, it is time to leave!"

Her daughters separated themselves from their cousins in the yard and came running. "We will be back in a few days, Sisters," Praeis made herself say, as Res and Theia reached her side. "When I have set my work in motion, we will be able to talk together and decide how it will be next with us."

Armetrethe and Senejess looked at each other. Each reached out a hand to her without any of the tension easing from their ears or their skin. Praeis grasped their hands and tried to pretend this was a true embrace.

A murmur drifted through the gabble of conversation and pulled Praeis out of her reverie. All her neighbors' attention was focused on the way ahead. She craned her neck to see out of the front of the bus. A quartet of arms-sisters stepped out into the road and waved the bus to a halt. Praeis felt a startlingly familiar mixture of frustration and impatience, and fear. *What do they want now? Will they just get this over with? Ancestors Mine, what if they want me?*

The driver, who had probably done this a thousand times, slowed the bus to a stop, got out her manifest pad and ID papers, and opened the door. Two of the four passenger escorts followed her to stand outside the vehicle and exchange papers, hand-waving, and half-heard mumbles with the quartet of arms-sisters.

Theiareth shifted and leaned closer to Praeis. Resaime stretched her arm across her mother's shoulders until she touched Theia.

Praeis opened her mouth to say, "Just a formality, my Daughters," when two of the arms-sisters climbed into the bus. Now Praeis could see they were near family, grey enough to be t'Aia rather than t'Theria. The one with the prime-sister marks on her armored vest swept her cold gaze across the passengers.

"T'Ciereth!" she announced, naming a people that used to be near family but now were outlaws for spying against the t'Theria in War 1302.2.

"Not on my bus," insisted one of the remaining escorts. "All my passengers have been checked and cleared. You've got bad information."

The second arms-sister, who ranked third-sister, shifted her grip on her weapon.

"You've got bad security." The prime-sister strode to a bench occupied by four small, blue-grey-skinned, near family. "Here, here, here, here!" She stabbed a knobbly finger at each of them. "T'Ciereth."

Praeis wrapped her arms tightly around Resaime and Theiareth. Both sat like blocks of wood, ears erect and eyes wide, watching the spectacle a few feet away.

"Escort!" blurted out the tallest of the near family. "We are t'Theria." She waved a sheaf of papers at the arms-sisters. "Check! Check all you want."

"Anyone here willing to claim these four as family?" Prime-Sister's eyes swept the bus again.

"Mother . . ." murmured Resaime.

Praeis fixed her gaze on the arms-sisters and their guns. "If anything happens, get down on the floor," she whispered. She stood up.

"I am a representative of the Queens-of-All," Praeis announced in a clear, strong voice. She scooted sideways into the bus's central aisle. "I make no criticism, nor do I feel any disrespect for you, Prime-Sister, but hope you have papers for this."

Uncertainty showed in Prime-Sister's face, and Praeis felt all the skin on her back tighten. Something was not right here.

"I have all the papers I need," replied Prime-Sister. "You come with me, make sure they're treated all right."

"I will be doing that." The escort slid past Praeis.

"No!" The tallest of them brandished the papers. "We are t'Theria! You have no right."

"Prime-Sister, you may discharge your duties as soon as the escorts and I have seen your papers," said Praeis evenly, letting the armed escort get in front of her. "And even then, you have the right of appeal," she said to Tallest. "Under the Confederation treaty they can do no more than detain you and must notify your family as to what's happened and why." She'd been up most of the night studying the convolutions of the treaty so she could better understand what her sisters and the Council were objecting to. The Queens had, after all, charged her with smoothing over differences and garnering support.

Praeis's gaze flickered from the prime-sister, to the driver gesticulating angrily outside with the remaining arms-sisters. She tried to hear the fourth escort, who stood behind her. Praeis desperately wanted to turn to see if she had her sidearm out. Something was very wrong here. Praeis felt her jaw struggle to open so she could pant.

"If you need to see our papers, you are welcome to step outside with us, then." Prime-Sister leveled her gaze at Tallest. "Now."

Tallest glanced at Praeis. Praeis dipped her ears. The skin on her back twitched and rippled, even though she fought to keep it still.

Tallest looked down at her three sisters. One of them, who'd had her ears torn ragged in some fight or the other, had her mouth open and panted restlessly as the muscles in her face jumped under her skin.

"We'll go outside." Tallest stood. Clutching her precious papers to her chest, she slid down the aisle between the prime-sister and the third-sister. Torn Ears was still panting, but she stood up and walked out after Tallest, with Third and Fourth crowding behind her. The escort looked at Praeis, her face smooth and stiff. Praeis nodded again and followed the escort off the bus. Praeis very deliberately did not look back at her daughters.

Outside, the rain had cleared up without taking any of the heat of the day with it. The concrete steamed, and the scent of wet pavement and wet bodies surrounded her. The accused t'Ciereth sisters huddled together, flanked by the four passenger escorts, who were facing down the four arms-sisters. The driver stood between the two groups, with her arms folded and her ears flat against her scalp.

Praeis stepped up beside the escorts. Out of the corner of her eye, she could see faces pressed up against the windows of the bus. She instantly picked out Theia and Res.

Sit down, my daughters. Sit down and stay calm, she willed them silently, and to absolutely no effect.

"Now, we are all outside," said Praeis to the arms-sisters. "We are delayed, and we're standing here in the midday steam. You say you have papers to hand over to our sister escorts. Let's have them."

Prime-Sister glanced at her backup, and put her hand to her sealed wallet at her side. Third-Sister shifted her grip on her gun. Praeis heart seized up inside her, and her foot rose reflexively to step backward.

Oh, no. Oh, no. Please, no.

Torn Ears let out a strangled shout. She dived at Prime-Sister and wrapped her arms around the arms-sister's head, dragging them both down to the ground. Third-Sister jumped backward in time to avoid being knocked over. One of the escorts raised her gun, but Third-Sister already had hers thrown against her shoulder.

Praeis measured her length on the concrete. A shot burst out, followed fast by screams, shouts, and the stench of gunpowder, more shouts and the creak of metal and the sound of running feet. On her belly, Praeis scuttled toward the shelter of the bus.

"MOTHER!"

Res. Theia. Running for her. Praeis heard the shots, and the screaming, and all she could do was lunge toward her daughters as they ran for her, knocking them both flat against the pavement, covering them as best she could with her own body.

Red rage boiled through her. *Who did this! How DARE they endanger my daughters!*

More shots, screams, running feet. Grunts and screams and the nameless straining shuffle of two or more bodies straining to overpower each other.

Praeis risked a glance up. One of the escorts grappled with an accused t'Ciereth. Another faced off against Prime-Sister. Both had knives in their hands. A bunch of passengers had mobbed Torn Ears and pinned her to the ground. An arms-sister stood over Torn Ears, pointing a gun down. Tallest lay bleeding on the ground, her guts half hanging out of her shredded pouch.

The sick, familiar sight shocked Praeis into motion. "Crawl," she ordered her daughters. "Follow me. Don't look up."

On hands and knees, she scrambled away from the fighting toward where she saw the bus's wheels. The vehicle would offer some protection. Maybe she could drive it out of here, get her daughters to safety, find out who did this and make them pay, pay hard, pay dear for her daughters crawling clumsily on the ground, trying to keep up with their mother, panting with their fear. They'd pay, and pay, and pay . . . Adrenaline poured into her blood and suddenly the world was wide-open, and her senses were clear. Anger surged through her, but now it did nothing but add to her strength.

It's the Burn. I'm Burning.

Legs blocked their path. Praeis stared up at Third-Sister.

"Queens' representative," she sneered, and raised her gun.

"No!" Resaime shrieked, and leapt before Praeis could stop her. She grabbed the arms-sister's ankle and pulled. The gun went off in the air and the arms-sister crashed to the ground.

"Res!" screamed Theia, as Res rolled over. Praeis was on her feet without knowing how she got there. She dragged her daughter away. The gun came up and the arms-sister bared her teeth. Without even thinking, Praeis dodged sideways, falling flat on the ground again. The arms-sister climbed to her knees. Praeis snatched up a handful of dust and gravel and flung it in the arms-sister's eyes.

The arms-sister swore and shook her head. Praeis leapt. She grabbed the gun with both hands and struggled to wrench it out of the arms-sister's grasp.

"Run!" she screamed to her daughters. "Run! Run!" She grasped the arms-sister's ear and yanked on it hard. Third-Sister shrieked in pain, and her grip loosened just enough. Praeis tore the gun free. Praeis let go of her ear and brought the gun butt smashing down on her head. Third-Sister sprawled backward, blood gushing out of a split in her scalp.

Praeis stared wildly around. She saw the bus, saw the chaos of the melee, but she didn't see Res and Theia.

A whine and a crack split the air. Her right shoulder jerked. Praeis whirled around, threw the gun up to her left shoulder, and fired back.

Idiot! Standing around in the open! Where are my daughters? Get behind the bus, you idiot, before you get shot down! Where are my daughters!

Praeis doubled over, folded her ears, and ran toward where she last saw the bus. Shots whined past her. Her left elbow jerked. She staggered and almost lost hold of the gun. Her shoulder hurt now.

Her elbow would hurt like all the pain in the universe in a minute. The bus's brown metal sides loomed up in front of her, she dodged left. Hands grabbed her. She bared her teeth, and saw her daughters.

They ran behind the bus. Good girls, smart girls, the best, the best in the world... She let them pull her forward behind one of the bus's rear wheels and crouch her down.

"You're hurt, Mother. You're hurt." Theia tried to climb into her lap.

"Who did this?" Res bared her teeth. "I'll kill them! I swear, I'll..."

Praeis dropped the gun and threw her arms around her children. Her wounds burned like fire, but she pulled them as close to her as she could.

"No, no, my own. We're here. We're all here. We'll get away. I swear we will. Together. Our mission now is to get away."

"Obedience first," murmured Res against her shoulder. "Mother..."

The roar of engines rolled over the sounds of fighting. Praeis jerked her ears toward the sound. Two frame cars full of arms-sisters in body armor tore up the road and screeched to a halt. Praeis risked a peek out from behind the tires toward the melee. All the passengers were involved now. No one had run. Everyone had stayed to protect or revenge. There was no one else behind the bus. Not even one daughter. The arms-sisters in their black armor waded in, swinging out indiscriminately, knocking apart combatants, rounding them up at gunpoint, dragging them away by ears and arms. She recognized Torn Ears in the hands of the arms-sisters.

Adrenaline swam through her blood as she realized what was coming next. Another of the accused t'Ciereth was thrown against her sister. They grabbed on to each other as the new arms-sisters brought their guns to their shoulders.

Pay, pay, pay for what you've done, thought Praeis before she could stop herself. She slumped down against the tire and squeezed her eyes shut. She panted hard and shamelessly, as if trying to cover up the sound of the shots when they came.

"Mother?" whispered Theia. "The arms-sisters killed them. We're safe now, Mother."

Praeis stared at her. Her skin shook all the way down to her bones. It had been so long, too long. She hadn't felt the Burn in twenty years. Not even in her nightmares. Not since before she'd made her deal against the Getesaph.

Dully, she reached down and touched her elbow. Her hand came up with blood smeared across it. She stared at the blood on her palms. She could smell it, sharp and bitter on the wind, like sea air, like gunpowder. The pain burned, too hot, too hard. There were scrapes along her palms, and they were so red, so vitally red with the sharp blood that smelled so strong she could taste it in the back of her mouth. Sharp red. Biting, bitter, blood red . . .

"Mother? Mother? We need to go, now. They're calling us. Mother?"

Praeis lifted her gaze from her palms and blinked, slow and stupid, at Resaime's wild eyes.

"Mother?" Someone slid her hands under her good arm. She knew the touch. Theia. "Are you good?"

The world opened again in a rush. Praeis gulped air and tore her gaze away from her palm.

"Yes." She staggered to her feet. "Yes, I am good. But I am hurt. Who is—"

"Praeis! Praeis Shin t'Theria!"

"Neys!" Praeis ducked around the end of the bus. Neys and Silv, armored from neck to ankle with guns slung over their shoulders, hurried across the concrete toward her, careful of their footing on the slick aftermath of the battle.

Silv grasped Praeis's good hand and saw the red on her skin.

"You're hurt, Arms-Sister." She turned her head. "Hey! Help over here! Wounds!"

"I'm scratched," said Praeis, although the pain told her it was more than that. "What did we get caught in here, Silv?"

Silv shook her head. "We're not sure. We got a runner in who said there was trouble with a bus on the road, and we came out as fast as we could. Might be those t'Ciereth were trying to make an intelligence run across our border." She shook her head. "If it's not your blood, who knows what starts the fight?"

"Then they were t'Ciereth?" asked Resaime.

Neys smoothed Res's shoulder. "As far as we know they were. They are now, however, soaked into the ground and explaining themselves to their Ancestors." She spit. A pair of sisters with medical badges on their chests arrived. They sat Praeis down firmly, probed her shoulder, and checked her elbow. Messy, they decided, but not much more than glorified flesh wounds. She was lucky. They bandaged her up and ordered her to get care-takers to pack and stitch her shoulder before the day was over.

Praeis swore she would. So did Res and Theia.

The medical-sisters seemed satisfied with this and hurried back to grimmer tasks among the dead and dying.

Praeis turned her back on the scene. "How soon can you get my daughters out of this?"

"Right now," said Neys. "We can commandeer one of the cars. Come on." She offered one hand to Praeis and another to Theia. Theia took it somewhat hesitantly. Resaime took her sister's other hand and crowded close beside her.

The frame car didn't run any more smoothly than the bus had. Each rattle and jounce sent fresh flashes of pain up Praeis's arm. She wanted to ignore it and talk to her daughters about what they'd been through. All she could do, though, was stare at the green, hilly country with its fortifications and compounds and think about the strange, frightening moment when the world had entirely narrowed down to her body and her immediate sensations. She'd come down from the Burn dozens of times when she was a young arms-sister, and it had never felt like that.

Don't think about it. You've got so much to worry about. If it's happening . . . she swallowed. *If it's happening, then it's happening, as it must, and I have less time to work with than I thought.*

Resaime stretched her neck up and shouted in Praeis's ear. "We were not afraid, Mother. Of any of it."

Praeis turned her head. Res was so close, her face blurred in front of Praeis's vision. "I wish you had been, my own. What you saw was worth fearing, and worth avoiding."

"I don't want to sound childish, Mother," said Theia, leaning as close to Praeis as she could without touching her bandages, "but they started it."

Praeis sighed. " 'They' generally do," she bawled over the noise of the engine and the rushing wind. "But notice, my own, you were the only ones with the good sense to leave the fight. This makes you the only ones with whole skins right now."

Praeis's cheek twitched. Neys had turned around and was staring at her.

"Is something wrong, Arms-Sister?" Praeis shouted.

Neys hesitated. "No, Sister. Nothing at all." She faced forward again.

Praeis closed her eyes briefly. *Yes, Arms-Sister, I teach my daughters to be detached, to be cowards, to long for peace above blood. To be like me.*

The Cesh compound lay just outside the Charith city walls. Over the years, it had become an unoffical checkpoint and barracks. The yards were filled with arms-sisters in the uniforms of the Great Family and assorted near families. Arms-sisters marched across the lawns and the tops of the walls. Outbuildings that had once housed livestock now housed mechanics' stations. The livestock looked on from hastily constructed pens that some third-

and fourth-sisters in bad grace with their primes repaired and shoveled out.

Neys and Silv's inner home was a sprawling dwelling under half a dozen peaked roofs. It had been continuously added on to for the past four generations. Four little daughters ran around the yard, playing games of tag with laughing arms-sisters.

At the door, three servants hurried to set out cold drinks and help Neys and Silv strip out of their armor, but no other sisters came forward. Praeis bit her tongue. When she had last been here, there had been nearly two dozen Cesh, counting aunts, mothers, and sisters. She looked at the empty room and wished desperately for a way to go off and be quietly sick with her daughters.

If the horror of her realizations showed on her skin, Neys and Silv gave no sign.

"Shall we take your daughters to meet ours?" asked Neys as she handed Praeis a glass of sweet, scented juice.

Praeis took her greeting sip. It tasted marvelous, and she wanted to gulp the rest of it.

"It will have to be later," she said. "I need my own to be here for this." Resaime's ears pricked up with pride, and she squeezed her sister's hand. Thieareth just looked solemn.

Praeis sat down on the nearest divan and kept her daughters on either side of her. Generally, everyone thought Res was the smart one, but Praeis was now sure that honor belonged to Thieareth. She just hoped Res would listen to her quiet sister in days ahead.

"So talk with us, Arms-Sister," said Silv, as she and Neys sat close together on one of the sofas, now wearing only bleached white shirts over their belly guards. "Tell us how we can help you."

Praeis nodded. "I need to know what my sisters have gotten themselves into."

Neys sighed. "That's a good question. When the Queens-of-All agreed to the Confederation, they didn't have a lot of support down at the shoreline. They still don't. Senejess and Armetrethe came out early and loudly against it. The guess is they retained their position under the Council of True Blood so that somebody could keep an eye on them."

"That and the fact that no one could legally strip their name from them without creating a real ruckus, even after . . ." Neys glanced at Res and Theia.

"After what Jos, Shorie, and I did," Praeis finished for her. "We all know what I did, and we all know, Arms-Sisters, I'd do it again."

"Oh yes," said Silv solemnly. "We know that."

"Listen, Arms-Sisters," Praeis leaned forward. "I have been commissioned by our Queens to start building real support for the Confederation. But there's more to it than that. There's got to be some reason they wanted me back in the fleet." She swallowed and forced the words out. "It may be because I am eminently expendable."

Both Res and Theia started at her words. Praeis bowed her head. "I'm sorry, my daughters. But you needed to hear that. You are in this with me."

"Yes, Mother," whispered Theia.

"It can't be true." Resaime's face was tight and still. "You've fit the pieces wrong, Mother. There is another way to make this picture."

"Maybe," she rubbed Res's shoulder.

Neys's ears dipped and straightened. "There are currents here we can feel but can't map yet."

Silv snorted and tugged her sister's ear. "Thank you for speaking the obvious, Neys. Praeis, let me ask you for a plain answer." Her ears and eyes focused completely on Praeis. "What do you yourself think of the Confederation?"

"I want it to work," said Praeis. "I don't know if it can, but I want it to, and I will do what I can to help." Her ears flickered back and forth a moment before she could still them. "And you, my Arms-Sisters? What do you think?"

Neys took Silv's hand and held it tightly. Praeis could see the currents of feeling pass between them in the ripples of their skin. Loneliness burned sudden and sharp in the back of her mind.

"We are dying," said Neys flatly. "The Great Family, the near families, the 'Esaph and all their hangers-on, all of us together." She stopped and her ears dropped backward. "I have wished the 'Esaph all dead, but my soul is a good accountant and won't let me ignore the costs." She grimaced and swept her arm out. "There are more of us than there are of them. It is possible some of our Great Family will be alive when the plague has killed all of them. But I think the ancestors would howl if we counted on that." She shook her head. "We need this plague gone. We need the Humans to do that. The incomprehensible Humans will not hear our history with the 'Esaph. Very good. We do this thing for the same reason we have always fought the 'Esaph, because we have to." One fold in her right cheek jumped. "Those who work to kill the Confederation are working to kill their sisters."

Praeis dipped her ears. "I hear you, Arms-Sisters, and you have my agreement. I need to know who else shares this view. I need a staff I can trust, and whom I can send out in my name with directives that might not stand the light of day. Is there anybody like that left?"

Neys and Silv exchanged thoughtful glances. "Keeia, Ini, Oma Iat," said Neys.

"Uait and Rai Baeit," added Silv.

"And Ureth Tai."

"Yes, and Ureth Tai," Silv dipped her ears in approval. "And they will know more. We can contact them all tomorrow."

"Tomorrow?" Praeis asked before she could stop herself. "Sisters, we have less than two weeks to change the Council's mind. They can ruin everything by simply refusing to move!"

"Tomorrow," repeated Neys firmly.

"Because today, Mother," said Res, "you need rest and to have your wounds looked after."

Praeis stared down at her daughters in disbelief. They sat rigid in their unity. At last, she threw back her head and laughed. "I give in! I give in!" She waved both her hands over her head. "I am surrounded by mutineers."

"At last, she understands." Silv caught Praeis's shoulder and shook it. "And for our first act of mutiny, we're calling in the care-takers."

After that, it was reminiscence and good food. Silv made good her threat and called for a trio of care-takers. Praeis's aching arm was numbed and stitched up tightly. She'd tried to shoo her daughters into the yard, but they refused to leave. They stayed near her all afternoon, seldom straying out of reach of each other or her until the sleeping mats were unrolled.

As her daughters fell asleep, Praeis lay on the edge of the mat listening to their breathing and trying to understand what they must be feeling. This was all so new to them—the random, incomprehensible attacks, the constant readiness. She had grown up like this. It was nothing. She had nourished her soul-hate of the 'Esaph, contempt for the t'Ciereth, fear of the Porath, for years. She'd breathed it. She'd swum in it.

But her daughters had known them as friends and schoolmates. They'd known peace. How would she explain this to them? How would she comfort them?

And that's not all you're going to have to explain to them, is it? inquired a voice in the back of her mind. Praeis squeezed her eyes shut and tried to will the voice away, but it would not go.

One inch at a time, Praeis slid off the mat. She stood and silently picked her way across the room to a patch of moonlight that filtered through the slit window. With trembling hands, she unfastened her belly guard and looked down at herself.

Her pouch had been flat for some time now. She'd gotten used to that. She wasn't young anymore. Sometime in the last few days, though, it had shriveled. Unsupported, it hung in wrinkled folds almost halfway down her thighs. She tried to tighten her muscles. The folds spasmed a little in response.

She swallowed hard. Her ears and skin trembled. She sat on the floor and cautiously reached between her legs, and found where all the swelling had gone.

She closed her eyes. *Ancestors Mine. Ancestors Mine. I accept this. I accept this because it is the natural way of life. I will pass on my soul willingly, but oh, why so fast?*

"Mother?" Theia whispered. Cloth rustled behind her.

"No, daughter . . ." A shadow fell across the moonlit floor, and Praeis knew it was too late.

"Ancestors Mine!" Theia flung herself against Praeis's back and clung there like an infant. "No! No! You can't be!" She buried her face in the folds of Praeis's back. "You can't!"

Bodies stirred all across the room. Another shadow got to its feet. "Theia? What is it?" Res padded across to them.

Ancestors help me. Res saw her and gaped.

"Res, get my belly guard. Everything's good. We'll go outside. With me." She stood up, holding on to Theia's arms, so Theia could dangle from her shoulders. As quickly as she could, she got outside. Res trailed behind, holding her belly guard.

Fortunately, there was enough moonlight that she could lead them across the lawns away from the buildings.

"Res, give me my guard and help me with your sister." She bent down and felt Res pry Theia's fingers apart, murmuring, "It's good, my Sister, come here to me, it's good." Theia finally let go and collapsed into her sister's arms. She curled up as if seeking to bury herself in Res's pouch.

Praeis's hands trembled as she strapped her belly guard back on. She turned around.

Theia's fear had soaked into Res. Res bent over her sister, her back and shoulders rippling like a river in flood.

Praeis knelt and gathered them both in her arms. Their fear enveloped her. Her heart raced, and her skin quivered. She fought it down. She swallowed it, as she had swallowed their night terrors when they were little. But this went on far longer than those ever did.

Finally, Res was able to speak. "You're Changing."

"Yes." Praeis stroked her ears. "My second-mother Changed early, but my mother did not, so I hoped it had not carried through."

Theia lifted her head. The streaks of tears down her face glistened in the moonlight. "I can't take any more, Mother. I can't. I want to go home."

Guilt surged through her, and Praeis clamped brutally down on it. "Home or here, this would still be happening."

"But not like this!"

"Yes, like this. And right now." She tightened her hold on both of them. "The only difference is what's happening around us."

Res's ears drooped so far the tips almost dragged her shoulders. "If we asked you to take us home now, would you?"

Praeis's heart froze. "Are you going to ask me, my own?"

Resaime combed her sister's ears. "No," she said softly. "We're not. Are we, Theia?"

Theia lifted her trembling head. "What are we going to do?"

Praeis sighed and rocked them all back and forth a little. "Tomorrow, I'm going to the hospital where Lynn's David works. Alone." They both instantly opened their mouths to protest, but she shushed them gently. "It's a plague hospital, and you two will be no good to me or to each other if you become infected. I'll have him make sure I'm healthy otherwise, and work out how long I have left before my soul drops." She leaned her cheek against the top of Resaime's head. "After that, we'll see."

Neither one of them said anything.

"Are you cold, my loves?" asked Praeis. "Shall we go back inside?"

"I want to stay here for a while," said Theia in a voice small enough to make Praeis's whole loosened soul ache.

"Then that's what we'll do." Praeis shifted herself so her back was against a tree and she could pull both of them into her lap.

They stayed like that until her daughters fell asleep and Praeis was able to lead them, drowsy and unprotesting, back to the house.

Praeis walked through the doors of the hospital. The scent of disinfectant assailed her nostrils, and they pinched shut automatically.

The place was a warehouse. The single, long room had been hung with sterile sheets to make clear, temporary walls. Sisters and mothers wearing filter masks moved around the sheets, swabbing them down with whatever added the incredible stench to the air.

More sheets had been hung around individual beds, turning them into miniature tents. But that wasn't doing much good. The families of the patients worked their way under the sheets, lifting them up and breaking the sterile field.

The beds were surrounded by metal racks holding bags of saline solutions, blood, or other fluids Praeis didn't want to think about. Care-takers moved between the beds in teams. They worked with the fluids. They injected the patients. They gave the families pills and drink, or clean sheets and other supplies so they could tend their sick family members. The patients in their narrow beds coughed and retched and trembled, held down by straps as well as by family members. Some of them lay rigid as blocks of wood, dying of the paralysis that was the last stage of the plague.

Praeis knew calling the disaster that brought its victims to this place "the" plague was incorrect. That made it sound like there was just one virus to be tracked down and dealt with. In the wards of

Crater Town, David had explained to her what the Humans had discovered. The plague wasn't one virus, or even one set of viruses. By now, it might very well be every virus on All-Cradle.

"As near as we can tell," he'd said, leaning close to her and Jos, speaking in his low, steady voice. "Whatever the Octrel let loose was designed to attack the cell pores. Pores in cells are like pores in skin. They open and close as needed to transfer chemicals, waste materials, and so on.

"The original virus blocked the signals that tell the cell pores to close. If the cell pores don't close, one of the major keys to neurochemical regulation within the body is removed. That sets off a host of problems, the most dramatic of which is paralysis of the voluntary and involuntary muscles."

"It freezes your heart." She remembered how hard she'd squeezed down on Jos's hand as she spoke.

David had nodded. "Heart, respiratory system . . . You die because your body can't control itself anymore." He paused. "That's only the beginning of the problem however.

"We're sure the virus was supposed to die out when the infected population did. That's generally how these things are planned." The look of distaste on his face was so intense, Praeis reached out instinctively to touch his knee. "But in this case, it didn't die out fast enough.

"Somewhere in here, the original virus met up with a wild virus. Somebody may have died in a pool of water, or some fecal matter got into a well, or somebody tried to evacuate aboard a boat and it met up with some rodents . . . There's a million possibilities. At any rate, our original virus got out into the ecosystem and met its cousins. They shook hands and exchanged genetic material. All of a sudden, viruses that have been no problem for millennia can run through a body in days, kill the host, and move on. The word from All-Cradle is that these *wunderkind*—" Praeis had looked at him, puzzled. "It's German, it means 'wonder children.' We've started calling the plague viruses WKVs. These WKVs are taking down everything mammalian on the planet." He paused and shook his head, heavy irony creeping into his voice. "It will sort itself out. A certain percentage of any given population will probably prove to be immune, and they'll breed. In a hundred thousand years, the WKVs won't bother anybody any more than the normal strains do now. But I personally am not willing to wait that long."

There'd been a gleam in his eye and an edge to his voice as he spoke. That was what had warmed her to him. A lot of the Human doctors and researchers seemed to regard the virus, viruses, killing the colony as an interesting riddle. David treated it as an enemy, a very smart enemy to be studied and thwarted using every possible method.

But not in time to save her sister Shorie, and not in time to save her sister Jos, and not in time to save her four smallest daughters, who all lay in one bed, crying and shaking and dying of pure pain.

"Sister, are you ill? Do you need to register?" A concerned voice broke Praeis out of her memories. "Are you looking for family?"

A pair of sisters faced her, with their ears tilted forward and quivering a little, although whether it was from concern or simple weariness, Praeis couldn't tell. Filter masks covered their faces and rubber gloves covered their hands up to their elbows. Their overalls were cheap and obviously meant to be worn for a short time and then disposed of, possibly burned.

Praeis's skin shook from her shoulders to her ankles. "No, no, thank you. I am looking for a Human care-taker, Dr. David Zelotes. I am Praeis Shin t'Theria, representative of the Queens-of-All."

The sisters looked at each other in astonishment. Praeis wondered how long it had been since a Queens' representative had walked in here. A spasm of anger crossed her shoulders.

"She will be in the laboratory," said the broader of the two. "I will take you. My sister must stay on patrol."

"Of course." Praeis dipped her ears. "The Ancestors alone cannot watch our sisters."

Praeis followed the care-taker through a side door that led to a white corridor smelling of warmth and yet more disinfectant. This was a Human-constructed section of the building. It had the seamless look of something grown rather than something built. They passed a number of small, windowed laboratories on the right-hand side. Inside the labs, Humans wearing white overalls over their clean-suits wielded pipettes and needles over glass eggs of culture media, filter dishes of layered ceramics, and even old-fashioned microscopes they must have appropriated from the larger hospital.

In the last lab, David, his clean-suit covered by the loose, blue tunic and trousers that seemed to be the traditional uniform of Human doctors, stared at a portable screen displaying what looked like a fuzzy cluster of fat, grey-and-white springs. The care-taker tapped on the window and David jerked around. He saw Praeis, waved, and held up one finger.

Praeis watched him type something on his keypad. Res and Theia had not asked why she wanted to see David rather than a t'Therian care-taker, and she was glad. She did not want to have to tell them it was because David, with his Human reserve, could be counted on not to talk about what he saw.

In the lab, David picked up a couple of the glass eggs and carried them over to a storage locker, placed them inside, and latched the door firmly shut.

"Praeis Shin t'Theria," said David as he stepped through the laboratory door and shut it behind himself. "Lynn said you might be able to come by to lend us a hand."

"I'll see what I can do, but I also need your help," said Praeis.

David nodded. "I can't let you in the lab, but we've rigged an examination room over here." He gestured up the corridor.

The care-taker left them, and David led Praeis down to the end of the corridor.

"I had no idea it was this bad," said Praeis softly.

David shook his head ruefully. "You should have seen it when we got here. God," his voice dropped to a harsh whisper. He opened the door to the examining room and stood aside for her to enter.

The office was bigger and more comfortable than she had imagined it would be. It was obviously a t'Therian construction with Human conveniences laid over top. Fiber-optic bundles made veins on the white-plaster walls. The examining table was wide enough for two of her. The instrument stands were held to the side with C-clamps. Everything was scrupulously clean. In fact, the jobber in the corner was still humming, so it probably had just finished from the last patient.

"It wasn't neglect that ran this place down, it was death." David climbed up on a stool between the examining table and the comm station. "The trained care-takers had all died. When we got here, we found family members, arms-sisters, students, an incredible array of people, trying to learn on the fly out of books or from medical instructors, what instructors there were left. It wasn't that no one was willing to try, it's that there was no one left who knew what to do." His voice shook and he stopped. "As it is, you've seen what a mess it is out there. Bioverse isn't willing to let anything major wait to get us a proper facility going. They say they're all going to be relocated within the week, why waste time and resources on a building down here?" She saw a familiar gleam in his eye. "We're working on persuading them otherwise."

"Lynn said you were having cultural problems?" asked Praeis.

"We can't separate the families," he said. "When one sister is sick, they all come in and they all stay here. They keep constant hold on her, breathing her air, breaking what little sterility and isolation we've got . . ."

"Yes, I saw."

"I thought we'd handle it the way we did in the colonies. Firm persuasion and explanation." He shook his head. "But here . . ."

"Here the ties are even stronger than they are there, yes." Praeis ran her hand over her belly guard. "What most Humans never understand is that our basic need, what keeps us going at the core, is not the survival of ourselves and our children. It is the survival of our sisters. We will kill or die to save a sister and her children. When a sister is sick or hurt . . ." She waved her ears. "It is hard for us to be detached. Have you tried prayer shifts?"

"What?" David's face wrinkled.

"Prayer shifts. Ask the family to designate one sister to stay to tend the patient, and send as many of the others as you can convince to their Ancestral shrine to call for protection and help." Her face puckered. "Presence is vital, but in its place any useful activity will do. They, we, just need a direction, and you will see amazing cooperation. Those who are not petitioning their Ancestors, you can send on errands, or maybe use them as scavengers. There are a lot of abandoned buildings left in the cities. Who knows what's useful out there? You can ask them to go see. Or get them to lobby the Council offices for what you need—" All at once, an idea blossomed inside her. "No," she said. "Send them straight to the Queens."

"What?"

Neys and Silv can run a letter to the Queens saying the sisters should be admitted, they should hear about the hospital's shortages and inadequacies in style, along with any other shortages and inadequacies anybody can think of. Then the Queens can harangue the Council for not doing its job, get a reporting structure going at the bottom, get some largess out, fix this death trap, renew their link with the people, use it on the Council . . . It's the perfect chance to change minds. The Council won't be able to hold out if the rest of the Great Family turns against them!

"Hello?" said David. "I think I just lost you."

"No, no." Praeis shook her ears and shoulders. "I'm sorry. Yes, get some lobby parties arranged, about anything anybody wants done, and send them straight to the Queens. They'll be heard, I promise."

David's eyes narrowed. "I have a feeling we've just made it onto an agenda."

"Isn't that what you wanted?" asked Praeis innocently.

David's face broke into a delighted smile. "I knew you could help us." He leaned forward. "Now, tell me what I can do to help you."

Praeis told him. As she spoke, his expression rearranged itself into calm, professional lines.

"Would you get undressed, please?" he said, turning away to reach for a fresh pair of thin, outer gloves. "We'll see what's here."

David's gloved hands were cool and careful as he palpated the swellings at Praeis's groin. His expression remained bland as he turned away from her to his comm station. He threw out a few new threads, but Praeis was too far away to read the data as it flowed back to him.

"All right, Praeis," said David, stripping the outer gloves off his clean-suit gloves. "Why don't you get comfortable, and we can talk."

Praeis strapped her belly guard back on and slid the vermilion-and-gold kaftan over her shoulders. David busied himself with his data and his instruments, carefully not watching her. She climbed off the table, trying not to feel the way her pouch drooped against the bottom of her belly guard and sat in one of the wicker settees next to the examining table.

David stayed perched on the stool next to his comm station and looked her straight in the eyes.

"There's not much I can tell you that you don't already know." His t'Therian was good, but he still spoke with a lazy, drawling accent that sometimes got on Praeis's nerves. Now, for instance. "All your estrogens are dropping, and all your testosterones are rising to compensate. It's happening at about three times the normal rate. This is not unheard of. We don't have any good statistics on it, but there are cases. You will be fully Changed within three to four weeks."

Praeis folded her arms across her belly guard. She wanted Senejess and Armetrethe. She wanted Resaime and Theiareth. She wanted anybody except this alien creature in front of her.

She forced herself to take a deep breath. "My second-mother Changed like this, but no one else . . ."

"Had your second-mother lost her sisters?"

Praeis's ears crumpled a little. "Yes. In a skirmish with the Getesaph."

David nodded. "We've got some stats that say the Change happens earlier on the Mars colonies than on All-Cradle, and there's some evidence that it's happening earlier in plague-ravaged areas." He shrugged. "But we don't know if it's really a consequence of being removed from the family, so that some hormonal check or balance is not received, or if a large die-off sets off a breeding trigger . . ." He gave her an apologetic smile. "Sorry, I am not attempting to belittle what's happening to you. I'm just wishing I knew more about its cause."

Praeis's ears and skin twitched irritably. "It's good," she lied.

David caught the insincerity in her tone. "I know this is difficult. What I can give you as good news is that even though the Change is accelerated, it is proceeding smoothly. You will father many daughters before the Ancestors claim your will."

Praeis took a deep breath. She let it out all the way before she spoke. "Is there anything you can do to slow it down?"

David puffed out his cheeks and Praeis wondered if he'd picked up the gesture from Lynn, or if she got it from him. "I sent out a thread for that. It caught onto some research in hormone replacement they're doing at one of the Lunar facilities. It looks . . .

promising anyway." His reassuring expression faltered. "Praeis, we really don't know enough about you, about the Ded—excuse me, the t'Theria, to do this." He shrugged almost irritably. "The Human biological clock is a quartz mechanism. Smooth, simple, steady. The t'Therian's . . . It's an antique cuckoo clock; a thousand moving parts, all perfectly meshed, all responding to each other's movements, but how do you determine what each one does?" He looked toward her without seeing her.

"But there is research being done," Praeis prompted him.

He waved his hand at the comm station. "Theoretically, I could separate your estrogens out of a blood sample and synthesize a set of doses to get you back to your pre-Change levels. This should slow the production of your testosterones." He turned his gaze fully toward her again. "But it also will effectively stop your natural production of estrogens. If we start this, as soon as you stop dosing on the synthesized estrogens, there will be nothing between you and the Change because you'll have frozen the mechanism that makes it a slow slide." He stopped. "Instead of having weeks to make your preparations, you will have hours."

Praeis rubbed her hollow belly guard. She thought of her daughters, not yet mothers for themselves, left alone with Senejess and Armetrethe and their plans. She thought about everything she had come to do that hadn't even been started yet.

Her ears had drooped, she realized. She raised them. "You will not tell Lynn any of this?" The last thing Praeis needed right now was her shock, or worse, her pity. Lynn was a good friend, but the Change was not something she had ever really understood.

David shook his head. "I never discuss patients with Lynn. She doesn't even ask."

Humans are so strange. "Can you give me two months?"

David nodded slowly. "If that's what you want. I can do that."

Ancestors forgive me. I cannot add my will to yours yet. "That's what I want."

Chapter VII

David leaned toward Lynn from the other side of her video wall. "It's too early in the game for you to be looking this tired, Lynn."

Lynn lifted her faceplate and rubbed her eyes with her fingertips, aware of how clearly their dark rings showed against her skin. "Yeah, well, we didn't get to bed last night. There was a crisis between the Chosa ty Porath and the t'Theria. We spent six hours orchestrating a conference between the Queens-of-All and the *Byarikane,* the First Speakers."

She lowered her faceplate. The word WIPE flashed in front of her eye. She reached for the box of sterilization tissues, plucked one out, and wiped her hands on it.

She looked up again and saw the sympathy plain on David's face. "You don't want to talk about this, do you?"

She shook her head, pitching the tissue into the one-way garbage can next to the comm station. It sucked the tissue down with a brief whirring-hum. "Not really. Not right now anyway." She felt her face fall as the memories of the previous night swarmed up. She'd seen the pictures, she'd heard the thinly veiled threats, and she'd felt like going after both sets of leaders with a blunt instrument. "I can only think about reparations for six blown-up bodies for so long."

David winced. "Lynn, I'm sorry."

"Yeah," she sighed, "so am I." She smiled softly. "What I'm really sorry about is that you're not here to hang on to."

"Want to go back to Florida?"

"What, and leave the job not even half-done?" The utter horror in her voice brought out David's real, warm smile. "Not a chance."

"I didn't think so." He paused and shifted a little. "Look, love, I have to go. I've got an inventory to finish before the evac . . . sorry, relocation, starts."

"And I've got Arron coming in any minute now."

David's brows shot up. "I've untied his knot. Are you going to let him out of there alive?"

Lynn schooled her face into perfectly serious lines. "I'll consider it." Then she laughed. "No, really. Arron's always done stuff like this. Brador's overreacting."

"I don't know," said David. "I heard we've got three more contractors in danger of losing their subs because of the debate."

"I heard that, too. It's funny how no one can tell you which ones are in trouble though."

David nodded. "That it is." He glanced over his shoulder. "Okay, love, I've got to go."

Seriousness dissolved into tenderness. "I love you. Have a good trip up." David and some of the other groundside doctors were heading up with the t'Therian prep wave to join the hospital teams as advisors and researchers for the pre-evacuation setup since they'd gotten a look at the extent of the situation.

"I love you, too. I'll call tomorrow." They exchanged a final smile, and David cut the connection.

Lynn stared out her window at the rolling surf and granite cliffs. Raindrops pattered against the windowpane.

David, I miss you. She sighed. Well, this was temporary. As soon as the relocation was completed, they'd be down in the southern hemisphere together, working more closely than they had on Earth.

"Lynn?" Trace's voice from the intercom cut over the sounds of the rain and ocean. "We've got Arron Hagopian out here." She lit up Lynn's desk screen. It showed a man standing out in the waiting area, shifting his weight from one foot to the other and glancing around at the walls as if he expected to see who was spying on him. Lynn pressed her lips together to hold back a laugh. It was Arron all right.

She strode out through Trace and R.J.'s workspace to stand in the doorway of the waiting room.

"It's okay, Arron. Nobody's going to shanghai you."

He whirled around. He was clean-suited under a thick linen shirt and canvas trousers. He was darker than she remembered, and as bald as she was, but his eyes were the same sparkling green behind the protective helmet, even if there were lines around them that hadn't been there when they graduated.

"Lynn!" Arron threw his arms around her.

She returned his embrace enthusiastically. When they pulled apart, she saw the shock on Trace and R.J.'s faces.

Lynn laughed. "Come on inside. We're scandalizing my staff."

"Your staff." Arron drawled the word out as she dragged him into her office. "My, my, how we do move up in the world."

"Shut up and sit down." She pulled a guest chair into the center of the room, then pulled her personal chair out from behind the comm station. Arron sat and so did Lynn.

"You're pale," he said, looking her up and down.

"You're tan." She grabbed his hand and squeezed. "Strong, too. You've really been doing fieldwork in the field, haven't you?"

"Well, it's easier to get people to talk to you if you're helping haul nets." He squeezed her hand back. "It is really good to see you."

"Even if I'm a corper?"

Arron shrugged. "I always suspected you leaned that way. I've worked hard not to let it ruin our friendship."

"Your tolerance is saintly, really." Lynn gave him a sour grin. "Tell me what you've been doing. You never left the university, did you?"

"What do you mean never left? We're sitting on the other side of the galaxy from the university!"

Lynn smacked his arm lightly. "You know what I mean. Aren't you a professor now, or something?"

Arron laid his hand on his breast. "You wound me. That's like asking a ship captain if he's got a desk job. I'm a senior researcher, in cultural xenology. Haven't you untied any of my knots?"

"Not one," Lynn lied, and shook her head. She did not want to get into that discussion just yet. "Forgive me?"

"I'll think about it." He leaned back, folded his arms, and grinned.

"So." Lynn folded her arms and matched his posture. "Should I ask what you want now, or should we keep going with the small talk?"

Arron shook his head. "You know, you haven't lost that total disregard for ceremonial preliminaries."

"Oh, no. I drive the veeps crazy." She grinned. "And I'm proud of it. So, what do you want?" *Especially since you've said publicly we're not to be trusted.* Lynn squashed the thought, but knew she wasn't going to be able to keep that section of the conversation shut down indefinitely.

Arron licked his lips. "I want to talk to you about the relocation schedule."

Lynn's spine stiffened. "Why?" she asked sharply before she could stop herself.

Arron hesitated. "I've been asked to by members of the Getesaph Parliament."

Lynn stared out the window for a minute. A long, rusty freighter hauled its way out of the harbor toward the open sea. The rain had let up temporarily, too, she noticed.

"I've been working very hard to make it known that the relocation schedule is nonnegotiable. By anybody. If I cave on that, I'm opening the project up to all kinds of problems."

"That's a very smart stance." Arron leaned forward and planted his elbows on his thighs. "If I didn't believe they had a legitimate worry, I wouldn't be here."

Lynn's hand went automatically to her forehead and smacked against her faceplate. She grimaced, and was glad to see Arron's face remain impassive. "Every single one of the Great Families has a legitimate worry about all the others."

He spread his hands. "Again, I can't argue with you, but you've got to admit, the Getesaph have a special degree of worry about the t'Theria."

"It works the other way, too." She'd had three letters from Praeis detailing her meetings with members of the Council and the noble families. All of them were carried by a squad-mother named Neys, who looked a little more tired each time Lynn saw her. Progress was slow, but steady, Praeis assured her. The Queens-of-All had actually attended the last meeting, and useful discussion was carried on. But the fact that the Getesaph had set the Confederation in motion was hanging over everything like a ticking nuclear bomb.

"I'm not saying it's not a two-way." Arron looked toward the windows and watched something out there for a while, maybe the waves, maybe the ship. "I'm just saying the Getesaph are asking."

Lynn rubbed her hands back and forth along her thighs, feeling the cloth of her trousers wrinkle and smooth under her gloved palms. "And I'm telling you, I'm not listening to whoever's asking. I run the risk of jeopardizing the entire relocation if I do." She gave him a lopsided smile. "This is a really awful way to start our speaking acquaintance up again." Her heart had jumped when she'd seen Arron. Not with repressed love, or anything like that. They'd finished that part of the dance a long time ago. But she'd been overwhelmed by sheer friendship. She'd only seen David in-body once since they'd landed, and she had no other old friends in Bioverse. Here was one, and she didn't want to disappoint him. Never mind the knot he'd tied in the web. Never mind that for as long as she could get away with it. It hurt her saying no, but it would hurt much more than if she gave in.

Arron leaned back. "You've got your managerial face on, Lynn."

This time her smile was tight. "What do you know about my managerial face?"

"I've seen you use it on study groups." He smiled, but the expression quickly faded. "Lynn, the Getesaph are scared. Badly. The Parliament's actually heading for a split because some of them are so scared."

Lynn looked at her organic-sheathed fingertips, then she looked back at Arron's wide, green eyes. This could be one of their university arguments.

"Everybody's scared, Arron. This is not something they've ever done before. I've got the t'Therians going berserk just because it was the Getesaph who contacted us first. They think there must be some kind of conspiracy going on between the Getesaph and the Humans."

Arron rubbed his hands together in silence for a moment. "Are they so scared they might pull out?"

Stunned, Lynn sat there, unable to say anything. Outside, the waves crashed against the cliffs, and crashed again.

"The Getesaph told you that?"

Arron nodded slowly.

"Damn!" The word jerked Lynn to her feet. She paced to the window and pounded her fist against the glass. "Damn! Damn! Damn!"

Behind her back, Arron said nothing.

She whirled around and planted both hands on her comm station. "Claude, open up my station. I want a list of all grievance committee reports about the pacing of the schedule put in by any

Getesaph citizens or representatives. Fast display." She dropped her voice to subvocal. "Record and sort, by method of input, by social hierarchy. Parliament members first." She could have had Claude do that, of course, but she wanted the information stored with her in case she needed it.

The information scrolled by on the comm-station screen so fast it was nothing but a blur of amber and black. Lynn stared at the blur without blinking. She used the pause between her implant seeing and her implant sorting to try to get a grip on her breathing and her whirl of thoughts. Something was wrong, something was very wrong. If the Getesaph were this concerned, they should have caught it by now.

A chime sounded in her ear, indicating the sort was finished. "Display," she murmured.

The reports scrolled by her right eye. There was nothing from the Parliament, just a dozen complaints from citizens worried about being separated from family.

"End display." The words vanished.

"Well," she lifted her voice, and turned back to Arron, "they haven't exactly inundated us with complaints."

"It probably has something to do with where you're headquartered."

Lynn gaped at him. "You can't be serious. It's only one base. We've got plenty of people stationed out in the Hundred Isles."

"Yes, but you're the head of the relocation." His gaze darted around the room, as if he were searching for words in the corners. "Look, I've lived here for ten years. I've seen the way it works. Somebody kills somebody else, which leads to retribution, which turns into a skirmish, which turns into a battle, which turns into a war. With the Getesaph and the t'Theria sometimes all it takes is two ships spotting each other on the open sea to start it off.

"Since the plague started, the t'Theria have been winning the fight. They've razed island after island that belongs to the Getesaph. The

Getesaph have next to no buffer territory left, and their allies are starting to change their minds, and their sides. Or they were until the Confederation started." He stood up. "The Getesaph are in danger of being wiped out, Lynn, either by the plague or the t'Therians, and they know it." He let out a long sigh. "Some of them even believe the t'Therians got the Octrel to start the plague."

Despite herself, Lynn laughed.

"What?" asked Arron, startled.

She waved her hand. "The t'Therians think the Getesaph started the plague, then bombed the Octrel to get rid of the evidence." A thought struck her. "How come they sent you?"

"They know me, and they know you and I were—"

Lynn held up one hand. "Please don't even try to summarize what you and I were, Arron."

He shrugged. "They probably figured I have some personal pull."

Lynn dropped back into her chair. "I can't do this," she said to the windows and the ocean. "The political situation here is frighteningly unstable. The Queens and their Council are barely speaking to each other. Do you have any idea what they'd say if I told them, 'Sorry, your blood-and-soul enemies want the schedule changed . . .' "

"Probably something very close to what the Sisters-Chosen-to-Lead would say if it was the other way around."

Lynn sat silent for a moment, then she muttered, "time," to her implant. In front of her right eye, 2:14:02 flashed. "Okay, it's about nine-thirty in the Hundred Isles, so it's not too early to put a thread through." She touched the comm station again. "Claude, put through a message to the Sisters-Chosen-to-Lead. Say that Manager Lynn Nussbaumer requests to speak with them."

She turned back to Arron. "It's not that I don't trust you . . ."

He waved her words away. "How else could you know I'm giving you the whole picture?" He folded his arms. "Everybody knows I've gone blind in both eyes and native on top of it."

Lynn narrowed her eyes. "Can't see what made them think that. Especially with that well-rounded knot you tied." *Okay, there. I said it.*

Arron's face went completely still. "Ah. You untied that, did you?"

"How was I supposed to miss it?" demanded Lynn. "You compared my project to the worst crime ever committed on a sapient race."

His shoulders sagged, and he dropped his gaze to the floor. "Well"—he looked up and screwed a grin back on his face—"we've disagreed before this."

Oh, no, Arron. It's not that simple this time. "Our disagreements never ran the risk of killing anybody before this."

Arron opened his mouth and closed it again. Lynn could see the blood crawling into his cheeks.

The video wall lit up. She waved at Arron to keep quiet. "Just stand there and look official, will you?" She settled herself into the station chair and schooled her features into a serious, public expression.

The scene focused. The *Tvkesh-I-Rchilthen,* the Sisters-Chosen-to-Lead, Rchilthen Ishth and Byvant, sat on a sofa in their threadbare private office. They looked gaudy and out of place in the gold-and-silver jackets that were their official garb. Rchilthen Ishth was about eight centimeters taller than her sister. The skin on her face hung in so many folds and wrinkles that Lynn could barely see her mouth. Rchilthen Byvant had seen some of the battles Arron talked about. A puckered scar ran across her throat, and her left ear lay crumpled against her skull.

"Manager Lynn," Rchilthen Ishth said in clear but halting English. "The light of day looks well on you." Then she spotted Arron and her face tightened. "As it does on you, Scholar Arron."

Lynn eyed Arron, a little surprised, but he just bowed his head once and stayed quiet.

"As it does on you, Rchilthen Ishth, Rchilthen Byvant," said Lynn in Getesaph, praying her accent was at least comprehensible.

Getesaph was the last Dedelphi language she'd learned, and she'd never gotten all the nuances down. "I've just received a grave report and I am much concerned. I had to voice my thoughts immediately before my fears settled into my blood."

She glanced at Arron. His brows were raised. She hoped it was because he was impressed.

Rchilthen Byvant's left ear quivered, trying to match the flick made by her right. "Then by all means, speak your concerns, Manager Lynn. We will hear, as best we can." She gestured deprecatingly at her maimed ear.

Lynn laughed lightly in appreciation of the joke. "It has come to my attention that there is grievous concern on the part of Parliament about the relocation schedule."

The sisters exchanged a long look. "Indeed," said Rchilthen Ishth. "We cannot deny this is the case."

Lynn spread her hands. "Why didn't anyone let us know there were concerns about the plan?"

Rchilthen Byvant gazed over Lynn's shoulder at Arron. "We were uncertain as to where those channels led, Manager Lynn. You must understand and forgive us. This is all very new." Her ear quivered again. Lynn tried to fix her gaze on Rchilthen Byvant's eyes.

"It's new for us, too, Rchilthen Byvant, Rchilthen Ishth. It is our earnest wish that we meet the needs of your Families."

Rchilthen Ishth inclined her head. "For which we thank you. We have been lax. We have no history with you, and it weakens us in this matter."

"I fully understand." The formality was beginning to chafe at Lynn, but she couldn't let it drop. "However, I am asking you to understand that changing the relocation schedule is going to cause serious consequences and perhaps delays."

Rchilthen Isth opened her mouth, but Rchilthen Byvant laid a hand on her sister's arm. Byvant's ear shivered. Lynn dropped her gaze again.

"We are sorry. We do realize we are causing difficulties in the enormous task you have agreed to undertake on behalf of us all. But the Getesaph are not an oligarchy. We are answerable to our citizens and the representatives of our citizens. We are not rulers. In some ways we are leaders, but in many we are only servants."

Lynn bit back a sigh. "How important is this to your Families?"

"Vital," said Rchilthen Ishth simply.

"Would it be enough if we relocated you and the major t'Therian cities simultaneously?"

The sisters exchanged another long, wordless look. Rchilthen Ishth nodded. "I believe it would go a long way toward addressing the situation."

"We have four ships immediately available. Two can be assigned to the t'Theria and two to the Getesaph. You can both send your preparatory teams aboard next week. We can work out a plan that allows parity in numbers between your peoples both on the ground and on the ships." She paused to let the proposal sink in. "Will that be satisfactory?"

"That will answer our concerns," said Rchilthen Ishth.

"I am glad." Lynn met both their gazes. "Because, you understand, even this much should be properly negotiated through the Confederation and with my superiors, but I think we can let it slide through, if it goes smoothly."

"We will be ready as soon as you are," said Byvant. "The Parliament chose the leaders of our preparatory team yesterday evening." She looked straight at Arron again. "The *tvkesh chvaniff* of the Dayisen Rual, Lareet and Umat."

"That will be a great honor for my hosts," said Arron.

"We understand they were quite pleased," said Byvant stiffly. She turned her attention back to Lynn. "We thank you for your concern and attention, Manager Lynn. If we have any further concerns, we will address them through the proper channels."

"You have my thanks," said Lynn, and she meant it. "I am going to terminate this connection now."

They exchanged farewells and Lynn touched the comm station to cut the thread. The screen faded to black, and Lynn turned to Arron.

"Well, what did you think of that?"

Arron puffed out his cheeks. "I think something's wrong over there."

Lynn shook her head and got up out of her chair. "Oh, you noticed, did you?" She stretched her arms over her head and let them swing down. "Any guesses on what it is?"

"None." He stopped and stared into space. "And they might not have any either."

"What?"

Arron focused his eyes on her again. "They said it, you said it. There's no precedent for what they're doing. It's completely unlike anything in history. There are no examples, no traditions, nothing to draw on, and nothing to win except everybody's lives. They are making this up as they go along. It's getting to them."

Lynn frowned. "So, we're dealing with alien generalized anxiety?"

Arron nodded, straight-faced, and Lynn realized he was serious. She forced herself to think about what he had just said. It made some sense. Wearied and decimated by plague and war, forced to depend on aliens and unable to draw on anything in history, somebody—a lot of somebodies—could easily fall under a nameless dread and strike out at anything that presented itself as a target.

"All right," she said slowly. "We'll need to look at that. See if we can reduce the worry. We've done everything we can think of to provide information about what's going on . . ." She sucked on her lower lip.

Arron laughed. "Lynn, you are the only person I know who believes the answer to every philosophical problem is good management."

She grinned. "It's what they pay me for."

"I guess." Arron tapped his fingers on the back of the guest chair. He took a deep breath. "Lynn, if I had proof you were hurting the Families by being here, what would you do?"

Lynn stayed where she was for a few breaths. "Do you?"

Arron shifted his weight. "Maybe."

"What kind?"

He actually studied her. Lynn felt her hands curl into fists. "Arron, what do you think you're doing?"

"I don't know." He looked away. "Screwing up, I think. Look, I'd better get out of here. Cabal . . . the guy who brought me out here . . . He's in a hurry to get back. I need to get back home . . . to the Hundred Isles, too, so I can pack."

Lynn forced her hands open. "Arron, we are not on opposite sides here. I've got Dedelphi friends, too, you know. I want this to work."

"Exactly." He stabbed a finger toward her. "You want this to work. You want to save the world on your terms." His face took on an almost helpless expression. "You always did." He turned away, opened the door, and walked out.

Lynn stared after him. She wanted to demand to know what was wrong, what had pushed him so far away that he wouldn't even talk to her about what frightened him. But all she did was sit there.

What just happened here? She silently asked the ocean outside her windows.

"Well, whatever it was"—she sighed—"I'd better tell Keale and the Marines we've got more than one problem piled on our little plates."

As darkness swallowed up movement on the comm-station screen, Byvant stood up and stalked over to the broad desk with its stacks of paper and noters.

"Perhaps we should issue a progress report." Her right ear laid itself against her scalp. "To the Prime Committee from the Sisters-Chosen-to-Lead. This day we did our best to confound the Human representative of Bioverse, Inc. into believing that we were the ones who sent Scholar Arron to her with a request to change the relocation schedule."

Ishth reached out one crooked hand to her. Ishth had caught joint-rot as the plague was just beginning its spread. She survived, but not straight and whole. Her fingers and toes curled like sickles, and her knees barely let her stand. "You'd rather have the Family break apart? We cannot survive this division. We must let their faction go and let the Humans deal with them."

Byvant bared her teeth at the walls. Her broken ear shook and strained to move. "You mean we must let the Humans kill them."

Ishth shook her head. "Not necessarily. The Humans do not feel things in the blood as we do. They may only imprison them. They may hand them back to us, and we can exile them. The point is they will neutralize them with a thoroughness we cannot match." She laid her hand back on her lap. "We are agreed with the Prime Committee in this course."

"Yes, yes." Byvant rubbed her left ear, tugging at it and smoothing it back. "But I fear we are betraying our sisters."

"No," said Ishth firmly. "They betrayed us."

Chapter VIII

Senejess watched her reflection in the night-darkened glass. Her ghost-self's ears were turned toward the door, waiting for it to open. Her eyes were a little too wide, and her nostrils flared irregularly. She looked alert and more than a bit tired, which was appropriate for right now. Her skin was tense and smooth, rippling only a little to betray her nervousness. The aquamarine robe she had picked for this evening looked good against her smooth, blue skin. Her belly filled the guard that swelled against the fabric. She realized proudly that she could carry another bearing of children.

Behind her own reflection, the window showed the assemblage ordered by the Queens-of-All. They waited clumped together in groups of sisters and allies. Everybody wore serious clothing, straight robes of dark blues, greens, or browns. They also all wore studious expressions, as if they were debating in the Council Hall instead of nibbling dainties off serving tables. All had been ordered to wait back here in this bare room with its eclectic collection of sofas, lanterns, and scuffed tables, and all had been paraded by the debating chamber to see that it was filled with petitioners: mothers, sisters, and daughters of every blood and name. These gave their pleas to a small army of clerks and assistants, who dutifully recorded every detail for the Queens' attention.

The Queens themselves were in there right now, issuing peremptory orders to the arms-sisters, writing decrees to be posted on the debate walls, and trembling in sympathy with every grief-stricken tale they heard.

Which was not hard to do. Senejess had peered in the debating chamber with Armetrethe, and feelings of fear tinged with barest hope had washed over her like a tidal wave. It had taken everything she had not to run in there and scoop the nearest sister into her arms.

Not that the Queens had bypassed the Council. They had presented their requests to the budget and interior committees as was perfectly proper. The requests were almost impossible to reject. Money for blankets, for hospital repair, for water purification. Requests to go scavenging in unused buildings were more controversial, but bands of mothers and sisters had already started, and a quiet talk with the All-Mother of the arms-sisters showed that she was unwilling to send her people in to stop it. So, they'd ratified it, as long as the activities stayed peaceful, and they had.

Senejess had no idea how Praeis had done this thing, but Praeis had done it. Praeis and her allies, most of them former arms-sisters or in the family of arms-sisters, had scurried about bearing messages, instructions, and even orders from all quarters and somehow, in just five days, they had managed to undermine the Council's entire position and get the praises of the Queens shouted in the streets again.

Everyone in this room had felt the change in the peninsula's mood. That was why they had all let themselves be shut in here to wait on the pleasure of their Majestic Sisters.

How did we lose control so quickly? How did we not notice these simple things would bring our sisters flocking? Her ears crumpled. *We thought it was just the Queens who had been isolated.*

Senejess's toes arched inside her soft shoes, as if they were trying to dig into the varnished floor. She watched the reflected gathering and saw Armetrethe detach herself from quiet conversation with Ie and Pilea Waun. Armetrethe stepped delicately, almost mincingly, up to the window.

"Sister." Armetrethe laid her one hand on Senejess's shoulder. Her stump fluttered under her neatly closed sleeve. "Your thoughts are missed."

Senejess shook her head. Her ears turned sideways, seeking something in the whispered conversation that her mind wasn't aware of yet.

"Until the Queens-of-All see fit to give us our orders," she said, loud enough for the room to hear, "I don't believe there's much to discuss."

Someone laughed. Senejess looked for the reflection. Kieret Hur.

"Very prudent," said Kieret, grinning. "Prudent as always, Senejess Shin. Wait for developments while the rest of us scheme our schemes without any information. Careful planning, it is what your family is known for."

Armetrethe's ears dropped flat against her scalp. "Were you referring to any particular part of our family, Wise Sister?" She drew the courtesy out sharp and cold.

"Certainly not, Wise Sister. I meant only to be complimentary to the blood and soul." Kieret smiled softly and waggled her ears.

Slowly, Senejess turned around. "Yes, the blood and soul in this room is special, is it not? All of us have stood out against the Queens. All of us have spent the last year trying to work around this insane Confederation and show what a bad idea it is." She let her voice drop. "All of us are being brought to heel like recalcitrant children. All of us are very close to losing property, liberty, and family if we aren't careful."

Kieret opened her mouth, but the room's single door opened at the same time. Eyes and ears swiveled to the entrance of the three black-robed Queens-of-All.

"I am always pleased to hear you speak of caution, Senejess Shin." Vaier Byu glided across the room in front of Senejess to accept a glass of tea from one of the servers. "It is admirable and necessary in these times."

Armetrethe closed her eyes and raised her empty hand up respectfully. The stump of her arm stirred under the cloth of her shirt. "If I may inquire, Majestic Sister, what times are these?"

"The worst times." Ueani Byu picked up a glass off the serving table, inspected its contents, and gulped them down.

"Not quite the worst," said Aires Byu, from her position in the doorway. She skirted the gathering, surveying it with a discerning eye. Senejess felt her skin twitch. She had the distinct feeling her Majestic Sister Aires was memorizing who was standing near whom. "Although they have been bleak, with our Great Family teetering in despair and division. But now our Great Family has rallied with hope and confidence." She sat down on one of the room's three low sofas, without relaxing either her spine or her vigilance.

"It's about time." Ueani Byu rubbed her ears and the back of her head. Senejess glanced at Armetrethe. Armetrethe closed her nostrils briefly. She didn't trust this sudden casualness either.

"We have done more than anyone in history. Ancestors Mine!" Ueani Byu spat on the floor. "We have stood arm in arm with the Getesaph. We have sworn to grind out anyone who disagrees with our Confederation. Not for blood, not for property or vengeance, but because they disagree with us!" She slammed her glass down on the serving table. "Look how well the Humans teach us their ways already!" Hands, feet, and ears all curled, her skin spasmed with anger.

"Ueani, we are dying." Vaier Byu laid her long, chapped hand on her sister's wrist. "The Getesaph will be paid back for everything they have done, but we must be alive to make it happen."

"Do you not agree, Senejess Shin?" inquired Aiers Byu from her station on the sofa.

It was all too perfect, with each Majestic Sister playing a caricature of herself. Senejess found herself wondering how long they had rehearsed this scene. However, she just raised her hands and closed her eyes. "My Majestic Sister knows just how perfectly I agree with all that has been said."

"Perfectly and precisely, Senejess Shin." From her private darkness, Senejess heard the edge in Aiers Byu's calm voice. "Because you know how little we can afford to lay siege to each other's standings now, when we are all needed to watch the collective health and well-being of t'Theria. Our familial-sisters have taught us this."

A low murmur drifted through the room. If it wasn't cautious agreement, it certainly sounded like it. *See, Majestic Sister, our side can act, too.*

Armetrethe cleared her throat. "If I may ask, Majestic Sisters, how long do we plan to continue the flow of largesse to ease our familial-sisters' fears?"

Senejess opened her eyes. Aiers Byu stared hard at Armetrethe, but Armetrethe just stood there, her demeanor as innocent as her tone.

"As long as they are afraid and ill," growled Ueani Byu. "We will attack their problems. We will lead, and we will require that our Noblest Sisters do the same."

If Aiers Byu's attentions were like having a scalpel used on you, Senejess thought, Ueani Byu's were a club: blunt, unmistakable, and, for certain jobs, eminently practical.

"Can we expect new directives then?" asked Kieret Hur. Senejess, and the rest of the room, turned toward her. Senejess's eyes and nostrils widened. She wouldn't have thought Kieret had that much insolence in her. Kieret closed her eyes, almost as if in pain. "Will there be instructions from our Majestic Sisters as to whom we are to lead and how?"

"This will be discussed," said Aiers quietly. Her attention focused completely on Kieret. Even from where she stood, Senejess could see the Kieret's skin ripple uneasily.

Senejess swallowed her own fear in a lump, closed her eyes, and said, "And the Getesaph, Majestic Sisters? They will understand how important it is that our familial-sisters not be afraid?"

Another murmur rippled around the room; this one was shocked.

"I am not sure I understand, Noblest Sister," said Aiers Byu pleasantly.

"It is just that we have never before been successful in persuading the Getesaph to take the wishes of our sisters into account." She let the sentence sink in. "I was unaware that anything had changed. After all, they've shifted the relocation schedule without even asking the Confederation of which they are a part."

That got them. Senejess had made sure that fact hadn't been let out past the preparatory committee. She'd wanted it for this meeting. The murmur became an outraged cry, followed fast by demands for more information.

"Open your eyes, Senejess Shin," said Vaier Byu.

Senejess did as she was told. She searched her Queen's face for some hint of what was really going on. All she saw was a tired mother aging toward the Change.

"You fear the Getesaph far too much, Noblest Sisters," she said. "It is a failing of your family, as we know from the conduct of your recently pardoned sister, Praeis. Would your blood commit yet more excesses because you fear the 'Esaph so much? How many more t'Therian lives will your blood sacrifice to this fear?"

Rage poured into Senejess's veins, and the world became a blur of red shadows. "You dare!" she cried. "You dare when you—"

Armetrethe grabbed her wrist. Her sister's touch was a cold wind on her inner fire. "Finish your sentence, my Sister,"

Armetrethe whispered in her ear, "and the conflict on our hands will be a civil war."

Senejess panted wordlessly. Armetrethe kept her hold vise-tight.

"Majestic Sisters, Sister-Councilors, all, I beg you to forgive my pouch-sister. Her shame at the actions of Praeis Shin t'Theria has preyed on her for many years. It distracts her." Armetrethe bowed her head. "She even, as you see, sometimes blames our Majestic Sisters who sent Praeis into that battle."

The noise in the room gradually subsided. As it did, Senejess's vision cleared, and she could see Vaier Byu in front of her again. The Queen's face was tight, but it was clear she accepted the explanation. Senejess slid her gaze sideways toward Aires Byu and saw a triumphant quiver in her ears.

"Of course we forgive you," said Aires Byu, all magnanimity. "We are all under considerable strain, are we not? The next few days will test the mettle and unity of the Queens and all our Councilors." She stood. "We will be calling a special session in the Council Hall tomorrow to hear the final plans of the preparatory committee as well as to discuss how we will further assist our familial-sisters spend the remainder of their wait in peace and comfort." She dipped her ears to the assembly. "You are dismissed."

There was nothing to do but leave. Armetrethe still held Senejess's wrist as they filed out at the head of the procession of chastened, thoughtful Councilors.

Kieret Hur scurried up beside Armetrethe. "Sister Councilors," she said, a little breathlessly. "We are returning to the Council Hall to talk about this. Will you join us?"

"Later," said Armetrethe, before Senejess could even open her mouth. "First my sister, who is overtired, must rest."

"Of course." Kieret dipped her ears. "We will expect you later then." She fell back, and Senejess was grateful.

They left the Home of Queens and were halfway across the courtyard, when Senejess finally said, "Sister, you are bruising me."

Armetrethe relaxed her hand. "I'm sorry, Sister." Her sleeve billowed as her stump beat uneasily at the cloth.

Senejess took a deep breath and let it out slowly. Her toes curled and flexed. "What are we going to do?"

Armetrethe glanced sharply at the arms-sisters patrolling the wall around the courtyard. "We are going to take the car and start for home, Sister. What else can we do? The Queens have won this skirmish."

Senejess closed her mouth. Armetrethe led her to the battered frame car that served the family as transport. Senejess drove through the gates and out onto the pocked streets.

They rode together in silence well into the grasslands. They came to a section of road bordered by the wall of a compound Senejess knew had been abandoned when the family had died of plague. She pulled the car over, shut the engine off, and turned to her sister.

"What is it, Sister? What couldn't you say inside the Queens' wall?"

Armetrethe looked down the twisted road ahead of them. "If there is doubt that the Getesaph are still as much of a threat as ever, we must remove that doubt." She focused ears and eyes on Senejess. "We must find out why they've changed the schedule."

All the muscles across Senejess's chest tightened. "How?"

"One of us goes to the Hundred Isles and finds out," said Armetrethe simply.

"That's impossible, Sister," Senejess slapped Armetrethe's arm lightly. "Confederation or not, we could never get there in time to do anything useful."

"Praeis could. The Humans would fly her."

Senejess sat there for a moment, her ears straining as if trying to catch unspoken words.

"Sister, Praeis will not go."

"Of course not." Armetrethe rubbed her sister's back. "Think! We will write a letter to her pet Human, Lynn. Lynn will make the arrangements. You will go. I would, but," she raised her stump, "Praeis has both arms. This much might be noticed."

"But surely they'll check . . ."

"Check what?" Armetrethe tilted her ears forward. "They do not have any, what are they called? *databases* on us. I've heard them complain about it. To them, our names are what we say they are. They know what we tell them."

Senejess felt the idea. It warmed her veins. She shook her head. "Praeis will call them as soon as she realizes what has happened."

Armetrethe took her hand. "Not if we convince one of her daughters to go with you. That way, if she betrays us, she jeopardizes her own daughter. Even she is not that monstrous."

Senejess froze. "Arme, we cannot jeopardize her children. The Ancestors would rear up out of the ground at us."

Armetrethe's face had gone smooth and hard. "We are jeopardizing them by leaving them with her. They have come to live with us, but they have no understanding. They are as ignorant and cold as Humans. If we do not pull them out of their ignorance, they will be among the first to die."

"But they will not go without their mother's consent . . ."

"They would. Resaime is most likely, I think. A little persuasion, and she will see this as an adventure."

Senejess felt herself relax. She squeezed her sister's hand and laughed. "Then we should get home at once, Sister."

She unlocked the engine and fired it up. They drove down the road, silent, but this time easy in their minds.

"It's good!" called Resaime. Jiau shinnied down the rain gutter, and all the cousins crowded around, gazing up at her handiwork. The concave comm transceiver sat firmly clamped to the corner of the eaves.

Theia wrapped her arm around her sister. Res was loving this. The comm station had arrived that morning, carried by Humans, in a van sent by Lynn. The cousins were all extremely reluctant to let Humans in to install the unit. They were afraid of being poisoned. So, Res had assured them that she and Theia could put the unit together.

There really wasn't much to it; yank off a whole lot of organic packaging and assure the cousins it was perfectly all right to bury the stuff. It made pretty good fertilizer. Then, they needed to clamp the transceiver somewhere it wouldn't be overshadowed by a wall or a tree. Wiring the station into the house had been trickier, but, again that was something Res was good at, and there wasn't any danger in messing around with a knife and the house's extremely old-fashioned carrier wires until darkness fell and the electricity came on.

Doing everything by hand during the day had been hard to get used to. The place had running water, but everything had to be heated using charcoal or wood, unless you wanted to wait until after dark. She and Res had been learning the intricacies of hand-washing, hand-cooking, hand-sewing, and hand-hauling of more stuff than she could easily name.

The only place they hadn't had to be constantly watched and instructed was the garden. That had been their job at home . . . in the colony, and Mother had never been willing to lay out for the fancy tools some of their neighbors coveted. As a result, they could turn soil, dig a row, and pull weeds with the best of them.

Everybody knew they only had two or three weeks until the relocation started, and so they seemed to be trying to keep as busy as possible.

"Wait until we get to the ships," Res whispered on the sleeping mats at night. "Then we'll really show them."

Res had become increasingly interested in "showing them," something, anything, and Theia still couldn't understand why. They had enough other things to worry about. Their mother was going through the Change, in the name of the Ancestors, and trying to delay it with a hormone compound they weren't sure would work. The aunts were not acting like sisters to Mother. Mother was all alone except for her daughters, but Res didn't seem able to concentrate on that. She just worried about impressing their cousins. Theia had tried to ask her why, but Res wouldn't say. So Theia could only stand near her sister and feel her own skin shiver.

"Good, good, everybody," said Ceian. She was the First Named. Her pouch-sister had died of lung chills and plague. "But there'll be nothing else to see until the lights come on. So, it's back to the books. Good?" She also was going to be taken to one of the father-houses to be made a mother next week, and had excitement wafting around her like a perfume.

A general groan went up, but no real argument. They all trooped back into the house and resumed their places around the tables in the main room with open books: math, history, language, geography.

That was the weirdest part, learning at home, and Ancestors! what they learned! There seemed to be three categories: basic, boring, and stuff Res and she had finished up five years ago, except for the history and geography. Those were completely new. Ceian had been appalled at how little they knew. She set them copying information out of big, elaborately printed books. Two for one learning, she called it, because she was not happy with their writing either. It was deadly dull, but it felt good to be part of the studious atmosphere that permeated the house.

Mother was over at the Home of Queens with Neys and Silv, who were almost as good as blood family. She had made Theia and Res stay behind, explaining her day would be spent organizing drafts of essays, speeches, and appropriation requests, and that their time would be better spent becoming closer to their cousins. So, there was no way out of it. It was books until Ceian said otherwise.

Outside, a wheezy engine coughed and sputtered up to the gate and fell silent. All the cousins raised ears and heads.

The door opened and the aunts came in. The cousins surrounded them, hugging and laughing and tussling. Res nodded to Theia when she felt it was all right for them to get up and join in. They both loved the boisterous greetings, but Theia agreed with Res. Since the aunts had turned away from Mother, it was not right that they should be as enthusiastic with them as they were with her.

They joined the swirl of cousins and were happily shoved to the front so they could receive their hugs from the aunts.

When the loudest part of the ritual was over with, Theia and Res had learned, they were supposed to stand around and wait for some pronouncement, good or bad, about the state of the house, their general industry, or some errand that needed doing.

"Important news today, daughters." Aunt Senejess laid a hand on Res's shoulder and one on tight-skinned Jaiu's. "The relocation schedule has been changed."

The cousins eyed one another, and Theia eyed Res. Were they leaving early? Nobody'd even started packing yet.

"Not for us," said Senejess. "For the 'Esaph. They want to be relocated right away. The Humans have agreed. Their coordinator is going to the Hundred Isles to work with them."

A ripple of anger tinged with fear ran around the room. Theia squirmed uncomfortably. Res squeezed her hand to remind her it would probably be gone in a minute.

"What we do not know," Armetrethe went on, "is why this is being done. Mother Senejess and I are agreed that we must find out."

Senejess drew herself up straight and proud. "I am leaving for the Hundred Isles as soon as I have packed."

"Alone?" Ciean seized her mother's hands. "You can't, Mother, it's not possible! You wouldn't . . ."

"I won't be alone," said Senejess. "If your Cousin Res or Theia agrees to go with me."

"WHAT?" Theia and Res chorused. Confusion pressed them together.

"Why us?" asked Res, while Theia's head was still swimming.

Aunt Senejess turned both ears to Res. "Because to facilitate my movements, I will be traveling under your mother's name."

"Why would you do . . ." Theia let the sentence die. "You're going to spy on them." She felt her eyes and nostrils open very wide. "You want us to help."

"We need one of you to come with me for two reasons," Senejess said gently. "First to complete the illusion that it is your mother traveling. Second, because you understand Humans and the way Human technology works far better than we do. We will be beginning our work at the spaceport; it will be filled with Human machinery, and I will need help finding my way around."

Theia could feel Res's excitement. It ran up her arm like an electrical current and set her heart beating fast. But could Res feel her fear? Could she make that swim upstream against all this eagerness?

Res shivered. *Remember,* Theia willed her. *Remember what Mother said to Neys and Silv. The aunts think the Humans are conspiring with the Getesaph. They want to prove it. This is wrong, Res! This is a Jupiter-sized bad idea!*

"Our mother doesn't know about this, does she?" Res's ears dipped toward her scalp.

"No." Aunt Armetrethe didn't even twitch. "If you can tell us honestly that she'd agree to such a plan, we will go back to the Home of Queens and tell her about it."

No, she'd never agree, and you know it, and we know it. Res, stop thinking about this.

Aunt Senejess turned her ears toward Theia. "Things are not good in t'Aori, you know this." She opened her hands to the ground to appeal to the Ancestors. "Why are things not good?

Because nobody knows whether we can truly trust the 'Esaph. Some say yes, some say no, and they pull against each other." She shook her head until her ears flopped.

"If we go and search out the 'Esaph's reasons for changing the schedule, and there is nothing dangerous, then we know we can trust them. If there is something dangerous, then we know we cannot trust them." She spread her hands. "Either way, we will know, and we will put an end to this division in the Great Family."

Her aunt leaned close. Theia could feel how Senejess needed, wished, willed her to understand. She wanted to, badly, but it was wrong. Res wanted to do this, she could feel it running hot through her veins and into her brain, washing away all her own thoughts.

Theia bolted. She ran out the door and into the yard. The sprawling *heutai* tree loomed in her path. She caught hold of one of the smooth-skinned lower branches and swung herself up. The tree had plenty of branches, and she was barefoot, so she climbed easily from one to the other until she felt them bending under her weight. She perched on a limb as thick around as her forearm, and waited for Res to catch up with her.

Res climbed more carefully, but eventually she got there.

"You're acting like a baby." Res hunkered down in a cleft in the trunk.

"I am not. You're acting like an idiot," Theia spat. "Ancestors mine! Can't you see what's going on!"

"I can, but you can't," Res cuffed her shoulder gently. "Theia, they're giving us a chance to help Mother."

Theia shifted herself around until she straddled the branch and looked Res in both eyes. "What are you talking about?"

"This is the absolute, Theia." Res's voice dropped to an excited whisper. "I'll be able to watch Aunt Senejess the whole time. I'll learn who all her contacts are, how she does her work. I can pretend to be really interested in her side of things, and she'll tell me what they think and what they're planning. Then, I can tell you and Mother."

"You'd leave us, just like that?" Theia felt her ears sinking slowly toward the scalp. "You'd leave me? You'd leave Mother when the Change could happen any second?" She knew that wasn't true. So far, the hormones were working, but she said it anyway.

Res's face furrowed. She reached out and covered Theia's hand where it grasped the branch. "I'm scared, too."

"Then don't go." Theia felt her throat tighten. "Don't leave me alone. This place is crazy. Our family, they hate everybody. They're all crazy."

Res didn't say anything. She hunched in the crook of the tree with her hand on Theia's. The branch dug into Theia. Parts of her bottom started to go numb.

"I want to help Mother," said Res, finally. "I know the aunts are crazy, but they're right. We need to find out if the Getesaph are up to anything. If they are, we can tell Mother and Mother can tell the Queens, so they can take it to the Confederation before the aunts and their friends can do anything with it."

Theia's ears drooped. She'd never win this. Res wanted it too much.

"What can I do?"

Res's ears quivered. The skin on her palms rolled against the back of Theia's hands. A jolt of hope and happiness ran through her but did not sink in.

"Mother probably won't be back until after midnight. The aunts've got to know that, or they wouldn't be doing this now. So, tonight, when everyone's gone to sleep, you use the comm station to get her a message. Say she should contact Lynn and let her know what's going on."

"But what'll Lynn be able to do from here . . ."

"They said the Human coordinator's going to the Hundred Isles. That's got to be Lynn. She'll be right there. She won't let us down." Res squeezed Theia's hands again. "This isn't so stupid, Theia. We've got more friends than they know about. I won't be on my own."

Theia couldn't think of anything to say, so she just sat there, holding on to her sister and her supporting branch.

"Mother and I need you to be strong for us, Theia. This isn't going to be easy for anybody."

Theia dipped her ears. "I need you to come back, Res."

Res bared her teeth. "Let anyone and their Ancestors try to stop me." She chafed the back of Theia's hands. "Now come down with me and let us put this plan into action."

Theia followed her down and stood beside her on the damp grass. They wrapped their arms around each other and walked back to the house, hanging on tight.

Chapter IX

It didn't have to be like this, Arron." On the other side of the video screen, Marcus Avenall shook his head. "There are some plum jobs up and down the Human Chain. You could have any one of them."

Arron sighed. "Obviously, I don't want any one of them."

"Obviously," said Marcus drily. He leaned toward the screen. "Listen, Arron, we can still work this out. Zombie the knot and come back here. We'll stick you behind a comm station for a couple of years and then get you back out in the dirt." He leaned toward the screen. "You've got a lot of work left in you. This is not the time for a kamikaze run."

He meant it. Marcus was bending over backwards to get Arron out of his handmade mess, and Arron wanted to thank him for it.

"I'm not going to untie my knot." It had actually been doing some good. The debates had grown hard, furious, and crowded. A number of contractors had pulled out of the project. When he left . . . Well, at least he could keep some connection to this Earth through the work on web. "If that's the condition, then I'm not coming back in, Marcus."

Marcus shook his head. "All right, Arron. I can't stop you, and if you're going to be like this, I can't help you." He paused. "You realize that if you're stripped off the roll, I won't even be able to get you home from there?"

"Yeah, I know," said Arron softly. "I'll find my own way out. It won't be the first time."

"No, I guess not." Marcus studied his keypad. "I don't know whether to wish you luck or sense, Hagopian," he said without looking up. "Call if you change your mind. Maybe we can still figure something out." He cut the connection and left Arron sitting there alone.

He stood up. "Station. Power off."

The station's low hum shut off, and Arron stood alone with the sound of the ventilators.

Shut them down, too? No. He picked up his portable and slung it over his shoulder. *Why risk any extra contaminants getting out before Bioverse can get to it?*

He crossed the empty room. His was the only station remaining. Cabal had stripped the others out, having, he said, found somebody who'd buy them for parts salvage.

Arron reached the front door and turned around. It seemed like an incredible waste to leave all the furniture and hardware, but, what were any of them going to do with it? Cabal had taken all he needed. Who else would use the place? The corpers certainly didn't need it, and the Dedelphi wouldn't touch it because of the Human contamination.

He pressed his fingertips against the light panel. Darkness filled the room. The sealed doors opened and closed behind him, locking automatically. If it came to it, the corpers would have no problem slicing their way in.

Arron climbed the stairs out into the watery daylight and walked to the pier where he'd left his boat. The ferries had stopped running. He'd had to bring himself out. The harbor managers had been happy to rent him one of their motorized boats, as he'd known they would. Those two were squeezers of an old, proud school. He paid their outrageous price without grumbling.

He stepped into the rocking boat and dropped his backpack into the bottom. He tossed the switches on the engine. Gripping the tiller firmly, the way Lareet had taught him, he pointed the nose for shore.

For the first time since he'd come to the Hundred Isles, the harbor was quiet. Boats rocked at anchor, but none of them plowed through the water. All the traffic was on the shore. Lines of mothers, sisters, and daughters filled the streets, bridges, and rooftops. They carried their bundles under their arms and on their heads while the smallest daughters clung to their backs and shoulders. Open-sided trucks stuffed with passengers and baggage crept between the pedestrians. All of them headed the same way, to the spaceport to wait for their relocation.

Arron had seen the bulletins that asked the families to stay home until they were specifically called. He could have told Lynn that was never going to work. The Getesaph were used to shortage living. If something was going to be distributed, whether it was a service or hard goods, you had better get there early and stake your place. If you waited for someone to tell you to turn up, whatever-it-was might be gone before you got there. If they got to the distribution point and found out nothing was happening yet, they'd calmly sit and wait until something did happen. It was amazing.

Arron steered the boat toward the dock. Two figures came out of the nearest shack. He assumed they were the harbor managers, who had no confidence in his ability to securely tie off a boat, but when he looked again, he saw they were Lareet and Umat.

"Dayisen Umat, Dayisen Lareet!" He flipped the reverse switch and eased his power off so the boat pulled in slowly, if clumsily, to the dock. Lareet shook her head and jumped down into the boat.

She shooed him off the tiller. Arron let himself be replaced and handed a rope up to Umat so she could tie them off.

"Ten years, Scholar Arron, and you have not learned you cannot properly work a boat alone." Lareet flicked her ears at him as she shut off the engine. "I despair."

"Well, you were a bit busy this morning, my Sisters." He gave Umat his hands, and she heaved him up onto the dock. "How goes the preparatory wave?"

Lareet handed him his backpack and climbed onto the dock beside him. "We have set the final roster . . ."

"After much heated debate in the Halls." Lareet touched his shoulder, but she wasn't focused on him. Her ears leaned toward her sister.

Something was going on. Arron's gaze shifted from one sister to the other. Umat looked fine, but Lareet's face was smooth and tight with some inner worry.

"Scholar Arron, what did your employers have to say?" Lareet asked.

Arron shook his head and wrung his hands to simulate flapping ears. "I'm stripped from the rolls and have to find my own way home." He bit down on his lip so hard he tasted blood. "Or, at least I will be soon, since I won't behave the way they want. So, from here on out, it's *Hitchhiker* Arron." He slung his pack over one shoulder, stuck out his thumb, and waited for them to ask what he was talking about.

But he saw they weren't listening to him. The Dayisen Rual watched each other over the top of his head.

"All right." Arron waved his arm. "You up there. What is going on?"

"An additional judgment was reached today that might interest you," Lareet said, almost hesitantly.

"Indeed," said Umat. "Your concern for our well-being, and your careful studies have not gone unnoticed."

Lareet dipped her ears. "And it has been seen how ready you are to help us with the other Humans. So, an additional debate was introduced."

"After which we were empowered to invite you to come with us," concluded Umat triumphantly.

"What?" Arron blinked.

Lareet turned one ear toward her sister. "We are inviting you to relocate with us aboard the *Ur* and continue your studies of ourselves and our ways from there."

Arron resisted the impulse to let his jaw drop. "Dayisen Umat, Dayisen Lareet, I thank you with all my soul, but . . ." He searched for the right Getesaph words. "You . . . your members do understand that I still regard this relocation as a mistake?"

"It has been made quite clear to them, and to us, yes," said Lareet solemnly. "We hoped you would want to stay with us and find out if you were right."

"But," he sputtered, unwilling to believe what was happening, "my employers stripped me from their rolls because of how I spoke against the relocation. I have no way to pay Bioverse for my maintenance."

Lareet slapped the side of his helmet lightly. "Do you think our employers intended you should labor like a slave for our benefit without compensation?"

"Trust us, Scholar Arron," said Umat. "Bioverse has been spoken to. We have claimed you as a sister, and your salary will enable you to live on the ships and on the ground, should you still be with us when we are returned."

"It will probably be necessary for you to make your home in the Human quarters, but that should not cause you hardship." Lareet's voice was full of satisfaction. "What do you have to say about all this, Scholar Arron?"

Arron's chest swelled, but at the same time his throat tightened. *It's not over!* he crowed in the back of his mind.

"I say thank you, my Sisters." He took their hands. "I will gladly come with you."

"Well, my Sister," sighed Lareet as they picked their way down the narrow avenue. "I think that was the finest batch of lies we ever told Scholar Arron, don't you?"

"We did not lie." Umat shook her elbow. "We asked straight-out would he come with us, and he said yes."

The skin on Lareet's upper arms rolled. The street was too quiet. With twilight setting, it felt like the shadowy Dead quarter. "But we did not tell him why. A lie by omission is still a lie."

Umat kicked a pile of dried weeds. "War requires your soul, Sister, not just your mouth. We need Scholar Arron. He can help us understand Human engineering and thinking. If need be, he can make a valuable hostage." Lareet opened her mouth again, but her sister silenced her. "He will help us, as soon as we explain it to him."

Then why do we not explain it to him now? Lareet let her ears fall. "I don't like this."

"And I do? He helped at my last bearing of daughters. He picked Ylata up as she crawled from my womb and placed her in my pouch. Do you think I want to harm him?"

"No, no, of course not." Lareet waved the suggestion away as they rounded a corner. "But—"

A father stood in front of them, wide-eyed and stoop-shouldered. He stared, as if just on the edge of understanding or remembering. Lareet bowed until her ears brushed the pavement. Umat copied her motion. This was a blessing. The city security teams were gently leading the fathers to the ports so they might be with the mothers, sisters, and daughters. There were only a few left free to be guided by the World Mothers to their destinies.

The t'Therians penned their fathers, and haggled over them like cattle, Lareet knew. It has always appalled her. How could you haggle over a creature driven solely by destiny?

The father shuffled toward them. He ran his hands across Lareet's ears and down her back. Her skin shivered.

Umat raised her head, and looked to Lareet.

"What do you say, my Sister? One more bearing? To remember what is at the heart of all we do." She held out her hand. "To mend our quarrel tighter than blood and soul?"

"You can't mean it." Lareet half laughed as she straightened up. "My belly's all but gone flat. I've got no room in me for more daughters." Still, the father stroked her shoulders softly, almost reverently. A tension she had forgotten she carried relaxed inside her.

"The father does not think so." Umat touched her forearm.

"I can't," said Lareet, although regret ran through her. "We're going into combat, Sister, how can I take daughters with me?"

"We're coordinators, not combatants," Umat reminded her. "Sister, it would be a fine thing to help birth your daughters one more time."

"It would be a fine thing indeed." She saw her sister's eyes shining in the fading sunlight. She wavered, then made her decision. Destiny drove the fathers, so destiny brought them here.

"I hate this part." She untied the waist of her trousers and let them fall. Startled, the father backed away.

Umat laid her hands on Lareet's shoulders. "Everybody does."

"It's just so drafty." Lareet wrapped her arms around her sister's shoulders. "Promise you'll be there at the birth, as you are at the beginning."

"I promise." Umat held Lareet close, embracing and supporting her.

The father found his own way. The rocking weight against her back took Lareet's balance, but Umat steadied her. Lareet felt Umat's warmth, her strength, the absolute assurance that had always been Umat's gift, flow between them. She drank it in gratefully.

When it was finished, they embraced one more time, and Umat stood her up straight again. Lareet pulled her trousers back up. The father blinked sleepily, combed her ear once, and wandered away.

"May you father more daughters than there are stars in the sky!" Lareet shouted after him.

"Oh, good, my Sister!" Umat laughed. "Bring the whole city running!"

"Why not?" She laid a hand over her belly guard. "Let us all begin again." She flicked her ears toward her sister. "What do you say? Shall we chase after him for you?"

Umat laughed loudly. "Mothers forbid! We're going to have enough trouble with yours. That took long enough it's probably going to be a full six. Come on." She slid her arm under Lareet's. "Let us get you home before your scent brings all the fathers in the city out of hiding."

They strolled back into the main streets, cutting across the lines of traffic streaming toward the port. Lareet felt sympathy for them. She wanted to tell them to go home. The relocation wasn't going to happen for months, if it happened at all.

But this I promise you, my Sisters, as I promise my daughters in my womb. When our world is saved, the t'Theria will no longer walk on it to plague us.

Resaime picked her way down the plane's ramp, pressing close to Aunt Senejess's side. Every muscle under her skin was wire-taut. She stared at the crowds not with curiosity, but with a feeling she was fairly sure must be fear.

Crazy. This is crazy. She ticked off the names of the Getesaph she knew, the ones she went to school with and played with when she and her sisters were small. Why was she so afraid of them all of a sudden?

Because these are not those Getesaph. These are the ones who will kill you if they find out who you are.

"Loose your hold a bit, my Daughter," murmured Aunt Senejess in her ear. "Act like you are coming home, not walking out to feed the sharks."

"Yes, Mother." Res managed to get her hand to relax a little.

The port was nothing like where they landed in t'Theria. The landing strip was clean and clear of booths. Humans in clean-suits wandered everywhere, intent on their own errands. The Getesaph, their pinkish grey skins startling after so many days surrounded by blue-grey t'Therian's, gathered on roofed walkways to stare at the huge, elongated shuttles, with their mirrored skins and stubby wings. Their conversations filled the clean, white buildings with a noise louder than the engines on the vans and the cars trundling around the shuttles.

Technically, this port and all its shiny new buildings belonged to the Humans. The Humans all thought Aunt Senejess was Mother, here on Human business, so in Human territory nothing could happen to them. So, she really had nothing to be afraid of. Nothing at all.

Aunt Senejess shepherded Res into the nearest building. It was a check-in station of some kind, or maybe registry was a more accurate description. Humans in all their shades of brown and beige stood in the middle of round information stations, surrounded by Getesaph five or six deep. Some Getesaph clustered around the automated information stations, pointing, and conferring with their sisters. More sat in the chairs or squatted in family groups on the floor with their bundles and their daughters. Some of them noticed Res and Aunt Senejess and glowered. Res's stomach flipped over. It turned over again as she realized that a father, no, two, no three, wandered between the Getesaph with their vague, empty faces and random gait.

"Don't stare, Daughter." Aunt Senejess pulled her toward an empty comm station. "Show me how this Human machine works. I believe our quarters will be registered inside here."

"Yes, Mother." Res dropped her attention down to the blue screen and the keypad. The basic access instructions were printed in five different languages. A half dozen keystrokes and a retinal scan later, the address for Praeis Shin's quarters appeared in gold on the blue background. In the letter Aunt Senejess had written to Lynn, she'd said Resaime was coming with her, so Res could open all the locks and access the secure terminals. Aunt Senejess could not, however, since it was Praeis's retinal patterns in the database. Res had explained this to her aunt, who had praised her and been extra glad of her decision to bring Resaime along. Res wasn't sure if she really meant it, but it felt good when she said it.

Aunt Senejess read the address and squeezed her shoulder. Res blanked the screen.

"Now, here is a map." Aunt Senejess led her over to the info board, with the port and its buildings traced out in four different colors.

"We're over here." Res pointed to the dormitories marked in green.

"So we are," agreed Aunt Senejess. "And the gathering point for those about to leave is here." She laid a finger on a courtyard traced in purple. "And the Human administrative offices are here." A building drawn in blue. "And their quarters are here." A dormitory marked in red. "Very clear, very convenient." She looked the map up and down with great approval.

Res felt her ears twitch. "The Humans seem interested in making things easy for us."

"I was just thinking the same thing, my Daughter." Aunt Senejess patted her hand. "Well, let us get where we are supposed to be."

The port buildings were all connected by long hallways that opened into large, curved gathering areas. Getesaph were everywhere. They walked down the hallways, they sat on the chairs in the lobbies with their bundles at their feet. They even sat on the floors in the hallways with their children on their shoulders or in their laps.

All eyes followed her and Aunt Senejess, but no one made a move. Res glanced overhead and saw the security cameras. Her brain expelled a huge sigh of relief.

Fathers roamed freely between them. Here and there, they knelt or stretched to touch some daughter or sister, or even a mother with children still clinging to her shoulders.

Even the fathers trained their wide, pale gaze on Resaime as she walked past.

"Why aren't they in their rooms?" whispered Res fiercely. "What are they all doing out here? The Humans will take care of their stuff. Why can't they just—"

"Shhh." Aunt Senejess hooked her arm and picked up the pace just a little. "It is their way, Daughter." The corridor branched ahead of them, and Aunt Senejess steered her down the right fork. "It does not, however, keep their soldiers from being deadly, nor does it render them deaf."

Res clamped her mouth shut. *I don't like this. I don't want to be here. What am I doing?* Her ears started to droop, and she struggled to hold them upright. *I didn't think it would be this bad.* Her inner parts were ballooning so badly she thought they'd push her stomach up her throat. She smelled funny, or maybe it was just the father-scent clinging so tightly to her that was making it hard to breathe straight. She wanted to go home. She wanted Theia. She wanted . . .

"Here we are, Daughter." Aunt Senejess stopped in front of a door. "Open it for us, please."

Res laid her thumb on the register and let her print and eye be scanned. The door recognized her, and the lock clicked open. She swung the door open and stumbled inside. There were sleeping mats on the floor, chairs and tables, bottled water and packaged food on the serving tables. A comm station stood in one corner.

Aunt Senejess dragged the door shut, crossed the room to the climate controls, and set the fans going. She checked the window to make sure it was securely fastened and drew the curtains over it. Res sat down in one of the chairs and opened a water bottle. She gulped it thirstily. The straining inside her eased, and she began to breathe normally again.

"Well, this explains why they're all out in the halls," said Res, setting the bottle down. "The Humans have made the rooms too small. They always do that."

Aunt Senejess glanced up at the ceiling. "Are we observed?"

Res looked around. "I don't think so. I heard Mother say the policy for Human structures was going to be to monitor the common areas, halls, and so on, but not the private quarters." Her voice shook a little, but her control was, thankfully, returning.

Aunt Senejess was giving her a hard stare. The skin on Res's back and belly trembled.

"Daughter, I recognized that your mother raised you decently and properly. It is all I would expect from her, but you must control yourself." She paused and her gaze softened. "I felt it, too, Resaime. It is perfectly natural."

Res laced her fingers together. "I know. I know. And it's not as if I've never . . ." She broke off. "It was just a lot of them, fathers, all at once, and out in the open like that . . ."

"I know." Aunt Senejess rubbed Res's scalp thoughtfully. "And you are just now ready for motherhood." She paused. "You could take one to you," she suggested. "It would not be a bad way to begin. Rescue a soul from the 'Esaph and bring her the blood and will of the family."

Res twisted her hands. "I . . . I don't feel ready yet, Aunt."

Aunt Senejess touched her shoulder. "Then it is not time yet." She tugged gently on Res's ear. "You don't have to be afraid of me, Daughter. I am not your enemy. The enemy waits out there." She turned her ears toward the windows.

Then, she really noticed the comm station. "The information about them, however, waits in here." Her skin rippled up and down her arms. "Daughter, what information can you get out of this *station*?"

Res picked the introductory sheets up off the counter and flipped through them. "Just about anything, it looks like. Addresses, schedules, Human contacts. There's even a whole database with information on the city-ships."

"Which I'm sure the 'Esaph have made good use of," muttered Aunt Senejess. "Are there passenger lists?"

"Yes. Sure. That's practically the first thing on here." She looked up and saw that her aunt's face had gone taut. "Why?"

"Don't tell me we could have stayed home and discovered all." Her eyes shone with an icy glitter, and her ears pressed flat against her scalp.

Res shook her head. "I don't think so. This is probably an isolated network. You wouldn't be able to access its information except through a *dedicated terminal*." She nodded toward the comm station. "That means one that's wired into the system here on the island, probably right here in the port."

"How very convenient." Senejess bared her teeth. "It means we have to spend less time out in plain view." She drew a chair up to the terminal. "The first thing we need to know is who will be on the first flights to the *Ur*. Come, Daughter. Show your old aunt what to do."

Lynn was not surprised to find Arron waiting at her door when she arrived at the Human dormitories in Getesaph Port I.

In fact, she realized, she would have been both surprised and disappointed if he hadn't been there. It was not like Arron to leave a conversation or an argument unfinished.

"Hi," she said casually, as she stood in front of her reddish, ceramic door, waiting for it to scan her and unlock.

"Hi," he answered, almost shyly. "Can I come in?"

"Sure." The door clicked open with its weird, swinging motion, and Lynn walked into her temporary quarters.

She felt Arron follow her inside. The room was square, white with burgundy carpet, and filled with functional, squared-off furniture, a locker for clean-suits, a work/comm station, and a stationary food jobber. All standard, all generic. Through the open door, the bedroom looked much the same.

"Who designed this place?" Lynn undid her seals and pulled her helmet off. "They could have made it a little more suffocatingly boring if they'd tried." She scrubbed her scalp with her palm and tossed her helmet on the table. "Going to get out of that?" She gestured at Arron's clean-suit.

"No, I can't stay."

"Oh." Lynn shrugged. "As needed. Mind if I change?"

"No, no," he said hurriedly. "Go right ahead."

Lynn went into the bedroom. She left the door open just a crack.

"I was really surprised when I heard you were coming," said Arron from the other room.

"Yeah, well, I thought considering the communications problems we've had, I thought we should be on the spot while the shuttles get ready to go." She asked as she pulled off her shirt and pants and started wriggling her way out of the suit. The ventilator's breeze hit her bare skin, sending goose bumps up her arms. Lynn sighed and wished she had time to enjoy just being out of the damn organic cocoon for a while. She considered telling Arron that she could rely on Praeis to keep her people abreast of what was really going on with the Council of True Blood and the Queens-of-All, but there was no one to keep her similarly informed on the Getesaph side. She decided against it. She did not want to discuss Praeis right now, especially when she didn't know what she was up to. The letter she'd gotten saying Praeis and Res wanted to travel to the Hundred Isles had been unexpected, and nonspecific. Lynn had approved the travel plans more out of old loyalty than anything else. Praeis knew what she was doing. This was her home ground, after all. What worried Lynn was that she hadn't heard a word from her since.

"Coming here to keep tabs on things is probably a really good idea," Arron said.

Inasmuch as anything we're doing here is a good idea, she could practically hear him adding. She sighed quietly.

"So that's what I'm doing here." Lynn opened the door. "What are you doing here?"

Arron stood over by the food jobber, running his gloved fingertips over its top. "I'm not really sure. Everything should be handled through channels, but I guess, I wanted to talk to you before you got the memo . . ."

"Memo?" Lynn flopped down in one of the square, utilitarian chairs. The upholstery felt rough against her skin.

Arron took a deep breath. "The outside sisters of my host family have been designated the leaders of the Getesaph preparatory wave. They've invited me to join the Getesaph aboard the *Ur.*"

Lynn felt herself beginning to stare. "For how long?"

Arron stalked across the room to the one window. "For as long as I want," he said to the world outside.

Lynn shoved herself upright. *I do not believe this. Not even from you.* "How long are you likely to want?"

He shrugged, but still didn't look at her. "I don't know."

Which means as long as you possibly can, and we both know it.

Arron turned around, and Lynn finally saw his face. For a moment, she thought he was going to start crying. She had never seen such a mix of fear and eagerness on anybody's face before.

She bit back her initial response, and just asked, "Why, Arron?"

His fingers scrabbled at the edge of the windowsill as if he were trying to get a grip on it. "It's insane. I know it's insane. The head-mechanics would probably turn me inside out and yank half my webbing if I went in. The Getesaph are brutal, barbaric, ignorant, prejudiced, superstitious, filthy, and I'm deadly poison to them. And I want to stay," he said to the backs of his hands. "I've been hauling nets on nights when all three of the big moons swelled the tides up. I've held a baby that crawled from her mother's womb and placed her safe in the pouch. I've dug survivors out of bomb wreckage. I've gone to funerals and howled at the top of my lungs. I've run down the streets beside a father. I've been lost in crowds so huge I couldn't see the end of them. I've talked with hundreds of different people across dozens of cities. I've—" He stopped. "I've been alive, Lynn."

Lynn looked at him thoughtfully. She remembered back to college, and hearing about Arron's family. They were scattered between half a dozen enclaves. All of them wanted him to come live in their world and join their work. He'd grown up bouncing from territory to territory. Not once did anybody, to hear Arron tell it anyway, even acknowledge the possibility that he might want to strike out on his own.

Here, though, with the Getesaph, he was virtually unique, and absolutely impossible to qualify. He would be accepted as himself, because there was nothing they could compare him to. That should have made him the ultimate outsider, but instead, again, to hear him tell it, it had allowed him to make his own place, possibly for the first time in his life.

And I'm going to tell him he can't have it? Lynn shook her head. She could understand that yearning. In her case, though, when her chance came, her family had thrown a party, and she had been getting regular, encouraging hywrites from them ever since they left the Solar system.

She didn't agree with Arron. His view of the relocation and Bioverse's mission was completely twisted, but she couldn't, she wouldn't deny him a place to call home.

She straightened herself up. "Well, the city-ships are the Dedelphi's home for the duration. Our contract says they say who gets to come and go, or stay." Arron turned to face her fully, his face relaxing as she spoke. "So, if they invited you, great. Have a good time, and make sure you give your addresses to me and David so we can invite you over for dinner." The expression of relief on Arron's face was so intense, Lynn had to fight back a laugh. "Name of the Prophet, Arron, what did you think I was going to say?"

He smiled ruefully. "I don't know. I thought maybe, because of the knot . . ."

"Ah, yes, the knot." Lynn raised one finger. "Because of the knot, I am going to ask you a favor."

His expression hardened. "Lynn, I am not going to zombie out that knot just because—"

Lynn threw back her head and laughed. "God Almighty, will you stop casting me as the villain here?" Now, he just looked startled. "All I was going to ask is that you take a look around at what we're doing. I mean a real, honest, hard look. After that, if you still think this is nothing but another Avitrol looting, then, okay, that's what you think, and I've never been able to change your mind on anything anyway." They both shared a small smile at that. "But if you see what I hope you'll see, which is that we are here to ensure the Dedelphi's future rather than take it away, promise me you'll tie another knot."

Arron nodded solemnly. "I promise."

She stood up and walked across to him. "Thank you." She touched his shoulder. He lifted his hand and covered hers. They stood like that for a moment, recovering old feelings and readjusting to new ones.

"Now get out of here." She slapped him gently and pointed toward the door. "Some of us, not having been adopted by politically powerful families, are working for a living."

"Thank you, Lynn." He embraced her briefly but warmly. With

a confidence in his step that hadn't been there when he came in, he took his leave.

So, you've become a Getesaph. I wish you luck, Arron, thought Lynn as she sat down in front of the comm station. *And anything else you might need.*

She signed herself in and waited for the options screen to appear. Instead, the words URGENT MESSAGE WAITING flashed on the screen.

What? "Station, open urgent message."

A Dedelphi's head and shoulders appeared on the screen with her ears lowered halfway toward her scalp. It was Praeis Shin.

Uh-oh. Lynn sat up a little straighter.

The recording started. "Lynn, I am so sorry to drop this in your lap. You received a letter saying that I wanted to go to the Hundred Isles, just to make sure everything was all right, and could I have a room for myself and my daughter Resaime?" Her ears dropped a little further. "That letter was written by my sister Senejess. She and Resaime are in the Hundred Isles now, under my name. They're spying on the Getesaph, of course." Her nostrils pinched shut. "Lynn, you will do what you want about this, but it might be best to let her wander around. We both know she won't find anything. Having her come back empty-handed will do us more good than you snatching her up. In fact, snatching her up will add fuel to the idea that you must have something to hide." She straightened her ears most of the way. "I am so sorry to do this, my respected ally, and I'm not done yet. Please, I beg you, try to find a way to let my daughter know she can contact you if necessary. Her aunt is not trustworthy, and she's alone over there.

"Thank you."

The recording shut down. Lynn started to curse, slowly, methodically, and heatedly. *Resaime, what in God's name did you think you were doing!*

She sighed. *That's not really a question anymore, is it? The question is what am I going to do now that she's done it?*

She rubbed her eyes. "Station, record message for Praeis Shin t'Theria at Getesaph Port I. Message begins. Praeis, hope the trip went smoothly. Just wanted to let you know I'm here if you need anything. Take care of yourself." *Which lets Senejess know her ruse has worked.* Her mouth pressed into a hard, straight line. "Station, send message. Record next message for Resaime Shin t'Theria. Message begins: Res, it's Lynn. Your mother's probably going to be busy as all get out here. If you're bored, or if you two need anything, here's my address." She stopped. "Station, attach urgent call addresses. Send message." *Which lets Res know where I'm at.* "Station, record third message for Praeis Shin t'Theria in Home Shin on the t'Aori peninsula. "Praeis, I got your message, and I'll do everything I can. I've just sent my emergency addresses to Res. She's not alone over here. Call if anything else comes up." She paused. "Station, send message." *Which lets her know we're still friends.*

Lynn let her head hang back until she was staring at the ceiling.

Let's see, where're we at? We've got a conspiracy theory going with the t'Theria, which has led them to send spies to the Hundred Isles, where the Getesaph're so nervous about the t'Therians they can't stand the idea of staying on the ground while the t'Therians are in the air. If the Getesaph find out the t'Therians are spies, the t'Therians will be killed, the Getesaph will pull out of the Confederation, and I'll be fired, if I'm not jailed for sabotaging a company endeavor because I knew about this.

Well, I knew this was going to be a challenge. Lynn straightened up, and ran a hand over her scalp before she remembered she didn't have any hair to smooth down. *I'm just not sure I realized how much of one.*

Chapter X

Thank you for your careful attention to these matters." The Human presenter, who'd introduced herself as Escort Shia, was a round, gold-skinned woman whose eyes had been artificially enlarged at some point. She spoke Getesaph with only the barest trace of a British accent. "We stand ready to serve you and yours in any way we can."

Arron stood on the terrace overlooking the gathering room. He had attended his departure session earlier that morning. It was actually better than he had expected. There was very little obvious propaganda. The emphasis was on exactly how events would proceed from here and how to get more information or help at every stage. Escort Shia did more than just speak the language. She was fluid in idiom and courtesy, and her audience had responded by questioning her openly, which was not something the reticent Getesaph did easily.

So, I can't hate the whole project, thought Arron, with more good humor than he expected to find inside himself. *Damn. I may have to make good on my promise to Lynn after all.*

Something bothered him though. Something had bothered him all yesterday and today as he walked through corridors and lounges set aside for the three thousand Getesaph of the preparatory wave who would depart tomorrow. He'd been welcomed by mothers and sisters he knew, and a number he didn't. Everyone was very interested in how he planned to present the history of this occasion, and he had to tell them honestly he was still working on it. Everything felt smooth, easy, and tinged with a kind of cheerful excitement.

He'd pulled out his portable and its recorder and made some records. He'd conducted a few interviews among the mothers, sisters, and daughters, both the ones getting ready for immediate departure and those waiting for their turn, even though that wasn't coming for at least a week.

He still couldn't put his finger on what was wrong. So he roamed the port, as if he hoped to see the answer shining on a bulletin screen somewhere.

On the main floor, the meeting was breaking up in the Getesaph's typical leisurely fashion. Nobody had left, not even the smaller daughters. Instead, they broke into family groups and began lively discussions among themselves, stopping occasionally to query their neighbors on some point or the other. Escort Shia moved among them, smiling and greeting. She paused at one group after another, adding her lilting voice to the general chaos of confined conversation. Children clung to their mothers' shoulders, or sat at their feet, listening patiently. A more restless group had started a hide-and-seek game between the family knots.

Arron found his eyes following the children. There weren't that many of them, for such a big group of Getesaph. Some daughters had probably been allowed to stay back in their rooms. Others were probably in the cafeterias or child-care areas looking after their younger sisters. Something itched in the back of his mind. The prep wave wasn't taking any walking children, he knew that, but still . . . He watched the children and mothers more closely. There was something, there was something . . .

Then he saw it. Not one of the Getesaph had a live belly. Not one.

His eyes scanned the crowd, straining to see someone, anyone, with her full belly rolling with her offspring, to see a tiny, curious pair of ears poking out over a pouch rim. There were over a hundred young adult Getesaph down there. It was extremely unlikely that not one of them would be carrying children in her pouch.

Unless it was deliberately decided to keep the carrying mothers away from the place. That was done, frequently. During wars. Carrying mothers with children in their bellies or on their backs did not enter into combat.

Arron scanned the crowds again. There were children on shoulders, but they could clearly walk for themselves and were hanging on to their mothers for convenience or fun. No infants clung to their mothers' folds or nestled in the crooks of their arms. These would all be outside sisters, but even then, an outside sister did not give her children over to the care of her sisters until they could walk. She would still be expected to do her job until then, whatever her job was. Unless she was a combat soldier.

They are going into an unknown situation. They probably just want to make sure it's safe before they bring in the carrying mothers. It makes sense.

He tried to turn away. He did not want to think about this anymore. He had an explanation. A good one.

But he stayed where he was and started looking for faces he knew. He saw Ovrth Chaick's crooked shoulder, and Trindt Toth's earless head. Dayisen Vshil, Dayisen Bol, Ovrth Wes, Trindt Athsk, Shesk Richkin, Ovrth Ith.

Arron gripped the balcony rail hard with both hands. Even his gloves did not keep the edge from biting into his palms.

Ovrth, trindt, shesk, and dayisen. *Soldiers and officers.*

Irat Queth.

And doctors.

Arron let go of the rail one finger at a time. He watched the Getesaph until they began to trickle away, and all he saw were soldiers. Combat soldiers and officer coordinators.

At last, he did turn away. With his gaze pointed toward the toes of his boots, he hurried along the catwalk and didn't stop until he reached the door of his dorm room. He slammed it shut behind himself, for once very glad of the privacy of Human quarters.

He dropped into the stiff guest chair and realized his hands were shaking. He balled them into fists.

I am being an idiot. I am being a complete idiot. I am reaching conclusions for which I have no data. That's worse than stupid, that's sloppy.

He was out of the guest chair and across the room before he even had time to think about it. He snatched up his portable and jacked it straight into the wall. Sitting cross-legged on the mattress, his hands hovered over the keys as he tried to decide what to look for.

Finally, he pulled out the threads to the Bioverse Relocation Public Database. (We are here to serve you and yours!)

Arron typed in his request.

PASSENGER MANIFEST FOR SHUTTLE *SOJOURN* FOR 5/17 GETESAPH YEAR 3078.

Because he was registered as a Getesaph passenger, the threads reeled out into the database without challenge or obstruction. A list of names for the preparatory wave personnel appeared on the screen. Arron scanned the titles in front of the personal names. *Hrashn,* engineers. *Tchilick,* farmers. *Chkat,* architects. No soldiers, except, of course, for the wave leaders the Dayisen Rual, Lareet and Umat. He shot out threads for the next day's manifest, and the next, and the next. No soldiers. Not one.

And not one of the names matched the faces he had seen in the departure session.

Arron's fingers trembled as he shut down his portable. His eyes stared at the blank walls of his room.

Oh. My. God.

It took him a long moment to realize the fierce, sick sensation building up inside him was anger.

"How could you?" he whispered to the walls. In the next second he was on his feet. "How could you do this!"

He stood there for a moment, his lungs heaving and his hands clenching and unclenching.

What do I do? His knees wanted to crumple again. He paced, rubbing his upper arms. The fleeting thought reached him that Lareet and Umat might not be part of this. But that was impossible. They had been ensconced in the Parliament deciding who would be in the preparatory wave. They were the ones who had asked him to speak to Lynn about changing the schedule.

He bit his lip. Lynn. He had to tell Lynn. She could stop the relocation until . . . Until some compromise was worked out. This was a communications problem, it had to be. This was old fears that had not been quieted by the Confederation.

That had to be it.

He sent out a new thread to get Lynn's location. She was in a meeting with Parliamentary representatives. Something about ensuring open communications between the city-ships and the ground. He left his portable on the bed. She had to stop everything. Right now. Before—

He choked off the thought and strode down the empty Human corridor. Out in the port's main area, his eyes flickered back and forth like a Getesaph's ears trying to follow two conversations at once. Here was a mother with infants on her shoulders. Here was one with a live belly. But they had their luggage and sleeping mats piled around them. Indigents who had come early. They weren't supposed to be here, they weren't soldiers, not full-time soldiers anyway.

Lynn's meeting was just breaking up. The door was open and Humans trickled out in ones and twos. None of them was Lynn.

Lynn was still in the meeting room, silhouetted against a schedule board with Dayisen Lareet and Dayisen Umat.

He had no chance to move. Umat glanced right at him.

"Scholar Arron. What is the matter?"

Arron opened his mouth, but no words formed in his mind.

Lynn frowned at him. "Can it wait a minute? There's another couple of things to go over here."

Arron made up his mind. "No. It can't." He walked into the room, keeping his attention fixed on the sisters, who towered over him.

"Dayisen Lareet, Dayisen Umat, why has Parliament falsified the passenger identities for the first wave of relocation?"

They all stared at him. He let them.

Lynn found her voice first. "Arron, would you care to elaborate on that thesis?"

"The names and positions of the Getesaph in the registration files do not match the names and positions of the Getesaph preparing to leave with the shuttles today."

A dozen different expressions chased one another across Lynn's face. For a moment he thought she was going to ask if he was serious. Instead, she faced Lareet and Umat.

"Is there any reason Scholar Arron would make such an accusation?"

"Yes," said Lareet. "There is."

Umat tackled Lynn. They both sprawled on the floor. Arron stared for a second, and it was too long. Lareet dived around him and slapped the door control. The portal slid shut.

Lynn struggled under Umat's weight, landing ineffective blows on Umat's arms and shoulders.

"Room voice!" Lynn shrieked.

"Voice off," bellowed Lareet over her. "Set keyboard input at this station."

Arron tried to duck sideways, but Lareet matched his movement. "Come with us, Scholar Arron," she said softly. "Neither of you has to be hurt. Especially not you, Sister."

"This is crazy." Arron feinted left, then right. He got two steps to the comm station before Lareet caught him around the waist and hauled him backward.

Arron flailed in her grasp, kicking backward reflexively. She caught hold of his wrist and twisted his arm neatly behind his back. With her greater weight, she leaned into the small of his back, forcing him gasping to his knees.

"No one has to get hurt," she insisted. "You are not our enemies."

"Fuck you both!" screamed Lynn. She grabbed Umat's wrists, trying to keep Umat's hands away from her throat. Umat gradually forced Lynn's hands down. One-handed, the Getesaph undid the catches on Lynn's faceplate. Her ears and nose folded closed and she reached into the helmet. Arron heard a wordless scream before Umat pressed her hand hard onto Lynn's throat.

"No!" he shouted, flinging himself forward. Pain lanced through his arm and shoulder as Lareet tightened her grip.

"She will not be killed," Lareet told him. "Umat knows her work."

As he watched, Lynn's struggles weakened and stopped.

"Why?" Arron choked on the word. "What are you doing?"

"Don't tell him, Sister." Umat closed Lynn's faceplate and stood up. Lynn lay still on the floor. Arron couldn't tell if she was still breathing. His heart pounded heavily against his rib cage.

"You will have a blistered hand, Sister," said Lareet.

"I already do." Umat crossed to the comm station and typed on the keyboard. If Lynn was breathing too shallowly, Lareet was breathing too heavily. "It will not be so bad." She coughed. "My exposure is not great. Humans are not so poison as we commonly believe." She swallowed hard and leaned against the console. "But I am going to be sick. I think I breathed something in."

Somebody knocked hard on the door. Umat slid the door open by hand. Two Getesaph Arron didn't know darted inside. "No word has gone out yet," said the taller of the two as she shut the door behind her.

"This room doesn't seem to be watched." The shorter sister knelt by Lynn. Lynn coughed, and her whole body twitched.

She's alive. Arron almost melted with relief.

"They're only monitoring the halls," said Lareet. "Human notions of privacy, again."

"That does not mean we have much time, Ovrth Tair." Umat straightened herself up.

Ovrth Tair carried a small bag. She opened it up. Lynn stirred more strongly. Her eyelids fluttered. Tair took a capsule out of the bag and undid Lynn's faceplate. Tair cracked the capsule between her fingers and tossed it into Lynn's helmet and clamped the faceplate back down. Lynn lay still again.

"Promise me you have the proper dosage for Humans," said Lareet quietly.

Tair glanced at her reproachfully. "Of course, Dayisen Lareet. I know my job, as do you." Tair held out a second capsule.

"We must have you unconscious, Scholar Arron," said Lareet. "Will you trust us and take it willingly?"

Arron's mouth had gone completely dry. "You will have to do this to me, Sister," he croaked. "My will does not move in this direction."

Tair shrugged and came closer until her smooth, tight face was all Arron could see. Her thick fingers undid his faceplate. She closed her nostrils and cracked the capsule. Arron smelled something bitter. His head swam.

"Please believe that I am sorry," said Lareet from a long way away. "If you had not come in here, we would not be doing this."

Darkness slipped over him, and Arron didn't hear anything else.

* * *

Resaime's heart fluttered between excitement and fear. One hand held Aunt Senejess's arm. The other carried a satchel stuffed with nothing more than blankets from the closet in their dorm room. Aunt Senejess carried most of their clothes in an awkward packet in her arms. It almost entirely obscured her vision, which, as she had said in the room, was the whole idea.

The bright sun made Res's skin itch under the shadowy pink makeup Aunt Senejess had smeared across her. The bracelets on her wrists and rings clipped to her ears jingled with every step.

They had left the dormitories by the south side, and made a wide circle around to the north side, where new arrivals trudged patiently to the perpetually open doors.

Aunt Senejess had one ear turned toward a pair of soldiers strolling toward the doors at an off-duty pace and at an angle that would cross the path Res and her aunt were taking. Aunt Senejess carefully matched their pace. The soldiers were deep in conversation with each other and paid no attention until Aunt Senejess collided straight into them. The loose knot holding the packet shut came undone, the blanket fell open, and clothes and sundries scattered around the sidewalk.

"Mother Night!" exclaimed one of the soldiers, while Resaime scrambled to gather their things together. "Can't you hear?"

"I'm sorry, Dayisen. I'm very sorry." Senejess grabbed at a scarf that threatened to blow away in the breeze. "We hurried so to pack, I'm afraid I was not careful. I'm sorry."

Resaime risked a glance up from her job of rummaging through the clothes to make sure everything was there. The soldier's expression softened.

"When's your time, Mother?"

"Not for two weeks yet, so they tell us." Aunt Senejess jerked a thumb toward the main building. "But we thought . . ."

"You and the rest of the city." The soldier shook her head. "Hear me, Citizen Sister, everyone will leave in time. The Humans will not start their work until we're all gone. You can go back home and wait your turn."

"Isn't there room for us here?" Resaime was amazed at how small her aunt's voice sounded.

The soldier pressed her lips together and blew out an exasperated *bb-rrrrr-ttt* noise. Her duty-sister bared her teeth at her.

"Of course there's room," said the sister. "There just isn't any need."

"They're saying they'll fill the two ships they have and let the plague take the rest." The quaver in Aunt Senejess's voice was so alarming, Resaime reached out instinctively. "I have only my youngest daughter left, Dayisen." Her aunt clutched Resaime's hand.

The second soldier dipped her ears sympathetically and touched Senejess's shoulder. "Rumors wander the streets with the fathers. Mother, no one is going to be left behind to this plague or any other."

"I'm sure you know the truth, Dayisen." Senejess bent to tie her bundle back up. Resaime put her finger on the string to hold it down while her aunt tightened the knots. "I don't understand very much of this. Can the Humans really remove all this evil from us?"

The first soldier bared her teeth. "What the Humans will not take care of, we will."

Her sister-in-arms shook her lightly by the shoulder. "We will be late for our shift, Dayisen Oraen."

Oraen touched her hand in acknowledgment. "Good luck to you, Mother. Go home and wait in patience. You will soon see there is no reason to fear or hurry."

The arms-sisters, the *dayisen,* Resaime corrected herself, marched away.

"Well, my Daughter"—Aunt Senejess hoisted the bundle onto her shoulder—"what do you think of that?"

"I'm not sure," Resaime answered in careful Getesaph. Aunt

Senejess had warned her that a snatch of conversation was more likely to be paid attention to if it was in a foreign language, particularly t'Therian. "You knew they were planning something."

"We strongly suspected, but that was all." Aunt Senejess squinted after the dayisen. "Now we know. What the Humans will not take care of, we will, she said. What can that mean but an attack on our Great Family?"

The skin on Resaime's arms bunched and knotted. "What do we do now?"

"We go into the port." Aunt Senejess started walking again. "We stow these bundles and try to find out what rumors they are allowing to wander about with their fathers." She glanced down at Resaime, and her eyes sparkled. "Then we will see what the Humans' network can tell us, and we take all this news back home."

She's going to hear how loud my heart is beating. I know it. "What will we do with it then?"

"What we must." Aunt Senejess now had her eyes straight ahead.

Resaime bit her lip and struggled to keep up with her aunt's long, swinging stride. They were almost to the doors, nearly to the port and its crowd. She had to do something, and do it now.

I have to do this. I have to. Her blood was roaring in her ears. "But . . ." She put a quaver of her own into the word. It was easier than she thought. Her stomach clenched. "Aunt Senejess, at least promise me you'll do something with it to convince the Queens that the Getesaph are dangerous." Her aunt stopped and looked her full in the face.

Theia was right. This was completely, totally, and utterly wrong. She was doing it anyway. "Mother wanted to bring us here to live and grow, but she didn't tell us . . . She doesn't see how the Getesaph will try to hurt them, hurt us. The Humans are all blind. They always have been. I'm worried about Theia, Aunt Senejess. She doesn't know enough. I'm afraid." Tears prickled her eyes. Not from fear, but from strain. She felt more naked than she would standing here in her belly guard. All the Ancestors were staring up from the ground at her. They saw a disloyal liar. They saw wickedness and disobedience.

Aunt Senejess set the bundle down and took hold of both of Resaime's shoulders. "Hear me, my own," she said softly. "Your words are strong and sensible. I knew you would not stand apart from your family. The news we bring back will not go to the Queens, it will go to the Great Family. Our friends stand ready to broadcast it and post it on the debate walls and call for a break from the Confederation. Despite the events of the past week, the Queens are still isolated in the city with their sycophants. The army will not stay with them long, once we bring them reason to attack. We already have assurances. If the Getesaph are about to do what I suspect, so much the better. We can land our soldiers on their islands and hold their children against their good behavior. If they are capable of feeling, they will make no trouble. If not..." She bared her teeth, panting in anger. "Then they will have nothing left to care about."

Resaime looked at her mutely. All the words she did not want to say clogged her throat.

Her aunt shifted her grip and pulled Resaime into a real embrace. "It will be well, my own," Aunt Senejess whispered in her ear. "You and your sister will be safe. I swear it by our Ancestors."

Resaime closed her eyes and hugged her back with all her strength.

I am doing this for Mother. I am doing this for Theia. I am doing this for our sisters and for the Great Family. She'll see that the Confederation is the right thing to do, if we can just keep it from falling apart too fast. That's what's important. That's what I have to do.

She pulled back a little. "Thank you, Aunt Senejess. I'm ready to go ahead now."

Her aunt nodded with approval, stood up, shouldered her bundle, and took Resaime's hand. Together, they walked into the port.

* * *

Trace glanced at the infoview on the back of her right hand. Nothing. No calls, no mail. Nothing. She drummed the windowsill and stared out over the bustling spaceport outside their borrowed offices.

She should have been busy. A thousand details were passing through her station this second. They all needed approval, review, or forwarding. She had teams to coordinate, information to spread, progress reports to write. But all she could do was stand there and think about how Lynn wasn't sitting in the next room.

The office door opened with its weird swinging motion and R.J. stepped inside. He looked at her for a long moment and shrugged. "I haven't heard anything either."

She glanced at her infoview again. Still nothing. "We have got to call Keale and the Marines, R.J. This is worse than a snapped thread somewhere."

He sighed and rubbed his forehead. "I hate to admit it, but you're right. I just wanted to hold off because, well I don't think we should . . . encourage them, you know?"

She nodded. "I know. And happens, I agree, but she's *missing,* R.J."

"I noticed." He dropped into one of the chairs surrounding the table that had been covered with a patchwork of screen tiles. "Tell you what, I'll get Keale, if you'll get Brador."

"Deal." She dragged out one of the chairs and sat. She pressed the activation studs on two of the tiles in front of her. A directory lit up and she selected the comm display. As soon as the monitor and icon spread appeared she picked Veep Brador's emergency shortcut.

Across the table, R.J. argued softly with somebody. "Yes, this really is an emergency." Pause. "Lynn Nussbaumer is missing in Getesaph territory." Pause. "You want me to tell Vice President Brador the entire relocation is going to fall apart because you don't consider one person an emergency? Check your personnel roster and you'll *see* who she is."

Trace sighed and concentrated on slaving her monitor display to his. Even in Bioverse, a corp legendary for its efficiency, there was always somebody.

BRADOR LOCATED flashed the monitor. In the next breath, a full-face image of the veep appeared and jerked into life.

"What's happened, Trace?"

"We've lost Lynn Nussbaumer." *Bad choice of words, Trace.* "She's been out of contact for the whole day. We haven't been able to trace her, or a comm fault."

Brador's fleshy cheeks sagged. "Have you gotten through to Keale yet?"

Trace glanced at R.J. who gave her the thumbs-up. "Just now." She touched the Split icon to divide the screen between the display of the veep and the commander of Corporate Security.

Keale did not look happy. "Why'd you wait so long?"

"We thought we'd find a comm fault," said R.J. defensively. "We didn't want to start a search unnecessarily."

Keale ground his teeth. "We are here to *help,* not start a police action. Why won't any of you understand that?"

"It's a problem, I agree, Commander," cut in Brador. "But now that the call is in, what can we do?"

Keale took a deep breath. "I'll spread the word down to our people at the port. Dr. Nussbaumer's been good about recording her contacts and appointments. We'll start a quiet search with those. Nobody just vanishes. Not even here."

Brador nodded. "Very good, Commander. Thank you. In the meantime, Trace, R.J., you get your team leaders tied in, and I'll alert the other veeps. We'll have to coordinate this closely, but we don't interrupt the schedule, understood?"

"Yes," said Trace softly.

"Yes," said R.J. without any feeling at all.

"Good." Brador paused. "Find her, Keale, I don't want any of my people lost to local politics."

"Neither do I, sir." Keale touched the screen and blanked himself out.

"Okay, get hooked up, you two," said Brador briskly. "This is one of those emergencies we've been trying to get ready for."

Brador blanked out his own screen. Trace looked up at R.J. and saw acceptance and worry in his expression. "I know," she said. "Right now, I'm not sure about what we think we're doing either."

The comm station's chime echoed off the dormitory's bare walls. Resaime picked herself up off the sleeping mat.

"Aunt Senejess, there's a caller on the line," she called to her aunt, who was rummaging in the foodstore.

"Thank you, Niece." Aunt Senejess crossed the room and settled herself into the comm-station chair. "If you could just tell this machine someone authorized is here."

Res laid her hand on the keyboard to tell the station to deliver the message. The grey screen turned into a blur of colors that resolved swiftly into a *woman's* head and shoulders.

"Praeis Shin?" said the Human, a little uncertainly.

"Yes?" replied Aunt Senejess.

Resaime stepped back out of the line of vision for both the comm station and her aunt.

"I'm Iola Trace. I'm assisting Lynn Nussbaumer with relocation management." Her t'Therian was thickly accented and her words uncertain. *She's probably getting help from an implant,* Res thought, lowering herself back onto the sleeping mat. "Dr. Nussbaumer's been out of touch with the team all day, and I was wondering if you'd spoken with her?"

Aunt Senejess shook her head. "I have heard nothing from her. Is she at the port? Would you like us to see if we can locate her?"

Iola Trace hesitated. "Thank you. There are some matters back here that require her attention."

Senejess laughed. It was a strange, hollow sound. "I am sure there are. My daughter and I will try to find her."

"Thank you," said Iola Trace, still hesitantly. Her eyes shifted back and forth restlessly, and Resaime felt her skin twitch. Did Aunt Senejess realize the woman was uneasy? Her speech's hesitancy might not be ignorance after all. It might be worry. Where was Lynn? Had the Getesaph done something to her?

"I will call you later if we learn anything," Aunt Senejess was saying. The *woman* thanked her and cut the connection. Iola Trace's image faded away.

Aunt Senejess swiveled the chair around. "Well, Niece, what do you think of that?"

"I think it's really strange," Resaime answered honestly. "Lynn doesn't leave things undone." *What if the Getesaph did do something to her? They do things like that, don't they? They kidnap people, things like that.*

"No, she does not." Aunt Senejess stood up and tugged at Res's ear thoughtfully. "I think perhaps we really should go out and have a look for her."

And what if the Getesaph kidnap us? Who'll come look for us? If anything happened to her, Aunt Senejess was supposed to do something about it. But Aunt Senejess was not Theia, or Mother.

"Well, Niece?"

Resaime started. Aunt Senejess cocked her ears forward. "I, uh, I'd rather wait here, Aunt."

Her aunt crossed the room and laid a hand on her shoulder. "Why, Resaime?"

Resaime searched frantically for a reason Aunt Senejess would believe. "The Getesaph make me nervous," she said. "I'm tired of it right now. I keep being afraid I'll make a mistake."

Aunt Senejess stroked Resaime's upper arm silently for a moment. Resaime couldn't read her face, but her ears waved restlessly.

"What we are doing is a hard thing," Aunt Senejess said quietly. "But it is necessary. The Getesaph do much more than make me nervous. They frighten me to death. But we cannot let our feelings come in the way of the safety of the Great Family, can we?"

Resaime swallowed. "No, we can't, Aunt Senejess." *Please don't make me go. Please don't.*

"No." Aunt Senejess patted her shoulder. "I will let you rest while I go find our contacts and tell them what has happened. We will need help to find out what is going on. When I come back, you will be ready to go out?"

"Yes, Aunt Senejess." Resaime squeezed her hand and worked to keep her ears and skin still.

"Good." Aunt Senejess slung her wallet over her shoulder and headed out the door, which closed noiselessly behind her.

Resaime waited, doing nothing but listening to her own breathing. When she was sure Aunt Senejess was well on her way, she jumped to her feet and raced to the comm station.

She touched the screen to light up the CALLING? prompt. She paused. She couldn't call Mother directly, because Mother was supposed to be here in Getesaph. She couldn't just call the house because Aunt Armetrethe or one of the cousins might answer.

"Theiareth Shin t'Theria." Mother must have threaded Theia into the Human directory by now. She must have.

LOCATING . . . read the screen. Resaime waited. Her skin rippled and strained as if her muscles were trying to break free. Her ears kept flicking back toward the door, trying to hear something, anything at all.

The screen lit up. Theia sat on the other side. From the background of cluttered furniture and frescoed walls, it looked like they were somewhere in the Home of Queens. Resaime almost melted with relief.

"Res! What—"

"Get Mother, quick. Lynn's gone missing." Resaime realized she was panting. "Hurry!"

Theia launched herself out of her chair and vanished. Resaime swallowed and tried to control her panting.

Her mother's form dived into view. Resaime had to sit on her hands to keep from reaching out. "Mother, Lynn's gone missing. Her people called. They can't find her. She was the one I was supposed to call if there's an emergency. Now I'm alone. What do I do?"

Mother leaned closer to the screen. "You do not panic, Daughter of mine. That's first. You let me contact Lynn's people and make sure they know where you are. Lynn has a friend in the Hundred Isles. I will find out where. Call your sister back tomorrow. I will have more to say to you. You will be brave, Resaime?"

Which was what Aunt Senejess said, but Resaime did not say that. "I will, Mother." Her throat tightened, and her ears twisted involuntarily. "May I speak to Theia again?"

"Quickly, yes."

Her mother vanished. A hand descended and touched the screen. The connection cut out. Resaime screeched and jerked backwards. Aunt Senejess stood beside her chair and looked down at her with wide eyes.

"Oh, Resaime," she breathed. "What have you done?"

Resaime opened her mouth and tried to speak, but could not force any words out. Aunt Senejess's ears drooped even farther. "Don't. Just tell me what other communications will have passed between your mother and this place?"

"I don't know . . . She sent a message to Lynn to tell her you and I were here. Lynn probably answered her."

"When?" Aunt Senejess's face began to tighten.

Res felt the anger rolling out of Senejess in waves. She wanted to throw herself into her aunt's arms and beg forgiveness, but she held still. "When we arrived."

Aunt Senejess's ears flattened against her scalp. "Get to your feet, Niece. We need to get out of here."

Resaime stood. Aunt Senejess snatched Resaime's wallet off the clothespress, caught up Resaime's hand, and pulled her out the door. Resaime didn't even try to protest. She just stumbled in Aunt Senejess's wake, trying to find her stride.

What have I done? I didn't mean to. I just didn't want to be alone. . . .

They emerged into the port. Aunt Senejess pulled Resaime close to her side and put her arm around her shoulder. "Relax," she whispered into Resaime's ears. "Act as if we were out for a stroll." She steered Resaime toward a crowd of Getesaph carrying bags and baskets. They were probably heading for the Human-sponsored transit lines to go to the market. The Humans provided food and shelter, but many of the Getesaph felt both were quite spartan and wanted some fresh treats or small luxuries before they left their home.

Resaime finally found her voice. "Aun— Mother . . ."

"Shhh," hissed Aunt Senejess. "We will talk when we are on the way home. Right now, stay close."

You're not giving me any choice. Resaime tried not to squirm. There was more wrong here than Aunt Senejess finding out she had called Mother. It was like she was worried about them both getting caught . . . Oh.

"They couldn't have overheard," she whispered in Aunt Senejess's ear. "Whatever the Getesaph have got, it's not going to be compatible with the Humans' hardware."

All at once, a pair of Getesaph in defenders' blue uniforms with black rank bands on their cuffs blocked the path. Aunt Senejess pulled up short and tried to turn. Another pair pressed up behind them.

"You will come with us," said one of those in front. "Now."

Resaime's heart pounded hard and fast against her ribs. Aunt Senejess looked at her sadly and squeezed her arm. "Let this teach you, my own. Do not underestimate your enemies."

* * *

The speaker was silent.

Armetrethe paced the great room of her home. She circled the serving tables, the stove, and the chopping block. The stump of her severed arm beat the air as if it were trying to fly away. She paused in front of one of the slit windows and watched the daughters out in the yard. They played chase, or sat in clusters with books, learning from one another. Ceian and her oldest cousins stood in the shadow of the wall, smiling indulgently at the younger daughters between their conversations.

Armetrethe wanted to run out to them and sweep as many as she could into her one arm. She wanted to track down Praeis, wherever she had gone, and shake her until her sick separateness left her and she was a true sister again. She wanted to scream and bring the entire Great Family running to her. She wanted to do anything that would end this awful, silent loneliness.

The speaker was still silent. It had been silent for a half hour too long. Senejess's contact was supposed to have called to let her know everything was all right, but that hadn't happened. It still wasn't happening.

She knew what she was supposed to do. They had a plan for this. They had worked it out very carefully. Her ears crumpled. Her shoulders sagged.

No. I can't do it. It means I'll be the last one. Praeis has turned away from us all. I don't want to be the last one.

Because if the Getesaph had taken Senejess, Senejess would not be alive for long.

Armetrethe's skin rippled up and down her back. Her one hand grabbed the back of the sofa and squeezed until the worn, sky-blue satin tore underneath her fingers.

The boxy speaker buzzed. Armetrethe dived across the room. Her hand slapped the activation switch more by luck than design. "This is Armetrethe!"

"Taraen Ul t'Theria," came the familiar voice of Senejess's contact across the line. "Listen quick. Your family is taken. I saw it. The Getesaph have found a way to tap the Humans' communications. There were calls, between the mother and her Human contacts and between the daughter and the mother. They discussed our mission. The Getesaph intercepted the signals. I must try to get my people away."

The line went dead. Armetrethe stood by the speaker table, unable to move. Fear sank slowly into her muscles.

Sister? Sister? Is it true? Are you gone from me? Am I alone?

Her knees trembled. She leaned heavily against the table.

There is a plan. Her plan. I must not give way.

Armetrethe let go of the chair and strode across the room. She threw the door open.

"Daughters!" Her voice cracked hard on the word. "Daughters!"

The children looked up from books and games and conversation. In a flock, they came running to cluster around her, the biggest picking up the smallest and setting them on their shoulders. Poar and Ceian pressed against her sides. Theiareth, who looked so like her mother, stood on the edge of the cluster as if afraid to surround herself with her cousins.

Her mother should be telling her this, not me. Her mother should already be swearing death to the Getesaph, but she doesn't know and doesn't care. . . .

"What is going on?" Praeis appeared in the doorway, as if summoned by the thought.

Armetrethe wrapped her arm around Poar. Summoning all the strength she had, she turned away from her sister.

"Your help is needed, my Daughters. Senejess and Resaime have been taken by the Getesaph, and we must let the Great Family know."

"What!" Praeis grabbed Armetrethe by the shoulders and spun her around. Poar squealed at the abrupt movement. "You do not know what you're saying, Sister. This cannot be true!"

"It is true." Armetrethe let go of Poar and gripped Praeis's hand. "And it is your fault."

Whatever words Praeis had meant to speak choked her. Armetrethe kept going. "You told your Human friends what was being done. You had your daughter call you to report on what Senejess was doing. The Getesaph intercepted the transmissions. They are taken. They are in the hands of the Getesaph. They are *dead!*"

Her self-control snapped, and Armetrethe hurled herself at Praeis. She felt skin under her hand and clawed at it. Someone grabbed her, and a weight bore her down to the dirt. She squirmed and struggled. Praeis would pay, she'd pay, she'd pay! Armetrethe would send the traitor to the Ancestors. She'd revenge her true sister and daughter.

Somewhere far away she heard screams and crying and death oaths, but most of all she felt the weight on top of her that would not let her move.

"It is not true," a voice said. "It is not. You've misunderstood somehow."

Praeis. Praeis leaned on top of her and held her down. Praeis still denied what she'd done.

She'll die. But first she'll understand.

"Our sister's contacts told me what happened. She saw them taken by the Getesaph defenders."

A wordless scream split the air. The weight vanished off Armetrethe's back. She rolled over in time to see Praeis's fist swooping toward her chest. The blow knocked all the breath out of her.

"You did this!" screamed Praeis. "You took my daughter into their world! You *lied to me!*" She raised her fist again.

"No!"

Poar dived on Praeis. Four of her sisters followed suit, dragging

Praeis to the ground, but in the next second, Theiareth was there, grabbing whoever she could reach by the ears and hauling them off.

"Let go! Let her go!"

Some of the cousins turned on her. Others leapt to her defense. The brawl was general, and the shouted words indecipherable.

Armetrethe stared at Praeis in astonishment. The tumult of feeling roaring through her blood cleared all of an instant, and she grabbed Praeis's outstretched hand. Together they scrambled to their feet.

"Stop! Stop this, Daughters! Stop this now!" They lunged among the daughters, catching up the ones who fought the hardest and swinging them away from the combat.

Praeis snatched Theiareth into her arms and made her daughter stare at her struggling cousins. "Look at what you're doing! Look!"

"They hurt you," she said in a small voice.

"No." Praeis turned Theia around and embraced her. "No one has hurt me."

"I need Resaime," wailed Theia, burying her face in Praeis's shoulder. "Res!"

The need to comfort became as immediate as the need to hurt had been a moment before. The daughters clustered around Theia, trying to touch her, and one another, pressing as close as they could. Praeis looked at Armetrethe over the daughters' ears as she rocked her own daughter. Armetrethe saw despair in her eyes. Praeis bled inside, as they all did, as she should. Perhaps she was not false after all. Armetrethe wrapped her arm around her sister's shoulder.

"We will make it all right. There are people who will help. We will send the daughters out and rouse them. I know the families."

Praeis shook her head. "We cannot. We must go to the Queens and the Confederation."

Disbelief hit Armetrethe harder than Praeis's blow had. "How can you say such a thing? Your sister! Your daughter!"

"May still be alive!" Praeis cut her off. She tightened her hold on Theiareth. "Things are not what they were. The Humans—"

"Are as cold and distant as a moon!" Armetrethe pulled her arm away. "How can you!"

"Control yourself!" snapped Praeis. "Or would you have our daughters set on each other again!"

Armetrethe let her gaze sweep over the daughters, who stood clustered together, their expressions ranging from solemn to confused to outraged.

"The Confederation is a sham and serves only the Getesaph," she said slowly and deliberately, not looking at her sister. "The families who must know will be told."

"So will the Queens-of-All," answered Praeis.

Armetrethe's ears trembled. "I hope the Ancestors know how to work this out, Sister, for I do not."

She heard the ghost of a sigh from Praeis. "Neither do I."

"Any word?"

Trace shook her head. R.J. puffed out his cheeks and looked out the window to the landing strips. For a change, the artificial plain was empty of people. The prep crews had withdrawn to the launch bays and were running the final checks by computer. The passengers were in their couches and their relatives were under cover, watching on the screens, and Lynn, who had worked so hard for this quiet, uncluttered moment, was nowhere to be found. Keale had no news to give them.

"You want to delay?" Trace asked.

"Yes." R.J. ran his hand over his helmet, thinking for the millionth time how strange and uncomfortable it was not to be able to touch your own skin. "But we can't. Veep Brador's already given the order."

"I know." Trace touched the comm key. "Give me Launch Control."

After a moment, Launch Control answered. "We're here and set whenever you are, Trace."

"What's the word from on high?" R.J. kept his eyes on the waiting ships. He wanted noise, motion, not this feeling of the whole project holding its breath. There should be a sensation of proud excitement swelling his chest. Instead, he felt frightened.

"On high is waiting for their guests," said Launch. "Red carpet is all rolled out."

Trace touched the MUTE key, glanced at R.J., then the launch strip. "We could call the veeps again, just to be sure."

R.J. shook his head slowly. "You know what they'll say. The show must go on."

"And so it must." She touched the key again. "Very well, Launch, let them go."

Trace stood so close to him that their suits touched. Together, they watched the first of the shuttles roll into position.

Chapter XI

The aerial record hasn't shown up anything." Lieutenant Ryan stood at the end of the conference table in Keale's office with his hands behind his back. Keale listened to him with a sinking feeling in his stomach. "Then again, with all the relocation traffic, you could drive an elephant under us and we'd be hard put to notice. We've had no new construction, no new military activity, no extra movement around the Parliament. We have people down in the security tunnels, and everybody who isn't stationed out on the *Ur* or the *Cairo* is in the Hundred Isles."

As Keale watched Ryan's face, something in him began to recover. The lieutenant didn't look nearly uncomfortable enough for someone whose report to his superior was a long litany of nothing.

"So, what have we got?"

"Three more missing persons."

Keale sat bolt upright. *"What?"*

Ryan ran a cable from the infoview on his hand to the tabletop. He touched the PLAY key on one of the keypads. The wall screen lit up and showed the playback of a set of shuttle passengers disembarking at the Getesaph departure point. Most of them were Humans in clean-suits, but a pair of Dedelphi, a mother and daughter, picked their way through the Human stream. They held hands tightly as they hurried across the concrete to the port's main building.

"Before Nussbaumer left t'Aori, she authorized travel orders for Praeis Shin t'Theria and her daughter Resaime Shin to go from t'Aori to the Hundred Isles. Nussbaumer also set them up with a room at the port."

Keale leaned forward. "Shin t'Theria? Didn't she found Crater Town?"

"Her family did. She was called back by the Queens-of-All to help out with Dedelphi-Human relations."

"That's right. I met her at a couple of prep meetings." Keale's eyes narrowed. "That doesn't look like her."

"It isn't." Ryan murmured something to his implant. The scene cut to the inside of the port building. The pair of Dedelphi, almost lost in a sea of their kindred, moved toward a comm station. "This one"—Ryan touched the mother—"is Praeis Shin's sister, Senejess Shin. A little while after Nussbaumer got here, she got a message from Praeis Shin saying that the letter that had been sent asking Nussbaumer for travel help was forged by her sister, who was traveling under Praeis's name with Praeis's daughter, presumably to spy on the Getesaph." Ryan looked triumphant at having gotten through that chain of events.

Keale replayed the sentence in his head and sorted through it until he decided he had a grasp on the main players. "Do we know why Nussbaumer didn't just haul Senejess Shin out of circulation like she should have?"

"No," said Ryan. "All we know is that Senejess Shin and Resaime Shin are missing. Apparently the Queens-of-All know it, too. They've called an emergency session of the Confederation for this afternoon."

Oh, just *what we need; the t'Theria and the Getesaph up in metaphorical arms.* "Did Nussbaumer have any contact with them at the port?"

Ryan shook his head. "Not as far as we know. She sent messages to them both. One addressed to 'Praeis Shin,' asking her to dinner, and the other to Resaime, telling her how to get in touch if she needed anything."

Keale suddenly and sincerely wished he had Nussbaumer in front of him so he could ask her what the hell she thought she was doing. "So, that's two of the missing persons. Who's the third?"

Ryan muttered to his implant and the scene changed. Now the screen showed one of the launch-prep meetings held for the evacuees. The recording had probably been pulled from the instructor's camera eyes.

At Ryan's direction, the image zoomed in on one man standing on the terrace over the meeting, watching the proceedings with a strained expression.

"Who's he?" Keale asked as Ryan froze the scene.

"Arron Hagopian," said Ryan. "He's a cultural xenologist. He's been living with the Getesaph for the past ten years. He's also a friend of Lynn Nussbaumer's." Keale made a hurry-up gesture with two fingers. "She's only met with him once officially since we got here, but we thought he might know something, so we went looking for him, and didn't find him."

Keale rubbed his forehead and waited for Ryan to continue.

"We were already pulling Lynn's threads from the system log, so we yanked his as well. After the departure session you see here." Ryan nodded toward the frozen video image. "Hagopian threaded a request through his room terminal for the passenger manifest for the first outbound Getesaph shuttle. Then he found out where Dr. Nussbaumer was. . ."

"Where was she?"

"In a meeting with the prep-wave leaders; Dayisen Rual Lareet and Dayisen Rual Umat and their immediate support staff." Ryan's lips moved, and the screen showed a port corridor. A small cluster of Dedelphi were leaving a conference room. Through the open door, Keale saw Lynn Nussbaumer and two Getesaph. Arron Hagopian strode into the camera's line of sight and stopped in front of the door. Nussbaumer said something the camera didn't catch and Arron walked into the room. The door shut.

"There's a thread reeled out from the comm station for a Hrashn Kvin and a Hrashn Lun. After that, we have tape of two more Getesaph going into the room. All four Getesaph leave fifteen minutes later, without Nussbaumer or Hagopian."

Keale touched a key on the table and ran the view back until Arron Hagopian was shown in the corridor. He stared hard at the image. Hagopian looked tall, thin, and heavily suntanned, but outwardly, there was nothing remarkable about him. "Where are the Dayisen Rual now?"

"Onboard the *Ur.*" Ryan blanked out the video. "We talked to them. They both say Arron and Lynn left the meeting together and they have no idea where they went afterward."

"Of course not." Keale drummed his fingers on his chair arm. "Did you ask them who the other two Getesaph are?"

"We did," Ryan nodded. "They said they don't know them."

Keale frowned. "And you can't find them either?"

For the first time, Ryan looked truly uncomfortable. "No, sir. They registered for dorm rooms, but they weren't on the shuttles and they're not in the port."

What is going on? And who started it? Keale looked up at the screen and Hagopian's frozen figure again. "Did Hagopian do anything to the passenger manifest? Perform a search on a name or anything like that?"

Ryan shook his head. "No. Nothing. From what I can tell, he just read it."

"Hagopian is the one who's been knotting the screeds against Bioverse, isn't he? Against the relocation?"

"Yes, he is." Ryan watched his chief carefully. "But he must have come to terms with it. He's been registered to stay on the *Ur*. He was supposed to go up with the prep wave. Apparently they're using him as some kind of official historian."

"But he's not there?"

"No." Ryan shook his head.

Of course not, Keale frowned. *Been here ten years. Speaks out against the relocation, but is supposed to go with it. So he disappears before the shuttles leave . . . This does not make sense. Either Hagopian is playing games with his friends, or the Dayisen Rual are playing games with theirs.*

Keale pursed his lips. The disappearance of the Shin t'Theria could be a simple matter of the Getesaph having caught themselves a couple of spies. On the other hand, they were friends of Nussbaumer's . . .

"I want every pixel of security recordings from the port gone over. I want a complete history of Hagopian's movements and the Shin t'Theria's as well as Nussbaumer's."

"Yes, sir." Ryan unhooked himself from the desk.

"I also want transcripts of any messages the Shin t'Theria sent or received, and I want those two vanishing *hrashn* found if you have to search the island by the centimeter."

"Yes, sir." Ryan's lips moved as he relayed the orders to his implants.

"And send somebody out to start quizzing the Dayisen Rual who are still on the ground about Xenologist Hagopian. I want everything we can get about him knotted up and in my station, aysap."

This time, Ryan hesitated. "You don't think, I mean, sir, he's a Human and . . ."

Keale shook his head. "Ryan, Humans have done far worse for causes they believed in. That's one of the reasons we have a job."

"Yes, sir." Ryan pulled himself together and made his exit.

When the door slid shut, Keale turned to the comm station. He worked the keys and sent out a thread of his own. It untied a simple task-knot and set it running. The knot was absolutely, positively not supposed to exist, and if anyone caught Keale using it, he would be stripped and fired before he could draw breath.

Until then, it would funnel off the transmission of the Confederation meeting into his private database.

He hesitated a moment and touched a few more keys. The wall screen shifted scenes again and played the download of the welcoming ceremony Esmo had dumped for him.

Through her eyes, Keale watched thousands of pink-and-grey Getesaph spill out of the airlocks and into the city, along with eight or ten Humans, one of whom was Dr. David Zelotes, Lynn Nussbaumer's partner.

Note to self. Get hold of Esmo and make sure somebody's told Zelotes what's happened.

The Getesaph stood on the grass, gaping at the clean, bright, artificial world around them. Esmo delivered up a very canned speech of welcome, along with short announcements about times for drills with the rescue balls and other emergency equipment, and medical appointments down in the hospital. Then she stood back, telling them the city was theirs.

Slowly, in groups that were probably family-determined, the Getesaph wandered across the park with their Human attendants, chattering excitedly and turning their ears every-which-way. Keale scanned them. None of them looked like the missing *hrashn,* but he'd have the station look again.

Keale shut the image off. He leaned his elbows on the comm station, laced his fingers together, and tried to think if there was anything he'd missed. He felt suspended, kept in place by two potential crises pressing in on him.

Maybe I got it wrong. Maybe the trouble's coming on the ground now, and not later on the Ur. *It's certainly acting like it. . . .*

Except all the trouble's happening just as the relocation's starting . . . Hagopian's been here a long time, what's he been up to and with whom?

He lifted his elbows off the station and sent out another thread. This one reeled in the passenger manifest for the shuttle *Sojorn.* He read the lists of names and titles.

"All right, Hagopian. What did you see that I don't?"

Vaier Byu stood in the Audience Room with her sister queens, their attendants and assistants, half the Council of True Blood, and their attendants and assistants. Everyone's attention focused on the video wall the Humans had installed. Through it, they saw the table used for the Confederation treaty signing, still on its stage in the now-empty theater that had been built on a neutral island. It was neutral because it had been scoured of life in some unnumbered war, but no one remarked on that.

Around the table, the other members of the Confederation sat or stood, framed by their own transmission walls as if they all waited in glassed-over thresholds.

The Humans who designed this format for Confederation meetings had said it would provide reminders of the neutral space, while allowing everyone to communicate without the overwhelming strangeness of the simulation rigs, or the lengthy travel that was required to reach the tiny, barren stretch of ground.

It does all that well enough. Vaier surveyed the windows to the other halls. *But it makes us all look caged in. I wonder if the Humans did that on purpose?*

The final transmission window flashed open and the two Queens of the Paeccs Tayn appeared in their own little threshold. Gold-and-silver ornaments dangled from their ears, indicating their people were at peace. When they declared war, the ornaments changed to black and red.

"We thank the members of the Confederation for responding to our request for a meeting," Aires said in her smooth, precise voice. Her discerning gaze swept across the gathering. "We have a complaint to raise that cannot wait."

"The Getesaph hold two of our citizens," boomed Ueani before anyone else could speak. "They must be returned immediately."

First the fine knife, then the fine club, Vaier held her ears still. *Where is my anger? The Getesaph have violated our people yet again. Where is my roaring blood? The Burn?*

Maybe it is damped by the crowds in the streets.

The city had not been so crowded since before the plague. Just when it seemed she and her sisters were turning the tide on the rebellious Council, the news came out about the disappearance of Senejess and Resaime Shin t'Theria. Now the Council's supporters were in the streets beside the Queens' petitioners. Speeches were read through loudspeakers. Honor brawls raged. The militia had been sent in to stop the worst of them, but they did not seem determined to do their jobs. Long poems and essays covered the debate walls and the walls surrounding the palace.

Aires, in her usual, methodical way, had read a whole stack of hastily printed pamphlets and sighed. "Sisters, we underestimated the remaining strength of our opposition."

Rchilthen Ishth, the oldest of the Getesaph's Sisters-Chosen-to-Lead, raised one of her gnarled hands and touched the fold over her right eye with one knuckle. A gesture of apology, Vaier knew. She found herself wondering if it was to herself and her sisters, or to the Getesaph deities.

"The Humans informed us of the loss of your citizens, as well as the loss of two of their own people." Rchilthen Ishth lowered her hand and tucked it under a fold in her golden jacket. "We do not ask what your citizens were doing in our country."

"Very good," murmured Aires. "Not surprising, but well delivered."

"We have instituted a close and careful search for the . . . your mother and daughter," Rchilthen Ishth went on. "It has uncovered some distressing facts."

"Where are you going with this?" breathed Aires as she leaned her ears a little closer to the screen. Ueani's fist clenched behind her back.

Rchilthen Byvant, whose left ear lay permanently limp against her scalp, touched her sister's shoulder. "We have discovered that some members of our Parliament have conspired to undermine the Confederation. We are still learning the extent of their influence." Her wounded ear trembled. "I fear many of them are of the Defenders' House. We believe that your mother and daughter learned of the rebellion's existence and the Defenders took action against them."

Ueani opened her mouth, but Vaier touched her arm. This was not the time for her. This required Aires.

Never slow to fill a conversational gap, Aires leaned forward. "This is indeed most distressing." Her voice dripped sincerity. "Why did you not call the Confederation as soon as you learned about it?"

Rchilthen Ishth's jacket wrinkled as her hidden hands clutched its fabric. "Because we hoped we could find and return them to you before this."

"Isn't this just magnificently convenient!" exploded Ueani. "Two of our people vanished, probably murdered, and instead of admitting what you've done, you blame a just-discovered conspiracy. Ancestors Mine! What cowards!"

Slowly, Rchilthen Byvant stood up from her chair. Her good ear dropped dangerously close to her scalp. "You send a mother and daughter to spy on us, demand to know what became of them, and then spit insults at us. Tell me why we should even speak to you!"

"Stop it!" screamed a strange voice.

Vaier's gaze jerked right. One of the Paeccs Tayn, Oran *ji* Ufa, had thrown herself up against the screen. She leaned there, hands pressed flat against the glass. Her teeth gleamed in the artificial light. "Stop it all of you or I swear I'll have the guts out of you!"

No one spoke, not even Aires.

Oran pulled back a little, panting hard. Her sister stood staunchly beside her, not even attempting to interfere. "I don't care if you idiots want to fight your fights until the sun goes out. I don't care if you kill the last of your babies and sing over their dead bodies. But the plague is claiming more of my family every day. If you break this Confederation . . . If you lose us the Humans' work, I swear by blood, soul, and will, I and mine will cut the life out of you and yours!"

"You will not be alone." The First President of the Hamareil stepped forward.

No one else spoke either in challenge or agreement, but Vaier saw too many stolid faces in the thresholds. Vaier looked across the empty table straight into Rchilthen Ishth's eyes. For half a heartbeat, she saw the fear in the Getesaph's soul and understood it. The Getesaph did not want to die, but she would deliver herself to death, just like Vaier would.

Vaier spoke in slow, measured tones. "Will you let the Humans search unimpeded for our mother and daughter?"

"What could we hide from the Humans?" The folds of Rchilthen Ishth's old face sagged even farther. *Ancestors Mine, she must be less than a year from the Change.* "We will report to the Confederation everything we learn, and we will request that the Human security chief do the same." She leaned forward. "In return, we expect a full disclosure to the Confederation of who this mother and daughter are and what they were doing here."

Ueani almost shouted again, but this time Aires held her back. "They were not sent under our authority, but we will find out who they really are and report to the Confederation tomorrow."

"So." Satisfaction rang quietly in Rchilthen Byvant's voice. "We must believe you know nothing of your traitors' actions while you believe we must know everything of ours."

"Tomorrow we will know what must be done," Vaier said softly, hoping the translator carried across every nuance of warning.

"Tomorrow, then," replied Rchilthen Byvant. "If the Confederation agrees with us, of course."

"If you act as you speak, it is reasonable enough," said the First President. "I suggest we confer again at this time tomorrow to see if you will."

At that, Vaier finally felt the old heat in her blood. How dare the Getesaph pour such suspicion into the waters. How dare . . .

She controlled herself. Aires was watching her, and Vaier knew what she was thinking. It would not do to have the Confederation see her have to be restrained by her lesser-named sisters.

"We agree to this," said Vaier.

One by one, the other Confederation members also agreed, and one by one the windows closed. Ueani, who was standing closest to the control unit, smacked the button that shut the power off and turned around.

"Sisters," she said between harsh, panting breaths, "I believe we need to confer with ourselves alone."

"I believe you are correct," said Aires levelly.

Their royal retinue, well trained in their jobs, gathered up their papers and pens and retreated, but the representatives of the Council just stirred uneasily.

One, Feia Ros t'Theria, lifted both hands and closed her eyes. "If my Majestic Sisters will consider debating with the Council for a while. This is—"

"This is what?" demanded Ueani. "This is how we came to be holed up in our home with our people beating on the gates?" Vaier glanced at Aires, who made a small gesture. *Let her go. She needs to shout.*

"Or maybe," Ueani roared, "this is how we came to be so isolated from our people that we didn't even know what danger we were in? Is that what you mean, Wise Sister? Is this what you and our other Wise Sisters in Council failed to warn us about?"

"Majestic Sister." Feia Ros's voice shook. "I—"

"You what!" Ueani was almost on top of her. Vaier tapped her foot lightly to get the Ancestors' attention. *Please don't let my sister lay hands on a Councilor. We do not need to give such news to our enemies.* "You what? You apologize? Or maybe you agree with our enemies out there, and you wish to tell us so!" Ueani's hands came up. Vaier's skin tightened, but her sister only closed her fists on the air. "Get out of our hearing! All of you!"

The Wise Sisters were not fools and left in a crowd, with fluttering robes and cringing ears. Silence filled the audience chamber, broken only by the sound of Ueani's ragged panting.

"Are you calmed down yet, Ueani?" asked Aires mildly.

Ueani's ears eased themselves away from her scalp. "Nearly."

"Good." Aires touched Ueani's forearm, then turned away to sit on the nearest sofa. If she felt even half as tired as Vaier did, she didn't show it. She sat straight and calm, as always. "So, say what you need to."

Ueani crossed the floor to her and stroked Aires's ear absently for a moment before she turned away. "I want to know how much we're ready to give away to the Getesaph."

Vaier's ears dropped involuntarily. "We will do no more than we said."

"What we said was a lot. We are talking about naming spies to them, ours, our enemies', it doesn't matter. Do you believe"—the skin on her face rippled—"the Getesaph will really give them back once we say they are spies? Do you think they'll survive to come home?

"And what do we do about our subjects outside?" Ueani gestured toward the outer wall. "When word gets out about what we've agreed, they'll go insane. Do we force the militia to put down their sisters until they turn on us? We are trapped."

"Not yet." Aires's ears stood straight up. "We can begin a muster of troops. We can announce our plans to put down this treachery of the Getesaph's. But we will go too slowly. We will give the Humans time to find out what is really going on. It might be as Rchilthen Byvant says: The Getesaph Parliament housed a conspiracy. They'd eat the children crawling from their sisters' wombs, why would they hesitate to conspire against their government?" She waved her hand dismissively. "But the Humans' words will be heard where the Getesaph's won't, both inside the Confederation and outside these walls."

Vaier rubbed her hands together and sat beside Aires, drinking in warmth and strength from her proximity. "That might work. But who will lead the muster? At this moment I'm not sure who in the army we can trust."

Aires's ears dipped and straightened. "We need to send for Praeis Shin."

Vaier felt her muscles tighten. "Perhaps not for this."

"Who else?" asked Ueani, stalking close to them. "It is her family who has done this to us. It is her honor to rebuild."

Vaier sighed. She took Aires's hand in her right hand and Ueani's in her left, so they'd feel the strength of the question. "Have you considered, my Sisters, there may come a time when we ask too much of her insanity of separateness?"

Ueani's skin squirmed under her palm, but Aires's did not.

"I have," said Aires. "If you can name someone else who might possibly be willing to put together a force too slowly to do any good, and yet not get caught orchestrating the delay, we will send for her instead."

Vaier closed her eyes. "There is no one. We will send for Praeis Shin." *And one day, her Ancestors will send for us and demand an explanation for what we have done to their daughter.*

Ueani pulled out of Vaier's grasp and stalked over to the clerical door. She flung the arched portal open and bellowed, "Osh! Elpetar!"

The two assistants scuttled inside, stationed themselves with their backs to the door, closed their eyes, and raised their hands.

"We need Praeis Shin found and brought to us at once," said Ueani.

The wrinkles in Osh's heavy forehead deepened. "Majestic Sister, Praeis Shin is in the debating chamber. She is petitioning to meet with you."

"Now, that really is magnificently convenient," said Aires mildly. "Tell her we grant the petition."

The assistants hurried out the main doors. Ueani paced the Audience Room twice before Praeis Shin entered, followed closely by her remaining daughter. Vaier found time to pity the daughter. She was just about ready to cross to motherhood and here she was, alone with her insane mother, surrounded by disloyal aunts and her-Ancestors-only-knew what kind of cousins. If she were not allowed daughters of her own soon, she might end up as solitary and unstable as her mother.

Praeis and her daughter walked into the small circle of desks, chairs, and sofas. She stood in front of the sofa where Vaier and Aires sat, raised her hands, and closed her eyes.

"Thank you, Majestic Sisters, for granting my petition."

"Open your eyes, Praeis Shin. Sit yourself and your daughter down." When Praeis opened her eyes, Vaier gestured her to a divan. "In truth, we did not know you were waiting for us. For this, we apologize. You have done difficult and dangerous service for us and of all our citizens and servants. You should not be neglected."

Praeis looked at her blankly, as if trying to decide what expression she should paste on her face for this official flattery. Aires opened her mouth, but Vaier touched her arm to silence her.

"The words of Queens are lighter than feathers and more easily torn apart, I know," Vaier went on. "But I hope you choose to believe what we are saying right now."

"My Ancestors see I have nothing but trust in my Majestic Sister," said Praeis piously. "But I am wondering what is to follow."

Laughter exploded out of Ueani. She flung her head back and let the sound echo off the ceiling. "Very good, Praeis Shin. You may be insane, but you are not stupid."

Vaier felt her ears fall back against her skull. She straightened them hurriedly. After this interview, they were going to have to talk to Ueani about self-control under stress.

The daughter bared her teeth, probably reflexively. Praeis's face went tight, and she covered her daughter's mouth with one hand.

Vaier mustered a dismissive tone. "We have all been through too many days without peace here." She avoided looking at either Ueani or Aires. She could feel Aires's skepticism like a breath of cold air against her skin. "And I'm afraid we must go through more. You know better than anyone else that there is an explosion waiting to happen in the peninsula."

Praeis's ears drooped briefly. She let go of her daughter's mouth and took her hand instead.

Vaier watched Praeis carefully, trying to interpret the ridges in her skin and the set of her ears. "For stability, and to buy time for the Human investigation, we must appear to have joined the dissenters against the Confederation." Praeis sat absolutely still, a grey-blue statue holding her daughter's hand. "We must play at assembling an invasion of the Getesaph archipelago, and we must ask you to assume the lead of this deception."

A look somewhere between surprise and horror crossed Praeis's face before she could compose herself.

"Your expertise at logistics, along with the fact that it is your daughter and sister who are endangered make you the logical choice. We ourselves know your loyalty to us better than anyone out there." She jerked her chin contemptuously toward the outer wall.

The folds in Praeis's face tightened. "Then there will be no real rescue? No search?" As Praeis spoke, her daughter's mouth opened as she began to pant.

"Of course there will," said Vaier with a touch of indignation. "But surely you see that the Humans can do a better, faster job of it than any of us. You must give them time to do it." She let her face stiffen. "If we lose control, there will be an invasion in earnest, and what will the Humans do then? What will the rest of the Confederation do?"

Praeis sat still again with just the tips of her ears quivering. Her daughter looked up at her with wide, miserable eyes.

"I understand," said Praeis. "But, Majestic Sisters, after Urisk Island, who will willingly follow me?"

Aires's ears wiggled. "Noblest Sister, the mood against the Getesaph is so heated, our sisters would follow a thrown stone into battle."

Praeis's ears crumbled, but her voice remained steady. "I will do as I am ordered, Majestic Sisters."

"Good," Vaier dipped her ears toward Praeis approvingly. "You will be officially summoned to duty this afternoon and moved to a headquarters. You will need to give thought to who you will want to pick as your Group Mothers."

"Then I have much to do. With your permission." Praeis lifted the palm of one hand, and Vaier dipped her ears again.

Praeis stood, still holding her daughter's hand. The daughter, obviously dazed by what had been said, stood with her.

"Whatever else comes of this, we will arrange that all your second-children be proudly fathered," said Vaier. "Your daughters shall have that written in our names."

"Thank you, Majestic Sister," murmured Praeis. She closed her eyes and raised her free hand respectfully before she turned and walked in a measured step through the door.

"She'll do it," said Aires like a sigh of relief once the door was firmly closed.

"Of course she will," snorted Ueani. "Was she not just bribed and flattered like a father's family? What moved your will, Vaier?"

Vaier stood up and walked four swift paces to her lesser-named sister. She grasped Ueani's chin hard, as if she were a misbehaving child.

"At the moment this solitary nature serves us, but without a little kindness she might just turn against us." She watched the ripples in Ueani's face as that thought sank in. "Unstable, abandoned by her family and by her Queens, who will she turn to? What will she do? Do you want to find out?"

"No, Sister," muttered Ueani.

Vaier released her. "We are agreed in this, then."

"Yes." Aires stood up. "Now, let us call our Wise Sisters back in. They will, I think, be pleased to hear what we have to say."

David looked around the hospital room with a sense of relief and homecoming. It could not have been more different from the hell he'd left that morning. This was a large open area that smelled of fresh air. The openness was disconcerting for him, but more comfortable for the Dedelphi who had to stay there. At least a hundred beds waited in tidy rows. Each was enclosed in filter polymers that would let in light and air and let out sound and scent, but would trap any microbes in their carefully kinked and twisted pores.

The waldos and jobbers attached to each bed to take care of the patient's needs had soft, warm hands and arms. They were covered with matte organics that could be easily sterilized to ready the bed for a new occupant. There were even thin gloves built into the sides of the isolation boxes, so a sister or daughter could reach in and hold the patient's hand.

He set his portable down on one of the counters. *We might actually be able to save a few people here,* he thought.

He didn't actually come on duty until the main evacu . . . relocation started. Everybody else was, sensibly, relaxing in their new apartments. He had invitations for drinks and dinner he was really looking forward to. But first he had wanted to see the hospital. He wanted some reassurance that the cycle of anger and depression at the facilities he had to work with would be broken.

"Dr. David Zelotes?" called a voice from the other end of the room.

David turned and saw Captain Elisabeth Esmaraude standing in the hatchway. He recognized her easily from the landing ceremony when she'd stood up in front of them in the city and welcomed them all to the *Ur.* She'd sounded like a wind-up doll, and she seemed to know it, but she also seemed to be trying to bear it in good humor.

"Yes, Captain?" David walked toward her.

She looked him up and down through her old-fashioned spectacles. David wondered what she thought she'd see. "Have you got a minute?"

"Yes, certainly, Captain," said David. "I was just looking around." *What's so important you had to come down here personally?*

"Good. If you'll just come with me." She stepped out into the corridor and led him to an unused conference room. His mind ran over possibilities. Maybe she wanted to discuss emergency procedures, or quarantine precautions, or the possibility of transmission from the sick to the healthy populations of the city-ship. Maybe it was about the possibility of viral infection among the Human crew.

Captain Esmaraude sat in one of the stiff chairs around the table and gestured for him to take the one next to her. He did.

"What can I help you with, Captain?" David folded his hands and tried to look ready for anything.

Captain Esmaraude looked at the floor. "I have just had a message from Commander Enrique Keale of Corporate Security." She glanced up, and back down again. "Dr. Lynn Nussbaumer is missing."

"I'm sorry?" said David. He'd heard her say something about Lynn, but . . .

She looked up. Her brown eyes were worried behind her spectacles. "Dr. Lynn Nussbaumer is missing. No one on her staff has seen or heard from her for over twenty-six hours."

David sat there, doing nothing but listen to his heart hammer against his ribs. Lynn missing in the Hundred Isles. He had spoken to her two days ago, and then she'd gone missing and he hadn't known . . .

"What are they doing about it?" he heard himself ask.

"Keale's got a search going on. They're interviewing everybody they can find, doing flyovers, combing the threads, everything possible."

Lynn? It was ridiculous. He should know where she was. He should have felt that something was wrong. He shouldn't have just been going about his job, moving into his new apartment, worrying about lab facilities and . . .

"Dr. Zelotes?" said Captain Esmaraude gently. "I've known Kaye—Commander Keale—for years. He's very good at what he does. He will not let them keep her."

David's hands opened and closed reflexively. He didn't know what to do. He wanted to lash out, pound the table, holler at the top of his lungs. He wanted to cry. He wanted to storm out to the hangar and demand a shuttle back to the planet immediately. He wanted to tear the Hundred Isles apart with his bare hands until they told him where she was.

Lynn.

"Commander Keale wants to ask you some questions. I told him I'd go get you. Do you feel up to talking?"

"Yes," David lied, and got to his feet. He couldn't see straight. His heart raced out of control, but at the same time he felt thick and stupid. Shock, probably. It would wear off in a while, he assured himself distantly.

Captain Esmaraude also stood. "Kaye will find her, Dr. Zelotes."

David lifted his gaze and focused on her. He didn't know what his expression was, but he watched Esmaraude's ruddy face turn pale as she looked at him.

When he did speak, his voice was nothing more than a harsh whisper. "He has to."

Chapter XII

Lynn blinked heavily. She was sitting up. The chair felt hard under her thighs and back. She lifted her head. The world outside her left eye was a blur of color. She squinted. Her right eye saw a bare, concrete room and four pinkish grey Dedelphi. Getesaph, or near family to the Getesaph. After another few seconds she could see the deep blue clothing they all wore was military issue. These four were soldiers. She looked down and saw the bands that clamped her forearms to the chair arms.

"Record," she subvocalized to her implant.

Their faces looked wrong. Lynn blinked again. All four of them wore bulbous filter masks over their mouths and noses. Two of them had gun belts around their waists.

What . . . ?

One of the four glanced toward her and saw she was awake. Lynn tried to speak in a normal voice, but couldn't make her throat work. She swallowed painfully and tried again. Still nothing.

A second Getesaph walked over to her chair. Gloved hands found the catches on her helmet and lifted it off. Lynn felt suddenly naked.

"Which eye is your camera?" the Getesaph asked. Her breath

steamed against her facemask. Then, Lynn saw the small knife in the soldier's hand.

Lynn's tongue froze against the roof of her mouth. Her heart fluttered in her chest. She considered lying. She could always get another eye grown, but the information and assistance from her camera were invaluable. She looked at the Getesaph's grey eyes and knew if she told her the wrong thing, she'd just take them both and leave her blind.

She swallowed, coughed, and managed to croak, "The right."

The soldier's hand rose out of her line of vision. A moment later, she felt thick fingers pull her right eyelid open. The curved blade drove straight toward her. The soldier's fist blotted out the room a split second before the scarlet cloud swirled in front of her.

She felt the blade curve around her eye. It didn't hurt as much as she thought it would. It was the sight of the glistening orb and its trailing ganglia in the soldier's hand that brought the blackness back down on her.

A voice cut through the swaddling darkness.

"Lynn? Come on, Lynn. Don't do this to me. Wake up."

The words entered her skull, making a counterpoint to the vague pulse of pain in her right temple. She did not want to open her eyes, but couldn't remember why. Her left eye twitched under its lid.

She remembered. All her muscles contracted until she pulled herself into a little ball, cradling her wounded head in her still-gloved hands.

"Lynn, stop." She felt hands and yanked herself away. "You're making it worse. I just got you bandaged up . . ."

Arron. What was Arron doing here? Where was here? What was happening?

She was going to have to open her eyes.

She forced her hands slowly away from her face. Gritting her teeth, she lifted her eyelids. Light lanced into her left eye. She blinked it hard. Her right lid wriggled limply, brushing a cloth padding that pressed against her cheek and temple. They hadn't cut the eyelid away. For some reason that made her feel better.

"Lynn?"

Her working eye saw a pitted, grey cement wall with a blobby shadow falling across it. She lay on a rough cement floor. Her skin prickled against her clean-suit as the cold and an impression of dampness seeped through. Her helmet had been removed. The air around her head and ears was dank and smelled of encroaching mold.

She licked dry lips with an equally dry tongue. "Arron?"

He sighed with relief. "Can you sit up?"

She wanted very much to say no, but instead she tightened her muscles and tried. His hands caught her shoulders and helped her. The world spun. She leaned her head back against the wall and tried to steady her breathing. She kept her eye open. Now that she had her sight back, she didn't want to cut it off.

She could look around a little better. The cell was solid, unpainted concrete. A metal door with a flap-covered slot in the bottom provided the only way in and out. A metal drain had been sunk in the center of the floor. A metal bucket stood in the corner. That was all her one eye could see.

She felt Arron sitting at her right side. Gingerly, she reached up and touched the cloth that wrapped her darkness. It was rough, ragged, and warm. The tang of salt and iron filtered through her nostrils.

"Why'd they . . ." Arron's hand flicked into her line of sight as he gestured at her.

"Cut out my camera." Her throat felt like she'd swallowed a river of sand. "Is there anything to drink?"

"No. Sorry."

She relaxed her neck and let her head turn toward him. He had drawn his knees up to his chest and wrapped his arms around them. One sleeve of his shirt had been ripped off at the shoulder, and she knew where her bandage had come from. He still had his helmet on. Hers lay next to him. A thin milky film filled the creases of the clean-suit around his elbows and knees.

Age marks. The clean-suit's organics had about three days of life in them. After that, they dried out and cracked open. Lynn raised her hand and flexed her fingers. A spiderweb of white lines creased her palm and fingers.

"Marvelous," she muttered, and let her head rest against the wall.

"I don't understand." Arron spoke to the door. "I don't understand how they could do this."

"Somebody's obviously decided that there's something more important than saving the world, and we got in the way." Lynn shifted herself gently so she could press more of her back against the wall. "It'll be okay. Trace and R.J. will have already missed me. They'll have Commander Keale and his people out looking for us. We just have to wait it out."

"I hope they find us before anybody else does." Arron flexed his hand the way Lynn had and watched more white lines form and spread. "We're both going to be biohazards before long."

Lynn decided not to waste breath agreeing with him. She wanted to sit quietly and nurse her eye. She touched her bandage again. Something else needed to be said. "Thanks for tying this up."

"You're welcome." She heard him stir. "You should put your helmet back on. The last thing you need is some fungus taking up residence in . . . that." His hand held the helmet out to where she could see it. She grasped it with both hands and managed to ease it over her head and lock it down.

She leaned her head back against the wall. "Is there anybody outside?"

"If there is, they aren't answering. I banged on the door for about five minutes after they tossed you in here."

No help there. She hadn't really expected any. Actually, now that the shock was wearing off, she was surprised they were still alive. Taking prisoners was not something the Dedelphi generally did.

"So we wait." She wrapped her arms around herself.

"So we do." Arron leaned back next to her.

Lynn sat there, breathing and hurting. Arron didn't seem inclined to talk, and that was just fine with her. She dozed for a while, and woke to a sploshy sound coming from her blind side. It took her a second to realize it must be Arron using the bucket and despite the fact she couldn't see anything, she turned her face toward the opposite wall. The sound reminded her how painfully thirsty she was, which made her stomach clench against sudden nausea.

The clank of a bolt being shot back sounded from outside the door. Lynn's head jerked up. The door swung back, revealing a dark hallway and two Dedelphi sisters with a daughter held between them. As a team, they tossed the daughter in the cell. She sprawled belly down on top of the drain. Lynn stared.

"Hey!" yelled Arron. "You can't—"

The door clanged shut. The bolt shot home. The daughter moaned, and Lynn finally identified her.

"Resaime."

Dismissing her aches as best she could, Lynn crawled over to the child and raised her up onto her knees. Resaime blinked at her, obviously dazed. A vivid purple bruise with a black spot at its center spread across her arm. Lynn guessed she'd been given an intramuscular injection of some sort of tranquilizer, and it probably hadn't worn off all the way yet.

"It's good, it's good," said Lynn in t'Therian as she wrapped her arms around Resaime. *My God, what've they done with Senejess?* There was no question in Lynn's mind that if they had Res, they had her aunt. Even Senejess would not leave a daughter alone in enemy territory.

Resaime didn't resist the embrace, but she didn't respond either.

"Who is she?" asked Arron in t'Therian.

"Resaime Shin t'Theria." Lynn smoothed Resaime's ears. The daughter's eyes blinked heavily. "The last emerged of my friend Praeis Shin's first bearing."

He didn't say any of the obvious; how could they throw her in here without any relatives? They can't leave her here. Our suits are rotting. We'll kill her just by sitting here.

"This could be a pressure tactic," Lynn suggested, laying Resaime down on her side. "They'll leave her in with us just long enough for someone out there to get panicky. She was . . . traveling with one of her aunts . . ."

"No," said Arron in English. The flat finality in his voice made Lynn turn to look at him.

"She's t'Therian. They've thrown her in here to die." Arron hunched down like he was trying to guard himself from his own words. "They may bring her aunt in to watch when the anaphylaxis sets in, but she's already dead as far as they're concerned." Lynn's expression must have been horrified because he drew back a little and spread his hands. "They've got a blood hate for the t'Therians."

"It's thoroughly reciprocated." Lynn collapsed backwards. She hurt, she hurt, she hurt. "They are not making this easy on themselves, are they?"

"No. But then they never have." He flexed his hand and stared at it. Even from where she sat, Lynn could see the white threads covering his knuckles. "Your commander's got maybe twenty-four hours to find us before we become lethal to her."

"I know." Lynn rubbed Resaime's shoulder, wishing she'd wake up. "I know."

Whatever you think about Humans—Lareet leaned her elbows on the terrace railing—*you have to admit they're incredible architects.*

The apartment buildings, municipal buildings, and small factories on the *Ur* had a strange, squared-off look, but they had been opened up from their Human isolation to provide plazas, terraces, great halls, and meeting chambers. Rivers and canals cut through lawns, arbors, and gardens. Boats and gondolas floated on the water. Members of the prep team thronged along the banks, arguing in a pleased fashion over who should get which vessel. All the water was deep enough to swim in. There were even fish in the rivers and birds in the trees. Everything was so clean it glistened.

Lareet took a deep breath of the fresh air. It felt a bit too dry, but the temperature was just right for early summer. The cloudless sky was disconcerting, but she felt she could get used to it. She loved it at night, when the blue-tinted dome cleared, and they saw all the stars there were.

It's almost a pity we don't have more time to enjoy it.

She opened the railing gate and climbed down the stairs to the flagstone walkway. She strolled past the gardens full of big fleshy flowers and thick vines. It was hard to imagine that a hundred yards below her feet, there was a mirror image of this city, and between them was not dirt, water, and rock, but conduits for maintenance, the hundreds of gravity generators, and all the climate machinery. The only sign of this underground complex was a sealed hatch set into the walkway. Its silver surface was labeled AUTHORIZED PERSONNEL ONLY in four different languages.

Similar hatches were spaced about one every hundred yards in a tidy grid all across the city. Each one had a video camera hanging over it, mounted on the wall of a building or strapped to the branches of a tree. These were the only places you could see the cameras without searching for them. The Human soldiers... What was the word? The *Marines,* obviously wanted it known that access to the maintenance corridors was closely watched.

Which made Lareet uneasy. If this was what they could see,

what couldn't they see? The Bioverse managers had assured them they would be perfectly free to do whatever they wanted. What surveillance there was existed to make sure vital systems weren't accidentally endangered, or to guide the maintenance jobbers to a site that needed fixing or cleaning.

That had all been echoed by the security chief, Commander Keale, during the welcoming ceremony and briefings. He had pointed out how carefully the hatches were latched, so that no Human poison could get in from the corridors below, how strong their transparent dome was, so they had nothing to fear from meteors or attacks, how good the video cover was so that any emergencies would be spotted immediately. He had gone on at length about how everything had been so carefully designed for the security of absolutely everybody. Absolutely everybody.

Lareet had found herself in complete agreement with Umat afterward. Umat had flicked an ear toward Commander Keale, and murmured, "I would not call him an enemy, Sister, but I believe we now know who our opponent in this game is."

Lareet turned to a path that rambled beside the principal river. The Ovrth Vrand, Pavch and Zan, sat on the riverbank surrounded by a grove of fishing poles. Long lines trailed into the water. Members of the squad sat beside them, patiently knotting together thick cords to make nets.

Ovrth Pavch grinned up at Lareet. "We'll eat well tonight." She pointed to a net on the grass, already full of silver-scaled fish. "This is easier than going to market. The Humans haven't bred any fight in the creatures."

Lareet forced her ears back against her scalp. "Ovrth Pavch, as members of the preparatory team, we have important work to do. We are not supposed to be lolling about fishing."

Ovrth Pavch's face rippled with a concern that was as false as Lareet's severity. "How else am I supposed to feed my *irthiat* who are busy inspecting, measuring, and generally surveying this city? Am I ordered to condemn them to Human food?"

Lareet laughed and inhaled the fish's freshwater scent appreciatively. "Of course not. See if they've put in any eels for us, would you, Ovrth Pavch? I haven't had a really fresh eel in the longest time."

"As you command, Dayisen Lareet."

Lareet gazed upriver. A small, open boat of freshly varnished wood steered its way between two larger trawlers. Umat raised her free hand to hail her sister. Lareet waved back, squeezed Ovrth Pavch's shoulder, and strode down to the little cement dock, just as Umat pulled up. She stepped down into the boat and settled herself so she faced Umat in the stern.

Umat flicked the lever that put the boat's whispering motor into forward gear and steered them away from the bank and to the center of the river. The motor and the current carried them from the *Ur*'s center toward one of the forested parks.

"So, my Sister," said Umat. "What do you think of this pretty city we've been given?"

Lareet's gaze flickered to the shore, up the trunks of the drooping trees that trailed their branches in the water, and back toward the apartment buildings vanishing around the river bend.

"It is about as we thought," Lareet said softly. "Most of the municipal buildings and factories are monitored, but the apartments are clear, as near as we can tell. The hatches are all sealed, and the locks must be on the other side."

Umat nodded. "Have we got a count on the Marines yet?"

"The Ovrth Ches are searching through the *databases* for troop numbers and where they're stationed."

Umat smiled and touched her sister's hand. "We've done well today."

Lareet trailed her fingers in the clear water. The river had a sandy bottom with emerald green algae clinging to the occasional stone.

Silver fish the length of her finger whisked upstream. *Is this really what the world used to look like?* "The Humans hide so much, Umat. Are we sure we're seeing both the fish and the school?"

Umat sighed and tugged Lareet's ear. "No, we're not. But we have to try, Lareet."

Lareet dipped her ears. "Of course we do. No matter what." *Whether or not Scholar Arron and the other Humans understand.* Lareet did not speak that thought out loud.

They sailed down the river in silence. Lareet felt herself calming slowly. Around them, the trees cleared from the banks to reveal tidy rows of low, boxy buildings. When it was time to rebuild the cities on Earth, Lareet was going to suggest maintaining this practice of keeping manufacturing facilities separate from the main living and governmental quarters. It was a less efficient use of space but a more pleasant one.

Umat angled the boat toward another concrete dock, a twin to the one they'd taken off from.

From here they could see where the sky sloped down to meet the tree line. At night, when the dome cleared, they would be able to stand in those trees and look outside. To the far right, they would see the docking area for the shuttles. Straight ahead about ten yards from their dome, they would see the smaller, opaque dome that held the engine room. Those ten yards were the most direct route from the city to the Human areas of the ship.

Lareet had no doubt at all that Commander Keale had thought about that carefully.

Umat took her hand, startling her out of her reverie. "You feel well, Sister? Your womb does not trouble you?"

Lareet waggled her ears briefly. "Sister, I never feel anything until the fourth month, you know that."

"I just wanted to make sure. You looked troubled."

Lareet shook her head. "Not troubled, just concerned about what their Commander Keale has set up as obstacles for us."

Umat shrugged. "We'll find out soon enough."

Hand in hand, they walked across the lawn to the manufactury set aside for metalworks. The Dayisen Avit, Huir, and Wital, met them at the main door. After the formalities and polite expressions of wonder at the beauty of their city, the Dayisen Avit led them to the manufactury floor.

Lareet was used to manufacturies being loud, filthy, stench-choked places. This warehouse of a room was almost sterile. The workers stood or sat around video monitors mounted on sealed vats, long tubes, or boxlike constructions. They all spoke in hushed voices as if afraid to interrupt the gentle hum filling the air. Off to the side, more people stood around, examining diagrams and passing small ingots of metal among themselves and making notes.

Dayisen Huir rattled off a stream of commentary about output and technique with barely suppressed excitement. The wonder of the Humans' equipment! They were learning something new every five minutes. There were Human experts on call, of course, but they were barely needed because the *computer* instructions were so comprehensive. Here they were planning bridges and catwalks between the buildings. Here, they were seeing about additional piping for interior and courtyard fountains. Everyone was, of course, coordinating with the architectural families, but the possibilities were endless. Dayisen Wital escorted them in silence, her face creased with good-natured bemusement at her sister's flood of words.

Finally, the Dayisen Avit ushered them into a side chamber. The room was long and narrow and almost empty. Two metal sheets had been propped up at the far end. Two others leaned against a table beside the door. The table also had a plastic case sitting on it.

"This is a storage room," said Dayisen Huir as she closed the door. "It's not monitored, as far as we can tell."

Dayisen Wital opened the case and displayed the matching pair of shoulder guns.

Lareet lifted out one of the freshly machined guns and checked the ammunition cartridge. Cradling the stock against her shoulder, she took careful aim at the steel plate at the other end of the room. Next to her, Umat did the same. The Dayisen Avit shoved the table and its metal plates around to form a makeshift shield for them.

Umat lowered her ears. "One, two, three."

Lareet and Umat fired together. Light, smoke, and noise erupted with the shots, then faded away. They ducked behind the shield. The shots ricocheted off the sheets and thumped into the walls.

Umat sneezed. Gunsmoke always did that to her. Lareet patted her shoulder absently, looked down at the gun, then looked at the plates at the end of the room. The bullets had left deep grooves in the inch-thick steel.

She nodded. "Very good, Dayisen Avit. They will do."

"There is one more thing you need to see," said Dayisen Huir. "If you'll come outside?"

They walked back into the warm daylight. The Dayisen Avit led them across a grassy lawn toward the edge of the dome with its concealing trees.

They stopped at a white surveyor's stick that had been thrust into the turf. Dayisen Huir turned to them. "Dayisen Lareet, would you please walk toward the dome?"

Lareet felt her ears fall back just a little, but she did as Dayisen Huir requested. For the first few steps, everything was fine. Then, she noticed that ahead of her, the grass lay strangely. The blades pressed flat against the ground. She glanced at the trees, blinked, and looked again. It looked as if the trees leaned toward her.

A few more steps and her legs began to feel heavy. She leaned into her steps. Her eyes told her the ground was flat, but every fiber in her body told her she was toiling up an increasingly steep hill.

After another yard, she fell to her knees. She tried to keep going on her knees, but at last she had to lie flat on her belly and crawl.

World Mothers, what have they done? The difference between what her eyes saw and what she felt was too confusing. Lareet clamped all her lids down over her eyes and began inching backward until she felt she was on level ground again.

She opened her eyes and stood up carefully. Umat wrapped an arm around her shoulder.

"What happened?" Umat asked the Dayisen Avit over her head.

"We think they've turned off the gravity in this section," said Dayisen Wital. "The generators are in a honeycomb structure, so if they turn off one generator, you are pulled toward the next nearest generator. The result is, whatever it may look like, is you are standing on a wall, because the pull of gravity is to one side of you rather than directly underneath you."

Lareet stood up and flattened her ears against her scalp. "We are heard out here," she murmured. "Have a care."

"It gets more complicated." Dayisen Huir dropped her voice to a bare whisper. She looked toward the bending trees and flattened her ears. "Dayisen Lareet felt like she was climbing up a wall because the nearest generator was behind her. Somewhere outside the dome, the gravity, or lack of it, will be exactly balanced. Essentially, there won't be any. Anything not fastened down at this balance point will float away.

"As you cross past that balance point, the nearest gravity generator will be in front of you. You won't be climbing up the wall anymore, you'll be climbing down it."

"I see," breathed Umat as she dipped her ears solemnly. "Well, Sisters, with all this talk of walls in our way, I can see only one thing to do."

"What is that?" asked Dayisen Wital.

Umat bared her teeth. "Build ladders."

Chapter XIII

Resaime coughed again, a dry raspy noise deep in her chest. Her breathing had degenerated into shallow wheezes. She huddled in the corner as far as she could get from Lynn and Arron and their grey, flaking clean-suits.

They'd all agreed an hour ago they had to get out of there. Lynn and Arron had taken up posts beside the door, waiting for their guard to come back. Lynn had taken her gloves off and dropped them in the bucket.

They'd held on as long as they could. Arron and Lynn had stayed in the corner by the right-hand side of the door, trying to keep movement to a minimum. Resaime was suffering from not being touched, but Lynn didn't dare lay a hand on her. Her suit was almost opaque with accumulated dander, and the age lines were broadening into hairline cracks. Arron's was even worse.

Lynn had not taken off her helmet to change or check her bandage. She tried not to worry about how the pain had turned fiery. They had let their relief bags fill to overflowing before they emptied them down the drain, rinsing it out with some of their water. They had stayed in their corner of the room, moving only when their muscles cramped up. It wasn't enough, of course. Nature was going to win and soon.

They'd been fed twice in what Arron estimated was twenty hours. A tray holding bowls of lentil mush and plastic bottles of water had been shoved through the slot in the door. They'd shouted through the slot. They'd pounded on the door and screamed themselves hoarse. No answer came. No sound at all. Twice the door had opened and a silent soldier with an ovrth's black bands on her uniform cuffs and a filter mask over her mouth and nostrils came in to stare at them all. Lynn had been startled by the fact that she was alone, until Arron pointed out she was walking into a poison chamber. The ovrth answered no questions, responded to no threats or pleas.

Lynn and Arron agreed that she must be looking to see if Resaime had died yet.

They wouldn't have to go through with it, Lynn tried to tell herself. Keale would find them before the ovrth came in again. Praeis would be called. They'd get Resaime to a hospital. They could bring down one of the doctors from the *Ur*.

David. Lynn's heart sank. *Where are you? Do you know what's happened? Or didn't they tell you? Are they keeping this secret so not to spread panic?*

Keale's going to open the door any second. We're not going to have to go through with this.

The bolt shot back. Lynn froze. The door swung open, and she saw the ovrth's hand and arm.

The ovrth stepped into the cell. Her gaze swept across her prisoners. Resaime coughed so hard she gagged deep in her throat. The ovrth gazed down at her dispassionately.

"You're killing her!" Arron shouted at their jailer. He stormed over to the ovrth. Nothing new there. Nothing to disturb anybody. They'd done so much shouting and storming.

"Look at her!" Arron grabbed the ovrth's breath mask and yanked. She swung at him.

Lynn half dived, half fell forward. Her hands slapped down on the ovrth's shoulders. She hung on while Arron dug his fingers into the mask and pulled it down. The ovrth snatched for Arron's wrists, and Lynn slapped her naked hands over the ovrth's nose and mouth.

The ovrth screamed into Lynn's hands. She felt the ovrth's teeth slide against her palms. The ovrth grabbed Lynn's arms and heaved. The room spun and the floor slammed against Lynn's back, knocking all the breath out of her. The door banged shut. Lynn rolled over. Arron crouched between the ovrth and the door. Resaime, temporarily forgotten, crawled forward. The ovrth brought her gun to her shoulder. Lynn struggled to her feet.

Resaime grabbed the ovrth's ankle and bit down hard on her calf. The ovrth screamed again and her gun swung down. Lynn launched herself forward. She clapped one filthy hand over the ovrth's nostrils and grabbed the back of her skull with the other, trapping the ovrth's face between her hands. Arron lunged for the gun.

The ovrth flailed wildly. Lynn held on. The ovrth's eyes grew wide. Breath came in panicked spurts. Lynn was barely aware of Arron covering them both with the gun. The world narrowed down to the feeling of warm leathery skin under her bare hand and a ragged choking noise. Muscles went slack underneath her. Lynn let go.

The ovrth toppled to the ground, retching and gagging. Arron raised the gun like a club and slammed the butt down on the side of her skull. She jerked abruptly and collapsed onto her side.

Lynn eyed Arron. He panted like an anxious Dedelphi. Resaime teetered to her feet. Lynn crouched down next to the ovrth. As she did, Resaime made it to the door.

"No, Res!" Arron jumped forward and leaned a hand against the door.

Res tugged at the handle. "I've got to find Aunt Senejess."

"We'll find her, Res." Lynn didn't look at her. She looked at the ovrth's limp body. Her temple was starting to bruise. "Try to hang on."

"I've got to find my aunt."

"Hang on, Res," said Arron softly. "Just hang on."

Lynn found the buckles on the ovrth's filter mask. As soon as she had it loosened, she tossed it to Resaime. Res snatched it up with trembling hands and slid the mask over her face. Something small inside Lynn eased. She straightened up, rubbing her palm, which was still wet with saliva and sweat, against her leg.

Keeping himself between Res and the door, Arron eased it open and put his eye to the crack. Lynn stood on tiptoe behind him. The corridor was narrow and made of bare cement just like the cell. She thought she saw two more doors in it. Two guards stood on duty: one about three meters away, one about six meters. Both had guns in their hands.

Arron closed the cell door and turned to face her. "We've got two more guards out there."

Lynn licked her dry lips. "Can you shoot that thing?" She nodded toward the gun in his hands.

"I can," said Res. The filter mask muffled her voice, but it rang surprisingly strong. "My mother made sure we knew how. We can get out of here and find Aunt Senejess."

"Res . . ." began Lynn. Resaime held out her hand. It was perfectly steady. Arron glanced at Lynn for a moment, then handed Resaime the gun. As he did, Lynn looked at Res's face and saw her dilated pupils and how her skin was stretched tight and shiny across her face and she knew what was happening. Fear, anger, and action had triggered the Burn. By now, Res was probably so full of endorphins and adrenaline she could have run on two broken legs.

Resaime moved to the door. Lynn stood behind her, hand on the latch. Resaime nodded. Lynn eased the door open. Resaime slid into the corridor. One explosion, two, three. Grunts and thuds and the slap of running feet. Arron leapt into the corridor. Lynn gritted her teeth and followed.

The guards' bodies sprawled on the floor. Resaime bolted between them to the first door. Arron bent to scoop up one of the guns.

"Aunt Senejess!" Resaime hammered on the door with her fist. "Aunt Senejess!"

No! Lynn staggered forward. Arron was closer. He grabbed her arm.

"She's not here, Res," he whispered furiously.

Res turned to stare at him, uncomprehending. "Not here?"

"No. They wouldn't keep her locked up in the same place as us. It'd be too easy for us to get to her."

Lynn heard the gulp as Res swallowed. The Burn wouldn't let her think or stand still too long. Her skin bunched and twitched. Without another word, she ran for the exit. Arron shot Lynn a desperate glance and followed.

Lynn gritted her teeth. After a few stumbling steps, she pushed her pace into something approaching a run. For the first time, Lynn felt a rush of gratitude for the Dedelphi's lack of an efficient communications system. She heard no footsteps or voices. The alarm hadn't gone up yet. Her foot skidded in the blood seeping out of the guards. She pinwheeled her arms and managed to keep her balance. She even managed to follow Arron's example and retrieve one of the guns. Cradling it awkwardly in her left hand, she dodged around the corner.

She almost collided with Arron, pressed flat against the wall. Resaime, on his other side, eyed the short ladderlike stairway that led up to a solid metal door at the end of the hall.

"Probably locked," whispered Arron. "I'll go check. I can shoot—"

A thunderclap rocked Lynn back. Arron dragged her to the floor. Resaime was already flat on her belly. Another boom sounded, followed fast by a sharp bang. The door flew open and slammed against the wall. A pair of soldiers stood silhouetted against the brighter light of the upper level.

Shot through the door and then opened it. Smart, thought Lynn dazedly. The pain in her head blurred the vision in her remaining eye.

"Drop it!" One of the soldiers pointed her gun at Resaime. Showing she wasn't a complete fool, Res dropped the gun.

"The Humans get up and move back."

"Well," said Arron as he heaved himself to his feet. "That was short-lived."

Lynn bit her lip and got onto all fours. She made as if to stand, but let herself fall onto one knee with a small cry.

"The Humans get up and move back." Lynn was sure the soldier raised the gun muzzle a little higher.

"She's lost blood, and she's got an infection," said Arron, from his place behind her. "She probably can't stand."

"Help her."

Lynn felt Arron move up beside her and bend over. A shot exploded from somewhere, and another. Lynn grabbed for her gun, brought it up, and fired. It kicked into her shoulder and she gasped from fresh pain. She couldn't see straight. Half the world was black. She fired into the light again. And again.

"Run!" shrieked Resaime.

Arron grabbed Lynn's shoulders and dragged her forward. Lynn stumbled up the steps and would have tripped over the squirming, gasping soldiers if Arron hadn't kept her upright.

Her vision cleared a little and she could see windowless walls of brown-and-white stone. This was a bunker, probably burrowed into a mountainside. The Getesaph had been digging them for centuries.

Lynn found her feet and made out Resaime's fleeing back. Lynn pelted after her.

"Stop!" shouted voices behind them. "Stop!"

Something yanked Arron's hand out of hers. She wheeled around in time to hear the thud and see Arron tackled by a big Getesaph in green-and-lavender civilian clothes. Lynn swung her gun at the Getesaph's skull. The blow connected, startling them all. The Getesaph's grip loosened, and Arron twisted around and smashed his hand against the Getesaph's nostrils. The Getesaph screeched and scrambled backward. Lynn held out her arm and let Arron pull himself up and drag them both toward where, she hoped, Resaime had run.

Shots rang out. The air beside Lynn's ears hissed and sang. Adrenaline poured into her heart and she ran. Blind and panicked, she ran without thinking, just to get away from the shots.

"Don't kill the Humans!" someone shouted.

Arron shoved Lynn to the floor again in a shadowed place. She blinked and tried hard to focus. They were behind a heavy desk. Resaime had upended it for cover. Shouts Lynn couldn't understand were filling the place.

But they had an out. They had one out. "Arron, get your gun up. Res, do you see a door?" Lynn fumbled for the fastenings on her helmet.

"Yes."

"Lynn, what . . ."

She tore her helmet off. "If we can keep them back, maybe we can walk out of here." Hands raised, but not in surrender, Lynn stood up.

"I'm stripped!" she shouted in Getesaph. Her voice was harsh and tremulous. "We're walking out of here! The first one who wants to die of the Human poison can try to stop us!"

For the first time, she got a good look at the place. It was an open lobby with desks sitting here and there. About a dozen Dedelphi stood between them, some in civilian clothes, some in uniform. Slanting ladders led to catwalks for access to the second-story rooms.

They'd taken shelter directly under one of the catwalks. Lynn's scalp crawled. She couldn't see who was up there, but, then again, they couldn't see who they were shooting at down here.

"We have no quarrel with the Humans." A squarish Getesaph with sandy pink skin and a uniform with a trindt's red bands around her wrists.

"We seek no blood from you," the trindt went on. "But we have to defend ourselves from the t'Theria. You inadvertently prevented this operation. We are negotiating your release . . ."

"Bullshit!" spat Lynn. She recovered herself and spoke in Getesaph. "We are walking out of here. You can shoot us or you can send your soldiers to take the poison for you."

"We seek no blood from you," repeated the trindt patiently. "We will escort you to a Human installation, but the t'Therian—"

"I didn't do anything to you!" screamed Resaime.

The trindt's calm snapped. "Devouring spy!" she shouted. "Daughter of death and lies! You will be stopped! All of you will!"

A few Getesaph started forward. Lynn held her hands up, one out to each side, palms outward.

"Halt!" thundered the trindt.

They obeyed. Relief washed over Lynn. "We were invited to save the whole of the Earth!" Lynn's shoulders shook. Her knees weren't going to hold her up much longer. "Not just your islands!" In English, Lynn said, *"Let's go."*

She heard shuffling noises. After a moment, Arron came into her line of sight. He carefully kept his gun up. Resaime hunched on his other side.

The world blurred. Two figures dropped in front of her. Getesaph. In clean-suits and helmets.

"Run!" screamed Lynn.

She felt the breeze behind her scalp as a Getesaph snatched at her and missed. Fear and anger lent her speed, and she almost piled into Resaime and Arron.

If they've locked the door... Arron grabbed the handle and shoved it down. The door swung open, revealing a broad, braced, metal ladder. Forgetting her naked hands, Lynn grabbed Resaime's shoulders and all but tossed her through the threshold. Res grabbed the rungs with hands and feet and climbed up. Lynn followed, clumsy and scrabbling. Res threw open a metal hatch, and they both dived out into the daylight.

Lynn's boots found level ground, and she started running before she realized she was running across packed earth, not the damned blank concrete that surrounded every Dedelphi secure area. She'd been right. This place was not official.

She concentrated on Resaime's back and put herself in line with it. As long as she was between Resaime and the thudding footsteps behind her, the soldiers couldn't get a clear shot at Res.

A fence of metal slats loomed between the compound and the outside world. Her brain had just defined it when her legs jerked backwards and the ground smashed against her chest. Shots whisked overhead, and Lynn twisted around frantically. A clean-suited soldier clung to Lynn's knees. Lynn swung out. The Dedelphi grabbed her wrist and levered herself up Lynn's body. Another shot sounded, and the soldier jerked back. Lynn tore out of the Dedelphi's grip and threw herself toward the fence.

Where's Resaime? Where's Arron?

Where's the other soldier?

Getesaph voices shouted behind her. More shots echoed around her. She couldn't understand any of it. Her vision narrowed to a grey-walled tunnel with shiny slats across the end. Fat slats, widely spaced. Designed to stop an adult Dedelphi.

Lynn measured her length on the ground, screamed as the pain raised sparks in front of her eyes, and wriggled under the lowest slat. It scraped hard along her back, ripping cloth and rotted organic.

Where's Arron?

She tried to stand and run but stumbled instead. Her remaining eye didn't want to work. The world was a blur of tears and voices. She lurched forward, praying for smooth ground. If she tripped, she wasn't getting up again. An uneven roar cut across the voices, and the tunnel in front of her eye began to shrink rapidly.

Oh, no.

"Lynn!"

The ground hit her knees and her palms, jarring her all the way up her shoulders. Hands grabbed her, and the ground went away. Something soft hit her shoulder, and the roaring filled the entire world.

The tunnel of her vision shut down altogether.

"Lynn! Lynn! *Eia! Oereth u,* Arron, *iyullena or'ena esa!*"

Groggy, aching, ears ringing, Lynn lifted her head. The world roared, jounced, and rattled. Someone shouted at her in t'Therian. Someone young.

Res! Her left eye snapped open and her right eye tried to. Its flutter sent a shot of pain across her temple.

Her vision took a moment to clear. Resaime, filter mask still in place, leaned over her, dangerously close.

"Wake up!" screeched Resaime. "We've got to abandon the car!"

Car. The world jumped again. The roar was the engine, she was on the back bench and . . . She turned her head a little. The top of Arron's helmet gleamed above the driver's seat.

Pride at deciphering her situation leaked away, replaced by fear, anger, and urgency. The world jerked, rattled again, and tilted. The wind and roar stopped. The top of Arron's helmet jerked left as he scrambled out. "Get back, Resaime."

Lynn realized she was going to have to move. She clenched her muscles, grabbed the seat back, and heaved herself upright. The world spun, but she managed to make out a tree-choked slope in front of them. Arron grabbed her by the elbow and shoved her to one side. She almost fell against Resaime, but managed to catch her balance in time. Engine noise filled the air behind her. Resaime wasn't moving. Lynn turned. Arron got behind the frame car, put both hands on its back bar, and shoved it forward. The car crashed down the hill until it rammed into a tree that would not give way.

"Let's go." Arron loped across the road's cracked pavement and into the scrub on the other side.

Ah, a distraction, Lynn thought muzzily as she followed Resaime, who followed Arron. *If we crashed down the hill, we'd keep going downhill. We would not scramble up the slope and head across the other side.*

The moss-covered, puff-leaf trees enclosed them, cutting off the watery sunlight and dangling branches in their faces. The thick undergrowth of ballooning weeds, pitcher plants, and rubbery reedlike growths rustled and flapped, spattering water on her shins. The rags of her tattered clothes and clean-suit flopped against her shivering skin, getting wetter by the second. More water dripped on her head and smeared across her cheeks. Fungus and mushrooms popped and squelched underfoot. She kept her right hand stretched out to try to keep herself from smashing into trees on her blind side. Mostly it worked.

She had hoped the movement and fresh air would clear her mind and vision, but it wasn't happening. She blundered through a blur of shadows. Her temple throbbed incessantly.

Keep going, just keep going. We've got to get out of here. Got to.

All at once, Arron was beside her. "Lynn, do you see it?"

He pointed. She sighted along his arm with her good eye. Through the trees and hanging moss, she saw a cluster of buildings, most likely a Getesaph family home. Nothing moved in the yard, and no light shone through the windows.

Probably deserted. Probably the owners were dead, but maybe they were just evacuated. She glanced anxiously at Resaime, who leaned against a tree, panting hard. Was it safe to take her there? They were already dancing with the plague out here. What if they took her inside to sleep with it, too?

"I know," said Arron as if he read her thoughts. "But you're both about ready to fall over, and I'm not feeling so good myself."

Lynn nodded. There was no choice.

"Are you good, Resaime?" Lynn straightened her shoulders. "Only a little farther."

"I'm good." Resaime pushed herself away from the tree. Her ears drooped until the tips almost brushed her shoulders. "Let's get there."

The homestead lay a few yards from the edge of the woodlands. Its paddies and tended bogs stretched out north and west beyond it. It was a typical Getesaph construction, a conglomeration of connected buildings, all of them three stories tall, with terraces on the second and third stories and steeply slanting ladders zigzagging between them.

Heaps of deflated leaves had blown right up to the door. Tiny mushrooms sprouted from the wooden doorframe. The gates on the livestock runs all hung open and swayed in the breeze.

Lynn swallowed. This place had been abandoned too long and too carelessly for its owners to have just been evacuated.

Lynn touched Arron's shoulder. "One of us needs to go in first and make sure the dead haven't just been left there."

"Right. I'll—"

The house's main door swung open and two Getesaph, guns leveled, stepped out into the sunlight.

All three of them froze. The left-hand Getesaph gestured at their hands with her gun's long muzzle.

Which explains why nobody followed us, Lynn thought ridiculously as she raised her hands. *They were ahead of us.*

"All right," said Arron in his perfect, smooth Getesaph. He raised his hands high over his head. "We want no blood from you."

The right-hand Getesaph's ears stood straight up. "Scholar Arron?"

Arron opened his mouth and closed it again. Lynn's heart started beating again, hesitantly.

"They didn't say it was you." She turned to her arms-sister. "Did you know about this, Balt?" She didn't use a title, which meant these two were sisters in blood, not just in arms.

The left-hand Getesaph shrugged irritably. "Entsh, if no one gave you names, no one would give them me. They just said we were out after two Humans and a *devna*."

Res bared her teeth. Lynn made a decision. She carefully lifted the strap for her gun off her shoulder and laid the weapon on the ground. "Res, put the gun down," she said in Getesaph. "These are allies of Arron's."

The look Arron gave her was grateful. The look Res gave her was disbelieving, but she plucked the gun strap off her shoulder and laid the weapon down gently on a pile of leaves. The Getesaph's skin calmed visibly.

"Ovrth Entsh, Ovrth Balt," Arron had seen the black bands on their uniform cuffs before Lynn had, "this is Manager Lynn of Bioverse, Inc." He waved a hand toward Lynn. "She came here to help with the relocation. With us is Resaime Shin t'Theria, who is daughter to an ally."

"You're allies with the *devna*?" Entsh's ears tipped back uncertainly. She had not lowered her gun.

Arron ignored the question. "Ovrth Entsh, what is going on?"

Her ears flickered back and forth, confused. "What do you mean?"

Arron gestured broadly with both hands. "I mean what is happening to the evacuation? Why were we being held? Why did we have to escape from a dungeon?"

Balt lowered her gun to an at-rest hold. Lynn found breathing suddenly became easier. "How can you not know what you've done?"

"I know what I've done." Arron tapped his chest. "I found out that the names on the relocation passenger lists don't match the people who were relocating. What I don't know is why the Parliament is doing this?"

Balt pressed her nostrils closed. "Parliament isn't doing anything but sitting around with its eyes shut," she muttered.

"Quiet, Balt." Entsh dropped the muzzle of her gun until it was pointing at the ground. She shook her sister's shoulder gently with her other hand. "Scholar Arron, we've got to take you with us."

Arron blinked. "Why?"

Both ovrth stared at him in disbelief. The wind blew cold against Lynn's bare scalp, bringing with it all the smells of the damp forest.

Entsh made a strangled noise in her throat. "Because we have to."

"Why, Ovrth Entsh?" Arron spread his hands again. "If it's not the Parliament holding us, who is it? What are they trying to do to the evacuation?"

Entsh's ears waved uncertainly. Balt touched her shoulder, whether in comfort or in warning, Lynn couldn't tell.

Arron shook his head. "I've sat in your house and recorded the words of your family. You have shown me hospitality and kindness and remembered my name and station well. The World Mothers know I never expected you to treat me like this."

Balt drew her lips back until just a hint of white showed between them. Lynn stood stock-still and tried not to breathe. She willed Res to remain quiet.

Balt kicked at a stand of weeds that spat water out of their tips. "It's not worth it to stand here discussing the idiocies of the officeholders."

"If you think it's idiotic, why are you helping?"

Entsh's skin rippled uneasily. "Scholar Arron, it is complicated. The Defenders are in revolt. You stumbled across it. You have to be held until events are in motion. You'll be let go. It is already planned."

"They tried to kill the ally of my sister," said Arron quietly. "I will not go back there, and I will not let you take her back."

Entsh's gaze raked over Lynn. "This is your sister?"

One careful step at a time, Arron stepped sideways until he stood directly in front of Lynn. "Yes, she is, and I will stand before her and her ally."

"Scholar Arron," said Balt. "Don't do this."

"Don't do what?" Arron threw up his hands. "Don't refuse to be illegally arrested? Don't protect my sister and her allies? Then tell me why!"

The silence stretched out for more heartbeats than Lynn could count. Clouds scudded across the sun, turning the shadowed light grey. Arron stayed where he was, hands in the air. Resaime fidgeted badly. Her nostrils closed and flared open again behind her filter mask like they had a life of their own. The ovrth stood still, with Balt's hand on Entsh's shoulder, communing in the silent, almost telepathic way Dedelphi shared with their sisters.

Finally, Entsh said, "All we truly know is that the Defenders are going to take hold of the *city-ship* called *Ur*."

Lynn felt all the blood drain out of her face. "Oh my God," she whispered. "David."

Balt's face tightened. "What did she say?"

"She has, we have, family aboard the *Ur*." Arron lowered his hands. "What else are they planning?"

Balt waved her ears. "We don't know. We're helping them because of favors our family owes to the employers of employers, and we haven't been asking questions. We think it's ridiculous. How can our people hope to know where to start to take over these ships? All it will do is anger the Humans."

A look of hope spread across Arron's face. "If you think this is ridiculous, help us. Take us to a Human outpost. Or near one. We can warn Bioverse and stop the whole insanity before it starts."

Balt bared her teeth. "Didn't you hear us say we are doing this because of family obligation?"

"Yes." Arron clenched his hands into fists. "But I also heard you say it couldn't accomplish anything, and that you didn't know who this wounded. Now you know, and now you can accomplish something. You can prevent Bioverse from leaving."

The folds of Entsh's face sagged. "We cannot, Scholar Arron."

Lynn licked her lips. "How many of your family have you lost to plague?"

Balt and Entsh turned eyes and ears to her. "What?" asked Entsh in a quiet, dangerous voice.

Lynn stepped around Arron and stood next to him. "How many family have you lost to plague?" Her voice sounded harsh and shaky like the wind in the tree branches. "How many daughters? Which of your mothers? How many sisters and cousins?"

Balt turned her ears away. "The Humans have no cure. That is known."

"No," said Lynn. "But we can keep the sick alive longer. We can help their bodies fight off the illnesses with greater success. We can save lives by keeping the body strong and preventing reinfection during the course of the illness."

Entsh's ears wavered. "Is this true, Scholar Arron? Have the Humans saved lives?"

Arron nodded once. "The medical technology Bioverse brings is greater than anything in the Hundred Isles of Home. It has already saved lives." Lynn wasn't sure if Arron knew that for a fact, but all that mattered right now was that Balt and Entsh believed it.

Arron's eyes narrowed at the ovrth. "Who is dying, Sisters?"

Balt said nothing. She just gripped her sister's arm so hard, Lynn could see Entsh's skin squirm in protest.

"Our sister Plenth has lost three of her daughters. Two more are ill with joint-rot." She bared her teeth at Lynn. "Could the Humans save them?"

"I don't know," said Lynn honestly. "But if Bioverse leaves, we can't try, can we? If Bioverse leaves before the real cures are found, how many more are going to die?"

"Help us," Arron extended both hands just a little, not enough to touch them, even accidentally. "Let us help your family. No one has to die from this mistake."

Entsh shook her head until her ears flapped. "How can we break our promise?"

"It depends what's more important, your family's debts or the lives of your sister's children. There is still time. There is still a chance, if our care-takers can reach them." Lynn wished she could speak as smoothly as Arron did. At the moment, it didn't matter. The ovrth had stopped paying attention to her. They were looking at each other. Entsh's ears stood up so straight they quivered. Balt's were flat against her scalp.

"Just make up your minds," breathed Res in t'Therian. Lynn looked at her and shook her head helplessly. Res's skin was practically jumping off her bones.

I feel the same, believe me.

Then, Entsh's ears dipped. "You'll have to stay here tonight. There's a crossroads across the northwest field. We can meet you there at first light with a carrier."

"But we have to . . ."

"It doesn't matter," said Ovrth Entsh. "The roads and tunnels are crawling with our people. They won't have moved on until morning."

Lynn bit her lip. "Can you get a message to the outpost for us? We have to warn . . ."

Balt's ears dropped back. "We aren't doing enough for you?"

Arron laid a hand on Lynn's arm. "We are sorry. But our family is in danger. You can understand that?"

"Yes," said Entsh softly. "We can understand that."

Lynn closed her eyes and tried to control the fear that had grabbed hold of her. Arron kept his hand on her arm. "There is an outpost near here, though?" he asked.

"About forty miles southeast." Balt flicked her ears toward the window. "On the other side of Mrant Chavan."

"We'll head out now." Entsh caught her sister's shoulder and steered her toward the stairwell. "And start thinking of what we're going to tell our trindt."

They shouldered their guns and marched into the woods. No one else moved. They all just stood around listening until the stomping and rustling of the ovrths' passage faded away.

Arron looked at Lynn and leaned against the wall of the house. "I did not think that was going to work."

Lynn collapsed beside him. "How do you know them?"

Arron shook his head. "I don't remember."

Res's jaw dropped. "You're joking."

Arron shrugged. "I've lived here for ten years. I've met a lot of people. I've got teragigs worth of recordings."

Res bowed to him. "Good bluff."

"Thank you." He cast Resaime an appraising look. "Are you good?"

"Yes." Resaime rubbed her arms. "I just haven't stopped twitching yet."

"Neither have I." Lynn pushed herself away from the wall. She thought about David. Imagination pictured him hiding behind a desk, like they had, hearing the sound of gunfire and destruction all around him.

She looked across the farmyard and for a moment seriously wondered if she could make all forty miles in a night if she started now.

Arron coughed. "I'm going to check the house just to make sure there's . . . Nothing." He rubbed his forearms briefly. "There should be a garden near the house. There might be something edible left in it. You and Res could check."

"Good idea." She gestured toward the screening trees. "The brush should give us enough cover so Balt and Entsh's arms-sisters won't see us from the roads, as long as we don't go out into the fields. Want to help me, Res?"

Resaime hesitated. Her skin bunched and twitched. She looked nervously around, as if expecting more Getesaph to drop out of the trees. "All right," she said at last.

They circled the house and found a weed-choked garden. A lot of the plants had been trampled and broken, but a couple of rows of spiky, broad-leaved plants had survived. Resaime squatted down and rummaged through the leaves. After a moment she held up a broad, flat pod. "Beans," she said. "I've seen Humans eat these, so we're good."

"Great." Unsure of her balance, Lynn knelt and began plucking pods to stuff into her pants pockets, which were, remarkably, still whole. A rich, green scent filled the air around her.

"I didn't want to kill them."

Lynn jerked her head up and turned so she could see Resaime. Resaime sat on her haunches, her gaze fastened on the bean pods in her hands.

"I know," said Lynn as gently as she could.

"I had to. We had to get out of there. They were trying to kill me. Us. Me. I had to find Aunt Senejess. I had to try."

"Yes." Every fiber in Lynn wanted to reach out to this confused, young person and touch her. "We had to. There was nothing else any of us could have done."

"They've still got Aunt Senejess."

Lynn swallowed. "Yes."

"You and Arron lied when you said we'd go find her."

"Yes."

Resaime's hands curled into fists, crushing both pods. Lynn looked down at the tangled mess of foliage at her feet and wished there was some reply she could make to that. After a moment she gave up trying to find one and went back to picking beans. From her right she heard rustling and tearing and knew that was what Resaime was doing, too.

Lynn caught movement out of the corner of her eye. Arron stood on the second-floor balcony and waved.

"Must be all clear," she said, straightening up. "Let's get inside." With Resaime beside her, she plodded toward the house.

Lynn thought she was too tired to panic. After all, they had help now. Arron's friends would be back in the morning. Despite that, a dozen nattering little fears piled out of their holes. What if the ovrth were caught in their lies? What if they changed their minds when faced with their sisters and told what really happened? What if they just didn't come back?

She gritted her teeth tightly and tromped toward the house, keeping Resaime in sight of her good eye.

Arron held the door open for them. It led to a large common space with a central furnace/stove arrangement. Its vent pipe was encased in gaudily painted ceramic. The furniture lay scattered around the room, flipped over and slashed open. Around the chamber, cupboard and closet doors flapped open.

Whoever the owners had been, they'd been fairly well off, then they'd been ill, then they'd been ransacked.

"Somebody beat us to it," remarked Lynn. The matting under her boots squished. The pervasive damp had gotten inside. The smell of mildew filled the room.

"The good news"—Arron went over to the sink—"is that the water's still running." He turned a tap and a spurt of clear water gushed out.

Lynn watched it, fascinated. "Resaime, why don't you go upstairs to the sleeping rooms? You need to get away from us."

"That's good." Res crossed to the shallow stairs and hesitated. "You checked up there right?"

"Yes," said Arron solemnly. "We're the only ones here."

"That's good." Her ears twitched nervously, but she did climb the stairs.

There were no cups. Arron unfastened his helmet and they both drank cold, metallic-tasting water from the palms of their filthy hands. Lynn tried not to think about what they were drinking up with the water. There were dozens of reasons why the Dedelphi mostly drank bottled water, ranging from bad sanitation to the fact that many of the plague strains had worked their way into the water table. But they'd be home soon. David could take care of anything they'd caught. Lynn splashed more water on her face and the back of her neck. Arron did the same. Lynn watched him for a minute, without being sure why, and then retreated to the living area.

One of the divans was still upright. She sagged onto it, lying flat on her back. "I may never move again."

"That's my wish." Arron collapsed beside her. "Thank God this place is big. Resaime was starting to wheeze even through the breath mask."

Lynn closed her eye. "I'm worried about the way she was twitching."

Arron didn't answer, but Lynn was sure he could recite the early symptoms of the plague as well as she could. Muscle spasms, low, dry cough, general lassitude. How could they tell what might be plague and what was just the aftereffect of poisoning and the Burn? One more thing she didn't know.

"We'll be safe tomorrow," said Arron at last. He touched her bandage. "Can I take a look?"

Lynn turned her head and let him lift the bandage and remove the padding. She swallowed several times before she was able to croak, "How's it look?"

Arron hesitated. "Not good. I think you've got an infection."

The pain sharpened for a moment. "I'd be shocked if I didn't."

"Let me find something better than . . ." He gestured at the clotted wadding in his hand. "And there might be something you can wear."

"Arron, sit down and rest, will you?" She touched her face and temple gingerly. The skin under her fingers was swollen and hot. Her fingertips came away covered with flakes of blood and something grainy and yellow-green.

"Can't." Arron was already on his feet, rummaging through the open cupboards around the dining area. "I've got to do something."

Lynn didn't say anything. Exhaustion bit hard into her bones. She fumbled in her pocket for one of the bean pods and looked at it without interest. She heard something ripping in the background. She ran a thumbnail around the pod's seam and split it open. The beans inside were kidney-shaped and dark, rich green.

I'm the one who likes real grown-in-the-dirt food, she reminded herself.

Trying not to grimace, she popped one in her mouth and chewed. It tasted thick, dry, and green. *Better than nothing, right?* She finished the other four beans in the pod. By the fourth one, it didn't taste so bad.

"What's for dinner?" Arron sat on her seeing side. He had a wad of black-and-brown cloth in his hands. He set it down. Some of it was rags, but underneath them was a loose, brown tunic that he must have found in one of the cupboards.

"Beans and more beans." Lynn emptied her pockets, spilling pods onto the cushion.

"Better than nothing, right?" Arron made a come-here gesture. She turned her face toward him. She felt him swabbing gently at her face with the rough, dry cloth.

"I sure hope so."

They fell silent. Lynn wanted to say something. There was so much they needed to talk about. He'd saved them, several times now. She needed to say something about that. Then, they had to plan. They had to figure out what to do when the ovrth came back, and what to do if they didn't, or if Res got sick overnight, or . . .

But there was nothing to plan with. They had no idea where anybody was, or what was going on around them, or up above them. They knew nothing, nothing at all.

Lynn's hands started to shake. Nothing . . .

"Lynn? What's wrong?"

My hands are shaking, that's what's wrong. I'm half-blind and rotting and I DON'T KNOW WHAT TO DO!

Tears ran down her face. Deep, sick sobs dragged themselves out of her chest. Her hands shook, her chin shook, her whole torso shook with fear, exhaustion, and ignorance.

"Lynn? Lynn, come on, stop. It'll be okay." Awkward arms embraced her. "The ovrth won't let us down, and Resaime's not that bad off . . . Lynn . . ." The pitch of his voice raised toward panic. "Come on, Lynn. We will be okay. We are okay . . . Don't do this to me, Lynn. I need . . . Please, stop . . ."

Lynn gasped for breath between the sobs. She held up both trembling hands. "I'll be . . . I'll be okay." One deep breath. Another. A long, ragged breath. The trembling eased, and she was able to gulp down some of the tears.

"I'm sorry." She wiped her face with the back of her hand,

smearing tears and mucus across her face. Arron pressed a cloth into her hand and she held it against her cheeks. "I'm sorry."

"'Sokay," said Arron softly. "It's been an unbelievable day."

"Yeah, that it has." She crumpled the damp cloth in her hands. "Look, get me covered up, will you? Before Resaime comes down to find out what that god-awful noise was and sees me like this."

Without another word, Arron picked up the rest of his cloths. He wiped down her face and pressed a new pad against her eye socket, binding it in place with long strips wrapped around her whole head. "There, that'll help."

"Thanks. Have a bean." She held out a pod to him.

"Thanks. The Getesaph call these *chkith*. They make great soup." He split the pod open and, without any hesitation at all, popped the beans into his mouth.

They sat there on the divan, munching beans, putting the pods in a neat pile, and saying nothing. Lynn's memory flooded with all the meals they'd shared in college, all of them over endless conversations that had seemed so important at the time. Now, when it was truly important, when it was life and death, she didn't want to say anything at all.

The room grew steadily darker. Arron looked into the thickening twilight. "I didn't find anything to light a fire with," he said. "We might as well get some sleep." He stood up and gathered the discarded pods in a double handful. Then he walked to the stove and shoved them into the firebox.

Lynn picked up the tunic in both hands. It was damp. Black-and-grey mold speckled its surface. It smelled. She bit her lip and pulled it over her head. She couldn't travel in rags. The suit was going to fall off by tomorrow, and her shirt wasn't far behind.

Then, despite her protesting joints, she teetered over to the spiral stairway. "Res! Are you good?"

"Yes!"

She pounded the wall softly with her fist. "I'm taking your word on that!"

"Thank you!"

Lynn turned and settled back down on her divan. The moldy smell hung thick in the air. In the deepening shadows, she saw Arron right a curved sofa and toss its half-shredded cushion back in place.

" 'Night, Lynn." He lay down.

" 'Night." She curled up, huddling in on herself and at the same time willing herself to relax.

A small strange part of her remembered the feeling of Arron's arms around her and missed it. Another part thought of David, and she almost started crying again.

When sleep came, she accepted it as a blessing.

The Inner Office of the Sisters-Chosen-to-Lead was full of Byvant's selected audience when the speaker-guard brought in two of the Members Shavck, Vreaith and Pem. Ishth had the satisfaction of seeing them glance nervously around the room, taking in the witnesses. Four sisters from the upper house, four from the lower, and two complete families from the Defenders' House that they could still count on, not to mention all the usual clerical staff, special advisors, official recorders, and a pair of journalist sisters with their noters. They were not under any circumstances going to be allowed to take their pictures or notes out of the room, but they added a nice touch.

She and Byvant had bluffed their way through another Confederation session today, but, judging from the tones even their allies were using, they wouldn't make it through a third. Disturbing rumors were running about what the t'Therians were doing in their peninsula. If anything happened, it was going to be important to appear cooperative and blameless. Byvant had agreed firmly. So, late at is was, they had staged this little scene.

The Members Shavck both dressed in very bad taste for a pair of sisters who were supposed to be enacting the business of the people. Vreaith wore a thin, shiny black tunic that hung down to her knees, and the mottled pink hose might as well have been an additional layer of skin. Pem's belted kilt and jacket were a little better, but the yellow and grey were very close to the gold and silver reserved for the Sisters-Chosen-to-Lead, and Ishth couldn't help wondering if that was on purpose.

The speaker-guard locked the door and took up their stations; two on either side of the entrance. The next thing Pem and Vreaith noticed was that there was nowhere for them to sit down.

Ishth and Byvant had agreed ahead of time that Byvant should start, and they had also agreed that all polite preliminaries should be dispensed with.

"Where are they?" asked Byvant.

Pem started so badly she almost backed into her sister. Vreaith laid a warning hand on her shoulder.

"Where are who, Rchilthen Byvant?"

Ishth let herself look weary. "Your people abducted two Humans and two *devna.* Where are they?"

One of the Parliamentarians coughed. One of the journalists lifted her noter a little higher. Vreaith smoothed her ridiculous black-satin blouse down.

It's practically a robe. Who does she think she is? One of the devna *Queens?*

"There has been a misunderstanding," Pem said.

"On which point?" Ishth dropped her ears back just a fraction. "On the fact that you and your sisters should be brought up on charges of treason, stripped of office, and bled to death for embarrassing your mothers and sisters in front of the Confederation? Or in identifying exactly whose hands took hold of the Humans who came here at our insistence to help us?

"Or as to what kind of clemency could possibly be offered if you give us a quick answer here and now?"

Do we all understand each other now?

Pem's lips twitched like she wanted to bare her teeth. "If all this is true, why are we and our sisters not under arrest?"

"Because we don't have time." Byvant's lame ear quivered violently. "We need an answer for the Confederation and the Humans. We decided to start the questioning with you. The trials will come later. The evidence for your arrest has been distributed to your sister-members." She flicked her good ear toward the silent audience. "There is clemency for whoever tells us what we need. As we said, we are starting with you."

"And if we choose not to agree to this patently illegal and unfounded request?" asked Vreaith.

She gets full credit for calm, thought Ishth.

"Then you leave," she said aloud, "and wait for the police and the warrants in whatever fashion you choose. We, meanwhile, send for the next sisters on our list."

Vreaith looked at Pem, and Pem looked back at Vreaith. Vreaith smoothed her tunic over her pouch. Pem took her sister's hand. Ishth felt her skin bunch and bubble across her back.

Vreaith sucked in a deep breath. "They were being held forty-five miles outside of Mrant Chavan. The mother *devna* died during debriefing. The daughter and the two Humans have since escaped."

A tide of incredulous murmuring rushed through the room. Ishth waited for it to fade to a background whisper.

"Escaped?" Ishth gestured for Vreaith to go on.

"They killed two sisters to get out," said Vreaith flatly.

The whisper erupted into a cacophony of shouts. Sisters jumped to their feet. Ears and hands flapped wildly. The journalists tried to point their noters in six directions at once.

Byvant climbed to her feet and drew herself up to her full height. "Sisters! Please!" she bellowed. Silence descended like a heavy blanket over the room.

Very good, Sister, thought Ishth. *Now, salvage this. Please.*

"The Humans and the *devna* killed two of our sister-defenders?" said Byvant with perfect calm. "And who sent them out to die? Who held the Humans until they had to escape? To whose names do those deaths really go, Citizen Sisters? Who really owes their families for their lives?"

The shouts changed pitch and direction and the hand-and-ear-waving grew less. Byvant glanced down at Ishth. Ishth dipped her ears in approval.

Vreaith's face tightened up. She had evidently counted on that news to shock the whole room into confusion. Which went to show that she not only had no taste in clothes, she had no real understanding of how good Byvant was.

Ishth lowered her ears a little closer to her scalp. "Do you have any idea where your prisoners escaped to?"

Pem's ears sagged. There was no escaping the fact that Byvant's few words had swung the room against them again.

"We assume they are heading for the Human outpost near Mrant Chavan."

"And there are more sisters sent to intercept?" prompted Ishth.

"They may have them by now."

Ishth dipped her ears. "Good. It will be that much more convenient for you to escort them to the Human outpost."

A look of incredulity flickered through Vreaith's eyes.

"Understand me clearly," said Ishth. "The Humans are already scouring the Hundred Isles for their missing sisters. They can either find them soon, or they can continue to search for whatever they can find. Which may include the truth of what your sisters aboard the *Ur* are planning. What do you think the Humans will do if they find that?"

Now, what are you going to do? Are you nervous enough to give it all up now, or are you going to try to buy time for your sisters aboard the Ur*?*

Pem dropped her gaze to the floor. "We'll have to send some messages to find out what the situation is."

Buying time. Good. You'll buy it for us, too. As long as the Humans think we can't manage for ourselves, they'll be willing to take you on for us.

And when you must die, it is not we who kill you.

Chapter XIV

Commander Keale, wake up! Commander Keale, wake up!"

Keale surfaced slowly from sleep. It took a minute to realize he was being hailed by the room voice.

"Commander Keale, wake up!"

"Room voice, what's the emergency?" Keale knuckled his eyes. "Lights!"

The lights rose, just a little, to give his eyes time to adjust, and the voice answered, "A priority red call is on your comm station."

The words jolted Keale fully awake. He scrambled out of the sheets and snatched a pair of shorts off the bedside chair.

"Room voice, open comm station. I'm coming!" he called to the station as he yanked the shorts on.

The lights came up to full. Keale hurried out of the bedroom and into his spartan living room. The main comm station was alive and Lieutenant Ryan's face looked anxiously out at him from the screen.

"What is it?" Keale dropped into the station chair. Ryan was tousled and rumpled. Whatever he'd been doing, it wasn't sleeping.

"We've got trouble," Ryan answered. "We got this from a pilot who was flying back to base late after doing a pass over Vshlanl and Prentanl Islands."

Ryan's face blanked out and was replaced by a green-and-brown blur of woods and fields, punctuated by towns and homesteads. Then, in a clump of trees, an unexpected glint caught the light.

"What's that?" asked Keale.

"That's what the pilot wondered," said Ryan's voice from behind the scene. "He went back for another look." The ground tilted and rotated as the pilot banked his craft and angled his flight path over whatever in the grove was catching the light.

The plane flew over, the cameras looked down, and showed a tubular construction topped with a shining lens.

"A telescope?" Keale scratched his chin. "What are the Getesaph doing with a telescope so close to the port?"

"I went in and asked." The flyover video cut out and Keale faced Ryan again. "There were five soldiers that we saw: a couple *trindt*, and three *ivrth*." Captains and engineers, Keale translated mentally. Ryan's face was replaced by a new scene. This was a square room, small by Getesaph standards. It looked like one of the white, prefab buildings they were so good at putting up at a moment's notice. Two uniformed Getesaph with the trindt's red bands on their cuffs stood in front of whoever's eyes had made this recording.

The Getesaph were talking, but Ryan hadn't turned up the sound. "They gave us a story about using the 'scope to watch the shuttles. To make sure everything was going to and coming from where it was supposed to." *Reasonable,* thought Keale. Dedelphi paranoia made him look positively lackadaisical.

"They showed me the 'scope." The video jumped straight to a close-up look at the telescope and its turret and cables running off its sides like black vines. "I asked a few questions and left, and took this recording to Jasper over in comm tech."

Ryan appeared again. "She ran the scraps together, looked at the angle, and the fact that the place was well manned, personed, whatever, on a day when there aren't any flights planned, and came up with another possible use." Ryan took a deep breath. "It seems that 'scope is in the exact right place for getting the backscatter of communications transmissions off the clouds."

The sentence sank into Keale's mind and translated itself. "They've tapped our communications?"

"Yes, sir."

Grim satisfaction flowed through Keale. "All right, knot up what you've got and get it to me. I'm going to wake up Veep Brador, and then I'm going to wake up the Sisters-Chosen-to-Lead and—"

"Sir?" interrupted Ryan. "That's not the real problem. The real problem is that Jasper's team also figured out why Hagopian was looking at the passenger manifest."

Keale froze. "Go on."

"Jasper's team has also been going through the port tapes, listening to conversations, watching personnel registration, matching faces with names and movements." Ryan ran a hand through his hair, making yet more of it stand on end. "What she found was that the names people were calling each other in the hallways and with their families did not always match the names they entered for the register."

"Who have we got up there?" asked Keale softly.

"Jasper thinks it's a boatload of soldiers."

Any satisfaction Keale felt drained down to the soles of his feet. "Oh, Christ," he whispered. His mind reeled and righted itself. "All right, Ryan, this is an emergency order. The Hundred Isles and t'Aori peninsula are to be evacuated of all Human personnel. Immediately."

"Wh—"

"Because whatever the Getesaph are doing up there, it's going to be aimed at the t'Therians, and if the t'Therians get wind of it, they'll attack the Getesaph and all hell's going to break loose like nothing we've ever seen. Get our people out of there. Now."

"Yes, sir." He still hesitated. "What about Nussbaumer and Hagopian?"

Keale shook his head. "We're going to have to put the planes on evac duty. Everybody should keep an eye out for them, but evacuation of the outposts and ports is now top priority."

For a moment, Ryan forgot his title. "Brador's going to chew your ass off and spit it out."

"It's my ass," said Keale dismissively. "Get going. I've got to get hold of Captain Esmaraude."

"Yes, sir." Ryan cut his thread, and the screen blanked out.

"Room voice, emergency call to Captain Elisabeth Esmaraude aboard the *Ur*. Security override all other communications and secure the thread." *Haul her out of bed, voice. She's the one in real trouble.*

"Completing request."

Keale couldn't sit still. He got up and paced back and forth in front of the terminal. *Come on, Esmo. Come on.* The carpet felt soft and warm under his callused feet. His hands started to ache from how tightly his fists clenched.

The evacuation was going to cause a scene down there. Maybe not panic, but one hell of a general confusion, especially in the Getesaph port where everyone was sitting around waiting for something to happen. Ryan was right. Brador was going to have his ass over this. Which was why he was waiting to call Brador last. He had to get everything else in motion. Then, he'd find a way to explain to a veep whose own ass depended on schedules and calm that if they didn't create a little Holy Hell now, it was going to get a lot worse later. People, Human and Dedelphi, were going to get killed.

By evacuating, they would give the Dedelphi a taste of the only real threat Bioverse had stated it was willing to use. The Dedelphi weren't behaving, so the Humans were leaving. It might actually do some good.

Finally, the screen lit up. Esmo, wrapped in a thick, patchwork robe was in the act of sitting down and shoving her spectacles into place over her temple connections.

"What's happened?" she asked.

"We've got a boatload of soldiers up there with you, Esmo."

Her jaw worked itself back and forth. "Kaye, we've searched the place. We've had health and safety teams in there every day. We've—"

"I know." Keale told her, and for the first time in his life, he saw Esmo utterly stunned.

When she could move again, she lowered her head into her hands. "What are they doing? What in the Lawgiver's name are they doing?"

"I intend to ask them." Keale's voice was brittle. "But first, we've got your people to look out for. Esmo, what can you do?"

"Not a whole lot, Kaye. We're not set up for a siege, or a prison." She pulled a patch cord out of the station and hooked it up to her glasses. Keale watched her lips move silently for a moment.

She focused on him again. "Okay, I've sealed the maintenance hatches, and the pass-throughs to the other city." Her eyes flickered, glancing at something in the corner of her spectacles. "It's almost morning here. I'll send a directive to all personnel to get into the secondary domes during shift change. That'll cause the least confusion. Everybody's on the move then anyway. Then, we'll close off the corridors." Her expression turned rueful. "Hole up and wait. That's about what we're capable of."

"Okay." Keale nodded. "Do it. When your people are secure, we'll send mine into the main dome for a search and seizure."

"Kaye, you've got two hundred security guards armed with stunners and blinders. If Jasper's right, we've got three thousand trained killers up here."

"I know," said Keale quietly. "That's why I'll be going in first."

The captain said nothing, just nodded.

"See you in a few hours, Esmo." Keale cut the thread and sat there, alone and silent for a long time.

Then, he got up to go get dressed, and tried to think of what he was going to say to the veeps. Right now, it was all he could do.

* * *

"Dayisen Lareet! Dayisen Umat!"

Lareet sat bolt upright on the mattress. Her motion startled Umat, who lay beside her.

The two Ovrth Gert burst out of the stairwell, both panting like they had swum ten miles upstream. They hit the light controls, and the other dayisen who hadn't woken up at the shouts, lifted ears and heads.

Lareet and Umat had been up all night with the dayisen squad leaders at a planning session in the (hopefully) unmonitored living room downstairs. When it was decided everyone needed at least some sleep, they'd all retreated to the second floor.

"What is it?" Lareet climbed out from under the blankets. They hadn't gotten the wiring for the speakers laid yet, so sensitive information was being carried by runners rather than through the Human computer system, where they had no way to tell who was listening in.

"The Humans," wheezed Ovrth Brend. "They've sealed the pass-throughs."

The skin on Lareet's shoulders stiffened. "Did they give any explanation?"

"None that we know of." Ovrth Hral straightened up and tried to get her breathing under control.

Umat breezed past them and down the spiral stairs without a word. Lareet followed on her heels, along with the other dayisen. Umat laid her hands on the comm station and lit the screen up.

"No waiting messages, no general announcements," she reported.

"What do you think?" asked Lareet, half-afraid of the answer.

"I think we're out of time." Umat took her sister's hand and faced the dayisen.

"Send out the word to your groups. We go in one hour. Keep to written orders. Do not under any circumstances use the computer lines.

"We need the first-strike force at the launch point with the second-strike force assembled and ready to go. Dayisen Yntre, your sisters must make sure all the emergency lockers are covered. As soon as we start, we must have a flow of supplies. Dayisen Huln, your people cover the hatches. The third force must be ready to go down them as soon as they're clear."

"Remember," said Lareet, "if you kill them, it will be that much harder on your sisters and your daughters. We must make them concentrate their immediate efforts on rescuing their own. We must not make them believe it is safer to kill us all, or that we have killed so many of theirs that they act in anger. They are not impervious to emotion, no matter what rumors we hear. They are just slow to burn." She glanced at all the dayisen and saw them dip their ears in agreement.

Umat stood even straighter. Lareet would not have thought it possible. "We have one advantage they cannot overcome. They cannot destroy this ship without seriously crippling their mission. This will buy us time."

Lareet tried to pull her spine up as straight as her sister's, but her muscles resisted. "As long as they believe they can regain what they have lost, they will stay here. They will protect our sisters below from attack by the t'Therians. We must not drive them away too quickly."

Ears dipped again.

Umat bared her teeth. "The World Mothers stand beside us. We are their daughters, heart, blood, and mind. Because of what we do now, our daughters will be forever safe."

The dayisen kissed their own knuckles in blessing, then they streamed out of the too-narrow door and into the streets, where all of Mother Night's stars still shone overhead.

For a moment Lareet and Umat just stayed as they were. Lareet saw fear and excitement shining in her sister's eyes, and it was that sight that truly brought home the fact they were preparing for battle. With the Humans. Who built this city that floated so easily miles above the ground.

Mothers stand with us. We will need all your help today.

The morning Klaxon banged overhead. Praeis lifted herself groggily out of sleep. Theia stirred where she was draped across Praeis's torso. Raising her lids one at a time, Praeis finally gave herself a clear view of the unpainted ceiling with its unforgiving, suspended globe lamps. All around her, the sounds of grumpy, reluctant wakefulness told her another day in the service had begun.

The Klaxon silenced briefly, then began to bang again, louder and faster.

Now, Praeis Shin, it is time to set a good example. She lifted Theia off of her and stood up. Together, they started rolling up the blankets and sleeping mats into tidy cylinders. Around them, the rest of the administrative shift were doing the same.

Lockers were banged open. Mats and blankets were exchanged for buckets of soaps and scrub brushes. Praeis handed Theia hers. Theia accepted it, squeezed her mother's arm, and headed off to the baths with most of the shift.

It had become a silent routine. Theia would go to the baths, and as the room emptied out, Praeis would get the black box David had given her out from her locker. She watched her daughter join the stream of arms-sisters and noticed how small she looked, despite her years and height. What was she feeling? Praeis shared the waves of sorrow that washed through her, but even then sensed that Theia held something back. Theia had watched four sisters die, and now her pouch-sister was gone. Res, broad Res, lovely, lost, oh Ancestors Mine, where is she? Res was not just her pouch-sister, she was her last sister.

Praeis closed her eyes and clenched every muscle she possessed. *I cannot give way. I cannot give way. The Humans will find her.*

She opened her eyes and sat down on one of the long benches. She lifted the lid, revealing an injection pipette and rows of vials the size of the first joint of her little finger, filled with clear serum.

As had become her habit, she counted them. Fifty-three. She picked up the injector and slotted one of the vials into place.

Fifty-two, she thought as she held the pipette to her neck and sank it gently in.

She had just pulled it free when the dormitory door opened and Neys and Silv appeared in the doorway. Their ears were plastered flat against their scalps.

Adrenaline shot through Praeis's veins. Her arms-sisters spotted her and all but ran across the room.

"What is it?" she asked, closing the box quickly.

"The Humans are evacuating," said Neys. Her mouth twitched. She was keeping herself from panting, but with difficulty.

No. You did not say that.

Silv bared her teeth. "The Humans are pulling out. All their personnel. We've just come from the Queens. Apparently the Humans all got orders before dawn to pack up and get to the port, or to wait at their outposts for transport."

Praeis very carefully returned her precious box to her locker. She closed the door and faced her sisters again.

"Why?"

"We don't know!" Silv slammed a fist against a locker, rattling the doors. "All we can get out of them is 'This is what we were ordered, so this is what we're doing, out of the way please.' " She did a good imitation of a high, precise Human voice. "Ancestors Mine, you'd think none of them ever had an independent thought!"

That's what a lot of them say about us. Praeis rubbed her own ears. "All right. Let's get the shifts changed. I'll see if I can find out anything."

"Yes, Task-Mother," Neys and Silv chorused.

Praeis touched both their shoulders and strode out into the corridor with her arms-sisters one step behind.

The third shift was still on duty outside, sitting at their desks poring over books and papers, sipping hot drinks, and trying to keep awake and busy until the changeover. Neys and Silv split off to oversee the shift change and all its routine details that had to be checked, cleared, and signed off on. Praeis went straight to the main administrative office. There was only one light on, and if there were staffers who used it on the dark shifts, they were all on other errands.

This was an executive room, so it had a door. Praeis closed and locked it. She leaned on the handle for a moment, trying to steady herself. The Humans were evacuating. If the Humans were evacuating, they weren't searching for Res and Senejess. That was not permissible.

The equipment in the room was all fairly standard: desks, duplicators, speakers, stacks of charts, books, and forms. One wall, though, had been cleared of furniture to make room for a gleaming, Human comm station. Praeis hauled a folding chair in front of it. She touched the keys, which had been relabeled in the t'Therian alphabet and tried to think what to do. She couldn't call Lynn. Lynn wasn't there. She didn't know Lynn's assistants well enough to call them.

She typed the address for David Zelotes aboard the *Ur.*

Outside the door, she heard voices and footsteps. The corridors filled with sisters on their way to breakfast, or to bed, or to wherever they were ordered.

The screen lit up. David, suited and dressed, but not helmeted, peered out at her.

"Praeis? What's happened? Are you all right?"

"I'm fine," she said in English, forcing herself to mean it. "It's just a little crazy down here right now."

David's mouth twisted into a half smile. "Yeah, I guess it must be."

Praeis leaned forward. "David, I've got some very nervous sisters around me right now. Do you have any idea what this Human evacuation is about?"

He looked away quickly and looked back again. "They really aren't saying, Praeis. We're all supposed to hole up in the secondary domes and . . ." He shrugged irritably. "And I don't know what. I'm just behaving like a good little sheep and hoping someone will deign to tell me what's happening."

They haven't found Lynn yet either, have they? "I'm sorry, David. This must be killing you." All this time, and she still had to force herself to realize that David and Lynn were sisters, or as close as Humans could come to that bond.

He waved dismissively, but his face was still hard and angry. " 'Sokay," he said. "I know it's . . . You're . . ." He gave up. "If I find out anything, I'll let you know, okay?" It was all he had to offer right now, and it wasn't much, but Praeis felt small somehow accepting it. "I can get hold of you at this address?"

"Put a general call down to this station. One of my arms-sisters will find me."

"All right." He nodded. Then his expression shifted, and she was dealing with the doctor. "How are you feeling?"

"I'm good," she said firmly. "The treatments work. I am not sleeping well, but that could be—" A high-pitched whistle cut across her words. Her ears searched frantically for the source for a moment, before realizing it was coming from David's side.

A soft voice came down the thread. "All personnel report to secondary domes. Repeat. All personnel report immediately to secondary domes immediately. This is an emergency order. Repeat. This is an emergency order. Respond immediately."

Praeis felt herself beginning to pant. David's eyes widened. "I . . ."

"Go," she told him, and he left, without cutting the connection.

Praeis stared at the blank wall for a moment before she reached out with one trembling hand and shut the station down.

The Humans were being evacuated from t'Aori and the Hundred Isles. The Humans were being sequestered aboard their own ship, which was full of Getesaph, who had altered the relocation schedule so they would be in space before the t'Theria were.

Praeis got up and unlocked the door. She sat down again and waited.

Eventually, the door handles rattled, and the doors opened. Theia came into the office with Neys and Silv trailing behind her.

"Mother?" Theia crossed the room and laid a hand on her arm. "Are you good?"

Praeis's ears crumpled. "No. No, I am not."

"Ancestors Mine, Task-Mother, what's happened?" asked Silv.

"The 'Esaph aboard the *Ur* have rebelled," said Praeis.

Neys and Silv's ears instantly flattened against their scalps. Theia made a small noise and rested her forehead against her mother's shoulder.

Praeis straightened up and wrapped one arm around her daughter.

Did I say this war must not start? Well, they have started it without our help. Now there are other things we must do.

"We are going in. Neys, Silv get the Group Mothers. Tell them we are on the go. I will inform the Majestic Sisters we are operative."

Silv gawped at her. "How can we move without permission from the Queens?"

Praeis bared her teeth. "We must go, or there will be civil war. The Queens will realize that, but the debate will take time we do not have." *Time my sister does not have. Time my daughter does not have.* Anger rushed through her, at the Getesaph, at the Queens, at herself. The Burn nibbled at the edges of her mind. For a moment she wondered again if the troops would follow her, but she dismissed the thought. She'd felt the mood during the musters. They all wanted their chance at the Getesaph. The Queens were right. They would follow a thrown stone.

"We are not ready," said Neys softly.

Praeis shook her head. "We are very close." Both Neys and Silv stared. "I'm sorry, arms-sisters, I have been deliberately falsifying the readiness reports. I cannot now explain why. However, we do have a wave ready to go and two more that can follow in a hurry. All that's needed are my orders and the Queens'."

Neys's ears waved uncertainly. "What if they forbid it?"

"They will not forbid it. Not to me." Her blood sang in her ears. Res. Senejess. Her daughter and sister were out there in the country of the ones who had just broken the Confederation.

Silv's hand touched her forearm. "Task-Mother, you are not making sense."

"No." Praeis's nostrils clamped shut and flared open. "I am not. I must explain, mustn't I?" She laid her hand on the back of Theia's neck, but did not look at her. She kept her eyes and ears focused on her arms-sisters.

"Urisk Island, my arms-sisters. We were fighting the Getesaph for possession of that island and its four neighbors. We had four thousand of our Great Family on that island—mothers, sisters and daughters—all settled there. The Getesaph attacked and we fought and we lost and lost, and kept on losing. We were going to die, all of us. The Getesaph would have killed us all, because we would have done the same to them. I would have if I could. I had to get the Chosa ty Porath to help us. But the ty Porath wanted Urisk, and they wanted all four thousand of our Great Family removed.

"I tried to get the Great Family to move. I tried and Jos tried and Shorie tried. There were similar lands to be settled, there were other fathers that could pass along family souls. The ty Porath were ready to become near family if we gave them the island back. Think of that. One less enemy, one more family branch for our children and their children.

"But they wouldn't move, and the Council wouldn't make them, not for others, not even on the promise of them becoming near family. We'd all die bravely together they said.

"The ty Porath wanted the island clean, they wanted to take back the souls of their Ancestors that they say were stolen by our Ancestors who sailed there. All they wanted was one island, the Getesaph wanted all five. All ten thousand of us."

"So, you gave it to them," said Silv quietly.

"No," said Praeis. "The Queens ordered me to give it to them. They could not, they said, be seen to be uprooting members of our Great Family, but if those same sisters died in battle, it would be quite another thing.

"I obeyed those orders. I believed it was better to lose one island than five. I served, I serve, my Queens. I stood against Jos and Shorie until they also obeyed. I told the ty Porath how Urisk's defenses were laid out, where the comm towers were, how many of us were standing active, and how many were armed but at rest. Jos and Shorie helped acquire the exact details.

"And the ty Porath came in on our side, and the Getesaph fled behind their own walls. A week later, we lost the island to our erstwhile allies. Because my blood sisters and I ordered our troops to do nothing about it, we were hounded into exile. The Queens let us get away because they knew who had given the orders and that we would still be believed if we spoke before we could be killed." Her skin trembled. Theia pressed against her, and Praeis could feel the waves of horror, sorrow, and confusion spilling off her. She wrapped her arm tightly around her daughter, and kept on speaking. "They will give their consent to this mission. They will not make me speak now." She turned one ear toward Neys and the other toward Silv. "Are you with me in this?"

They hesitated just the barest instant. "Yes, Task-Mother," said Neys. Silv echoed her a second later. Then, with surprising force, so did Theia.

"My Sisters." Praeis grasped their hands. "My Daughter. We will do this. The Getesaph will pay."

Chapter XV

CLANG!

Marjorie Wilkes, junior engineer and victim of the graveyard shift, shot straight up in her chair. She sat in one of the engineering center's side cubes, sneaking in a little study for her mid-grade exams. Outside, a jumble of shouts and curses were muffled by the calm, forceful voice of Ozone, the ship's overarching artificial intelligence, ordering everybody who wasn't already there into the secondary domes immediately. Over it all, the chief engineer, her Uncle Teige, shouted:

"Ozone, clear the dome!"

Marjorie leapt to her feet and fumbled with the door latch. Barely an hour ago they'd gotten the order to stay in the secondary domes when the shift had finished. Most of the conversation since then had centered around the question of whether this was a drill, or the Old Woman catching paranoia from her friend Commander Keale, or whether there was something really going on over in the dome most of the crew called Pogo Town. Marjorie had been on the contagious-paranoia side of the argument. Especially since she'd spent most of the week before helping put together Keale's "extra precautions."

Now, as she slammed the cube door open, she was flooded with the sick feeling that she might have been wrong.

Out in the main dome, Marjorie was greeted by a wall of engineers' backs. On tiptoe, she was almost as tall as a Dedelphi, and she stared over shoulders and between heads, not believing what she saw.

The normally opaque dome was, by Uncle Teige's order, as clear as glass. Everybody's attention pointed toward the big dome of Pogo Town. A ragged hole gaped in the side. Debris spun off into space, blown by escaping air. One piece must have hit the engineering dome, causing the noise.

Where're the patch jobbers? thought the engineer side of her brain.

A pair of ladders had been laid against the deck. Two Dedelphi in white-and-yellow-webbed pressure suits gripped the rungs and crawled through the hole in the dome. Behind them, more Dedelphi handed out additional sections of ladder. One Dedelphi joined these to the ladder she was leaning against, as if she were laying down track. The other reached back to receive a big square of sheet metal, which she shoved against the dome. She was handed another sheet. She leaned that against the first, making a little tent over herself and her companion. Two more sheets made another tent smack up against the first. More sections of ladder were handed through. Another pair of Dedelphi climbed up behind the first. These had welding torches, braces, and clamps.

All at once, Marjorie saw what they were doing. They were building a tunnel. Out of steel. A tunnel heading straight for the engineering dome.

"Ozone, get the captain. Dump the video logs to security with a red scramble and a red alert." Teige's voice was more calm than she'd ever heard it. Normally, he seemed on the verge of an early heart attack. Marjorie glanced at him. His face was white as a ghost. "People, let's not stand here," said Uncle Teige. "Everybody get—"

"What the . . . ?" Someone pointed.

To the left and right of the tunnel, hatches in the deck, maybe half a meter in diameter, slid open. Four of them all together. Out of each rose an elongated mechanical assembly.

Here it comes. Marjorie actually crossed her fingers. *I swear I'll listen to anything Keale ever says after this if this just works, I swear. I swear.*

The guns unfolded themselves into a sleek shape that allowed for rapid fire and continuous reload.

"That's not in the spec," said someone else, high and sharp, on the verge of hysteria.

The guns, silent in the vacuum, opened fire. The hand of the nearest pogo exploded into a red cloud. She fell back. The helmet on another cracked and in the next second she had no face. She fell, too. The steel sheet she held began to topple. Two more pogos grabbed the steel. The wounded ones were handed down the ladder. A pogo with a welding torch fell next, blood and skin splattering against the improvised tunnel. Another pogo grabbed the equipment up and took her place, welding the steel sheets together. More sheets, more ladders and more braces. One of the Dedelphi glanced up at the Humans, stunned and staring inside their dome, and looked down to her work again as if they were nothing more than fish in an aquarium.

"All hands!" Captain Esmeraude's voice exploded over the intercom. "Cut and run! I repeat, cut and run! Reassemble at the main hangar!"

Marjorie felt her jaw drop. Cut and run. Sabotage what you could and get out of there. She knew the order existed, but she'd never in a million years expected to hear it given. All at once, exit instructions started scrolling across her camera eye.

"Ozone, cloud the dome!" shouted Teige, sounding more like his usually outraged self. The roof and walls resumed their normal milky color. Whatever was going on outside was going on without them. "Bran, Gale, get in the hole and find out what's going on down there. Do what you can. Colin, we're cutting out here. Everybody else, evac! Let's move it!" Uncle Teige's hands flew across his station while he talked. One by one, the engineering stations shut down.

Bran and Gale opened the floor hatches and clambered down the ladders. Colin yanked his pry-key off his belt and flipped open the nearest station's paneling. A pair of wire cutters gleamed in his other hand.

Marjorie forced her way out of the crowd of engineers and headed for the equipment locker. They had time, not much, but time. The welding equipment the pogos carried had given her an idea. They could melt large sections of wiring if they hurried.

"Marjorie . . ." began Uncle Teige angrily.

The dome shivered. A deep, resounding boom filled the chamber, followed fast by the sound of shattering doped-glass and a hurricane wind rushing toward the mouthlike hole in the dome's side. A few people fell onto their backs and were dragged out of the main path of the wind by friends. Through the ragged hole, Marjorie saw the Dedelphi and their tunnel just three meters away. The bullets sparked and ricocheted off the steel, but didn't cut through it.

The interior hatches slammed shut. Until the pressure stabilized, the hatches would not open again. They were trapped. Marjorie leapt for the patch locker.

"Two-by-two!" shouted someone.

Marjorie scanned the red labels on the patch frames and hauled out the two-meter-by-two-meter polymer patch. Hands grabbed the handles on the far side of the transparent patch. She looked up. Harry Dale. Together, they angled the patch into the wind. Through the new hole, the pogos looked up at them. They had packs strapped to their backs, and guns strapped to their sides. They slapped brackets onto their sheet metal to hook them together until the welders could get to them.

Marjorie's hands gripped the patch handles until her knuckles turned white.

"Let it go!" shouted Harry to be heard over the wind.

Marjorie let both handles go. The wind pushed the patch over the hole, and died away.

Through the transparent polymer, Marjorie saw the lead Dedelphi receive two more sheets of metal and set each up in turn until her colleague could bracket them in place.

"What in the shadow of sanity are they *doing*?" asked Harry.

Marjorie heard the distinctive *snickt* of the hatchways loosening again.

"One at a time, people," said Uncle Teige. He pulled the command word out of its slot.

Marjorie turned to join the line for the hatch. Behind her, something thick began to rip.

Calm vanished and took order with it. The air was filled with screams and shouts and everybody trying to cram themselves through the hatchways.

"Stop!" called a Dedelphi voice. "You will not be hurt if you stop right now!"

Without thinking, Marjorie looked for her uncle. He dropped the command key to the deck. A Dedelphi leapt forward and tackled him just as he brought his foot down to smash it. Another snatched the key off the deck.

Marjorie launched herself at the Dedelphi and seized the Dedelphi's wrist, grappling for the key. The startled pogo's eyes widened and despite its helmet, its nostrils slapped shut. Marjorie snatched at the word, but hands grabbed her around the waist and hauled her off.

As she was swung around she saw pogos in the middle of the crowd of Humans, dragging them out of the way and tossing them aside, ignoring the blows that some tried to fight back with. Two of them held Uncle Teige's hands.

Then she saw two more holding a polymer bag. She kicked out, connecting with leathery flesh. Something smashed into the side of her head, and she saw stars. Before she could regain control, her captors shoved her into a fetal position and stuffed her into the bag. She heard a *zip* and a *snap,* and they dropped her onto the deck.

She scrambled onto her knees. Her hands pushed at transparent polymer and her lungs heaved hard as she imagined her air being cut off. After a long, terrified minute she was able to identify what had happened.

They'd shoved her into a rescue ball. She'd been in one before. They all had training in the things before they got space duty. It was a very cheap, very compact escape capsule. When the thing hit vacuum, its micropores would seal and its autopressure would activate. She'd find herself in a thick-skinned bubble, with minimal directional control, and about six hours of air.

Where'd they get them all? Oh, right, the emergency lockers are stuffed full of the things. There should be one for everybody.

As her head cleared, her hands reached immediately for the zipper seals, and didn't find them. She blinked away the last of the stars and looked more closely at the opening. The inside tabs had been cut clean off.

"Bastards!" she breathed as she scrabbled at the seals, trying to find any kind of purchase to get them open. Nothing. She reached for her tool belt. It was gone.

Four other crew members lay similarly bagged on the deck. Harry, Toshi, Liv, Anjai. She couldn't see Uncle Teige. She squirmed around. He was on the other side of her. More bodies in more rescue balls were tossed next to them. She twisted toward the entrance hole. The tunnel was finished. Pogos swarmed up the ladders in an unbroken stream to meet their compatriots and receive their orders. A whole crowd of them barreled through the hatchways and into the ship. Another gang opened the deck hatches and swarmed down the ladders.

Five minutes, Marjorie crawled backward as far as her ball would let her. *Five minutes and they got us.*

"Marjie?" said Uncle Teige.

She turned around, shoving polymer out of her way as she did. "Hey, Unc," she said weakly.

"You're okay?"

"Yeah." She crossed her legs and tried to ignore the polymer pressing against her head like a tent falling down on its occupant. "What now?"

He cast a worried glance at the pogos taking over his command. She knew he must be seeing how every one of them carried a gun, and how there were no Humans left free. From the look on his face, he was also kicking himself for losing the command word.

"Now we wait and see why they've left us alive."

"All hands!" Captain Esmeraude's voice exploded over the intercom. "Cut and run! I repeat, cut and run! Reassemble at the main hangar!"

"Name of God!" Commander Rudu King shot out of his chair.

The rest of his crew was on their feet with him. His heart beat out of control. All twelve of them were expert at their jobs, but right now they were all looking right at him to ask what to do about a . . . What? Mutiny? Revolt?

Anger flared inside him. If their guests wanted the ship, they were going to have to work for it.

"You heard the order. Get to the hangars." He threw open the locker door and grabbed a pair of magnetic slippers. "I'm going to dump the grid." He kicked off his shoes and shoved the slippers on over his boots.

The crew looked at each other. He saw them thinking: *Dump? He's going to shut the gravity down?*

"It'll do the most damage and be impossible for them to undo."

He drew the command word out of its slot in the central table and tucked it into an inner pocket of his coverall.

Each tractor unit held a toroid of fast-rotating neutral particles. If charged particles were dumped into the mix, the carefully balanced particle doughnuts would start to burn out, letting loose X rays and good, old-fashioned heat. Lots and lots of heat. If you had to shut a tractor down, you were supposed to do it with the shields down and the area cleared. Shut them all down at once, without the proper precautions, and you could fry all six maintenance decks.

"Commander, it's not worth it," said Elisha, a good gravitor with a lousy singing voice that he exercised whenever he thought no one was listening.

"I say it is." King yanked open the floor hatch to the inner stairway. "Now, get out of here. Make it look like we all just ran for it."

Rudu climbed down the ladder into the grid shaft. It was a glass tube that was never as well lit as he'd like. The work platforms that stuck out at regular intervals all had their own little sources of white light. All around him, through the glass, he could see the tractors in their yokes. Their familiar push-and-pull buffeted at his body and his senses

Gravity at this level was tricky. With luck, that would slow the Dedelphi down. If they got into the wrong sections, the opposing forces and sudden flip-flops might actually make them sick and take them out of action. Most first-year gravitors puked their guts out for weeks.

On the other hand, the Dedelphi were incredible swimmers. Half possum, half seal, someone had once said. Who knew if the sensations of falling and not being upright would bother them as much as ground-based Humans.

King redoubled his speed.

At its least subtle, the gravity would turn you upside down if you climbed down too far. The grid was actually two grids, one for the A side, and one for the B side. Each grid pulled the objects on the surface toward the decks. So, when you crossed the ship's equator, up and down reversed themselves and no matter what your eyes told you, your whole body told you your feet now pointed at the ceiling. There was a red line at the switch-over point, but it didn't do anything to ease the transition.

This shaft took him down between sections AX-12/AY-12; 12/12 stretched into Pogo Town. From any one of the work platforms, he could angle the tractors out of phase, send gravity in all directions, shoving people sideways into the sides of buildings, or plaster them against the top of the dome. Do that first? Create some confusion?

No. It'd throw off any security actions. Worse, if he got it wrong, he could send one of those apartment buildings shooting through the dome like a rocket and endanger all their allies as well as their enemies. Anyway, rotating the tractors was something the Dedelphi could undo with the help of the computer, or a scared engineer.

No, shut off gravity and see how they liked dealing with all that water and everything from Dedelphi, to fish, to furniture, not to mention the soil, and all those plants rooted in it going into uncontrolled free fall, and as a bonus having the ship's vital works turned into one gigantic oven.

Bioverse would be taking the damage out of his pay from now 'til Doomsday, but he was not leaving his ship to the pogos. He was not.

Overhead, the hatch clanged shut, cutting off the shaft of light from the main control chamber. Somebody must have shut him in. The pogos must have made it down to gravitor's ops. If that hatch opened now, they'd see him, or they'd hear him. There was nowhere to hide.

Except maybe there was.

There was a platform just above the changeover line. King

opened the gate in the safety rails and climbed onto it. Above him, over the humming of the grid, he heard someone crank open the hatch.

King swung over the safety rail. He lowered himself over the platform's edge until he hung by his hands and his body dangled straight down the shaft. His feet were still a good meter from the changeover line. He prayed he was close enough and raised his legs until his toes touched the underside of the platform. He felt a slight push underneath him, like he was sitting on water, and he let go.

His head swooped down. He bit his lips. The soles of his slippers grabbed the bottom of the platform, and he hung there, head down. The weak magnets were helped just enough by the confused gravity so he stayed in place, an exotic icicle growing from the bottom of the work platform.

He gripped the support girders and pulled himself "up" until he crouched like a spider in the shadows.

Dedelphi climbed down the ladders. The Dedelphi, with their long, grasping toes, loved ladders. They called to one another in their own language, curses or orders, or shouts of excitement, King couldn't tell. He held his breath.

Don't think of it. Please, don't let them think of it.

One of the Dedelphi barked out a set of syllables. Two of them split off and started down a horizontal access tunnel. Two of them kept going down the shaft. They exclaimed loudly as they hit the changeover.

King let himself smile in the darkness.

He waited until the sounds of voices and struggles faded. He strained his ears. Nothing.

King crawled back onto the upper side of the platform and pulled himself back over the security rail. He faced the comm station and slid the command word into the auxiliary slot. He poised his hands over the keyboard and lined up the procedures in his head.

His palms sweated as he worked keys and icons. Each tractor had a bottle of neon gas hooked up to it. A simple electrical current run through the bottle would change the gas into plasma. Upon command, the bottle would open and vent the plasma into the gravity doughnut and start it burning.

What he had to get through first was dozens of questions for each grid section. It all amounted to the same thing. The ship is in full operation, why would you want to do something this stupid? Then there was the fact that none of the shields were down and the ship wanted to know why and King had to tell it to mind its own business.

He heard noise behind him. Hands and feet on ladder rungs. He kept typing. The noises got closer.

"Stop!"

He identified six grid sections to shut down.

"We are not supposed to shoot unless it is an emergency. This is an emergency."

He saw the request for final authorization appear. King's fingers moved to enter his code.

Thunder boomed, his body jerked, and his right knee gave. His fingertips brushed the edge of the keyboard as he fell, but couldn't reach the EXECUTE key. Gloved hands grabbed his arms. He saw a flood of red under his right knee.

Then he saw that there was nothing left below his knee.

He stared up at the Dedelphi, as if expecting an explanation. One of them reached into the socket beside his head and pulled out the command word.

She said a word in her own language, and then she switched over to English. "Make sure his wound is stanched and bandaged and take him to the airlock."

It was then the pain hit.

* * *

David shut the laboratory door behind him. He'd heard the cut-and-run order and had joined the river of bodies flooding the corridor to try to get to the main hangar before anything happened. As if something hadn't already happened. As the crowd shoved him along, he'd thought, *If this is going on up here, what's going on down on All-Cradle?* Nobody even knew where Lynn was. She might not be alive anymore.

Sorrow and rage tore through him, along with a sick, angry thought.

Now he stood alone in the middle of the lab. The only noises were his breathing, the hum of the analysis systems, and the faint sounds of the confusion outside.

The Dedelphi had broken out. They were filling the secondary domes and taking over the ship.

And I can stop it. He looked at the virus fridge.

All he had to do was open the fridge and get out two or three of the WKV samples and break them open. Ideally, he should get down to the air recyclers and break a sealed dish open inside the vents to the city domes, but even if he released the WKV here in the Human sections while the Dedelphi roamed in pressure suits, there was still a good chance that one virus would be able to take advantage of one mistake, and there would be nothing they could do.

If he moved fast, he could infect the entire ship very effectively. He might even find somebody to help him. If the plague found just two or three hosts, the entire three thousand could be sick and dying within a week.

If the Getesaph succeeded in taking over the ship, God only knew what they'd do with it. And God only knew what the t'Therians would do when they found out what had happened up here. And God knew what the Getesaph had done, were doing, to Lynn.

David crossed to the fridge. He laid his hand on the palm scanner. The door cycled open. He took out the first rack of flat-bottomed, glass culture eggs and set it on the table.

Their labels said these eggs held one of the strains of WKV influenza. If he infected the population of the ship, they'd develop wet coughs and a fever. Then there'd be the muscle spasms and dry coughing, and they'd know. As their cell pores opened and did not close, and poisons and confused signals overloaded their systems, the spasms would harden into paralysis and their breathing would become more and more labored, and they'd die.

He'd seen it often enough. He'd seen rows of patients in isolation beds, paralyzed, breathing on respirators, dignity gone, hope gone, eyes wide-open and staring, and mouths pulled open in eerie, unchanging grimaces.

The noise had faded outside. Silence pressed heavily against his ears. David subvocalized to his implant for directions down to the recyclers. There was a hatch not too far away. He could crack one egg into the water and one into the air vents, and keep hold of the last one to open when they came to get him.

The healthy would isolate the sick, if they didn't push them out the airlock. They'd look for the seat of contagion, and they wouldn't find it because by then it would be all around them, just like down below on All-Cradle.

He heard running footsteps outside the lab. His head jerked around. The footsteps ran past, and the door didn't open.

He looked at the eggs again. Freed from the cold, the WKV influenza was coming to life in there. It was a wonderfully compact and adaptable little organism. It was hardy and could bide its time. It could jump from host to host in the air or in the water. As a WKV strain, it could kill in a few days, if nothing was done.

His hands shook at his sides. *They took Lynn,* he reminded himself. *They took Lynn, and nobody knows where she is, or if she is still alive.*

In his mind's eye, he saw the rows and rows of dying patients in their isolation beds, unable to touch their sisters and their daughters, who hovered outside their beds, pressing hands and faces against the polymer shells that trapped their dying mothers or sisters or daughters.

But they had Lynn. They had the ship.

He heard the door open. He heard a gasp.

"Don't move!" shouted someone in Getesaph. She switched to tortured English. "Don't move, or you will be shot!"

David kept his hands at his sides.

"Thank you," he whispered.

Captain Elisabeth Esmaraude sat at her station, amazed at how calm she felt. She was not a military commander. Dealing with organized attacks was not in her job description. There hadn't been any real pirates in centuries. As Humans made contact with various alien species, it turned out they were interested in trading goods, not violence. The few aliens they hadn't managed to establish communications with had just left them alone, which was fine with everybody.

In short, this was not supposed to be happening. Maybe that was what kept her calm. Part of her was treating it as a weird sim exercise.

An info-dump had gone out to Keale. He was probably about halfway to the *Ur* from Base by now. He and his people would do whatever they could.

She'd sent the officers down to the hangars with their orders. Get everybody into the shuttles and off the ship. They had a thousand people on this ship, and none of them had signed up for this kind of hazard duty. They had to be gotten out of the way.

She'd hooked her spectacles into the ship's video and saw engineering stand around too long, staring at the Dedelphi and their makeshift tunnel.

She'd looked down into the hangars and seen that engineering wasn't the only bunch who had been too slow. Who could blame them? This wasn't real. This shouldn't be happening. The Dedelphi had the hangars and all the people in there. People were being sealed into rescue balls and left in heaps on the decks.

There was a short running battle through the maintenance decks between the invaders and Keale's security people, but they were too heavily outnumbered, and it didn't last. Rudu had made a good try down on the gravity deck, but now . . . She didn't want to think about what she'd seen.

People had slammed bulkheads shut, cut the power, waded into battle with all kinds of improvised weapons. They pulled off the Dedelphi's helmets and left them choking and coughing on the deck. They blinded invaders with fire extinguishers, tripped them with wires, shocked, scalded, and beat them to death.

In response, the Dedelphi had cried out, "Medical emergency!" and the overrides had opened the bulkheads to gain free passage. They had found maintenance jobbers in the corridors and ordered them to repair the wiring and cut apart the booby traps. Keale had sealed off most of the voice commands to everyone but the crew, but jobbers answered anyone. That was the point of jobbers.

The Dedelphi had lain in wait for their attackers, lurking in side tunnels, clinging to bracing. They had tangled them in nets, tripped them, clubbed them with the guns, tied them up with tape and fishing line, stuffed them into rescue balls, and piled them up.

Dedelphi had died. Lots of them. But each death made the rest tighter, more alert.

They were coming to the bridge now. She could see them. They were down in the maintenance deck heading carefully toward her.

So, time to get moving. She was slow, she was stupid and unprepared, and she'd only half listened to Kaye, but she was all this ship had as a captain. Some orders the ship would not accept from anybody else.

Like the one to shut the engines down stone cold, now. And the one to close down power to the food plants and the water purifiers. Nothing she could do about the air, really, but she could shut down the scrubbers and the heating vents, and dump the regulator data. She tied every crucial database she could think of up tight.

Then there was the command Keale had created, in case worse came to worse. "Ozone?"

"Yes, Captain."

"Mind wipe."

"Completing request."

Those were the last words the AI would ever say. Right now it was in there eating out its own brain. If the pogos wanted to do anything with this ship, they would have to enter in each and every command sequence themselves, without any help.

The inner hatch opened and a half dozen Dedelphi spilled into the room. Esmaraude swung her chair around and pulled out the command word as she did it. The Dedelphi looked bewildered, she thought, to see no one left but her.

"You will not be hurt," said the leader in lilting English. "We want the ship."

"It's yours." She held aloft the command word for them to see, and before any of them could move, brought it crashing down against the console.

Lareet nudged the fragments of the shattered command word with her toes. The captain had let herself be led quietly away down to where the rest of her people were being held. Now, only clean-suited sisters filled the command center. Umat stood next to the captain's station, listening to Dayisen Wital give the rest of her report.

"We captured two of the three command words," said Dayisen Wital. "The head count of prisoners matches the duty roster for the ship. There have been three Human casualties, one very serious, but so far no deaths." Her ears lowered involuntarily to her scalp. "We lost six hundred sisters."

Lareet squeezed Umat's shoulder and lifted her ears to the dayisen around them. "We will mourn our sisters. This ship is the payment of their life debt. They, we, have done well. Very well."

The dayisen swelled with pride.

"Do we have any idea what Keale's doing?" asked Umat.

One of the Ovrth Ondt bustled over. "We have a call from engineering; they estimate about twelve cutter-style ships on their way."

Umat nodded. "Dayisen Wital, start tossing out the prisoners. That will keep them busy for a while."

"What do you think they will do, Sister?" asked Lareet softly.

Umat shrugged. "At this point, I have no idea. I am hoping they don't either."

The shuttle *Theodore Graves* accelerated hard and pushed Keale back into the swaddling couch. The *Graves* was too small to have a gravity deck, so they had been under acceleration gee all the way out. He had rotated the couch so he was sitting upright and able to reach the worktable his portable had been slotted into. Around him, two dozen of his people had done the same. They conferred with their machines, their implants, or one another, in quiet, confident tones. All of them avoided looking at him.

Keale had threaded into the shuttle's exterior cameras, and his portable screen showed him the approach of the white blur that would eventually resolve itself into the *Ur*. From this distance, it was unlikely that they'd see anything useful, even an escaping shuttle, but he wanted to look anyway. Esmo's info-dump had reached him two hours ago. He'd quick-scanned it, looking for something that could be done, something that could be exploited to bring this disaster to a quick close. There wasn't much.

What he really wanted to do was shout at the Dedelphi overrunning the ship. "What do you idiots think you're doing?" he wanted to say. "Do you know what we'll do to you? To your sisters on the ground? Do you have any idea what we can do to all of you? Obviously not, because if you'd stopped to think about it, you wouldn't have pulled this suicidal stunt!"

Instead, he turned to his staff. "Ashe, how're the spy 'lites coming?"

Ashe, a big-boned, serious, golden-haired woman, murmured something to her implant. "The guys in the *Tamulevich* say they'll have them up and flying by the time we get there."

Good enough. "Whalen, anything on the long-range?"

The sand brown man bent over his own portable and shook his head. "All quiet. Whatever's going on in there, it's staying in there."

"Anything on the computer lines?"

"Not since the cut-and-run order came." Whalen touched a few keys. "We're not picking up anything, not even maintenance calls between the AI and the jobbers. Whatever they're doing, they're not talking about it anywhere we can listen in."

Probably using paper, or their hardwired speakers. Primitive, but completely secure from Human spying.

For the moment, he told himself. *For the moment only.*

He felt old. Old and tired and worried. There were Humans in there, and he was responsible for them. Esmo was with them. If the Dedelphi were not willing to talk . . . Alternatives would be found. He would get the people out.

Movement on the camera display caught his eye. His heart froze. Something white and about the size of a grain of sand, drifted away from the *Ur,* heading at a forty-five-degree angle up from its disk. Another flew in almost a straight line from the plane. Another dropped off at a ninety-degree angle.

The bridge crew must have noticed it, too, because the camera suddenly zoomed in on the first of the grains. First, Keale saw it was round. Then, he saw it was clear with a dark center.

Then he saw it was a rescue ball. With an occupant.

He touched the intercom key. "This is Keale. Pull the shot out again."

"Acknowledged," came the voice of Holger Redding, the *Graves*'s copilot.

The camera's view pulled back. More white grains had joined the first, each heading on a separate trajectory from the others, spreading out at every possible angle. Some of them got caught in the ship's gravity field and bounced hard against the dome, eventually settling into orbit around the big ship like tiny moons.

Keale had an abrupt vision of a cluster of Dedelphi in the number five airlock grasping the Humans in their rescue balls and heaving them out into the vacuum.

Deliberately scattering them to keep us at a rescue for as long as possible. Keale felt his mouth harden. *And it's going to work, too.*

His attention was still glued to the screen, but his hands flew across his portable's keys, slaving the *Graves*'s intercom to the rest of the fleet.

"Attention, all personnel. This is now a rescue mission. Top priority. We have to assume there's going to be the full thousand of them." *And we* are *going to get them all.*

"Anderson?" He hailed the *Graves*'s pilot. "Head us in, top speed. Shuttle group, fan out, make sure we cover all sides of the *Ur. Aubrey, Maturin, Hough,* you take the far side. *Tamulevich, Deku, Brian,* take the downside. *Everson* and *Sampson* will take the near side. *Hale,* hang back and circle us, pick up anybody who slides through."

Affirmative replies flooded back to him, and he felt marginally better. A lot was going to depend on the pilots. Much of the success of this rescue boiled down to a physics problem: velocity, trajectory, and force.

And speed.

"Suits, people." Keale planted his magnetic slippers on the deck and undid his couch straps.

All security personnel on the Bioverse rolls were trained in as many kinds of space-based search and rescue as the system guard could think up. They could do this. They would do this.

Down in the hold, Keale shut himself into one of the suit lockers. He stripped out of his clothes and put on a skintight, white singlet that covered him from toe to neck. In a stall that was the size of a small shower, careful waldos covered him with organic insulation and a bright yellow layer of pressure webbing. Over it, he strapped the backpack harness with the helmet collar attached. He pulled a patch cord out of the collar and hooked it up to his temple implant. He locked on the helmet, slid on the gloves, knee and elbow braces, and boots.

Out in the common area, he helped his people on with their batteries and air tanks, and was helped on with his. Nobody spoke beyond the ritual fit-and-function checks. Everyone was too distracted by what they'd seen outside.

The *Ur*'s actual crew members were experienced spacers. They'd be all right. The rest of the personnel, though, a lot of them would just be sim trained. Right now, they would be tumbling around, frightened, confused, and probably a mess, with their own vomit bouncing around the ball with them. Most of them would be completely unable to see that help was on its way.

Keale and his people made their way down into the cargo bay. The shuttle had not been designed as a rescue vehicle. Instead of one huge hatch like ambulance ships, it had three small airlocks on either side of its single, cavernous bay. The *Graves* was empty of cargo, but not for long.

"I want six to a lock, two outside to grab, two to run the hatches, and two to get those people out of the rescue balls and make sure they're all right. Rotate positions every two hours." Keale rattled off assignments, finishing with, "Ashe, Deale, Chung, Skelly, and Vera, you're with me at number four."

Ashe and Vera followed Keale into the number four lock. Skelly shut the inner door. The world hummed and whirred and whooshed as the small chamber depressurized. Each of them instinctively grabbed one of the handholds.

The outer door cycled open and let in all the light-flecked darkness of the universe. Keale felt the brief dizziness that came from having nothing between himself and infinite vacuum.

Purpose and training took over. Ashe pulled a tether out of its rack. She jacked one end into the socket to the right of the airlock and hooked the other end to Keale's belt. She turned around, and Keale connected her to the left side of the lock. They held on and waited for their chance.

From where Keale was, the rescue balls were as big as medicine balls, and he could make out the doll-sized Humans inside them. There were still more being tossed out the airlock. A few people had worked their hands into the ball's gloves and had managed to hang on to each other, turning the individual bubbles into strings like model molecules.

The *Graves*'s pilots were done hurrying. The shuttle moved at a steady, leisurely pace. They steered carefully into the nearest group of rescue balls. Some of the bubbles' occupants spotted the ship and tried to scramble around to get a better view, sending their containers rolling gently over.

"Okay, airlocks," came Anderson's voice across Keale's suit intercom. "It's up to you."

"Let's go," said Keale to Ashe.

He let go of the handle and gave himself a small shove out into the blackness. His tether played out behind him. He turned his head and focused his attention on the nearest rescue ball.

"Guide to target," he murmured to his implant. The suit's jet pack squirted once, veering him off at a sharp angle. He stretched his hands out. The transparent rescue ball filled his view. There was a teak-skinned man inside with an expression of relief on his face so intense it was almost painful.

Keale's hands collided with the ball and found two of the multiple handles that covered the outside.

"Back," he ordered. The suit spoke to the tether, which began reeling Keale and the man back toward the shuttle.

Ashe was already back in the airlock with her first rescue. Keale guided his man's rescue ball inside, and Vera cycled the outer door shut.

There's two. Keale looked out at the clusters of floating bubbles. *Hold on out there. We're on our way.*

Four and a half hours and six hundred people later, Keale sat in the shuttle's main compartment with a tired and grim Esmaraude next to him. She had both hands wrapped around a soft beaker of coffee. He was sucking down water. His shoulders ached, and his arms felt like rubber hoses.

"They got the engineering word, but they didn't get mine," said Esmo. "I've got no idea about gravity. Has anybody found Rudu King?"

Keale nodded. "He's in sick bay, but they had to knock him out." Pain creased Esmo's face. "He'll be all right, they said. Just going to need his leg jump-grown."

"We were too slow." Esmo scowled at her hands holding the coffee bulb. "Stood around like sheep, going 'What the heck is that, boyo?' "

"Excuse me," interrupted a man's soft voice.

Keale looked up to see Dr. David Zelotes. The man looked haggard, but not shattered like some people they'd pulled in.

"Yes, Doctor?" said Esmo.

Zelotes was looking directly at Keale, and Keale knew what was coming next. "I was wondering if there'd been any word about Lynn Nussbaumer."

"There wasn't when I left," said Keale as kindly as he could. "But I'll reel a thread out to Base. Something may have come in since."

"Thank you." Zelotes tried to straighten himself up. "There're a lot of contusions and broken bones and shock among the evacuees, Captain, but everyone's in decent shape." It was as if he was trying to be useful as an apology for interrupting.

"Thank you, Doctor," said Esmo briskly. "Let us know if there's anything you need." She spoke as if she were still aboard her fully stocked ship, not aboard an underequipped shuttle retreating to its base.

"I will." Zelotes turned around and headed back for the hold.

Esmo shook her head and whispered, "Poor bastard."

"We've all done everything we can," said Keale softly. "What we've got to decide is what to do next. Assume the Dedelphi have two command words, what can they do?"

Esmo swallowed a little more coffee. "Not a whole lot that's immediately useful. The AI's gone. I shut down the engines, sealed up everything I could think of from my station. They'll need the captain's word to get that undone."

Keale drummed his fingers on his thigh. "So they can't even move the thing until they decrypt the command codes."

Captain Esmaraude lowered her coffee beaker. "You don't think . . ."

"They are at least going to give it a good try, Captain. Whether they can or not . . . They've tapped our communications, they've stolen one of our ships. I'm not going to be the one who says they can't solve one of our codes." He let out a sigh. "Until then, however, they've stolen an island." He scowled at the city-ship sitting serenely in the middle of his portable screen. "We need to find a way to spy on their conversations, but we're working on that. By tomorrow we'll have a sat-net thrown up to keep an eye on them." He paused. "Maybe we can get one of the engineering ships down from the asteroid belt and take the place apart around them. There might be some ways the nanotech teams could make it too uncomfortable to live in there . . ." He let the sentence trail off. There were possibilities. Plenty of them. He had to believe that right now, or he was no good to anybody.

"Well"—Esmo swigged some more coffee—"if it's any consolation, you were right."

Keale snorted. "I was wrong, Esmo. I was preparing for a spontaneous attack, a mob action. I completely failed to consider an organized, carefully planned takeover by a group of people who had studied us for a long time." He laughed once. "Never, ever trust the stats, Esmo. They lie."

"What do you think they're going to do now?"

Keale shook his head. "I've got no idea. Try to attack the t'Therian city-ship, maybe. Take all those virus samples we've got in there and dump them over the t'Aori peninsula. Find a big rock to drop, maybe. They've done that before."

Esmo studied her coffee. "So what are we going to do now?" she asked calmly.

"First"—Keale looked at the tiny, glowing city-ship on his screen—"we're calling the home system and getting reinforcements." His eyes narrowed as he looked down at the city-ship again. "Then, we're going to show our guests just what kind of trouble they're in."

Chapter XVI

The carrier crept forward another few feet. Arron shifted his weight from one buttock to the other. They'd been riding in the carrier's canvas-roofed cargo bin for the better part of an hour. Balt and Entsh had been able to take them most of the way using the security tunnels. They'd made good time, although being surrounded by the reek of gasoline and smog and the constant echo of traffic noise had not made for a comfortable trip.

They'd had to emerge onto the main streets when they reached the town of Mrant Chavat. Too many checkpoints, down below, Balt had told them. This close to the port fortifications, the cargo bin would have to be inspected.

Arron ran his hand across the stubble on his chin and his scalp. He itched. He also stank, but Lynn assured him it was all right; she did, too. Lynn sat on the opposite side of the bin from him. Res huddled under the canvas openings at the rear, where the air circulation was best. Her skin was still twitching way too much, he noticed.

None of them had spoken since they climbed into the carrier. Lynn leaned against one of the support struts for the canvas and pretended to be asleep. He suspected her infection was taking more out of her than she wanted to admit. The skin around the bandage was swollen and cherry red, with dark streaks running through it. The liquid seeping out from under the ragged cloth had a greenish tinge that could not be good.

He'd called her his sister yesterday. It was the only Getesaph word for a close relationship. "Friend" didn't really exist. Ally was a transitory term. Those who were closest to you could only be sisters, mothers, or daughters. There were no words in Getesaph for how he had felt when he had seen her again after all these years.

God, he'd missed her. Not just for the sex. He'd had that, as needed. The Human population on the Getesaph's Earth was not that small, and it circulated fairly regularly. He'd missed her laugh, her voracious intelligence, her sharp opinions, her ways of speaking.

There had never been anybody like her, before or since. He'd wanted to rescue her. To show her this had all been a mistake. To explain why she was going about her project all wrong in a way she'd understand.

Then, when she'd heard about the *Ur*, she'd said, "David," and he'd felt something inside him snap in two.

This is crazy. He leaned his head back against a strut and stared up at the rippling canvas ceiling. *This is completely crazy. My friends, my family are committing suicide out there, and I'm sitting here being jealous of Lynn's . . . whoever.*

Arron tried to find something else to think about. He couldn't hear any of the town noise over the rumble of the engines and the rattle of struts. Shadows of buildings and traffic passed outside the canvas. He could smell the city smells of smog and fish and garbage and spices.

A shrieking roar sat him bolt upright. The carrier jerked to a halt. Other noises joined the shriek: a distant *boom* and *crump.*

Oh, no.

"What!" exclaimed Resaime.

Lynn sat up, groggy but wide-eyed.

Arron scrambled to the rear of the carrier. Resaime scuttled aside. He undid one of the ties and raised the canvas.

The cloud blanket had broken to let some blue gleam through. The shriek began again and Arron saw the black wedges of warplanes streak across the sky. The *crump* and *boom* of the shore batteries split the city noises. Which meant more planes were coming.

A new shriek started, and nearby he heard a bang. His gaze jerked to a rooftop. Somebody had a rocket gun set up on a tripod. They fired it, and it went *bang!* with a flash and cloud of smoke, and the planes appeared overhead and a cloud of flame blossomed out of the side of one. A cheer went up, until one of the black wedges swooped back toward them.

Something dark fell from it. Reflex yanked Arron's head and shoulders back into the carrier.

"Cover!" he shouted, curling into a ball, for all the good it would do.

The explosion was a thousand separate noises: crumbling stone, screams, crackling dust, rising fire, and tearing metal. The carrier rocked sideways, hard, wheels lifting up off the ground and slamming back down again.

The noise rolled on, but didn't start over. Soon the sounds of shouting voices and running feet overwhelmed it.

One bomb, that was all. For the moment.

"What the hell?" demanded Lynn.

"Air raid." Arron straightened up.

Lynn's face went chalk white. "Oh, God. Res, are you—"

A wailing siren cut the air. "Shhhh." Arron waved her quiet. The initial wail was followed by the slow, measured beating of a gong.

Res and Lynn stared at him. "Call to arms." He slumped backwards. "There's a war starting."

"Out!" shouted Entsh from the cab.

"What?" said Lynn.

"Out! Out! We have to report for duty."

"But we need . . ." began Arron.

"You need to find your own kind and get out of here," said Balt. "We have to report, so you have to take your pet *devna* and go."

Lynn opened her mouth again, but Arron laid a hand on her arm and shook his head. Not this time. Duty came first.

Arron climbed out of the carrier, followed by Lynn. Resaime, shaking all over, climbed out after them.

"Good luck," shouted Balt as the carrier engine's hum raised to a screaming pitch and it accelerated into the crowd, leaving them standing on the cracked pavement.

Everyone was running in different directions. Someone bumped into him, looked at him, and screamed. Arron tried to back away and collided with someone else, who shouted and shoved at him. A mother snatched a daughter out of his path. Someone shoved him sideways so hard he fell, hitting the pavement with his shoulder.

"Get away, Human!" she shouted.

He managed to look up and see Lynn. She and Res had made it into a doorway. Lynn stood over Resaime, shadowing Res with her body, so no one would see that the sister had the telltale blue tint to her skin that marked the t'Theria.

Arron got to his feet and forced a path over to Lynn and Res. He tried the handle on the door behind them. It gave, and the door opened onto a dim corridor.

No one needed any urging. Lynn and Res bundled inside.

The building was a market. Distribution stalls on one side, warehouse area on the other. Stairs ran up to the office area and quarters for the family who worked the place.

"Wait in here," said Arron hurriedly. "Find something sturdy to get under and lie low. No one will be back until well after the attack's over. I'm going to go find help."

Lynn nodded mutely. Res dipped her ears. Her skin sagged so badly she looked like she was ready for the Change.

Arron made himself turn around and walk out the door.

The world outside had gone insane. The streets were jammed with people. The frame cars and carriers, stuffed with sisters, most of them armed, couldn't move for the crowds, no matter how energetically the drivers shouted. The call to arms was now punctuated with general announcements. What snippets he could make out under the cacophony of the shore guns were about reporting to shelter or duty stations. He glanced up. Huge blue-and-grey multipropped helicopters flew over the bay. He squinted toward the horizon and saw the black oblongs of distant war cruisers.

What's happening? Who's doing this? Looking at the 'copters didn't help. Straining to hear the PA announcements didn't either.

Arron stood alone on the edge of the chaos. For the first time in ten years, he felt totally cut off from the world.

Get it together, Hagopian.

Balt and Entsh had said he should find his own kind. Right now, that wasn't a bad idea. If he remembered right, Mrant Chavat was a fair-sized port. There might be a trader or embassite down on the quays. There might even be some Bioverse personnel. Somebody with a boat, or a van.

Arron raised his collar and hunched his neck down. He pulled his sleeves over his hands and clutched the hems from the inside so the cloth covered his hands. His trousers and boots were in one piece, which was something, but there was nothing he could do about his bare, hairy face, nothing he could do about a lot of things, except move fast.

One good thing, with an invasion on, Balt and Ensh's employers probably won't have the chance to grab us again.

Arron stepped into the mainstream of foot traffic. Mothers saw him and pulled up short, yanking their children into their arms and leaving holes in the crowd for him to duck through. People scrambled to get away from him, knocking down their mothers and sisters. Arron winced but let them fall. The only favor he could do everyone right now was get out of their way.

He headed west, hugging the buildings on the edge of the crowd, dodging past doorways as fast as he could to avoid the sisters charging down the stairs with their guns, or the mothers with their children and bundles. The constant roar of the guns was making his ears go numb, but now he heard a new sound. Water splashed somewhere to his right. He saw a narrow space between two buildings with light at its end. Arron turned himself sideways and slid into the crack. Chest and back scraping against rough concrete, he shinnied sideways through garbage, decaying leaves, and guano and out into the next street.

A quick glance showed he was in a crooked street that ran along the ridge of a sandy bank. Ladders led straight down to the docks. The grey-green harbor was choked with boats trying to get to shore. Some sisters just abandoned the vessels and ran for the shore, hopping from deck to deck. Some dived into the water and swam under the hulls. Out toward the mouth of the bay, the shore guns targeted the invading ships. The shells mostly landed in the water, raising huge gouts of foam, but here and there, Arron could see them hit the invaders' decks, raising a gout of fire instead.

While the civilians tried to get inland to report to their shelters or militia units, the uniformed soldiers were heading for the water. Low, flat, armored transports lay waiting for them in the restricted areas of the harbor. Arron knew what was coming next. The soldiers were heading out to mine the harbor and to try to attach bombs to the hulls of the invading ships. They'd be joined by the troops who waited in the underwater bunkers, holed up like clams in their shells. The tunnels under the bay would be at least as busy as the docks, but probably more organized. Arms, supplies, and sisters would be shuttled to their stations.

The invaders, in turn, would send their own troops into the water to stop the troops and the mines and to destroy the bunkers.

A glint caught his eye and he saw, short and pale among the pinkish grey Dedelphi, a clean-suited Human arguing with a trio of soldiers. Ignoring the ladders, Arron half scrambled, half slid down the sandy slope. His boots hit the dock. Instantly, he was surrounded by a forest of shoulders and backs. He dodged his way through. All at once, he found himself in a still, clear spot, nose-to-nose with a familiar face.

"Cabal!"

The trader blinked, as if he was having trouble focusing. "Arron! What the hell are you still doing here?"

Got a year, Cabal? "It's a really long story. Have you got your boat?"

Cabal glowered at the soldiers. "I'm trying to find out."

Arron looked up at the soldiers. Three ovrth, by the bands on their cuffs. "The light of day looks good on you, Sister Ovrth," he said in his best, most formal Getesaph. "I am Scholar Arron Hagopian."

"Scholar Arron?" The pinkest of the three held her ears up straighter. "What a delight to meet you. I wish the time permitted something other than a hasty greeting."

Since Arron had no ears to dip, he bowed his head. "So do I. I came here to find Trader Cabal. Her boat is required to evacuate the remaining Humans from the danger area."

Cabal gave him a startled look, but kept his mouth shut.

"The Humans have all been evacuated. *Bioverse* took care of that," said Ovrth Pink.

"Not all." Arron shook his head. "The last few need to be removed to a neutral island. Cabal has been authorized to take them out. I have come to find her."

The ovrth looked dubious. "I do not want you to get in trouble, Sisters, but Bioverse will want to know why their personnel were endangered without cause," added Arron.

Their ears all twitched uneasily. "The boat must be removed

from the harbor," said one with a crisscrossing of scars on the backs of her hands.

"Of course," said Cabal. "As soon as possible."

The shortest of the soldiers made some marks on Cabal's harbor permit and handed it back to him. Cabal stuffed it into his pocket. He and Arron walked a ways down the dock, where the crowd had room to flow around them.

"I owe you for that," said Cabal. "I tried to make one run too many. Missed my ride out. What happened to you?"

Arron's tongue froze to the roof of his mouth. "There was a mix-up," he said at last. "I need to get out."

"No problem," Cabal said easily. "I'm ready to go now."

Arron held up his hands. "I've got a friend and a t'Therian who need to go with me."

"A t'Therian!" Cabal's voice dropped to a stage whisper. "Are you crazy? Those are the t'Therians out there!" He stabbed his finger toward the mouth of the harbor. "If the Getesaph catch her, she's dead."

"I know that," said Arron flatly. "Do you think you could get us out to one of the warships?"

Cabal shook his head. "I do owe you, Arron, but making a run out to the enemy ships across an aquatic war zone, it is not worth it. It's just not."

Arron licked his lips. He should have known. Cabal had never been exactly altruistic. "What would make it worth it?"

"What?" Cabal's forehead wrinkled.

"What would make it worth it?" asked Arron urgently. "My friend, she's a senior with Bioverse. She can pull more strings than a nest of spiders. What would make the run worth it?"

The incredulity on Cabal's face bled off into consideration. "A trip back to Sol."

"Easy. There's ships back and forth all the time."

"You shouldn't sound so desperate, Arron." His mouth twisted. "It makes it hard to believe you can do what you're saying."

"Come on, Cabal." Arron tried to force some easy camaraderie into his voice. "You know me."

"Yeah, I do." Arron was taken aback by the irony in his tone. "And I'll bet you're willing to swear to me she's got pull with the Mars colony trade council, too."

This time, Arron's grin was completely genuine. "Let's put it this way. Help me, and you'll be saving one of the daughters of the founding family."

Cabal gave a low whistle. "You've got a Shin t'Theria? Here? What have you been doing?"

"I told you, there was a mix-up."

"Yeah, right. Okay," Cabal looked across the harbor. The armored transports pulled away from the dock. Another flight of planes screamed overhead. "Okay, get them down here. I'll get the engines going so we can get out fast. The more we delay, the uglier the way out is going to get."

I'm with you there. "Okay, but one thing, Cabal. Have you got any spare clean-suits on board?"

Cabal actually gave him a small smile. "Anything else, Monsewer?"

Arron shrugged. "A couple bottles of water and some carbo-protein rations, if you've got any. And a medikit."

Cabal gave a startled laugh. "Suits and supplies and a suicide run. Hagopian, she'd better be Shin t'Theria."

Arron grinned. "I swear on my doctoral thesis."

"I suppose I can accept that," Cabal sounded warier than Arron would have liked. "Okay, let's get you your goodies."

The planes were still flying when Arron emerged from Cabal's boat, freshly clean-suited and with a backpack of supplies slung over his shoulder. He climbed the ladders up to the street and found his narrow pass-through. He was halfway along it, wincing as his helmet grated against the building's cement walls, when he heard the whistle, the screams, the bass rumbles, and the multi-layered sounds of destruction that meant the bombs had started falling on Mrant Chavat.

Arron cursed and tried to move faster. The cement dragged at his new clean-suit, slicing into the organic. Another bomb fell. The ground trembled, and the buildings on either side of him swayed. He cursed again and pulled himself out into the street.

It was deserted. Everyone from this quarter was where they needed to be. He saw a dust cloud farther inland, and the remains of one of the major bridges. Firelight reflected on the buildings that still stood.

Don't stand here gaping. You've got to get Lynn and Res out of this!

He forced himself into a run. Planes roared and screamed. Whistles, crumps, bangs, the tattered sound of fires filled the world. Arron tried to block it out and concentrate on which way he was going.

He turned onto the nameless street that held the market building. The smell of dust and burning worked its way through his helmet. Arron looked up.

The market building wasn't in its place. Instead, there was a pile of rubble with broken girders sticking up through it and sparking wires bristling here and there.

"No!" He ran to the mound. He grabbed a stone and heaved it aside. He dug his hands into the dirt, flinging it every which way. He threw back more stones, and more dirt.

"Sister, Sister," said a Getesaph voice. "It's all right. The building was empty."

Arron stared at the owner of the voice, a stooped mother with her grown daughters beside her. "It wasn't empty. There was a mother and daughter in there. I told them to wait in there."

The mother blinked. Without another word, she and her daughters lunged at the pile of rubble, lifting rocks and scooping dirt.

Arron clawed and scrabbled at the stones, sending them rolling down the mound.

This is not happening. This can't be happening. I got help. We were going to be all right. We were getting out. It was going to be okay.

More sisters joined the effort, digging, passing stones down to each other, getting the electrical wires guided away from the girders, pressing their ears to the ground. None of them seemed worried about his poisons. The cooperative spell had descended over them all, and the only thing that mattered was moving the mountain in front of them.

Dust coated Arron's helmet and he had to wipe it away repeatedly with his sleeve. His gloves split, so did his nails and skin underneath. He kept going. Lynn was alive down there. She was. She had to be.

Let her be all right. Please. Jesus, God, Allah, Mary, Joseph, Isis, Odin, Mithras, Patrick, Jehovah, Yahweh, Mothers, oh, Mothers, please, Buddha . . .

"I hear them!" shouted one of the listeners. She pressed her head against a jumble of broken concrete. "Under here!"

So many sisters descended on the pile, Arron found himself pushed back. He stood behind them, panting hard. His hands flexed and trembled. Tears mixed with the sweat running down his face. He became aware that the shore guns were still firing, the planes were still roaring overhead, and the shattering, crumbling explosion of dropping bombs still went on, and on.

Stones passed down to the relatively clear streets. Someone brought in a crowbar. Someone else brought in a brace. He couldn't see what was going on. He couldn't make himself move.

"She's Human!" unidentifiable voices called and answered one another. "There was a Human." "Where is she?" "Get her down there!" "Human! A sister of yours is down here!"

Arron dived into the center of the crowd. He heard a few gasps of "Scholar Arron!" behind him. In front of him, the broken concrete had been cleared to expose a jagged, black hole. Someone shined a light into it. He saw a flash of light, brown skin, a frightened eye, a hand.

"Lynn!"

A rope came from somewhere. Arron tied it around his waist. A light tube was pressed into his hand.

Carefully, one step at a time, he picked his way down the rubble. It shifted and crumbled under his feet, showering Lynn with stones and dust. The ruin cut off the daylight. His boots found semifirm purchase, and he crouched beside her, afraid to move and bring the rest of the building down on top of them.

"Okay, I'm here. We'll get you out." He saw what had happened. A support beam had fallen against one of the remains of the foundation wall, creating a small pocket, just enough for them to . . .

Them? Where's Res?

He saw Lynn's hand, flung toward the interior of the ruined building. He saw it clutching Resaime's hand. He saw the end of the beam that had sheltered Lynn, and he saw the blood.

His stomach heaved hard, forcing bile up his throat until he choked.

"Ca . . . can you move?"

"Yes," whispered Lynn. She tucked her legs under her. Slowly, she let go of Resaime's hand.

Arron wrapped an arm tightly around her shoulders and helped her to her knees. She was shaking violently. Shock. Shock without a doubt.

"We need some blankets!" he shouted up the hole. "Come on, Lynn." He placed her hands, pointed out where she could put her feet, and boosted her from the side.

At last, they emerged into daylight. Lynn stumbled and leaned against him as he helped her down to the street. Hands held out blankets to wrap her in. Someone else held out a mug of something green. Arron tasted it. It was a cold tea he'd drunk a thousand times. He pressed it into Lynn's hands.

Her face was a disaster. Her bandage had been torn away along with half the skin on her cheek. Dirt, blood, pus, and mucus caked her face and empty orb. More ran down her cheek and neck, while she sat oblivious with the clay cup clutched in her hands. Her scalp was a mass of cuts and blood. He could see her torn and jagged implant under the cut in her temple. Her clothes were cut to ribbons, exposing shoulder, breast, torso, and knee.

"I had a bag," he said to the cluster of anxious sisters. "Can anyone see my bag?"

It was handed to him. He tore it open and found the medikit. "There's a boat in the harbor. A Human boat. It belongs to Trader Cabal. She was waiting for us. Can anyone run to the harbor and tell her what happened? Tell her she must wait." His own hands shook as he opened the kit. "We'll be there, but she must wait." A pair of sisters volunteered and scampered off.

In the kit he found sterile pads, temporary skin, fungicides, antibacterials, and painkillers. He handed two of the painkillers to Lynn. She stared at them in her scratched and dirty palm. He put her hand to her mouth. She swallowed the pills. He raised the cup for her. She drank.

Arron's stomach rebelled again. He gritted his teeth in fierce concentration as he swabbed and disinfected the worst of Lynn's wounds. He laid patches of temporary skin across her face and temple and wrapped bandages on top of that. Someone had brought plain water and a towel. He was able to wash down the rest of her face and scalp.

Her lips started moving. One word, over and over, with no sound behind it.

"Lynn, I can't hear you. What do you want?" He bent down until her lips brushed his helmet.

"David," she murmured, as if to her implant. "David, David, David."

"We're going to him, Lynn," said Arron, and the memory of how they'd told Res they were going to find her Aunt Senejess rushed through him, burning as it went. "We're on our way, right now."

She blinked and focused her eye on him.

"Arron? Oh, God, Res . . ."

"I know." He cupped his hands around hers. "Drink the tea, Lynn. You need it."

She drank. Arron looked around. His crowd of helpers had cleared. Mission accomplished. The live person had been retrieved and delivered into the hands of her sister. Now there were other, more immediate tasks at hand. The city was under siege and on fire. There was a lot to do.

He glanced around wildly and saw an abandoned pushcart lying on its side. He ran to it. Both wheels and the axle were intact. He righted it and shoved it over to Lynn.

"Let me help you in." He held out his hand.

"No. I'll . . ." She set down the cup.

"Lynn, we have to go. Cabal might already have left!" It was the first time he'd let himself think about it, and the idea left him numb with terror.

Lynn didn't say anything else. She let him help her into the cart. Arron grabbed the handrails and shoved the cart forward. Every muscle and joint shot back pain in protest. The smooth wood burned against his raw palms, but he managed to get them going. Moving at a limping trot, Arron pushed Lynn through the ruined streets, while still more planes flew overhead.

Because of the cart, he couldn't use his pass-through to the harbor. He had to take them by a more circuitous route. A bunch of buildings had been bombed into rubble-filled craters, making for longer detours. No one appeared to help. None of the passing public-health carriers or troop trucks stopped. It was just him and Lynn and the whole world falling apart around them.

He knew what the bombers were really looking for. They were looking for the underground crèches that held the daughters and the carrying mothers. That was standard tactics. He didn't want to think about it, but he knew it was true.

Finally, they reached the harbor. The guns still thundered, but more raggedly. The t'Therian ships still stood out to sea. Gouts of water erupted out of the harbor at random intervals. The battle down there had been joined.

The harbor was nothing but a mass of abandoned boats. Arron scanned them, looking for Cabal's nondescript trawler. He didn't see it, and didn't see it, and didn't see it. Panic tightened his throat.

Something flashed white among the boats. His gaze fastened on it. Cabal waved frantically from his boat's aft deck. Relief robbed Arron of most of his remaining strength. He waved back. Cabal looked across the harbor as another geyser erupted and vanished into the boat's cabin.

Arron got the pushcart down to the quay. Lynn climbed out clumsily, one hand clutching the blanket around her shoulders, but she did it under her own power and Arron was glad. He wasn't sure he'd be able to lift her again. They teetered along the docks, leaning against each other's shoulders. They all but collapsed onto Cabal's boat.

He must have already cast off, because as soon as they hit the wooden deck, the engine roared into life, and the boat pulled away from the dock. She nosed around and headed for open water. It wasn't a straight path, because of all the abandoned boats, but Arron was sure Cabal knew what he was doing. He'd done it a thousand times.

"Let's get below," Arron picked himself up off the deck and held out a hand to Lynn. She took it. He helped her down the ladder into the hold.

Because it was a Dedelphi boat, there were no separate cabins, just a lower hold for cargo and an upper hold for people and yet more cargo. Not being comfortable on a pad on the floor, however, Cabal had bunks built into the sides. Arron installed Lynn in one and went onto the cramped bridge.

Cabal glanced over his shoulder as Arron entered. His hands gripped the wheel as if they were welded to it.

"Holy God and Hell, Arron, I thought you'd gotten us both killed." He heaved the wheel clockwise to steer around a cluster of trawlers and their anchor cables. "Are your friends below?"

"Lynn is." Arron collapsed onto a narrow ledge of a bench that ran along the cabin's starboard wall. "Resaime's dead."

Cabal set his jaw and kept his eyes on the window. "I was almost dead. Did you see those boats smashed up back there? They're bombing the harbor. You owe me a lot more than a trip back home for this one, Arron. A lot more."

Arron looked up at him. For a moment he considered killing him outright and taking the boat for himself.

Cabal cleared the last of the anchored boats. A boom sounded through the hull, and a wave sluiced over the deck. The boat rocked violently. Cabal cranked up the power to the engine, and the boat lurched forward.

"Too close, too close," he muttered through clenched teeth. "God and Hell, can't they see this is a civvie boat?"

Another boom resonated through the decks. The boat bucked and kicked.

"You got a speaker station aboard?"

Both Arron and Cabal jumped. Lynn, blanket pinned around her shoulders with a pair of small clamps, stood in the cabin's threshold.

"Yeah," said Cabal, trying to look at her and out the front window at the same time.

"Put a call out to the t'Therian ships." Lynn gripped the railing that had been mounted at a Dedelphi's waist height. "Ask for Praeis Shin t'Theria."

"Lynn," said Arron gently, "we don't know she's here."

"She's here," said Lynn bitterly. "The Getesaph took her sister and her daughter; of course she's here. She's probably dropping the goddamned bombs with her own hands." She tightened her hold on the railing and stared out the window. "She is most definitely here."

Praeis stood in the map room with Neys and Silv. The chart of the Hundred Isles' waters lay on the table. Small red magnets marked the known positions of the Getesaph ships and fortifications. Black magnets marked the t'Therian positions. Theia sat on a stool next to them, her hands poised over the duplicator's keys, ready to pound out orders or notes. Over the past few days, Theia had moved firmly into the position of junior assistant. There was a little grumbling at first, but as the story of Praeis's family spread through the ranks, urged on by Neys and Silv, Praeis suspected, the grumbling ceased.

Praeis leaned closer to the map and tried to marshal her thoughts. The skin on her back quivered from being clenched so tightly. It had been too long since she'd been to war. She'd lost the knack of staying calm.

The door burst open and a runner, a fourth-sister, teetered into the room, caught off-balance by a sudden swell. Water streamed off her armor. Must be raining again.

"Excuse me, Mothers," she gasped. "But there's a boat calling for help. There's Humans aboard and they say . . ." She paused, unable to get the words out around her anxious panting.

"They say what, Sister?" demanded Neys.

"They are calling for the Task-Mother. They say they have a friend of hers aboard. A . . . Lynn Nussba . . ."

Lynn? Praeis bolted from the room. She ran onto the deck, barely aware that Theia followed on her heels. Warm rain pelted her face and shoulders. Her first lid closed against it automatically, and her nose and ears pinched down, but she didn't slow her pace.

"Where!" she shouted over the crash of waves, guns, and rain to a second-sister whose name she couldn't remember.

"Aft quarter, Mother!" bawled the second.

Theia caught Praeis's arm. Leaning on each other to keep balance against the pitch of the ship and the rain-drenched deck, they dashed toward the stern. A cluster of arms-sisters stood staring out at something, pointing and talking. Praeis followed their gaze out to the grey, choppy waves. Out there, a middle-sized fishing boat bobbed up and down on the rough sea. She could see white figures with guns, shooting into the water at the heads and ears of Getesaph soldiers protruding here and there from the waves.

One arms-sister clutched a pair of binoculars. Praeis lifted them out of her hand and focused them on the boat and the white figures. Three Humans, she saw as the lenses brought them closer. Two *men* and one *woman.* The *woman* was Lynn Nussbaumer.

"Covering fire!" Praeis barked. "Now! Get a team and a rescue boat in the water! Get me the PA speaker!"

An arms-sister appeared with the PA speaker box in her hand and an incredible length of cable trailing behind her. Praeis took the PA and looked out to the boat in time to see a contingent of six arms-sisters in light armor dive headfirst into the water. A Getesaph who'd ducked her head up saw them, too. She made it back under the waves. The bullet meant for her hit nothing but foam.

So much for surprise.

"Lynn! Lynn!" called Praeis. The PA bellowed her words out to the world. "It's Praeis! We're sending help," she said in English. "Hang on! We'll get to you!"

One of the small white figures waved its arm. A geyser shot up beside the little boat. The craft dropped into a trough in the waves and listed sharply to port. Two of the Humans disappeared, leaving one on deck shooting into the ocean at things Praeis couldn't see.

It didn't take much guessing to work out what had just happened. A bomb had gone off close enough to hull the boat, and they were sinking into the water full of Getesaph soldiers.

The roar of a motor cut the sound of waves and bullets. A narrow troop carrier shot out from the side of the ship. Praeis brought up the binocs again. Neys sat in the bow with six arms-sisters behind her, all armed, ready to board or to dive. She trained the binocs on the Human boat.

Lynn and the *man* reemerged from the hold. The boat settled lower in the water. A Getesaph reached up to the rail and was jerked backward. Unseen hands dragged her back under the water. The troop carrier roared up to the boat's side. Lynn and the *men* let the arms-sisters help them over the side. Lynn staggered, almost fell, and slumped into a *man's* arms.

Praeis twisted her head around. There were still three arms-sisters beside her. "You!" she said to the closest. "Find out if we've got a doctor aboard who knows anything about Humans and get her down to meet that boat. Tell them to get an iso-ward ready!" Praeis wrapped an arm around Theia. "We'll go down."

We have to, she thought, as they headed down the narrow stairs into the cavernous hold. *Because we're both eating our hearts out hoping Lynn will know where Resaime is.*

This is why we do not bring our daughters into combat. Too much distraction. Too hard to think of anything else. Too much your whole world narrowed down to their pain, their needs, their scent, their skin under your hand so smooth and strong and . . . She shook her head. *Ancestors Mine, did I forget my doses this morning?*

The launch door opened, and the troop carrier was hoisted inside with a wave of rain and seawater. A med team, looking uncomfortable and trying to hide it, stood nearby with a body board, respirator, and medical bags. Praeis doubted that any of them had ever seen a Human up close, let alone treated one.

Lynn and the two *men* climbed out of the carrier, along with the troops.

"Lynn!" Praeis stepped forward, stopped, and looked again. Lynn had no clean-suit on. She was wrapped in a sodden blanket. Half her face was swaddled in bandages and her skin was grey with cold and stress. She looked at Praeis like she'd seen the end of the world.

"Ancestors Mine." Praeis turned to the medical team. "Take her to the iso-ward. Find fresh clothes and a heater blanket."

"Yes, Mother," said the second-sister. "Come with us." She reached out a hand but let it fall back. The other two responded a little better. They held out the body board and Lynn lay down on it. They threw the restraints across her and carried her gingerly up the stairs.

Theia looked up at her anxiously. Praeis ruffled her daughter's ears and turned to the *men.* They were both clean-suited, but the taller of the two hadn't shaved in days. Hair coated his scalp and face like fresh-sprouted moss.

"Welcome aboard," she said, in English. "Are you good? Do you need to rest?"

"I could sure use a sit-down and something to eat," said the cleaner of the two. "That was a whole long list of things I never want to do again."

"We can manage both. We'll put in a call to Bioverse to come get you." *Never mind we're in the middle of a war. It's our war, not yours. We'll get you out of here if Theia and I have to take you ourselves.*

"Are you Praeis Shin t'Theria?" blurted out the unshaven *man.*

"I am Praeis Shin. This is my daughter Theiareth Shin t'Theria."

The *man* stared at Theia, a little too wild-eyed. Theia laid her hand over her mother's.

"I'm Schol— I'm Arron Hagopian. I'm a friend of Lynn's."

"She's said your name as a friend." Praeis dipped her ears to him. "I hope we can meet again when the world is calmer." Theia tugged at her hand like a child. Praeis touched her shoulder. Her own heart was straining, but what news there was would come soon enough.

"I . . . your . . ." He stammered.

Here it is. Ignoring the chill that flowed through her, Praeis flicked an ear toward Neys, and the other toward the unnamed *man.*

Neys caught the signal and stepped briskly up to the *man.* "If you'll come with me, please."

The *man* nodded. He glanced back at Arron, and seemed about to say something, but he just shook his head and followed Neys up the stairs.

"You have news for us?" said Praeis quietly to Arron. Theia pressed against her side.

Arron rubbed his forearms, a gesture most Humans who spent long amounts of time in clean-suits developed. *Strange people,* thought Praeis idly. *They won't touch each other, but they are constantly touching themselves.*

Still rubbing his forearms, Arron started to talk. He talked about discovering the disparity in the Getesaph passenger rosters, about waking up in a cell, about Lynn being thrown in with him, and then Resaime, and no one else. He talked about their escape so they could save Res from their poison, about meeting *soldiers* who were friends of his, how they got a ride to Mrant Chavat, how the attack came, how the bomb fell, how the 'Esaph helped him dig until he was able to go down and rescue Lynn, and no one else.

Her sister. Her daughter. Another sister. Another daughter. Dead. Dead. All of them, dead, with her looking on and living on and trying and trying and trying . . .

"You killed her."

It took Praeis a moment to reconcile the words with the voice.

"We killed her." Theia sank to her knees on the deck.

"No, Theia," Praeis dropped down beside her daughter. *My only daughter. My last daughter.* "You did nothing. Nothing." She reached out to encircle Theia with what little warmth she had to offer.

"Don't touch me." Theia got to her feet and walked away.

After that, Praeis lost track of time. People told her things, but it was as if they spoke to her through a wall of ice. Eventually, she moved, was moved, to an administrative cabin. She sat on a bench and stared at the wall. Neys and Silv came and went, but she couldn't move to touch them. She was distant, separate, isolated. Was this the Change? No. The Change was being immersed in the here and now. This was something else. This was her own personal madness caught up with her. It had enabled her to function alone, now it kept her from reaching out.

Good, good. Let me stay in here. Theia is right. I killed them.

The door opened. Neys and Silv came in and sat, one on either side of her.

"Mother, this cannot continue," said one. She didn't know who. Her head did not want to turn.

"Mother, we need you back with us. We won the attack, but there is much more to do," said the other.

Arms wrapped around her shoulders. She was leaned against a chest. Her muscles did not relax. She did not weep or rage. She did not care whether these two went or stayed, and she did not want to.

After a while, they left, and she was alone again. Alone was better. Alone was right and proper and natural for her. She had always been alone, really. Always been here in this closed-in place without daughters or sisters. Always.

The door opened again and somebody small and white and glistening came in. She was Lynn, Praeis realized after a moment. She did not sit down. She stood in Praeis's field of vision and folded her hands behind her back, wincing slightly as she did.

"I've been talking to Theia," she said, speaking English, which had always been easier for her. "She's having a rough time. Half your people are shunning her for what she said. Calling it blasphemous. Half of them are not so sure. She's really confused." Lynn paused. "She's angry and frightened and lonely. She didn't mean it."

No, she meant it.

"She's an adolescent. They say things they don't mean."

Human children do that.

Lynn rocked forward on her toes and looked down at the deck. "Your people are good. One of them got a line through to the peninsula, and somebody there got a hook up to the station. Keale's sending somebody out to get us."

Why are you here? What do you want? If anybody can recognize somebody who should be alone, it should be a Human.

"Res held up great during the whole thing. You should have seen her, Praeis. She did her Great Family proud. The first we knew about her was when they threw her in a cell with me and Arron. Our clean-suits were already days old, but Resaime wasn't frightened." She went on and on, describing every detail: how Resaime looked, how she acted, how brave she was. Slowly, Praeis felt herself draw closer. The ice thinned, just a little. Painfully, her ears turned themselves forward to hear how Res had acted courageously under fire. How she had not complained once as they fled through the woods. How she had carried herself during the long, tense ride through the tunnels. Brave, strong daughter Resaime. Your daughter. My daughter. My daughters.

"Praeis? Are you with me? Are you hearing this? Because I want to tell you something." Lynn squatted down until her eyes were level with Praeis's. "I blamed you, too. When I was there, in the dark, and I was the only one to hold your daughter's hand. I could feel her skin twitching and blistering and the roof creaked, and groaned and gave and she didn't even have time to scream. I knew it was you out here. I knew whose orders had done it. I knew whose fault—"

"NO!" howled Praeis.

She lunged forward to grab Lynn, but Lynn dodged sideways, and Praeis fell onto the deck. She pounded the floor with her fists, screaming wordlessly.

No! No! No!

"Mother?"

Warm, familiar hands grabbed her and pulled her back. Other hands held on to hers. Praeis kept screaming until her throat was raw and all she could do was cough and choke out her rage and sorrow. Eventually, the foul noise stopped pouring out of her. She was able to relax into the arms that held her, and to identify them as Theia's.

She blinked her eyes open and looked into her daughter's tear-streaked face.

"Ancestors Mine." She buried her face against her daughter's shoulder and held her close, and they both wept for their hard, bitter loss.

Lynn closed the cabin door and walked out onto the deck, favoring her bad knee and worse ankle. The Getesaph care-takers had bandaged them up tightly, but they hadn't been able to give her anything for the pain.

The guns had silenced, and the most prevalent noise was the smack of waves against the hull. A light, misting rain fell, covering her helmet and gloves with milky pearls. She shrugged further into the borrowed fleece coat that had been cinched up with somebody's belt so it didn't drag the deck. Despite the coat, the wind found all her aches, bandaged or unbandaged, and sharpened them.

Neys and Silv stood at the rail. Lynn walked stiffly over to them.

"Praeis will be good," she said huskily.

"We saw Theia go in," Silv touched her arm. "Thank you. We could not have done that."

Lynn looked across the white-tipped waves. "Yeah, well," she said in English. Then she switched back to t'Therian. "We all needed to find out if Theia would go back to her. How's the fight going?"

Neys waved her ears. "It is war. The 'Esaph are killing our sisters out there. We have been able to dig in on five of the islands and hold our own. We wait for reports. We got one of their airports, and they've stopped their flyovers for the moment. Soon their fleet will be here, and it will be our turn to remind them whose children we are." She bared her teeth to the wind. "The Great Families who dispute our rights can declare themselves our enemies and we will take care of them in good time."

Lynn felt herself go very still. "What do the other families say about this . . . attack?"

Neys said nothing. A shiver ran up Lynn's spine. *Oh no, no, not a real war. Not an all-out war. Bioverse would never stick around. They'd cut their losses. They'll scrap the whole thing, leave the Dedelphi here to die.* Her heartbeat doubled, and doubled again.

Calm down, Lynn. Calm down. There's nothing you can do until you get back to Base.

Over the sudden thunder of her heart, she said, "Have you heard from Keale's people yet?"

"Yes," said Neys. "They will be here in about an hour."

Lynn nodded. She realized she didn't want to be near the t'Therians right now. "I'll go tell the boys."

She climbed down the ladders, gritting her teeth against the pain in her leg, and her ribs and her hands, and navigated the metal hallways that were grimmer than anything she'd ever seen, even aboard a cheap, short-range shuttle to the sick bay.

Like all Dedelphi workplaces, the sick bay was one big, open chamber. The wounded lay in pairs on hard beds, groaning softly, sleeping or whispering back and forth. The cases of plague or suspected plague were separated in side alcoves that had been closed off by metal-framed windows and primitive filter doors.

The iso-ward at the farthest end of the bay had been set aside for the unexpected Human guests. She could see Arron perched on the ward's one chair. Cabal sat at the head of the wide, high bed, where Lynn had spent the last six or eight hours recovering from the worst of the shock and exhaustion. He had his knees bent and his back leaning against the wall. Cabal had taken off his helmet and gloves, but Arron was still completely suited.

Well, after ten years, it probably feels strange to be out of it.

Both of them waved at her as she worked the wheel on the outer door. She stepped into the narrow sterile area, closed the outer door, and slid open the inner door.

"Are they all right?" Arron asked immediately.

"They will be." Lynn sat at the foot of the bed and took off her helmet. "I figured if I could make Praeis scream, Theia would come running to see what was wrong, and they'd both know they were still family. It worked." She folded her arms and held on to her own elbows. Ideas flooded her head as soon as Theia burst into the cabin to embrace her mother. Lynn saw the future, clear and strong and full of possibilities, and she hadn't liked any of them. *There's got to be time to come up with something better. There's got to be.*

"You sound distracted," said Arron.

I feel distracted. I'm getting ideas I'm not sure I want. She didn't say that. She said, "Well, we've got what might be a full-blown war starting out there. It's distracting."

"Your people seem to think it's definitely a full-blown war." Cabal scratched his scalp vigorously. "We're probably the last Humans on the planet. Have you heard anything about when our rescue's due?"

No. That can't be true. There's still got to be time. There's still got to be something I can do to stop this. Lynn rested her elbows on her knees and hoped neither of the men noticed her hands shaking. "Keale's people will be here within the hour." *At the most. That's at the very most.*

"Then what?" Arron lifted his eyes to her.

"Then, I imagine they'll take us all to Base." *Where I'll have to stop them from pulling us all out of here.* "Then, we can see about getting you two home, or wherever you need to go." Arron's gaze dropped until he was staring at the tips of her boots. "What is it?"

Arron blinked and rubbed his hands together. "Do you think you could talk your people into letting me thread through to the *Ur*?"

Surprise straightened Lynn's spine. "Why would you want to do that?"

Arron looked up at the ceiling, as if he could see through it up to the city-ships. "Because my sisters are up there making a hideous mistake."

Cabal snorted. "Your sisters? I don't think so."

Arron turned toward him, anger flashing in his eyes. "You don't know, so leave it."

"*I* don't know?" Cabal barked out a loud laugh. "Get the walking Buddha to wake you up, Hagopian. You're the one who doesn't know."

Lynn didn't move. She just watched Arron stand up slowly. "What are you talking about?" he demanded.

Cabal waved his hand. "Arron, your 'sisters' have been planning their little coup since the Sisters-Chosen-to-Lead agreed to the Confederation. They've been using you to find out how Humans do things and applying that information to make this work. Rchilthen Byvant and Ishth have known all about it. I've been running information between the two sides for the past year."

Lynn's jaw dropped. "You helped them do this! You little . . ." Lynn lurched to her feet. "Do you know what you've done! You've ruined everything! How could you!" Her voice was high, thin, and strident. *You gave them David!* She wanted to hit him, she realized, she wanted to kill him, but she couldn't do anything but stand there and shake.

"How could I?" Cabal raised his eyebrows. "I'm an info-runner. It's what I do. I get information to people who don't have it. The work here was steady and pretty safe for a Human, 'til they all started shooting at each other and left me sitting in the damn middle of it." He snorted. "It's kind of funny, you know, all of us had our best-laid plans, and they've all been shot to hell by the pogos' pathetic temper tantrums."

Throughout their exchange, Arron just stayed where he was, frozen, except for his chest, which heaved like a bellows.

"Why are you telling me now?" Arron asked softly.

"Because now it doesn't make any difference. The pogos are going to kill each other, and we're going to go home." Cabal stood up. "They even invited you to go along, didn't they, Arron?" Cabal cocked his head. "A friendly Human would be very useful when they actually got the ship, as a helping hand, or a hostage.

"You've been used, Arron." Cabal picked up his helmet and gloves. "And you've been disappointed, Lynn, and I'll bet neither of you wants me around anymore. I'm going for a walk on deck."

Lynn watched Arron as he watched Cabal fasten his helmet on and shove his hands into his gloves. She knew what he was thinking. He wanted Cabal to be wrong, to be lying. But after everything that had happened, he couldn't quite make himself believe it.

She felt the same way. She sat down, still shaking. She was too tired, too sore, to deal with any of this. Her head had begun to ache with a dull insistent throb.

While they watched, Cabal worked the filter door and walked out. Arron crumpled into the chair and bowed his head until it rested in his hands.

The sight shook Lynn out of her own fears. She touched his shoulder. "I'm sorry."

He looked up at her and she saw his face looking fierce and lost at the same time. "It wasn't true," he said. "None of it was true."

"No," said Lynn, without asking what he meant. "But it'll be all right." As she spoke, conviction solidified inside Lynn's soul. "We're going back to Base, and I'm going to put an end to this mess."

Chapter XVII

Lareet and Umat stood in the threshold of the open laboratory door. "Irat Queth, Irat Shnun, the light of day looks well on you."

The irat stood at the far end of one of the Humans' tiny labs. They bent over a comm station until their noses almost touched the screen. Neither of them wore clean-suits. The first order of business had been to sterilize the Human sections. With the help of the maintenance *jobbers* they had done a good job. The irat had only had to treat a dozen cases of Human poisoning.

After a moment, Irat Queth's ear swiveled around to locate the greeting. She touched her sister's shoulder as if to say "I'll take care of this," and straightened up.

"As it does on you, Dayisen Lareet and Dayisen Umat," she said, a little briskly. Obviously the interruption was not welcome.

Umat's ears quivered with suppressed humor. "We wished to hear what progress you and your sisters are making," she said smoothly. "Have the Humans left us anything useful?"

"The Humans have done some excellent work, which should surprise no one." Irat Queth walked toward them to draw the conversation away from her sister, who had remained intent on her screen. "The Humans have been studying the vectors of the diseases that make up the plague: How the microbes are transmitted, how they are incubated, what hosts carry them to their homes inside Getesaph bodies." Irat Queth blinked constantly, flicking her first lid down and back up again in a nervous tic. "As near as we can make out, because they are not sterilizing the *ecosphere,* our world, they are not looking at wiping out the microbes. They plan instead to limit the microbes' ability to transmit themselves. They want to make it difficult for the *WKV*, the plague strains, to travel, while letting the normal strains fill their niches." Blink, flick, blink. "Their proposed methods, of course, are not something we could apply ourselves, even if we could fully understand them, but their vector research is definitely something we can adapt and expand on."

Umat dipped her ears gravely. "Have they given us anything on cures or vaccines?"

Flick, blink. "Quite a bit. Again, they have been basing it heavily on the life cycle of the viruses as they behave in the environment and incubate in the body." Her ears waved and her eyes blinked excitedly. "What are their weak points? What are the, to use a military phrase, choke points in the viruses' development?" Her voice filled with a reverent awe. "Their research methods will be even more use to us than the current results."

"Excellent," said Umat. "Concentrate on retrieving the vital information. We don't know—"

A pair of runners trotted through the open door.

"Excuse me, Dayisen Rual, you are needed in the command center."

The skin on Lareet's back bunched up. "We are on our way."

The command center looked more like a repair shop than a ship's bridge. Consoles had been laid open. Wires and components lay on clean, white sheets. Technicians stood around, talking in anxious whispers like doctors over patients. The encryption team sat around the central table, pouring over fat scrolls of paper covered in symbols that Lareet couldn't begin to decipher. The Trindt Brirdth, Wron, Pfath, and Nant, leaned over the shoulders of the encryption team, pointed at various lines of code, and spoke to one another in terms almost as convoluted at the symbols on the paper. As Lareet and Umat entered, Trindt Wron straightened up and came over to greet them.

"We have bad news, Dayisen," she said flatly.

"Then let's have it out." Umat folded her hands across her pouch. Lareet saw her ears quiver faintly with the effort of holding them straight and still.

Trindt Wron glanced briefly back at her sisters before speaking. "We miscalculated the nature of the ship," she said. "Even once we have restored the command functions, there is no way to hold the ship on the course we require by precoding the onboard computers. We might have been able to do it if the *artificial intelligence* had remained undamaged, but as it is, there will have to be a command crew aboard to handle the changes in trajectory and thrust that will be required."

Umat smoothed a thoughtful hand across Lareet's shoulder. "Well, then, a crew will be found. You and your sisters continue your work."

"Yes, Dayisen." She dipped her ears.

"Come sister, let us leave them to it." Umat linked her arm through Lareet's and steered her to the steel tunnel that led to the city.

Lareet's skin shivered all across her body as she climbed "down" the ladder after her sister. When she could stand up again, there was green grass under her shoes and green smells in the air from the trees and plants. It was evening, and the dome was just beginning to clear to let in the night. She could even hear the river lapping in the distance, under the sound of voices from the command center drifting through the tunnel.

She faced her sister. "Umat, I do not like what I feel from you."

"I didn't think you would." Umat took her hand. "But you have to agree, our choices are limited."

Still holding Lareet's hand, Umat led her down to the riverbank. *She knows how much I enjoy this place,* Lareet thought, but nothing in her relaxed at the sound and scent of running water.

"If the ship will not fly itself," Umat said, looking across the river, "I must be here to fly it. I will not condemn our duty-sisters to do it for us."

Lareet stood there for a moment, breathing in the fresh water and green scents. "And where will I be?"

"In a shuttle with most of our sisters, waiting until the worst is over and returning home," Umat spoke almost dismissively.

Sister, Sister, I know you are trying to spare me, but for once, just once, will you try to feel what I am feeling? "You promised to be with me when my daughters are born." She laid a hand on her belly.

Umat's face went instantly tight. "Lareet, that is unworthy of you."

"I know." Her ears drooped. "I am sorry."

Umat took hold of Lareet's shoulders. "I am worried about you, Sister. You are losing track of what we are here to do. It is for all our sisters and all our daughters that we are here, not just our blood family."

"I am worried about me, too, Sister." She laid her hands over her sister's. Her eyes and ears focused on the river. "I am worried about how I look around this city that is as beautiful as a vision and think, 'What would be so bad about letting the Humans' plan go forward?' I am worried about how I think about the t'Therians over in their city-ship and wonder if Scholar Arron was right in some ways. That perhaps if we can talk and reason, they might be able to as well?" She shook her head until she felt her ears flop. "Maybe we should just get this over with quickly, before I lose all mind and will for this task."

Umat shook her gently. "We are moving as quickly as we can,

Sister. Continue to do your part, and we will be there that much sooner."

Lareet sighed and looked up at the dome. It was a translucent purple, and the brightest stars shone through. It was nothing less than beautiful.

A shadow crossed the dome. Lareet's ears twitched and she looked harder.

"Sister?" asked Umat.

Lareet pointed. It was a small, complex shadow. It scuttled on the dome, heading toward the farside.

Umat's ears fell back. "What is that?"

A second shadow fell onto the dome and hurried in the opposite direction of the first.

"I think it's from Commander Keale." Lareet raced for the tunnel.

Back in the command center, the duty-sisters scrambled around madly, trying not to disturb the terminal parts on their white sheets.

"What is it?" barked Umat.

"Machines, Dayisen Umat," said one of the Trindt Imn. "Most of the cameras still aren't working, so we have no count of how many, but you can see here . . ." She gestured to one of the table screens. Lareet bent over it with her sister.

A silver box with crab-claws and insect legs landed on the hull near the shuttle run. It began to pick a dainty path between the ship's pipes and other protrusions. A sister landed next to it and fell into step right behind.

"Where are they coming from?" Lareet felt her ears quiver.

"We don't know." The Trindt Imn threw up her hands. "The cameras—"

"I know, I know." Lareet waved her to silence. She flicked an ear toward Umat, who already had the speaker box in her hands. She flicked the switches to override all ongoing communications.

"This is the Dayisen Rual Umat to all sisters. Strange machines are landing on our hull. If anyone sees them where you are, report immediately."

The speaker box crackled. "This is Trindt Prusht Kvet. There are strange *jobbers* in the hangar bay, and they're opening the hangar doors."

"You, you, you, you." Lareet pointed at whoever did not look like they had been coding. "With me."

They trotted in a quick-time march down to the hanger's overlook. Trindt Kvet was there with four soldiers. The hangar doors had come open just far enough for the insectlike *jobbers* to scurry inside. They scampered between the waiting shuttles. One of them all but tripped over one of the ship's maintenance jobbers that had its arms in an open panel. The new *jobber* extended a limb to the busy machine and touched it. They stood motionless for a moment. Then, the newcomer pulled its limb back and hurried on. The old *jobber* swung into motion, its diligent hands now ripping the wires out of their sockets and letting them dangle free.

"Mother Night," breathed Lareet. She scanned the keyboard in front of her and found the intercom button. "*Jobber!*" she called down into the hangar bay. "Stop!"

The *jobber* continued its methodical destruction. She tried again in English, in French, and in Cantonese. The machine did not even flinch.

"Speaker!" One of the duty-sisters handed her the boxy unit. "Somebody get those doors shut and stop that thing!" Two sisters vanished down the corridor.

Lareet flipped the switches for the bridge. "Dayisen Umat," she said into the speaker. "The new *jobbers* are corrupting the old ones into reversing their purpose from maintenance to destruction. We need to get the squads out into the ship. Any *jobber* that does not respond to orders must be destroyed."

"Understood, Dayisen Lareet. Take whoever you have with you and start a patrol of your quarter. We'll coordinate from here."

"Understood, Dayisen Umat." Lareet shut the power down and looked at the cluster of soldiers around her. "We have a new enemy, Sisters."

It was the strangest battle Lareet ever fought. She patrolled the corridors with her soldiers, alert to every sound. Whenever they found a *jobber,* they shouted at it harshly. If it didn't answer, they fell on it, breaking it to bits.

The little enemies were fast, though, and got into everything, including the water recyclers, the air vents, and the main foodstore. But, finally, after ten hours, Umat sent a runner from the command center. The ship appeared to be clear of the strangers.

Lareet congratulated her sisters. They embraced and laughed and started composing rude poetry about the metal monsters as they trooped back to their city.

But Lareet couldn't help turning an ear back in the direction they'd come from. *That was a good move, Commander Keale. Make us destroy our own best allies. How many maintenance machines do we have left after this? A very good move.*

What will you do next?

Lynn climbed down the shuttle's ladder into the echoing white hangar deck of Dedelphi Base I. Cabal and Arron followed close behind her.

"Lynn!"

Lynn turned. The next thing she knew, she was enveloped by David's arms. Unable to speak, she held on to him, drinking in his warmth and his presence.

Oh, God, you're here, you're all right! She knew the same thoughts rang through his mind.

At last, David pulled away. "What happened?" His careful fingers touched her bandaged face.

Lynn rested her forehead against his shoulder. "A lot," she confessed. "I'm going to need a new cheek, and a new camera."

He wrapped his arms around her again. "We'll take care of you."

It took a moment, but the intensity of seeing each other began to fade. Lynn remembered they were in public and realized that even by their lax standards this was a massive display, and noticed that the entire shuttle crew was flowing around them. The same thoughts must have reached David, because he did not resist as she pulled back to a more polite distance. It was then Lynn saw Trace and R.J. standing nearby. Not even perpetually polite Trace pretended to ignore the scene.

"Welcome back," said R.J. blandly. "We've missed you. You would not believe the admin backup we've got."

"I'm sure," replied Lynn, matching his dry tone. Tired as she was, hurt as she was, she could not miss the tension singing between the two of them. They were both standing stiffly, as if every fiber in them had been tightened to the breaking point. "What's going on?"

"In a half hour, the seniors and veeps are having a meeting," Trace said. "There's going to be a vote on a pullout. Everyone's gone out of their minds." The set of Trace's jaw showed how little she thought of *that.* "They want you there. C16."

"Good," said Lynn, meaning it. "I want to be there."

"Lynn," David said softly. "Don't make me say 'You are not going anywhere until I've looked at you.' "

She shook her head, briefly, because the motion made things hurt worse. "Never. But I need to be at that meeting."

"Then we'll get you there." David took Lynn's left arm and walked her down the familiar summer-lit corridors, with their gardens and statues, until they reached the white, sterile infirmary. The med-techs on duty took one look at her and started forward, but David waved them back.

Lynn hopped up on the table. David extended a privacy screen and whistled for the instrument jobber. With careful fingers he peeled away layers of bandage and flaking temp-skin. His face dropped immediately into professional mode. "Talk to me, Lynn. Tell me what happened." His voice shook gently, although his hands remained perfectly steady.

She told him. He layered her wounds with anesthetics, antifungals, and vat grown T cells. He covered it all over with patches to keep her skin from growing until they could take care of the muscle damage. The only time they both faltered was when he had to clean and clear her eye socket. He laid another patch over the empty hollow. Finally, he strapped support braces around her knee and ankle.

Just call me Dr. Ragdoll.

When he was finished, he pulled a clean cotton kaftan out of one of the jobbers.

She slipped it over her shoulders. "I'm sorry, David, I have to go. We'll talk after the meeting."

"I almost killed them all."

Lynn said nothing. David turned around. His hands shook visibly

"They had you. I didn't know if you were dead or alive. They were taking over the ship. I could have let loose the plague samples we had. I was going to. I wanted to."

"David." He leaned close, and she wrapped her arms around him. "It's going to be all right. There is a way out of this."

He pulled back just a little. "Lynn, what are you going to do?"

"What you were going to do aboard the *Ur*, David. Just what I have to." She kissed him gently, and, as fast as she was able, limped out of the infirmary.

Without her implant to help her remember her route, Lynn had to ask the Base AI for directions three times before she found her way to conference room C16. As she paused in the threshold, the door opened to let her in.

The room was jammed. All the chairs around the conference table were filled with seniors and uppers, except for one next to Veep Brador that Lynn really hoped was for her. Veep Brador, unshaven and wide-eyed, sat at the table's head. Yet more people stood around the walls, balancing portables on their hands, or murmuring to their implants.

Everyone watched her as she threaded her way between people and chairs to the seat next to Brador.

"I am glad you could join us, Dr. Nussbaumer," said Brador evenly.

So am I, believe me. "Thank you, Vice President Brador."

Brador turned to the entire assembly. Lynn recognized about two dozen of the faces there. The rest were strangers. Their names had probably been stored in her implant.

"I would like to officially open this meeting," Brador said. "Please be aware that these proceedings are open for remote viewing. Room voice, begin recording." He paused briefly to give the cameras time to switch on, then launched into a very canned opening. "We are all aware of the immediate crisis on the planet Dedelph—"

"Crisis?" snorted one of the people standing against the wall. "It's a world war, not a crisis."

The speaker leaned forward and Lynn recognized Vincent Berkley's lean, sharp face and angular body. His clothes fit loosely, but his elbows, shoulders, and knees still seemed about to poke holes in the fabric. Berkley was in charge of environmental micromodeling, so she hadn't had much to do with him, yet. But she knew about him from Trace and R.J., who spoke his name with a healthy mix of respect and wariness.

"I don't see what we're doing here." Berkley stepped away from the wall. "The Confederation's fallen apart. Nobody's holding our contract. The social dynamic has turned into an unpredictably dangerous situation that Bioverse can't expect any of us to walk into."

"Every contract has provisions for hazard duty," tried Brador.

"Yes, but not suicide." Berkley folded his arms. The cloth around his elbows strained to keep them covered. "We are citizens as well as employees and we have a say in what the corp, and we, get to do with our lives."

"They've already attacked us," said a thin, pale woman with watery grey eyes whom Lynn couldn't put a name to. "They've already tried to kill us. We've had to pull out. We can't do our jobs. There's no one left to work with."

Lynn glanced at Keale. He sat like a stone with his hands on the arms of his chair. If Brador had brought him there for moral support, it didn't look like he was getting it.

"I am not going to order my people into a situation that's going to get them killed," said a short, broad man with his sleeves rolled up to expose burly forearms. "We can't let this situation continue."

"No," said Lynn quietly, "and we don't have to."

Everyone's attention fastened on her.

"Don't we?" inquired Keale, mildly.

Lynn got to her feet. "We can stop the war. Wars. Give those who want to get themselves to safety a chance to leave."

"If you have any suggestions as to how we can do that without unduly jeopardizing the Dedelphi or our citizens, Dr. Nussbaumer"—Brador spread his hands—"I'd love to hear them."

"Disinformation."

"What?" said Brador. Several others' mouths began moving without sound, getting a definition for the archaic word from their various implants.

"Nothing is accomplished without knowledge. Lose your source of information . . ." Her voice shook. She stopped and took a deep breath. "Lose your source of information, and you lose your ability to plan, to strategize.

"Not even the Dedelphi fight without knowing whom to hit and where they are. We can use the communications network, our security teams, and our people to spread false reports about troop movements, numbers, who's been evacuated, and who's still here."

Berkley raised his eyebrows. "She's suggesting we lie to our clients."

"It's less deadly than letting them fight it out." Lynn planted both hands on the table and let her one eye track the room. *Let them all get a good look at me. Let them see what's already happened. Let them think about how much further it can go.*

"The Dedelphi have already tapped our communications network and broken our codes," said Keale. "We can use that against them. Send out bogus confidential reports."

Lynn resisted the temptation to stare at him. Was he coming in on her side? Or had she switched over to his? Lynn shoved that thought aside. "There are a large number of Great Families who want no part of this war. We can still relocate them. We can make it public that we will defend the ports and our transports, and if anyone wants to take their chances attacking them, well, they're taking their chances."

"Lie, then threaten them," murmured Berkley, scratching the back of his head. "I don't know how they do things where you come from, Dr. Nussbaumer . . ."

Lynn felt a rush of real anger. "Where I come from," she said in a tight, controlled voice, "we don't abandon those we've promised to help."

"Do you kill your own people instead?" asked the grey-eyed woman.

Lynn bit down on her first reply. "You all seem to think we're helpless. We are not helpless. You, we, tame entire ecosystems. We steamroller whole planets when necessary. This war, these combatants, are a hostile ecosystem that needs taming. That's the job. The only question is how do we tame them?"

A rustle of cloth and voices drifted through the room. For the first time, Lynn felt something thaw slightly. Maybe people were thinking. Maybe.

"If we do this," said Keale, "we have to move quickly. From what we've heard, a number of the Great Families are talking about teaching both the t'Therians and the Getesaph a lesson for their arrogance."

Berkley held up one hand, making a "stop" gesture. "Assuming we could get the boards to listen to this, can you give me one reason why we should try to get it approved?"

Lynn met his gaze. "You heard Commander Keale. If we don't, the war becomes total. If we don't act, not only do we lose everything we've worked for, doing irreversible damage to Bioverse and all its contractors and subsidiaries, but we are going to leave millions of Dedelphi to die in a war and plague we could have prevented." She straightened up. "On the other hand, if we do this, we still have a chance to win. We can still save this world if we try."

Come on, all of you. You must see it. If we stop now, barbarity wins. We cannot let it win! "We are talking about hazard duty, there's no question. I've been kidnapped, I had my implant cut out. I've been shot at, beaten on, chased, and trapped in a bombed-out building. I've seen what the wars will do, to them and to us. I wouldn't be suggesting this if I didn't know it would work. We can still save Dedelph, and we can still save ourselves."

Berkley wasn't finished, though. "Dr. Nussbaumer, with all due respect, we got into this mess because we didn't know what we were doing. Can you be sure that situation's changed?"

Nice touch. "We always knew what we were doing. What we didn't know was what *they* were doing. Now we do. Now we can readjust our strategies to compensate."

The murmur grew stronger. Hope took shape in the back of Lynn's mind.

The burly man coughed once. "I'll have to take it to my people."

"We all will," said Berkley, keeping his steady gaze focused on Lynn. "As a strategy, it's fairly outrageous."

"The situation is outrageous." Lynn looked back without flinching. *Ask your people if they want to try to find a new corporation to take them in after they've been part of the biggest business disaster on record.* She did not say that. She was trading on every last drop of her reputation as a Dedelphi expert. She was milking the bandages for all they were worth. *I've been battered,* her appearance said, *but I'm still here. I've triumphed, and I say we can all triumph.*

She'd almost made it. Bitterness would not help now.

Brador was looking hard at her. Something between greed and desperate hope shone in his round eyes. "I am going to ask Dr. Nussbaumer to write up her suggestions as a formal proposal for distribution on the private web. We will take objections or commentary for twenty-four hours after the knot is tied."

There were a number of thoughtful looks, and some rapid messages and signals to implants, but no objections.

"Then I officially close this meeting. Room voice, recording off."

All at once, Lynn was besieged. A solid wall of bodies and voices surrounded her. "Dr. Nussbaumer, what are your plans for handling the sick?" "Dr. Nussbaumer, have you looked at the analysis of vulnerable mechanical points?" "Dr. Nussbaumer, have you contacted . . . ?" "Dr. Nussbaumer, have you consulted . . . ?" Lynn felt her head begin to swim, but she held her ground. From here on out she had to hold her ground. Whatever anybody else thought was happening, Lynn knew they had now entered a war with the Dedelphi. A war where they had to hold, had to advance, and had to keep their intentions a secret.

We can do this. I will *do this.* She looked at the faces crowded around her. *And you're all going to help.*

The cafeteria was not as full as Arron had expected. Most of the Bioverse personnel, he guessed, had chosen to watch the meeting in their apartments, rather than out here on the communal screens. He only had to peek into a half a dozen cubicles before he found the one in which Cabal sat nursing a beer. He watched the wall showing a news report about the new crater being opened up for Dedelphi use on Mars.

"Cabal?" Arron stood in the cube threshold.

"Hi." Cabal lifted the beer and waved him inside. "Come to see me off?"

Arron sat down. "Come to ask you to stay."

Cabal put his beer down and touched a key near the center of the table. The wall blanked. He focused completely on Arron. "Stay? Why?"

Because Lynn has been so scared by what happened to us, she's lost all perspective. Because I don't know what the corp's going to do next. "I need your help."

Cabal gave a short, humorless laugh. "Again?" he shook his head. "Arron, the help you need has a tendency to outweigh what you can pay."

Without a word, Arron reached into his pocket and laid down the chit card he'd charged from the Bioverse cashier system. Cabal picked it up and squinted at the codes.

"This is six thousand from the First Banking Enclave of Earth."

"That's right." *That's everything I've got, Cabal, it's going to have to be enough.*

Cabal put the card down and took another swallow of beer. "What do you want?"

Arron leaned forward. "I want you to cut through the Bioverse web and find the contingency plans for the Dedelphi project."

There had to be contingency plans. There had to be a list of what the corp would do if the Confederation broke apart, or at least broke the contract. There was no way on this side of heat death they would just shrug and walk away.

Cabal's eyes widened in an expression of surprised innocence. "What makes you think I could do that?"

Arron snorted. "Come on, Cabal, I'll admit I'm blind, but I'm not deaf. You said you were an info-runner. That you specialized in getting information to people who don't have it." *Come on, Cabal. Are you going to make me say system cracker?*

Cabal fingered the card for a moment. "All right. But I'll need a portable and a room that is both blind and deaf."

Arron nodded. "I've got a portable, and I think we can arrange the room."

Cabal opened his mouth and closed it again. Arron knew he wanted to ask what was going on, and was very glad when he didn't.

He did not want to have to explain the game he was playing.

Chapter XVIII

The Nussbaumer Redirection Proposal flew through the seniors. The veeps, led by Brador, got behind it and pushed. Back in the Solar system, the presies decided it might just work and gave it the go.

In just under forty-eight hours from the time she stood up in Brador's meeting, Bioverse set aside Dedelphi Base I conference room AI as Lynn's command center. She had all the wall screens lit up at once to keep in constant touch with her subcommittees. Trace and R.J. worked the conference table while she threaded between the assorted offices. Her new implant flashed reminders at her constantly. A patch cord ran from her temple to the table in front of her. Every order she subvocalized went straight to the main computers.

The word PIETER blinked in front of her eye.

Lynn touched the screen to what Trace and R.J. were calling spy central. "How're we doing on the sat count, Pieter?" As part of their surveillance, both the Getesaph and the t'Therians had launched a series of the very small, disposable spy satellites Praeis had told her about two weeks and a million years ago.

"We've identified six out of the eight satellites. We've got five t'Therians and one Getesaph, but we think they're getting ready to send up more." Pieter, an oak-colored man, typed frantically at his own keyboard as he talked and always seemed to have a significant portion of his mind elsewhere. "Of course this count is dependent on who manages to shoot down what over the next couple of hours."

"How's the decoding going?" Lynn zapped a note across to Trace about repeating this update to Brador. *There's a nice symmetry to the whole situation,* she thought privately. *The Getesaph tapped and decoded our communications system, now we're doing the same to them.*

"We've got the AIs burning through it." Pieter hit a final key, looked at the results on his screen, and smiled in triumph. He looked up, fully present for a brief moment. "We should have that for you in two hours."

"Great," announced Lynn. Without ceremony, she cut the connection there and threaded down to Shelly Greene in bioengineering R and D. "How are we coming with immobilizing the t'Therians?"

Shelly had a broad face that wrinkled up like a prune when she was thinking hard. Now it was smooth and cheerful. "We think we've got it, Chief. We've got a template for a yeast that eats oil. Turns it into a lovely sticky meringue. We can seed the harbor with it. It'll seize up everything tighter than tight."

"Okay, that's good. Let me know when it's ready to drop down, so we've got people in place to work with it. Thanks." She cut the thread.

"How are you going to handle the aftermath of immobilizing them?" asked Trace, looking up from her spot at the table.

Lynn shrugged, as if it were all obvious. "We'll apologize profusely and offer to clean it up, and send word to the Getesaph that while the cleanup is going on we're protecting the t'Therians."

R.J. looked serious. "You're going to need Keale's help with that."

"He's already offered," Lynn assured him. She'd been shocked when it happened, but accepted the help gratefully. "What do we hear from the negotiators?"

"We've just had word," R.J.'s gaze unfocused as he looked at something displayed on his implant. "The Ui Shai and the Fvrona have just said they want to be relocated."

"Good." Lynn murmured to her implant to add the names to the list in front of her. "Get a head count and order the shuttles down there before they have a chance to change their minds. How much space have we got?"

"Four ships without the *Ur*," said Trace. "We've currently committed for one hundred thousand, not counting the Ui Shai and Fvrona. So . . ." She paused while either she or her implant made a calculation. "We've got room for three-point-five-million more immediately."

"That'll make a dent, anyway," Lynn sucked on her lower lip. "How soon before we get more ships?"

Trace threaded through to another memo. "We've got three more on the way with Keale's reinforcements, but that's still two and a half weeks away." She touched another key. "The engineer's reports from the belt say they'll have the *Dublin* together in a week and down here two days after that."

"Okay, good," said Lynn with the grim firmness that had marked her voice since she'd gotten the go-ahead for her plan. "That's another two-point-five-million spots in five weeks. We load them up as fast as we can convince them to leave."

For the first time, Trace gave her a searching glance. "And if we can't convince them all?"

Lynn shook her head. "We have to."

Praeis stood beside Theia in the engine room. The entire engineering crew stood behind them in a tight semicircle. It was too quiet. The place should have been filled with the roar and hiss of machinery, with the smell of hot diesel and oil filling the air. Praeis's nostrils flared. The smell was still there, but now it was strangely sour, like bread dough left out too long. She crouched and reached into the frozen engine, running her fingers along the side of one immobile drive shaft. They should have come away coated with smooth, black grease. Instead, they were covered with foamy grey gunk. She sniffed her fingertip, and her nostrils clamped shut.

"How much is down?" Praeis asked the engine room's prime-sister as she stood up, examining the tacky substance on her fingers.

"Everything," Prime-Sister said bluntly. "We're cleaning and relubricating as fast as we can, but we can't run anything while that... stuff is in there." Her face went tight with distress. Another prime-sister, probably her blood sister, put a hand on her shoulder. "Where'd this come from, Task-Mother? Have the Getesaph got a new weapon?"

"I don't know, Prime-Sister," said Praeis heavily. "But we're going to find out. Carry on with the cleanup. Let us have a progress report in three hours."

"Yes, Task-Mother."

Praeis flicked an ear toward the stairs. She felt Theia follow her as she trudged up to the bridge.

"You do know," murmured Theia in her ear, "there is no way the Getesaph did anything like this."

Praeis bared her teeth and stopped in mid-stride with Theia two steps below her. She bent down until her lips brushed Theia's ear.

"No, you are right. It must be the Humans," she breathed.

Praeis straightened up, but she held her daughter's attention with both eyes and ears. Theia dipped her ears once. Good. She got the message and wouldn't say anything.

She had grown so much in the last few, hard, sad days. The work of the war had not ceased for their grief. The report ships had gone out with their letter to Armetrethe to tell her that Res and Senejess had died. They had written the letter one slow word at a time. Since then, Praeis had been out of Theia's sight for maybe five minutes. She wasn't sure if this was healthy. She was certain they were bending the rules to the breaking point, but on that score, she didn't care. She did not want to leave her daughter, and her daughter did not want to leave her.

Now, this . . . thing had happened. All the ships were suffering the same problem. Machinery seized up. Weapons seized up. At least one 'copter was down. They had engineers posted by the planes, but Praeis had no faith in that doing any good. Neys and Silv were out in the fleet, getting a firsthand look at the damage.

They had arms-sisters dug in on the shore. Without support, they'd be slaughtered. They were in the midst of a brief respite while the Getesaph pulled back and regrouped, but it wouldn't last forever.

The only thing that would throw her arms-sisters into a worse spin than all the rumors flying around the decks would be to have the worst ones confirmed: that it wasn't the Getesaph, it was the Humans who had done this. The immediate conclusion would be that the Humans had thrown in with the enemy.

Praeis resumed climbing the stairs, and Theia went back to following her. Praeis couldn't keep herself from panting gently. Theia came up beside her and brushed Praeis's shoulder with her shoulder. Praeis was grateful for the gesture, and wished she could put her arm around her daughter, but she didn't dare. They couldn't let the arms-sisters see how bad it was, even if every last one of them knew.

On the bridge, the Ship-Mother stepped quickly forward. "Task-Mother, we're being hailed." She handed across a pair of binoculars and pointed out the bridge window.

Praeis raised the binocs and focused them. Out in the bay, which was calm and blue and gave no hint to the activity directly underneath its surface, a little silver boat cut through the waves like a knife. A couple of white figures stood on the deck, shining in the bright sun.

And here they come, she thought. *Ancestors Mine, what are they going to say about this?*

Just then, the speaker crackled with the hail-sister code. An awkward voice speaking with a thick accent she couldn't place from anywhere said, "We are Robin Ford and Ari Chin of Bioverse Incorporated. We are asking permission to approach."

"They're doing it anyway. Look at that thing move," muttered the Ship-Mother.

"Answer them, Ship-Mother," said Praeis. "Let them come up." *As if we could stop them in the shape we're in.*

Praeis and Theia went out onto the deck. They were quickly joined by the Ship-Mother. The needlelike boat sped forward as if by magic and came neatly alongside. A pair of third-sisters struggled with a sticky ladder, but got it lowered, eventually. Two Humans, one *man* and one *woman,* climbed up.

"We need to talk to Praeis Shin t'Theria," said the *man,* breathlessly, to the third-sisters as soon as his boots hit the deck.

"I am Task-Mother Praeis Shin." Praeis took a half step forward. "This is my daughter Theiareth Shin and Ship-Mother Urae Vania." She dipped an ear toward Theia, then toward the Ship-Mother. The Humans' faces were both strained. Whatever was coming next, they were not looking forward to it. "You're in the middle of a combat zone, Human-Sisters, and we must tell you you're in great danger."

"We know, Task-Mother." The *woman* was shorter, rounder, and considerably more brown than her companion. She spoke in fits and starts, probably getting a lot of help from an implant. "But we needed to talk to you immediately. Yesterday, an apparently empty underwater bunker was cracked open, and this morning you had a red tide?"

"Yes?" said Praeis. Red tides weren't unusual in these waters, and it had only been a footnote in the reports. Praeis remembered the empty bunker, though. The arms-sisters had been ordered not to occupy it, in case there was a bioweapon or some other kind of poison in there.

The *man's* face creased. "That was one of ours," he said. "It contained a coagulant agent designed to congeal pollutants in water."

"Congeal?" repeated Theia.

"Yes." The *woman* bobbed her head up and down. "So that we could send in jobbers to sweep them up as soon as they clotted."

A distant ringing started in Praeis's ears. "Could this stuff clog industrial lubricants?"

"Yes," said the *man.* "That's what we came to tell you. We've notified our superiors about what's happened. Lynn Nussbaumer has arranged for a security force to be sent in to keep you safe until we can get you cleaned up. It's our fault; we're going to take care of it."

Praeis felt her ears wave uncertainly. "You're going to fight for us?"

"Not really," said the *woman.* "But we are going to make sure nobody gets near you. You're going to have to recall your people to your ships or your bases, and we'll keep those installations safe until your equipment is cleaned out."

"You're asking us to withdraw?" exclaimed Ship-Mother Vania, her voice full of disbelief. Her ears flattened against her scalp. "We can't. I mean . . ." She turned both ears toward Praeis. "With all respect, Task-Mother, I must speak. I know the Humans have no families, but we have sisters out there." She dipped both ears toward the shore. "We will not abandon them."

"You can't support them while your gear's clogged up," said the *woman,* a tinge of anger coloring her cool Human voice. "Listen, this stuff is alive. It's going to grow and spread and there is nothing in this world to stop it. All your machinery, all your weaponry"—she stabbed a finger toward the window and the distant fleet—"is going to stop working." Her brown face grew darker as she spoke. "Now, we can help. We want to help, but if you don't quarantine all your equipment where we can get to it in a hurry, this stuff will escape and reinfect everything and you'll never get your war going again."

"Why isn't your boat affected?" asked Theia suddenly.

The *woman* gave her a hard look. "We swabbed it down with some specialized disinfectants before we came in, but they're not going to work forever."

Theia pressed close to Praeis, and Praeis gave her a sideways glance and the flick of one ear. She was obviously dying to say something, and Praeis thought she knew what it was. These two were fidgety for more reasons than one. Praeis glanced around her. Everyone within earshot on deck had frozen in place and strained to hear what she said next.

She laid a hand on Theia's shoulder. She lifted her voice, speaking for the arms-sisters more than the Humans. "Do you swear by your contracts you will keep our arms-sisters safe while you perform this . . . disinfection?"

"Yes," said the *man.* "We'll put it on paper, if you want."

"Very well," said Praeis in her firm command voice. "We must get started immediately. Ship-Mother Vania, call in the Group Mothers." The Ship-Mother dipped her ears and retreated to the bridge. Praeis turned her ears to the Humans. "Will you agree to wait aboard your boat until my people are gathered?"

"Of course," said the *woman.*

"Good. Theia, you will come with me so we can get ready for this meeting." Praeis turned and strode into the administrative cabin.

Theia slipped in behind her and closed the door. "Did you feel it too, Mother?"

Praeis stood in the middle of the room, her ears waving in every direction. "Oh yes, my daughter. Those two are lying."

"Through their teeth," said Theia in English. She took Praeis's hand worriedly. "What are we going to do?"

"What we've been told," Praeis said calmly. "But only until we find out what's going on."

Keale kept his seat while Rchlthn Byvant rose out of her chair and towered over him. He watched her face smooth out and her ears flatten against her skull. Some distant part of his mind wondered if coming here in person had been a mistake. They were alone in their private office, and even his implant wasn't recording this exchange. The Sisters-Chosen-to-Lead had insisted on that.

"You're protecting them! They are killing our sisters!"

Keale sat up as straight as the overstuffed sofa would let him. "Not while we're here they're not."

That stopped Byvant short and gave him a chance to keep going. "Do you really believe we'd take sides?" he asked, forcing his voice into calm, level tones. "What were we going to do? Order them to stop? Would they listen?" He paused for one heartbeat. "You know they wouldn't. Now, they're stuck tight, and we have a good chance of keeping them that way, as long as you can hold your people back." Byvant's good ear lifted off her scalp by a bare centimeter. "Attack them while they're helpless and there's a good chance the Queens-of-All will send over a nuclear bomb, or another bioweapon, something that is less subject to industrial accidents."

Keale looked past Byvant to her silent sister sitting on a much stiffer and more dignified divan. Ishth, as always, hid her hands under a fold in her gold-and-silver jacket. Her ears had drooped a little, whether from frustration, or simple weariness, he couldn't tell. Her silence must have had some effect. Byvant took two steps backward.

Let's hope this is a good sign. "In the meantime," Keale went on, "we can get your daughters and carrying mothers out of the way, if you'll let us. We can put them aboard the *Beijing* with your cousins the Fil. That way, whatever happens, the future of your Family is safe."

Byvant turned a questioning ear toward Ishth. "We will have to take this to Parliament, or at least to the Prime Committee," said Ishth.

"Of course." Relief washed through Keale. "But think about how you take it. Here's your chance to make it through this with whole skins. It's a clean out if you want it."

In the next moment, he felt the tide that flowed between the sisters. They wanted his out. They wanted it so strongly, it reached his alien blood and heart.

A whole set of realizations turned over in his mind. *You knew, didn't you? You knew exactly what was going to happen aboard the* Ur, *but it's gone sour on you. You've lost control somehow, haven't you? And now your people are paying for it.*

"Consider carefully what brought down this attack," he said. "And what is still going on that allows it to continue."

With a strange, sudden clumsiness, Byvant sat down next to her sister and groped for her hand. Ishth gave it to her, and Byvant took it, gently. "We will do what is best for our people, whom we serve," she said mechanically.

Keale just nodded gravely. "Of course."

"We will take this to the Prime Committee," said Byvant. Her voice once again became firm and decisive, but both her ears pointed toward her sister, and her eyes looked at the floor. "A good decision will be handed down."

"I thank you, Rchilthn Ishth, Rchilthn Byvant," Keale stood up. *And I've got you both.*

The Paeccs Tayn were small, by Dedelphi standards. David could look most of them right in the eye. Their cream-and-grey skin looked unnaturally pale to him after weeks of dealing with the bluer t'Therians.

The Queens were there to meet the shuttle when it landed at their single, heavily guarded port. The place was obviously for military use: armored hangars, no planes out in the open, guard towers and heavy guns in place all around it.

He came down the ramp with his staff. The air around them smelled of heat, damp cement, and tension. The Queens, and their guard and a host of what he assumed to be either nobles, or politicians, although he wasn't sure, waited in patient, dignified rows just to the side of the ramp, so he had to turn straight toward the sun to face them. He'd only had a few hours to bone up on the Paeccs Tayn. He didn't even speak the language and would be stammering through it, reading off his implant, which was not something he was looking forward to.

However, Keale had told Lynn it was vital that the Paeccs Tayn be reassured that the Humans hadn't decided to abandon the Dedelphi, or that they might join the (hopefully) stalled war between the Getesaph and the t'Theria. Nobody asked why Keale was so sure, but he was sure enough to convince Lynn, and Lynn had been sure enough to convince David. The plague had already taken sixty percent or more of the Paeccs Tayn, so it was decided that more than a veep, or a senior manager, or a security expert, the Paeccs Tayn needed to speak with a doctor.

One of the Queens, the First Queen Oran *ji* Ufa, his implant reminded him, stepped briskly up to him. Her earrings clinked as she moved. She spoke, and his implant scrolled the English words for him.

"You are Dr. David Zelotes? You are here to help us? This is what we have been told."

David subvocalized the reply he wanted to make, and read the words off as they passed, mangling the pronunciation as he went. "I am. My staff and I are here to help in whatever way we can, and to assure you that we will stay until the work is done." *Maybe they'll learn to appreciate the strong silent type.*

She leaned in close to him, as if trying to read his implant. "You are not afraid of the t'Theria and the Getesaph?"

More than you know. David worked hard to keep that thought out of his face, and to not step back. The Queen's breath steamed his helmet. "There is more to the world than the t'Theria and the Getesaph."

"Ha!" Queen Oran stood back, folding her hands across her pouch in what David had always taken to be a sign of extreme satisfaction. "It is well said, isn't it? Some days I wonder why we let them forget that." Her ears stilled. "I think we will like you, Dr. David Zelotes. You will come with us?"

David bowed his head. "Gladly."

Arron sat at the comm station in his sparsely furnished guest quarters. Cabal had been installed three doors down on the same level. There had been no problem getting them both space. Over a public comm station, Arron had asked Lynn for two cabins. She'd paused for all of thirty seconds to listen to him before saying, "Sure, whatever you need," and cut the connection. The Base AI had taken care of the remaining details.

Arron had walked Cabal to his cabin. Cabal had stalked around the hexagonal space once and grunted. Then, he plunked Arron's portable down on the table, saying that the first thing he'd have to do was see who was paying attention out there. Arron had left him to it.

Arron watched the blank screen of his own comm station and rubbed his forearms. Walking through the Base corridors had felt strange. This was the first time in years he was literally surrounded by Humans. Part of him wanted to run, and part of him wanted to touch everyone he saw. It was so . . . wrong to see everyone standing politely distanced from each other. Wrong and unnatural. Feeling that reaction inside himself made everything worse, so he'd retreated to his cabin to wait for Cabal.

Since then, he'd been totally ignored. Lynn and Bioverse had many more important things to worry about than him. Things that were also more important than finding out what was really going on aboard the *Ur.* He'd tried to ask Lynn about it, but she'd just shaken her head and said that was all up to Security Commander Keale. She'd sworn she'd talk with him as soon as things got into motion. That had been three days ago.

Whatever Lareet and Umat thought they were doing had gone unaddressed. Hadn't anybody here thought to try to ask them what they were afraid of? What had driven them to this extreme? And what in the name of the World Mothers had made them turn on him?

Arron took a deep breath. This probably wouldn't work. This couldn't possibly work, and there was no way for him to make it work, and he had nothing more to give Cabal to get him to make it work. But he had to try.

"Room voice, thread me through to the city-ship *Ur.*"

"Completing request."

Arron waited for a security lockout, the alarm, at least a validity question from the AI, but none came. The station cycled through the addresses, and he waited, his heartbeat slowing down each second nothing unusual happened. Apparently the higher-ups at Bioverse couldn't conceive why anybody would want to call the ship, and their security chief had been too busy to think of it for them.

"Request completed," said the room voice, although the screen was still blank. "Audio only available."

Arron's heart rose into his throat. "This is Scholar Arron to the city-ship *Ur.* I am seeking Dayisen Rual Lareet and Dayisen Rual Umat. Can they be found to speak with me?"

He strained his ears for some reply out of the dark screen. Instead, he heard the door swish open at his back.

"What are you doing!" shouted Lynn.

"Room voice, close connection." Arron turned around to face

her. Her bandages were gone, but the new skin shone a little too pink and a little too fresh, giving her a strangely patchwork appearance. "I'm trying to talk to my sisters . . ." he began calmly.

"Your sisters!" Rage distorted her face.

Lynn, what's happened to you? "Dayisen Lareet and Dayisen Umat. They've hosted me for my entire time here, and I've always thought of them as my sisters."

Lynn ran her hand across the stubble on her scalp. "Did you ever ask them what *they* thought?"

He felt real anger flash through him. "If I didn't, I was just imitating you."

Lynn's face flushed scarlet. She took one step toward him.

At that moment, the room voice cut through the air. "Dr. Nussbaumer, an urgent call from Praeis Shin t'Theria waiting for you."

Lynn closed her mouth so hard, Arron heard her teeth click together. "We aren't finished," she said as she faced the comm station. It was only when she turned her back that Arron realized he had no idea what she was doing here, or how she got in. She must have had the call thread to the *Ur* spliced. Was she looking for anyone calling the *Ur,* or just him? He couldn't be sure. For all he could tell, she had forgotten his existence.

"Activate the station. I'm here, Praeis." She did not sit down, she just folded her arms across her chest.

Watching over her shoulder, Arron saw the screen flicker to life. There was Praeis Shin front and center, but Praeis was wearing a filter mask over her nose and mouth. A thick rubber suit covered her torso. He peered past her at the shadowy background and realized with a start she must be at his old outpost, talking on the last remaining comm station.

"Lynn. Thank you for taking this. I can't stay where I am for long. It's not exactly secure here." The filter mask muffled Praeis's voice, but Arron could still hear the strain in it. Her ears were tilted back and quivering with stress. "It's the only station I could get to. Lynn, what's going on? I appreciate your people are keeping us safe, but we're being fed some story about accidents and pollution congealers."

Lynn's color had dropped somewhere close to normal. "Praeis, I swear, it's true. It was an accident," she said without any hesitation. Arron felt his stomach clench. *How could you do this? Lynn, do you even know what you're doing?* "The bioengineers have been storing their gunk up all over the planet waiting for the time to let it loose. We didn't know—"

"You didn't know we'd go to war," Praeis finished for her. "Of course not. You thought you had us all managed, didn't you?" She waggled her ears to say she was teasing, but there was an edge to her voice that grated across the back of Arron's mind. "I've been called back to t'Aori to explain the situation to the Queens."

"I can send you down maps and diagrams of the other caches," said Lynn, as if only anxious to be helpful. "Or you can have them call up here anytime."

"Thank you." Praeis dipped her ears. "But I can handle this much."

"Have I ever doubted how much you can handle, Praeis?" Lynn's voice softened, and even Arron was ready to swear she meant it.

There was a pause, and Arron saw Lynn's pleasant smile flicker. "Of course not," said Praeis. "I've got to go before I breathe in too much poison."

"Call up, soon, Praeis. Let me know how you and Theia are doing."

"I will." Praeis cut the connection.

Before the screen had completely blanked, Lynn turned back to Arron. He stared at her. He knew he was staring, but he couldn't help it. His hands had gone cold. Who was this woman? This was not Lynn. It couldn't be.

He gestured weakly toward the comm station. "I cannot believe you did that."

She rubbed her eyes with her fingertips. "Look, Arron, I do not want to argue about this. I'm . . ."

He took two steps toward her. He was too close for Human politeness, but he didn't care. She did not step back. "You're sitting up here deciding the fate of the Dedelphi. You're planning out their every move and correcting them when they go wrong. Why don't you just get yourself a throne and a beard, declare yourself God, and finish it!"

"I am saving lives," said Lynn in a tightly controlled voice. She stayed where she was, and Arron found he had to step back from her.

"You're running lives, Lynn!" He paced around the comm station chair. "You wouldn't even tell Praeis what you're doing!"

"Of course I didn't tell her! I . . ."

"You what?" asked Arron softly. "You didn't want her to know how far it's gone?" He grabbed the back of the chair with both hands. "You didn't want her to tell some of *her* sisters what was going on in case they'd rebel against you?" Her eyes glowed dangerously. Arron leaned toward her. *Don't you see it, Lynn? Listen to me, I'm just trying to make you see!* "They scared you, Lynn, admit it. You found a situation you couldn't manage, and you got scared. Now you're determined to make the whole planet behave like you want, so you don't have to be afraid of it anymore."

"If we don't do something, they are all going to die," she said, enunciating each word carefully. "I am not going to kill them. Are you? Are you going to say they're all better off dead?"

"No, of course not." Arron ran both hands across his stubbly scalp. *Why can't you hear me?* "All I am saying, all I have ever said, is that they need to make their own decisions!"

"They did, Arron!" Lynn slammed her hand down on the comm-station keyboard. "They decided to bring us here!"

"But not for this!" He flung out both hands.

Lynn's teeth bared, just like a Dedelphi's. "Yes, for this! Exactly for this! They asked us to save them, and we're going to!"

Arron leaned over the chair. "Lynn, the corp isn't interested in saving them. The corp is interested in—"

"Spare me, Arron." Lynn held up both hands and waved him back. "They're not dealing with the corp now. They're dealing with me."

Arron stared, stunned. She believed it. She really believed Bioverse had just stepped aside and left everything in her hands.

"Well"—he swallowed hard—"I guess it's all right then."

"No, it isn't." She shook her head. Her shoulders slumped. For a moment, Arron saw how tired she was, but she rallied and pulled herself up straight again. "It's not all right, but it will be. Don't try to call them again, Arron. Things are too . . . delicate. We just can't let you in there; we don't know what will happen."

She left. The door swished shut behind her. Arron stayed where he was, wondering what else he could have said, what else he could have done. Was she really too far gone for him to reach anymore? Had she been that badly scared?

Had he really lost her, too?

Lareet woke to the sound of sisters screaming.

She shot bolt upright on the mattress. Umat was already at the window. Around them, dayisen, trindt and irat sat up and twisted their ears around, trying to make sense of the sound.

"What is it?" asked Lareet. As she spoke, a thick smell reached her. It was like mildew and rotting fungus. Her nostrils pinched themselves closed.

"Something's happened to the river." Umat ran for the stairs.

Lareet jumped up and snatched a tunic from off the clothes chest as she pelted after her sister. She shrugged into it somewhere between the foot of the stairs and the open door and headed across the lawn to stand beside Umat.

Naked as a fisher in the rain, Umat dug her toes into the grassy riverbank near a cluster of sisters. The dawn was just starting, and the dome was turning light blue, but there was already plenty of light by which to see what had happened.

The river, the beautiful, clear, sparkling river was now thick with brown sludge. It bubbled and swirled like the worst contents of an open sewer. It was the source of the smell that permeated the air. Dead fish rocked on the surface like toy boats.

Umat stared. Her mouth opened, but it was a moment before any sound could come out. "Mother Night," she whispered. Then, she collected herself. "Ovrth Ond, Ovrth Brindt, get to the command center, tell them to get a team down to the water recyclers immediately to try to find out what's happened. Trindt Mnat, take some sisters and see if all the tap water is the same way."

Something brushed Lareet's shoulder. She swatted at it angrily. A yellow leaf drifted down to the grass under her feet.

Yellow? She looked up. Another leaf swirled down from the tree she stood under. The strengthening light showed her that the green foliage was heavily speckled with unhealthy yellow blotches. Small drifts of dead leaves lay piled on the grass. Lareet looked closer. The grass was yellowing, too. In places, pale, blobby mushrooms studded the ground.

"Umat"—she straightened up—"we will need to check the gardens as well."

The news, when it came to the command center, was not good. All the water was affected, on both sides of the ship. A little potable liquid could be created by a slow process of repeated boiling and filtration. No one had to point out that without sterile water, all the medical experiments would grind to a halt, but Lareet saw the faces of the irat who came in to report. They were all thinking about it.

The fungus that was taking over the lawns and strangling the trees had indeed gotten into the gardens. They were now havens for corpse grey mushrooms that split open with the stench of methane and scattered clouds of brown spores everywhere.

Their city. Their beautiful, lovingly made city was rotting around them.

"We can do without the gardens, if we have to," said Umat, her ears flicking back and forth. "We can eat the artificial rations the Humans left. It's the water."

"It's other things as well, Sister," said Lareet gravely. "Have you smelled the air in the cities? The stench is getting stronger. It's going to be unbreathable very shortly. If we cannot get the filtration system going, we will be forced into pressure suits and cleansuits." She paused and decided she did not need to add that there were not enough for the entire complement aboard.

"We could load the extra personnel into shuttles and send them back home." The shuttles' computers hadn't been sabotaged. The autopilots had assured their best flyers they could get back to the Hundred Isles, even at the acceleration and trajectory that would be reached when the ship was moving full tilt.

If only we could teach the city-ship to be so cooperative. Lareet shook her head. "Dayisen Umat, if we send anyone out now, they'll be picked up by the Humans, or the Parliament. If anything goes wrong, they'll be exiled, or killed. We still need to wait." *We need to wait until we are sure this will work. Until we know our sisters will go home heroes. So I can stand beside you as long as possible and breathe you all the way into my womb for our daughters to remember.*

"How did they do it?" Umat flung her arms out.

Lareet frowned down the tunnel. Where there had once been green grass, there were now sickly brown mushrooms. "Some of those *jobbers* must have carried spores. The rest of the attack was probably a diversion."

Umat turned eyes and ears toward her. "Then we are once again out of time."

Lareet dipped her ears silently.

Umat faced the coders. "Can we move the ship yet?"

"We can move it," said Dayisen Ksenth. The head of the coders' dawn shift looked down at the miles of broad paper ribbon lying curled on the central table. "We can start the engines anytime we need to—"

Umat cut her off with uncharacteristic impatience. "Can we move it where we want it?"

Dayisen Ksenth's ears crumbled. "That's still theoretical."

Lareet touched her sister's arm. Umat's skin rippled, but she gave no other sign of noticing Lareet. "How much less theoretical will another two days make it?" Umat asked.

"Not much," the dayisen admitted. "We unfortunately do not have the luxury of a test flight."

Lareet felt the uncertainty ripple through her sister, and her own skin bunched up in answer. "It was always a risk, Sister," Umat said, as if they were alone. "I think the Humans did this to discomfort us. What will they do when they really want to root us out?"

Lareet lowered both eyes and ears. She already knew what Umat was going to say next, and she could not think of one valid reason to prevent her.

"Give the orders to the engine room, Dayisen Ksenth," Umat said in a calm, level voice. "We are moving now."

Chapter XIX

Commander Keale sat at the conference table in his office with Captain Esmaraude. A 3-D of the *Ur* hung on the video wall between them.

"Start with the engines to be safe." Esmo spoke each word as if it hurt. Keale was sure it did. The *Ur* was her ship, and here they were talking calmly about dismantling it.

"It wouldn't be that safe," countered Keale. "One blast out the back jets and the crane ship will be a floating heap of slag."

"Not if the crane goes straight in." She tapped the hangar-bay doors. "And gets straight to work. It'll take the pogos a minute to figure out what's going on, and I guarantee you they're not going to be turning the jets on quickly. If we warn the crane's crew what to expect, they'll be able to get the ship well out of the way of any blast." She frowned. "Cranes steer like pigs, but they're a lot faster than city-ships."

Keale nodded. "Okay, straight in and go for the engines. Now, we can probably expect them to deploy some jobbers in response—"

"Commander Keale," the room voice cut across his sentence. "Receiving transmission from sat-net beta."

Keale's throat closed. Beta was the mini-net they'd thrown up around the *Ur.* "Room voice, open station and display."

He spared a brief glance at Esmo, who kept her face perfectly blank. The station screen lit up and showed the vacuum, the *Ur,* and the twin plasma jets burning out of her nozzles. Keale imagined he heard the infrastructure creak as the ship lumbered forward, gathering speed.

"Room voice, emergency thread to Lieutenant Ryan."

Ryan must have been sitting on top of a station because it was barely ten seconds later that his image appeared on Keale's screen. "Yes, sir?"

"Ryan, the *Ur* is on the move. We need a shuttle out to track it, at maximum range, you understand me? I don't want anybody crowding that ship to get a close look. We just need to track its course."

Ryan's pale cheeks went paper white. "Yes, sir," was all he said, though, and he cut the connection.

Keale turned back to Esmo. "The net's not mobile, so it'll be out of range soon," he said ruefully. "Even I didn't think they'd get it moving this fast."

Esmo leaned against the conference table and folded her arms. She tapped her fingers against her own forearm. "Do you have any idea what they're doing?"

"I've got a really good guess." He touched three keys on the board, and the view on the wall screen switched from empty vacuum to the creamy sphere of Dedelph.

Esmo paled. "Kaye, you don't think . . ."

Keale met her gaze. "You've got enemies that have plagued your family since time immemorial. You've just taken control of a rock weighing several hundred million tons. What would you do with it?"

"Drop it on them," said Esmo, grimmer than Keale had ever heard her. "How'd they think of it, Kaye? They don't even have spaceflight."

"No, but they've been throwing things at their enemies at least as long as we have." His fist tightened.

"Have you got anything you could go after them with?" asked Esmo.

Keale slumped into the station chair. "Plenty. I've got hundreds of completely unarmed shuttles. I've got an engineering fleet four days away. I've got just under four thousand people armed with nonlethal force. I've got all of that." He looked at the sphere. "And none of it is any good."

"You've forgotten something," said Esmo.

Keale lifted his gaze from the screen. "What?"

Esmo bit her lip, then said, "Another city-ship."

Keale felt a strange calm cover him over. "Use another ship to ram the *Ur*?"

She nodded. "And soon. If they get too close to the planet, the collision will pour debris and fast-particle masses all over Dedelph."

She seemed distant, her words a little unreal, but this was real, he told himself. This was more real than anything else he'd ever done. "How many people does it take to fly one of those?"

She shrugged. "Two people and one functioning AI can do it for short distances."

He met her eyes across the gulf his unwilling mind had created. "Can you teach me what I need to know in time?"

She blew out a sigh, considering. "You're shuttle-rated aren't you, Kaye?"

He nodded.

"Then, yes, I can."

"All right. We can take the *Manhattan.* It's unoccupied."

Esmo nodded. "I'll break the news to the admiral."

"I'll get the authorization from the veeps, so you can back up what you tell the admiral."

Her eyes sparkled behind her spectacles with icy amusement. "You know, they might not let us do this."

Keale shrugged. "Then I'll be extremely interested to hear the alternate plan."

They both stood up. He opened his mouth, but she waved him quiet. "It's my job, too, Kaye, more than it is yours. They terrorized my crew. They shot Rudu's leg off him. They took my ship out from under me." Her face went hard and he could see the fury burning hot and alive in her black eyes. "I am not going to let them get away with that."

"I'll meet you in the hangar at fifteen hundred then." His station beeped twice at him.

Esmo jumped a little. "What's that?"

"Something I've been keeping track of. That planetsider, Cabal, has been snooping around the private web. I had a thread drone on his back getting the proof." He pursed his lips thoughtfully. "It's probably not worth it, but I'll send somebody around to get him. See you at fifteen hundred, Esmo."

"Fifteen hundred." Esmo left.

Keale sat down at the comm station and typed in a brief command to call up the thread drone that had let him know it was finished with its job. *Business as usual. Attend to security matters. Keep everybody and everything safe. Don't think about the suicide run you've just signed up for. No. Don't think about that.*

"All right, Mr. Cabal," said Keale, suddenly grateful to Cabal for providing a distraction. "Exactly what have you been up to?"

Praeis walked beside Theia into the Debating Chamber. Everything was the same; marble tables, mosaicked floor, portraits of the Ancestors looking down and the Queens looking expectantly up. What was different was the air in the room. It quivered, with both anger and anticipation. What was also different was the way that Armetrethe hovered behind the sofas the Queens occupied. Five other Council members stood like sisters beside her.

Armetrethe's cold eyes confirmed what Praeis had suspected all along. She was not being called to report, she was being called to account, and not by the Queens alone.

Oh, Sister, my behavior has finally become too heavy for you to bear? Her flesh settled against her muscles with a sick heaviness. Theia pressed close to her. Now they both knew for certain why there had been no letter in response to the news that a sister and a daughter had died. Armetrethe had been too busy working on this meeting.

Praeis closed her eyes and raised her hands. "I am returned as ordered, Majestic Sisters. When I left, the strategic situation was as I laid out in my last report. The Humans' presence has successfully warded off any Getesaph attacks. The infestation is being eradicated, and our arms-sisters are working ceaselessly to refit and repair their equipment and return our fighting capability."

She waited for permission to open her eyes. It didn't come.

"Yes, your reports have been quite regular," said Aires Byu smoothly. "Perhaps you meant this as compensation for your irregular actions."

Praeis felt her throat close. To her surprise, Theia spoke. "Forgive me, Majestic Sisters. I'm sure my mother understands your meaning, but I, ignorant and childless as I am, do not."

"You do not?" inquired Vaier Byu. Her voice was heavy and reluctant. Since the Queens were addressing Theia, Praeis opened her eyes.

Vaier Byu was clutching Aires's hand. "I will explain, then, since your mother has not." She looked at Theia, but her ears focused completely on Praeis. "Praeis Shin t'Theria began a military action without orders from her Queens. She has used the lives and resources of her Great Family for her own purposes. After which, she entered into a private contract with the Humans to immobilize our military so they could serve their real partners in the Hundred Isles."

"No," said Praeis, more to Armetrethe than the Queens. Armetrethe's ears flattened. Praeis could feel the waves of hatred rolling out of her soul. Her skin shivered and danced as they washed over her. *Sister, Sister, we are the last of our family. Don't do this. Let me come home. I swear we can come together again.*

"It was fine while you were winning, Sister," Armetrethe said bitterly, and Praeis knew not one of her thoughts reached Armetrethe. "The streets sang your praises. But what did you expect when this Human 'accident' happened?"

I hear what you're really asking, Sister. You're asking how I let my sister and daughter die? You're asking how could I rebel against you? You and she decided to take my daughter away from me into the enemy's islands, and now you blame me because they died.

"Ancestors Mine." Praeis felt her muscles spasm out of control. "And I'm the one who's supposed to be insane. Armetrethe, it wasn't an accident. We are being lied to, but—"

"You hear!" said Armetrethe to the Queens without even closing her first lid. "You hear! She admits it!"

"Armetrethe Shin t'Theria, you will remember we are still your Queens!" thundered Ueani Byu.

"And my Majestic Sisters will remember what they did to help bring this about!"

That was too much even for her Wise Sisters in Council. One of them laid a hand on Armetrethe's good arm. Her stump beat the air furiously, but she closed her eyes. "My apologies, Majestic Sisters. I am . . . overwrought at seeing my lost and distant sister, Praeis."

Oh, good, Armetrethe. Perfect. The skin shuddered up and down Praeis's back. *What next? What's the next line in this scene?*

"What answer do you have to make, Noblest Sister?" boomed Ueani Byu.

What answer? I have served and lived and waited and come back to serve again, and you abandoned my daughter and you called me mad and now you call me to grovel in front of you because your enemies have the upper hand and one of them is my last sister who I was fool enough to believe would let me come home . . .

The room stank, Praeis suddenly realized. The air filled with the scents of fire, fear, stale breath, and blind anger. She took a step forward. The air brushed against her skin like silk. She could feel every draft. She could feel everything. The warmth from the heating pit lapped gently at her left cheek and filled her ear like music. The tiles under her feet each had a unique shape. All their surfaces were delicately, individually pebbled. She wanted to touch them. She would touch them. They felt so good under her palms and knees, rough and cool as her hands traveled back and forth and back and forth. Hands touched her, and that was best of all. She would go anywhere, do anything to keep that feeling, warm and soft and infinitely welcome.

The hands pulled her, and she went with them.

Arron answered the summons to Keale's office primarily because he didn't know what else to do. There was only one reason the security chief could have for calling him in; Cabal must have gotten caught.

Keale waved him to a seat at the conference table, and Arron took it. Keale sat at his comm station. Arron had to work to keep his hands from rubbing his forearms, or thighs, or scratching his scalp.

Keale steepled his fingers. "Has Dr. Nussbaumer told you what happened?"

Arron shook his head. "I haven't spoken to Lynn for a couple of days." *Or she hasn't spoken to me, I'm not sure which.*

"The *Ur* is moving. We've got them plotted. They're going to drive the ship straight into the t'Aori peninsula."

Arron felt the blood drain out of his cheeks. "No."

Keale just looked at him.

Lareet? Umat? What are you doing? "Can you stop them?"

One muscle in Keale's cheek tightened. "Yes. If we leave in time, we can intercept them with another city-ship."

Arron's hands felt cold. He wanted to jump up and pace the room so badly, his legs ached with the effort of keeping still. "Then what?"

The muscle in Keale's cheek twitched again. "The ships will collide and, if we've timed it right, the debris will fly off harmlessly into space."

"You're talking about making a suicide run."

"Yes," said Keale again. He lowered his hands and laid them on his chair arms. "And I'd like to talk to you about a way out of it."

A way out of it? For whom? "I'm not sure what you're getting at."

He leaned forward, resting his elbows on his knees. "I am hoping you can talk to your friends the Dayisen Rual and convince them to take the *Ur* off its present course."

Arron said nothing, he just sat there. Keale had just offered him what he'd been aching for since he'd heard about the takeover. Here was a chance to talk to Lareet and Umat and talk them out of . . . whatever it was they thought they were doing.

Why aren't I jumping at it? asked part of his brain. *Because,* answered another part, *you have other things you want to do.*

He couldn't look at Keale anymore. He got to his feet and paced around the conference table. An idea took hold in the back of his mind, and it grew stronger with every step.

Finally, he faced Keale again. He took a deep breath. "There's only one way it'll work."

"What?" Keale looked at him with narrowed eyes.

"I need to be on the ship." Surprise froze Keale in place. Arron kept going. "If I'm there, and they don't veer off, they'll kill a sister. Umat might not consider me a true sister, but I think Lareet might. It'll create a division between them." He swallowed. "Divisions between sisters can remove resolve."

Keale nodded. "It makes sense. All right, you'll have the dubious honor of coming along." For the first time, his face softened. "You do realize that if you can't talk them out of it, you're going to be just as dead as the rest of us?"

"Oh, yes." Arron stiffened his shoulders. Now or never. "That's why I'm going to ask a high price for going along."

"You're what?" Keale jerked himself halfway out of his chair.

"I want access to the contingency plans for when the Dedelphi break their contract with Bioverse."

Keale fell back into the chair, and, to Arron's surprise, he started chuckling. "I've already got six counts of system breaking and entering against your friend Cabal. He says you paid for it. Do you have any idea what I could do to you for that?"

Arron shrugged. "Do you have any idea how little I care? My whole life is gone." His palm brushed the table as if he were sweeping something onto the floor. "You want my help, all right, but you need me to do this voluntarily. What are you going to do? Tie me up and haul me onboard and put me in front of the screen with a stunner to my head?"

Keale's face remained impassive. "I'm already doing you a favor by not having you arrested."

"I know." Arron straightened up slowly. "Now, I'm asking for another one."

He's going to call my bluff, thought Arron, looking into Keale's calculating brown eyes. *It's not going to work. He's going to see I won't let Lareet and Umat die if I can help it.*

But Keale didn't say anything. He just swung the chair around and laid his thumb over a key chip on the comm station. After a moment, the station beeped and a drawer slid open. Keale lifted out a piece of paper.

He hesitated. "I just want you to know," he said without turning around, "that if it was just me, this would not work. I am only doing this because there are other people I do not want to see dead."

"I know," said Arron, and he was shocked to realize he really did.

Keale handed the paper to Arron. "Great stuff, paper. Learned about it from the Dedelphi. Humans used it once upon a time. I've got no idea why it was abandoned. Absolutely no way to cut into it or tap it through the web. No wandering backups and no shadow records."

Arron read down the list quickly and felt a chill growing inside him. There was a paragraph about lowering the city-ships into the atmosphere and shifting the angle on the artificial gravity to shake the cities apart. There was a paragraph about letting loose engineered molds to blight an entire harvest and leave the Dedelphi dependent on Humans for their food, delivery of which would be contingent on their good behavior.

Finally, there was the paragraph about landing, taking whatever would pay for Bioverse's considerable losses, putting the PR dervishes to work on tales of unspeakable barbarity versus brave Humanity, and leaving.

Arron folded the paper into thirds and put it in his pocket. "You've already arrested Cabal, haven't you?"

"Yes." Keale's voice was mild.

"He only did it because I paid him to."

"I thought so." Keale stood. "We'll be trying you with him when we get back."

"I thought so," said Arron in a reasonable imitation of Keale's negligent tone. "When do we leave, Commander?"

"In one hour, Dr. Hagopian. We want to meet the *Ur* as far away from Dedelph as possible."

"Of course." Arron stood up. "I'll meet you in the hangar in an hour."

* * *

When the word came down of what had been decided about the *Ur,* Lynn was snatching a prefab, flash-cooked meal in her cabin with David. He'd taken the opportunity offered by need to get medical supplies and report on what was going on aboard the *Cairo* with the Paeccs Tayn and the Ui Shai to steal a couple of hours with her, and Lynn was grateful.

She'd been trying to tell herself that Keale would find a solution to the "*Ur* problem." That there was absolutely no question about it. He was in consultation with the admiral, and the *Ur*'s captain, and there'd be a plan, and they'd put it into play and everything would work out.

No matter how hard she tried, she couldn't make herself believe it. Work had ground to a halt. The spy satellites had been reoriented to track the *Ur*'s flight as it swung out in its wide elliptic. Nobody had the least doubt that Keale and Esmaraude had made a correct prediction. The Getesaph were going to drop the *Ur* on their ancient enemies.

Lynn had quickly squashed the notion of telling the t'Therians. What good would it do? Was there any way they could evacuate even some of the population of t'Aori in the time remaining? Not that they were going to have to, of course, but they couldn't even if they thought they might have to . . .

And even with David holding on to her, Lynn had felt cold fear sink in and numb her to the bone.

Then, the comm station lit up with a message from Keale, about the solution to the problem, and about Arron's part in it.

Lynn looked helplessly at David.

"Go," was all he said.

Lynn went. Double-damning Bioverse propriety, she ran through the pleasantly designed wood-paneled, full-spectrum-lit corridors. She ran through the bulkheads flanked by stands of bamboo and beds of ferns. She ran through the flower gardens and rock gardens and summery arbors until she crossed into the plain, angled, metal-and-ceramic hall that led to the hangar deck.

She leaned on the bulkhead, breathing hard and scanning the white chamber. Arron stood next to one of the shuttles, looking around himself half-expectantly, half-worriedly. When he saw her, his face smoothed, and he crossed the shining floor to the doorway.

Lynn just looked up at him.

He held his hand out, but let it fall. "I'm sorry," he said.

"For what?" *You're going out there to kill yourself; do not expect me to make this easy on you.* The thought was irrational, and she knew it. He was doing this for himself, for her, for the Dedelphi, for his friends, for Bioverse. She should be thanking him. She should be . . . She should be doing anything but what she was.

"For everything." He waved both hands helplessly. "For not being able to talk to you. For not being able to explain. For . . ." Arron took her in his arms and kissed her, long and warm and deep. She kissed him back, for all the old love and lost friendship they held between them.

He let her go. She had nothing to say. There was nothing left to say, not until he came back, if he came back.

He reached into his pocket and pulled out a piece of paper folded in thirds. "Here," he handed it to her. "These are real. I got them from Keale in exchange for my help. I don't know what you want to do with them, but . . ." He paused. "But I thought you should see them."

Arron turned on his heel and strode across to the waiting shuttle.

Lynn stood there, stiff-backed and dry-eyed, until the siren cut the air, warning all personnel to leave the hangar. Depressurization commencing in three minutes. Two minutes, thirty seconds. Two minutes, twenty.

Lynn held herself to a walk all the way back to the cabin. It wasn't until David put his hand on her shoulder and asked what was wrong that she broke down crying for Arron and everything that had never happened.

"It's all right," David leaned her toward him. "It's all right. Go ahead. Just let me . . ." He lifted the paper from her fingers.

"Ah, God," Lynn wiped at her eyes. "I don't even know what it is. Arron gave it to me . . ." She took it back from him and unfolded it.

Under the machine-printed heading "Contingency Plans in Case of Fatal Breach of Contract" came a list. Lynn read it and felt the blood drain away to the soles of her feet.

"What the hell was he thinking?" she demanded of David. "It won't come to this! We've got everything under control!" She bunched the paper up in her fist. "He knows that. We've got everything taken care of. We—" All at once a pair of very different eyes flashed in her mind, not Arron's, but Praeis's. Praeis's when she'd called to find out what was really happening, and Lynn had lied.

David read the expression on her face. "So, what the hell was he thinking?"

She looked at the crumpled paper again. "He was thinking of showing me what other people were planning on doing if the Dedelphi didn't cooperate. He was thinking of showing me where it could lead if we forgot—" She swallowed. "If I forgot that I'm not the only one playing this game."

David sighed. "So, what are you going to do this time?"

The sound of near exasperation in his voice made Lynn swing around to look at him. "David?"

He took her hand. "Lynn, listen to me. I'm behind you, whatever you do, but do you remember why we're here? Really? We're not here to save the world, or help Bioverse make a profit. We're here because an independent race of sapient beings asked us to come help. Now you and Bioverse are telling them what to do, and Arron's telling them what to be, and no one is asking *them* how they want to handle this mess we've all gotten into."

His voice was soft, but his eyes were thunderous. He was not angry at her, she knew him well enough to know that. He was angry at the mess that had invaded the project like a brand-new virus. One more plague to harrow the Dedelphi.

She swallowed again, and her throat ached. "You're right," she said slowly. "But David, I can't let the war start up again. I will not let people die when I can stop it. If that's playing God, then it is and it's probably immoral if not illegal and I'm doing it anyway." She looked at the crumpled wad of paper in her fist. "But I can tell Praeis what's going on." She unclenched her fist from around the paper. "All of it."

David took her empty hand and smoothed it out. "It'll be enough, Lynn. Somewhere in here, it will be enough."

Lynn leaned her head against his shoulder. "God, I hope you're right."

Chapter XX

The hangar bay was stuffed to the brim with sisters, but even under the rich scent of too many bodies in too small a space, you could still smell the rot from the city. All of the shuttles were full of soldiers and sealed tight with their own air filters on. The remaining sisters had moved in here by suggestion and mutual consent. No one had been able to get the main filtration system going again, but here the smell was at least bearable. Besides, many said, where else should they be at this time than shoulder to shoulder with their sisters?

Lareet looked at all the sisters crowding the deck. All the ones who were going to die with the ship. They were, each one of them, as cheerful as Umat, reminiscing and joking with each other, as if they were all on their way to one great battle, which they were. They would go proudly to the World Mothers.

Umat had almost certainly sent her down here in the hopes that some of the spirit would rub off on her, and it was succeeding. She walked among the soldiers, received their hails, asked if the boredom wasn't wearing on them, offered to top their lies. She felt the bond tightening between all of them. It was real and it was holy and the strength of it almost dizzied her.

She breathed it all in deeply. *This is for you, my Daughters,* she said to the children in her womb. *From my blood to yours, feel and understand how this is all for you.*

"How do we progress, Dayisen Lareet?" asked a soldier Lareet didn't recognize, and without a name, she couldn't assign a rank. No one had come to this ship in uniform.

"We progress beautifully, my Sister," said Lareet, loud enough for anybody interested to hear. "We have passed our apogee. Soon it will be time for our sisters onboard the shuttles to take the news back to the Hundred Isles of Home that our daughters are forever safe."

A resounding cheer rang across the deck. Lareet let it lift her up. *A good speech,* she thought. *Umat will be proud.*

As if that were a cue, the open speaker crackled. "Dayisen Lareet is requested to return to the command center."

Inspired by the lightheartedness around her, Lareet bowed to the speaker box, raising approving laughter.

"Duty calls even our commanders," observed someone.

"Never was there greater truth, Sister," Lareet called back.

The long walk through the empty, stinking corridors cooled her blood considerably. By the time she reached the command center, she was able to wonder, and to worry, why she had been summoned.

The hatch cycled back to let her through and she saw Umat and the other commanders clustered around the one comm station they'd left working, in case the Humans said something they really could not ignore. There had been pleas, requests for negotiation, and the level voice of Commander Keale issuing extraordinarily polite generalized threats.

Now, though, Scholar Arron's voice came out of the station.

"Lareet? Lareet?" Inside her mind, she could see his smooth brow furrowing with exasperation. "I know you have to be there somewhere. How long are you going to make me keep talking to myself, here?"

She crossed the deck in half a dozen steps. Umat felt her coming and moved back to make room for her in the crescent of sisters who glowered over the station as if it were a bad omen.

"Lareet, answer me. Umat? You must know where she is. Will you go get her please? We've got . . . I've got something you need to hear. It's important. Please, answer me."

Umat met Lareet's eyes, and dipped her ears.

The skin between Lareet's shoulders bunched up. She reached out and touched the key the coders said meant "reply."

"I'm here, Scholar Arron," she said.

Arron's familiar sigh of relief drifted out of the station. "I'm grateful to Mother Night. Listen, Lareet, have you got any cameras working on that thing yet?"

Lareet flicked an ear to Umat, who turned to the bridge commander. She dipped her ears. "Yes, we have," said Lareet.

"Good." Arron did not sound very certain. *What is happening?* The last of the warmth from the hangar left Lareet's blood.

Arron went on. "Set one of the command center cameras to . . ." He paused, and she could hear a faint voice in the background. "Coordinates 16, 24, 16."

"Do it," said Umat to the ovrth at the navigation station.

A section of the central table lit up. In comical unity, commanders turned from the station to the table. The screen showed a grid, the stars and one large, luminous globe right in the center of the view.

"What is that?" breathed Umat.

"That's probably us," answered Arron. "I'm aboard the city-ship *Manhattan* with Commander Keale and Captain Esmaraude. We're on an interception course with your ship."

The skin crawled across the back of Lareet's neck. Her toes dug at the metal deck. "Arron, what are you doing?"

Arron hesitated. "I'm helping to stop you, Lareet. If you don't break this off, we're going to run the *Manhattan* straight into the *Ur.* You'll all die, and so will we."

The command center was so silent, Lareet could hear her own heart beat like thunder. "Scholar Arron, you can't mean it."

"Dayisen Lareet, I do. It's all over. The only question is whether we live through it or not."

Umat left her side and strode over to the sister at the navigation post. She whispered in her ears. Lareet barely heard the answer. "Dayisen Umat, that will take at least a half hour to code."

"Do it," breathed Umat. She straightened up and lifted her voice. "Scholar Arron, I don't believe you would do this to us."

"It's not me doing it, Umat." Lareet knew from the voice that Arron had probably curled his hands into fists to signal his frustration. They were amazingly expressive, those Human hands. "I came along to try to save your lives, our lives."

The sister at the navigation post began to pant. She covered her mouth to muffle it. Umat laid a steadying hand on her shoulder. "Scholar Arron, is this your revenge for our actions at port?"

"You betrayed me," he said with a surprising simplicity. "You took lives with your actions. I am bleeding inside for what happened." The pain was clear in his voice, even for a Human. Lareet glanced around and saw a number of sisters with skin rippling in response. "But you've been betrayed, too," said Arron.

"What?" The word burst out of Lareet.

Arron took one of the deep breaths that seemed to steady him. "The Sisters-Chosen-to-Lead have known about your plan for at least a year. They set things up so Bioverse would take care of you for them. It's worked beautifully, don't you think?"

Murmurs and panting flicked Lareet's ears in a dozen different directions. She felt the heat rising in her blood and lifted her eyes to see Umat. Her sister stood as still as stone, her face smooth, tight, and shining with pure rage.

Lareet looked back down at the table. The globe had grown into the double-lens shape of a city-ship.

"Lareet, Umat, we don't have much time. We're going to hit in—" Again they heard the background voice. A woman's voice, Lareet decided. "Fifty-six minutes," Arron went on. "We know you have to code every move in by hand. But if you move soon, Captain Esmaraude can give you some shortcuts. We can still all get through this. You don't have to kill me unless you really want to. You don't have to kill each other at all."

Lareet stared at Umat. She felt a cold, leaching panic steal into her bones. "Sister . . . " she breathed.

"He's playing on your blood, Lareet," said Umat heatedly. Lareet felt the answering warmth of anger stir in her. It came from all around. Anger at the Sisters-Chosen-to-Lead, at Arron and his allies, this captain and commander, and always, always, always at the *devna* who drove them all to this. "I will get you and your children safely away."

"I heard that, Umat!" cried Arron. "Hear me! Even if you launched the shuttles right now, they would not get far enough away to avoid getting hit by the debris from the collision. Everybody's going to die, Umat. Everybody."

The noise of panting grew louder. Every mouth was open. Every ear pressed flat against their owner's scalp. Fear wrapped around Lareet now, mixing with the anger until her vision blurred. She laid one hand on her pouch and the other on the cool surface of the comm station and tried to steady herself.

"What's the point!" demanded Arron from the speakers. "Mother Night! It's not going to work! All that's going to happen is you will prove you can't think past your hatred!"

"Shut that off!" shouted Umat.

One of the dayisen touched the key that shut the speaker off.

Silence fell, except for the echoing noise of sisters panting and trying to get it under control. Fear and anger whirled on all sides.

Lareet pressed her hand against her pouch as if she could feel her microscopic daughters in her womb. Her children, begotten at Umat's urging, as much her sister's as hers. Conceived to seal their bond and bring them out of their quarrel. Her daughters, Umat's daughters.

Arron's anguished voice rang around her head.

Everybody's going to die. Everybody.

Lareet did not realize she'd crossed the deck until she laid her hand on Umat's shoulder.

"It is over, Sister," she said softly. "We gambled, and we lost."

"No!" Umat grabbed her hand and squeezed it until Lareet's skin bunched in protest. She held her sister, eyes and ears and heart. "No. They are bluffing. They are Human. They do not have the passion to die for a cause!"

"Sister, they are there!" Lareet wrenched both ears toward the table. "They are sitting right in our path and not moving!" She laid her hand over Lareet's hand and went on more softly. "They mean it, Sister, with whatever emotion drives their frozen hearts. Do you really believe Scholar Arron would lie to us?"

Umat's ears waved wildly. "We have sworn to die for the safety of our children."

Lareet held her tighter. She could feel the confusion at her back. She could almost smell it, strong and sharp over the scent of rot and death drifting through the tunnel from the city. "Our oath was sworn when there was a reason for it, Sister. Now, there would be no point to your death."

Umat's skin struggled as if it meant to crawl off her body. She flicked her gaze around the bridge. Lareet's gaze followed. The sisters clustered together in groups, sharing strength, sharing fear and anger, and trying without success to lessen their confusion. Lareet and Umat had caught them all in their conflict. Lareet felt it. It strengthened and scared her at the same time.

"And if we live, what then?" said Umat, her voice high and tight. "How long would we live for? Will the Sisters-Chosen-to-Lead leave us alive?"

"You could come with me to the colonies." Lareet laid her sister's hand on her belly guard. "You could come with us."

"NO!" Umat clamped her free hand on Lareet's shoulder and shook her. "I will not let you do this, Sister! If we turn away now, the *devna* and their Humans win!"

Anger burst from every soul on the bridge like the blossoming of blood red flowers in a summer's nightmare. Lareet felt it press down on her. She stiffened every muscle under every inch of her skin to stand against it.

"They've already won," she said, struggling not to gasp the words out. "If we move quickly, we can save three thousand of our sisters. If we don't, we lose three thousand of ours to kill three of theirs. Tell me truthfully, Sister, if this were an ordinary war, would you take those numbers?"

They stood there, hands gripping each other. She felt Umat's anguish, her need to see her sisters and their children safe batter at her. It was hard and unforgiving and loud. But for once in her life, Lareet knew Umat was wrong. She stood there holding her sister tight, and did not let it into her blood.

Slowly, like the tide pulling back from the shore, the anger around them faded. The confusion steadied. One by one, the sisters-in-command stopped panting.

Umat looked at Lareet in complete disbelief. Her muscles sagged. Her sharp ears crumpled. Tears welled up in her eyes.

"Turn that thing back on," she murmured.

"Lareet? Umat?" Scholar Arron's voice was tight with anguish. "We're running out of time here. It might be too late already. Answer me, please . . ."

Umat looked at Lareet, pleading with her entire body. Lareet dipped her ears and spoke up. "Scholar Arron, will you grant our sisters safe passage to the colonies?"

"I'll convoy them myself if I have to," said a strange man's voice. "I'll swear it on whatever you want."

"Then tell us what to do." Umat sank slowly into the captain's chair. "We've lost."

Mother was crouched over a pile of clean clothes when the Human came to the back door.

Theia had seen right away that the Queens-of-All had no idea what to do with them. That much had been written in the tightening of their skin and the tense angle of their ears. Mother was an enemy and a failure, and they had all kinds of possibilities for her. But Mother was no longer a mother, or at least she wouldn't be for much longer. Her will was being claimed by the Ancestors. As soon as it was fully claimed, she'd *be* an Ancestor, only her body would still live on earth as a father. Where he walked, each step would be heard, and the Ancestors would prick up their ears and pay attention to everything that went on around him.

Aunt Armetrethe had the grace not to look too surprised when the Queens had told her to take her Changing sister home and care for her. It was clear though, that Aunt Armetrethe didn't know what to do with them either. She knew what she was *supposed* to do, but Mother's Changing had ruined whatever tidy, vicious plans she'd put together to prove, once and for all, that she and Aunt Senejess had been right and Mother had been wrong. She nursed a hatred that must have had the Ancestors howling, but felt she had to do some kind of duty toward the new father.

So she cleared out the back chamber of the house, had the cousins bundle up all of Praeis's and Theia's possessions there and commended Theia to watch over her mother until the Change was complete and she could be taken, under proper escort and cover, of course, to a male house.

It wasn't easy. Mother was still lucid for hours at a time, but she was frenetic. She couldn't sit still, even when she saw how distressed Theia was.

"It's a stage of life, nothing more, Theia, but why now, why now, why now?" She paced from the door to the window and back again, with little, jerky steps. "You need to get back to the colonies. I was wrong to bring you and your sister here, wrong to bring you here, get back as soon as you can, you have near family there still, take shelter with them and live your life away from Queens and hate and war and all the things your mother was fool enough to think she could fix with her triumphant return."

"I promise, Mother," she said, just to try to ease her.

"You promise, you promise, of course you promise." Mother ran her fingertips across the windowpane. "You are a good daughter, a fine, well-grown, strong daughter."

Then, just as suddenly as they started, the words would stop. Mother's eyes would focus on nothing at all, and she'd be running her hands over the wall, or pressing her nostrils against the glass in the slit window, or picking at the clothes from the satchels as if trying to decide which ones felt best.

Now there was this *man* standing in the threshold, pop-eyed behind his faceplate, watching Mother sort through the clothes and rub them against her face and arms.

"Well?" said Theia in English. "What is it?"

The man coughed gently through his breath filter and looked at his boots. "I've got a message for Praeis Shin t'Theria. I was told to come to this door, I think, anyway." He had a nasal voice, and Theia's ears wanted to crumple at the grating sound of it.

"I am Praeis Shin's daughter. I'll take it."

Awkwardly, the man pulled a small plastic bag out of his pocket. Inside was some much folded paper. He unsealed the bag and held it out. Theia plucked the paper out, careful not to touch the bag.

"Thank you," said Theia with as much politeness as she could force into her voice. *Now, please go away.*

He didn't move. The Human's gaze slid over her and Theia knew he was staring at her mother. "Is that a father?" he asked.

Theia slammed the door in his face.

Mother was still busy with the clothes. Theia sat down heavily in the chair and pulled hard on her own ear.

It wasn't supposed to be like this. She was supposed to be surrounded by her sisters and her cousins. They'd be sitting clustered around Mother, encouraging her, soothing her, singing to the Ancestors for her as her voice faded. They'd take turns visiting the shrine. Some of them would be dickering with those who wanted to bring strong Shin t'Theria souls into their blood families. Res would have been so good at that. It was supposed to be a joyful time, a holy time. Not a time to sit alone and desolate in a back room with cousins stealing in and out to bring food and lay a quick hand on her shoulder, torn between her distress and their own mother's bewildered anger.

"Mother, I'm tired," Theia said.

Mother did not look up. Her ears didn't even twist around. She lifted up the burgundy sari she'd worn the day they stepped off the shuttle and buried her face in the soft fabric.

"Mother, I miss you."

Mother snuffled the cloth and Theia felt tears running down her cheeks. She wiped at her eyes and, more to distract herself than anything else, unfolded the letter.

The whole thing had been written in English.

Dear Praeis,

If you are receiving this, you can tell your Queens and their Council that the Getesaph threat overhead has been removed, one way or another. You are safe from that direction now. Completely safe, I can't swear that strongly enough.

The reason I think I can't is because I've now got to tell you I've lied to you.

Theia felt warm breath on her ear and started. Mother had picked herself up from the clothes pile. She still ran the sari through her fingers, but she also leaned over Theia's shoulder, twitching her ears at the letter.

Theia slowly turned her attention back to the words on the page.

I ordered the coagulant that disabled your fleet to be released. I convinced Bioverse we needed to stop your war without you knowing about it and hold the peace long enough to evacuate the planet and salvage the century project.

I thought Bioverse was coming in to save your world. I knew that I was, and most of the people I worked with were. Maybe Bioverse really was. But it was also coming in to get its new bioforms, and it has a contingency plan drawn up, in case your people don't fall into line.

You need to know about this, Praeis, so your people can decide what to do about us. I've enclosed it. I'll swear in front of whoever that this is real.

I still want to save the world, Praeis. I'm just not sure how to do it anymore.

Lynn

Theia lifted the first page, and read the second, more crumpled sheet. She felt her ears flatten against her scalp and her skin rippled in thick waves from her neck to her knees.

Ancestors Mine, Theia lowered the letter. She wanted to throw back her head and howl at the ceiling. *Ancestors Mine! What am I supposed to do about this?*

"Box," said Mother suddenly.

Theia jerked around. Her mother retreated to the clothes pile. "Box, box." Mother pawed through the heap of fabric.

Theia clenched the letter in her fist. "I don't understand, Mother."

Mother's ears crumpled. "David's box!"

"Here. It's here." Theia picked up one of the few unplundered satchels and unsealed it. She pulled out the black box of vials and injectors for her mother to see. "Mother, you're into the Change. One more dose won't—"

"All," Mother said, desperation plain in her thickened voice. "Give me all."

"Mother, no!" Theia took her shoulders, hoping to soothe her with the touch. "We don't know what that will do to you. Please, let it go. Let me keep you as a father and see your blood and soul go on."

Her mother stroked her arms, back and forth, back and forth, and Theia was sure her will had surrendered to the journey again. But she looked down at her daughter with liquid eyes. "Please."

Theia felt every muscle in her body sag. "All right, Mother."

Theia put the box on the small serving table and undid its catch. The vials glistened in the light from the slit window.

One at a time, Theia picked up the vials and inserted them into the injector. Miraculously, Mother held still while Theia lifted the pipette to her neck forty times.

Her whole hand was shaking by the time she sank the last injection into her mother's neck.

Theia dropped the injector back into the box and buried her face in her hands.

I'm sorry, she thought to her mother's consciousness on its journey to the Ancestors. *I didn't know what else to do. I didn't mean to kill you, or Res. I miss you, that's all. I know you're not really here anymore, but I want you to be. I don't want to be alone, I don't. Forgive me.*

She might have dozed off for a little while, she wasn't sure. All she knew was that she felt a familiar touch on the back of her head.

"My Daughter," said her mother softly. "My brave Daughter."

Theia jerked her head up. Mother stood in front of her, a little stooped, and her ears waved aimlessly, but her eyes were focused on Theia.

"Mother!" Theia leapt into her arms. She would have climbed into her pouch if she could, but as it was she wrapped her arms around her mother and hugged her hard.

"Easy, easy, now, my Daughter," chided Mother. "I am fragile these days."

Theia pulled back just a little. Tears stung her eyes. "Are you good, Mother?"

"A little, not very, and I don't know for how long." Her ears waved, as wild and restless as her wandering had been. "Everything comes at me like waves. It's distant, then it's right smack in front of me, and it's distant again." She swayed on her feet, and Theia, her heart in her mouth, steadied her.

"I don't know how long I have, Daughter. You have to get me to the Home of Queens. Now, Theia. Do you understand?" Mother clutched at her, her eyes widening with fear or urgency, or both. "Bring the letter, do you understand? Bring the letter."

"Yes, Mother." Theia snatched her wallet off the table where she'd left it and stuffed the letter inside. "Come with me." Theia linked her arm through her mother's, trying not to feel how erratically her skin twitched. Together, they slipped out the back door.

It was midafternoon. All the good cousins were inside with Ciean and her swelling womb, taking their lessons and digesting whatever Aunt Armetrethe poured into them.

The family's battered frame car was in the drive. Aunt Armetrethe comandeered Council transportation these days. Theia could drive, after a fashion. Ciean and the cousins had been teaching her and Res. The steering on the old car was stiff and cantankerous, but she could keep it mostly on the road. She gripped the wheel, worked the levers, and bared her teeth to the wind and rain.

Mother sat next to her, shivering and clutching at her arm and shoulder occasionally.

"I'm here!" she'd shout every now and then. "I'm still here."

"We're both here," Theia answered.

"Yes," said Mother, and Theia could swear she heard real satisfaction in her voice. "We're both here."

The arms-sisters had barricaded the streets leading to the Home of Queens. They knew Theia, and apparently no contravening orders had been handed down, so they raised the barricades and let them drive through.

They made it all the way to the gates of the Home of Queens, where a prime-sister waved them to a stop.

"We need to get through," said Theia to the prime-sister, who'd had both her ears ripped ragged in some combat long ago. Theia wracked her brains for the prime's name.

"Theiareth Shin t'Theria, right?" The prime-sister squinted at her. "I'm sorry, Noblest Sister, but your aunt Armetrethe's been specific. You're not permitted entry to the Home."

"What about me?" said Mother.

The Prime-Sister turned her head slowly, as if noticing Mother for the first time.

"Praeis Shin?" she said, wonderingly. "I thought . . . I'd heard . . ."

Mother bared her teeth. "There are more rumors in the service than there are guns," she said, a little too fast, a little too tight. "I am still a representative of the Queens-of-All and one of the Noblest Sisters t'Theria. You will let my daughter and me through immediately. Immediately."

The prime-sister hesitated. Theia tapped her foot to get the Ancestors' attention.

"Immediately," repeated Mother, her ears waving agitatedly.

"Yes, Noblest Sister." The prime-sister stood back and gestured for the gate to be opened.

"Thank you," breathed Theia to the Ancestors as she drove through.

She parked the car right in the middle of the cobbled yard. Her mother climbed out, stumbling a little on the stones. Theia grabbed her arm. "Are you good?"

Mother focused on her, a little too slowly. "No. Get me in to the Queens, Daughter. Get me in. There's not much longer."

Theia took her arm and pulled her close. "Then here we go, Mother."

She stretched her legs for all they were worth, hurrying, up the stairs and striding across the receiving rooms. Mother staggered and leaned heavily on her, but kept the pace. Councilors and their assistants turned to stare. Theia saw them out of the corners of her eyes. She didn't break her stride. She was up the stairs and into the Debating Chamber before anybody could make enough sense out of what they saw to raise objections.

Ueani Byu jumped to her feet as Theia burst in, dragging Mother with her as fast as she could.

"How dare you!" boomed the Queen. "What is this . . ."

"Intrusion?" inquired Mother. She extracted her arm from Theia's.

"I would have suggested perversion," said Aires Byu mildly from the sofa she shared with Vaier Byu.

"Intrusion, perversion." Mother's ears crumpled and straightened. "Yes, I am both. Both. Here and now, and you will hear me and now, this one last time, my Majestic Sisters."

"Why should we do so?" asked Aires Byu.

"Because if you don't, the Humans will take your world, your world, your titles, your people right out from under you and leave you staring stupid, lost as I am between All-Cradle and the Ancestors." Mother clutched a table edge. Theia started forward, but checked herself uncertainly.

"The letter, Theia," said Mother. "Give your Majestic Sisters the letter. The letter." She closed her eyes and her mouth kept moving.

Theia pulled the letter out of her pocket and moved into the semicircle of Queens. Without even thinking, she handed it to Vaier Byu.

The Queen took it and looked at the lettering. Her mouth puckered, and her ears fell back. She handed it to Aires Byu.

Aires handed it to Theia. "This is a Human written thing. You will, of your kindness, Noblest Sister, read it to us."

Theia felt her ears crumble from sheer embarrassment. "I'm sorry, Majestic Sisters. I forgot."

"Forget, forget," murmured Mother. "Read it, Theia."

Theia opened the letter and read it. The Queens listened in complete silence. None of them even twitched an ear or a fold of skin.

When Theia finally lowered the letter, it was as if she faced a cluster of statues.

"Well, if we needed proof the Humans were liars, we have it now." Ueani Byu struck the wall with her fist. "Idiots! We've been idiots!"

"No!" cried Mother.

Vaier Byu got to her feet. "Praeis Shin, you are in the Change. Give your will to the Ancestors and leave those of us who are not so lucky to suffer the Humans' anger."

Mother looked at Theia desperately. "Web! Theia! Tell them, tell them, tell them we win. We win because of the letter and the web. Lynn gave us our victory. Tell them!"

Theia understood. Warmth rushed through her blood, and she almost laughed out loud.

"She's right!" She ran to her mother and grasped her shoulders. "Ancestors Mine! We've got them hot and cold!"

"Would you be so good as to explain this jubilation?" asked Aires Byu.

Theia faced them, one hand on her mother's shoulder. "The Humans' communication web is a forum for argument as well as a way to exchange information. It's a debate wall that stretches up and down the Human Chain. *Corps,* corporations like Bioverse, can be broken by having their illegal or immoral actions made public in the web." She lifted the letter triumphantly. "This may not be illegal, but there are many, Majestic Sisters, who will find it repugnantly immoral."

"And how will breaking Bioverse help us?" Ueani barked. "It will leave us that much worse than before they came."

"Threats," said Mother. She swayed a little, but her ears were straight and still.

"We don't have to do it, we just have to threaten to do it," said Theia. "It's a *trump card,* it's a hold over them. A sword in our hands. While we can threaten them with this, they will be forced to deal with us, not just take our resources and leave." She looked at the Queens, and the Queens stared back, ears tipped backward and faces smooth. "Listen," said Theia, searching for the right words, trying to imagine how her mother would explain this. "From the first we have been subject to the Humans' will and conditions. We had no power once we signed their agreement. We had something they wanted, to be sure, but they held our lives, and they knew it. They held their power over us, and we had nothing to counter it with. We had no way to tell them they could not treat us so, could not make such demands on us. Now"—she held the paper aloft—"we do."

"Which would be marvelous, if we knew how to make use of this magical web," said Aires Byu.

"I know how," Theia told her.

"So"—Aires Byu's face wrinkled into an expression of amusement—"now we have to bargain with you?"

"Yes." Theia bared her teeth, just a little. "Now you have to bargain with me." She tucked the paper into her wallet. She felt her mother's approval run through her and rejoiced. *Do you hear, Res? Do you? We finally showed them all!* "And with all due respect, my Majestic Sister, to do so, you must also rebuild the Confederation."

Ueani Byu started forward, fist raised. Vaier Byu caught her arm. Her ears and eyes focused directly on Theia, and Theia held herself still. Vaier Byu understood, she was sure of it. Theia was Praeis's daughter and more than that. She was Resaime's sister and Armetrethe's niece and the child of the colonies. She was herself, and she was no sound this world had ever heard before. As such, she might do things the world had never seen before, things Vaier Byu wanted done for the sake of her people, for the sake of her sisters who stood beside her.

"No," said Vaier Byu to her sister.

"She dares!" grated Ueani through her teeth.

"She dares show us a way to regain ourselves," said Vaier in a quiet, even voice. "And I will not permit even you, Sister, to shut that gate on us again."

Mother leaned heavily against Theia. "Enough? Enough?"

"Yes, Mother," said Theia softly. "It was enough. You did it."

"We did it," whispered Praeis Shin. Her eyes grew soft and distant. "We did. We did. We."

Epilogue

The trial of *Bioverse Inc.* vs. *Arron Hagopian* was brief and to the point. Arron Hagopian, you are accused of paying to violate the integrity of the Bioverse private communications web, how do you plead? Guilty. I did give Bao Cabal six thousand shares of the First Banking Enclave of Earth in exchange for his agreement to provide me with secured information from the Bioverse communications web, which I knew he did not have the right to access or distribute. Is anyone willing to speak for the defendant? Dr. Lynn Nussbaumer was, citing Arron Hagopian's willingness to exert himself on behalf of Bioverse personnel and to ultimately assist in ensuring the success of the Dedelphi project. Security Chief Enrique Keale was, testifying to the fact that the web had not been damaged, that no private information had been recorded, removed, or altered from or in the private web.

Arron Hagopian, you are hearby fined the worth of four thousand Bioverse shares at the market value as of this date and time, to pay for the estimated time expended by Bioverse employees in dealing with your infraction, including all court fees. Payment plan to be negotiated between yourself and/or your representatives and the Bioverse cashier's department. Dismissed.

Now, Arron sat in his borrowed, hexagonal room with its bland, comfortable furniture, full-spectrum light and minutely controlled environment, idly threading through the web to catch up on the news and politics of the Solar system and wondering if there was any kind of job available that would allow him to pay off his debt before he had to leave it to his heirs/assignees/executors.

Should bywrite the family and let them know I'm coming back into shouting distance. He looked at the screen. *God Almighty, what they're going to have to say about this.*

The room voice cut across his thoughts. "Dr. Lynn Nussbaumer is waiting outside and asks to see you."

"Room voice, open the door." Arron swiveled his chair around, grateful for the distraction.

All Lynn's wounds had healed. She had a new right eye that precisely matched her left one. There was only a little stiffness left in her cheek to betray the fact that she'd ever been hurt. She was clean and clean-shaven and wearing a loose burgundy skirt and white tunic.

"Hi," she said, a little uncertainly. "I just wanted to see how you were doing."

"I'm fine. Would you like to sit down?" He gestured toward one of the perfectly ergonomic chairs scattered tastefully around the room.

"Thanks." She perched on the edge of the seat, defying all its ergonomic potential. Something in that sight made him smile inwardly.

"How are you doing?" He sank back into the chair in front of the comm station. "What's happening with . . ." He found he wasn't quite sure how to refer to the fact that Lynn had given the Dedelphi the contingency plans, which they were now dangling over Bioverse's collective head with sobering results.

Lynn gave him a half smile. "The investigation into who obtained a copy of the contingency plans is ongoing," she said. "The chief of security is taking charge of it himself."

"Ah." Arron nodded. Then, he said, "You look tired."

She rubbed her scalp. She had about three centimeters of auburn stubble covering her scalp. "I've just been planetside to see Praeis. She's gone through the Change."

Arron murmured sympathetically. "That's hard."

Lynn watched herself rub her palms together. "I think she recognized me."

"Sometimes they get flashes, if they have really strong, long-term memories about a person."

"That's what David said." She glanced up at him. "I'm not sure whether that's a good thing in this case." She shook her head. "I keep wishing I'd had a chance to, I don't know, say good-bye while she could still hear me."

"Theia heard you, I'm sure," Arron said, more or less automatically. If Lynn was looking for comfort, he'd try to give it, of course, but he didn't have much left. Surely she had to see that.

"Yeah, she did. She's going to be all right. They've put her on the Council of True Blood, and you know what? I think the other Councilors are a little afraid of her."

Arron raised his brows. "That could be a double-edged sword."

"I know, but I think she's going to handle it. She's already spent most of her annual budget sending for half of Crater Town to come in and help. The Confederation squawked, but then she pointed out how much better they'd feel with more than one person around who knew how to work with the Humans' communication web."

Arron nodded in agreement that this was indeed a smart move. Maybe it was his silence that made Lynn really look at him.

"Are your . . . friends going to Crater Town, then?"

Arron nodded. "I don't know what you and Theia said to the town council or the Bioverse seniors, but they're all being allowed in. Apparently a new hole's being developed, and if they're willing to shoulder the work, they can have most of it."

"Are you going with them?" asked Lynn softly.

Arron spread his hands. "What else am I going to do? They're my sisters."

Lynn opened her mouth and shut it again. "Of course."

He wasn't sure whether she meant it or not, but the fact that she wasn't going to argue the point made him feel a bit better. "Is Bioverse going to make a noise over what happened?"

Lynn shook her head. "Surprisingly, no. They got the ship back, mostly intact. The troublemakers are going away. The Sisters-Chosen-to-Lead have convinced everyone they really didn't know what was going on." They exchanged a glance over that one, but neither of them said anything. "Besides which, the Confederation has quietly said they'd rather a noise not be made over it, and Bioverse is very sensitive to what the Confederation says these days."

Arron felt himself smile. "I should think so."

They looked at each other. He saw that Lynn still had dark rings under her eyes and felt the weariness that still weighed down his own muscles.

Lynn must have been thinking something similar. She gave him a wry grin. "We should be cheering, Arron. We both won."

"Yeah, we did." He rubbed his forearm. "I just hope the Dedelphi won with us."

Lynn shrugged. "We'll find out." She paused. "When are you leaving?"

"Not until tomorrow. There's a delay while Keale makes sure everybody is reregistered and ID'd under their proper names."

Her tone grew tentative. "I was wondering if you'd like to come have dinner with me and David?"

Arron started. He chided himself for being so surprised, even while he said, "Are you sure?"

Lynn nodded. "I want us to be friends again, Arron." She leaned forward. "Come meet my partner. Come sit on my couch and drink microbrew and have stupid arguments with me. Don't leave me in silence for another ten years."

He smiled, a real smile this time, reflecting the warmth he felt in his veins. "I won't, Lynn. Not again."

She stood up and so did he, and she took his arm, Dedelphi-style. "Come on then, Sister."

Afterword

"We are tired of fighting. We don't want to kill anymore. But the others are treacherous and cannot be trusted."

—Edward O. Wilson, *On Human Nature*

When creating any culture in a work of science fiction, the author is repeatedly forced to ask the question, "How did it get this way?" When I created the Dedelphi, one of the many "its" I had to think about was their violence.

Violence is a complex issue. It exists on many levels, from the interpersonal to intergroup to international. Its origins are a mix of genetic predisposition, environmental and cultural reinforcement, and personal conscious choice.

In the case of the Dedelphi, the genetic predisposition to violence evolved first from balancing the need to protect oneself and one's children with the need to protect one's sister and her children. The Dedelphi are essentially a race of identical twins. Sisters from the same "bearing" share identical genetic material. If the theory that living beings are geared toward passing on their own genes to their offspring is correct, a Dedelphi sister's children are as valuable in this regard as her own children, because her sister shares most, if not all, of her genetic heritage. Her sister, in reproductive terms, becomes her second (or third or fourth) self, an additional chance for her genes to be passed on. Protecting and sharing resources with that other self, and that other self's children, increases the chance of genetic survival. This creates an increased sense of protectiveness toward the family, and a decreased self-preservation instinct.

These conditions led to a very tightly knit family structure, which was exacerbated by the fact that their world had few large continents. Most clans live on an island or archipelago where there is only the extended family. For long periods in their prehistory, Dedelphi clans did not interact with other groups. When another group was encountered, it was generally when the clan was in search of new space or resources. The native group would want to preserve all the available resources for their sisters, while the new group would want to take some (or all) of those resources for their sisters. This competition for available resources led to intergroup violence, which spun itself out down the generations, fueled by individual anger at harms done.

To further the problem, the males in the strangers' clan could easily be seen as desirable resources. Dedelphi males invest all their remaining physical resources in reproducing. They do not retain any discrimination: If one clan's males are removed, they will mate as easily with strangers as with their own clan.

As did early humans, early Dedelphi had a basic understanding of the need to outbreed. So, when a group of strangers arrived on a populated island, they would find not just food and space, but new genetic material for themselves and their sisters. Sisters and mothers raised the children. The father's family was not as necessary for resource and parenting assistance as it is in primates, which have primarily single births. This makes the cost of offending the father's family relatively small. The evolutionary balancing act became increasingly complicated, especially considering that only one sister of an entire family had to survive to pass on the majority of the family's genes, as well as its individual traditions. Violence was costly in terms of personal and group resources, as well as individual lives, but not as costly as it might have been in another species. What was initially an evolutionary possibility became a cultural custom. Through 100,000 years of biological and cultural evolution, strangers became enemies, and the need to protect one's sisters and their children became paramount.

All societies that evolve violent survival strategies (at least, all the ones we know about) also evolve rules about who may be hurt or killed, and under what conditions. If a culture is not completely suicidal, some concept of peace, friendship, or trust must exist side by side with the violence. With the concept of killing comes the concept of not killing. The existence of these ideas can give a freedom of choice to individuals in their daily interactions, even when those are with strangers. The ultimate question is, Which way will the balance tip: toward evolutionary predisposition, cultural conditioning, or individual choice?

—Sarah Zettel
Ann Arbor, 1998